BUTTERFIELD STATION

REBA RHYNE

Hey Bev —
Enjoy the ride

Reta Rhyne
(alias Carolyn Meiller)

Butterfield Station

REBA RHYNE

Published by EA Books Publishing a division of Living Parables of Central Florida, Inc. a 501c3 EABooksPublishing.com

Dedicated to
Harry D. Russell, Ph.D.

Because you encouraged me to keep writing, Harry, you were my Barnabas for your thoughtful comments on several pages of my first scribblings. Otherwise, I would have found other activities to keep myself occupied during the many weeks and months while living and working for Tracker Boats in Springfield, Missouri and other customers in the southern states. You are much loved and appreciated.

This book has been suggested as a well-researched read for home-schoolers, because there are so many interesting places, historical figures, plants, animals, rivers, and states to find exciting details about.

The time period in 1858-9 is set just before the Civil War, after the Gold Rush to California, before the Pony Express, at the beginning of the Cattle Trails from Texas, after the Trail of Tears, and at the start of the massive amount of wagon trains crossing the prairie to the western states.

CONTENTS

FOREWORD

How did Butterfield Station come to be written? I love history, and I love reading romance novels. So, my favorite pastime is reading the two mixed together. Doesn't matter the time period. Another preferred activity is traveling. I'm ready to go any time and any place.

On a trip with a church friend to a writer's conference in Glorietta, New Mexico, I passed the Guadalupe Mountains National Park. I never go by a national park if I have time to stop. Walking through the museum, I noticed a reference to the Butterfield Trail, and remembering some history I'd read in high school, I decided to visit the site which was close to the park headquarters.

Standing there in the midst of Pinery Station's rock ruins, the idea for Butterfield Station was born. I took some pictures of the area and continued on to the conference.

Months passed as I worked on my idea, researched, and traveled to soak up any information pertaining to John Butterfield and his establishment of the mail route. The Tipton name is part of my heritage here in East Tennessee, so why not combine my heroine, Gracie Tipton and her father, with the founding of the new trail?

Therefore, Jay Tipton is on the way to the Guadalupe Mountains in Texas to become one of Butterfield's employees at The Pinery.

As a Christ-follower for many years and sometimes a scribbler, writing a book was a far-off dream. But, given the opportunity and time, I sat down and patiently let the thoughts flow. It is my hope that this story will bring glory to God and that the reader will take away a better understanding of how love and abuse sometimes go together, usually in a negative way, I hope you, the reader, will enjoy the story as much as I enjoyed writing it.

And therefore will the LORD wait, that he may be gracious unto you, and therefore will he be exalted, that he may have mercy upon you: for the LORD is a God of judgment: blessed are all they that wait for him.
Isaiah 30:18 (KJV)

But they that wait upon the Lord shall renew their strength, they shall mount up with wings as eagles, they shall run, and not be weary, and they shall walk, and not faint.
Isaiah (KJV)

Now let's join Grace Tipton and her Pa on the way to Butterfield Station.

PROLOGUE

The cold metal of the steep barn roof sent an ominous chill through my prostrate body. Black darkness surrounded me. I inched my way across the corrugated surface—desperate not to slip on the wet, icy dampness of the building's covering. In my dream state my terrified mind asked, "How did I get here?" No answer.

My fingers slipped bringing the appalling realization of sliding—sliding downward faster and faster—bumping on the grooves of the rusty metal—my mouth open in a sickening shriek. I grabbed frantically for a handhold in the dark night. Anticipating the roof's edge, I plunged into the air—falling, screaming, and landing with a solid thud on the wooden floor of my bedroom.

Though I was jolted half-awake, the nightmare continued with a woman's comforting voice in the black darkness. "Gracie, Gracie, you're all right, sweetheart—only a bad dream." Her arms surrounded me, holding on tightly. Rocking back and forth, she comforted me. I clung to her, needing her affectionate presence, wanting her nearby.

"Mama, I'm scared. I dreamed of falling."

"And you were." She laughed softly, her moist breath brushing the side of my face. "...Right out of bed." Although she soon expected another child, she gently picked me up off the wooden floor, and placed me back beneath the warm covers. I felt her silky cheek on mine. She kissed me goodnight, and assured, "Gracie, you're safe."

BUTTERFIELD STATION

REBA RHYNE

❧ 1 ❧

May 30, 1858

A man's voice broke the refuge of Mama's protection.

"Gracie, it's Pa. Are you all right?"

I heard his concerned words in the semi-darkness. I was now fully awake in my secure bedroom, and Mama's assuring vision and words spoken years before went quickly away.

From my position on the floor, I could see his figure in the door's moonlit frame.

"Yes, Pa. I fell out of bed...again. Sorry I woke you."

He chuckled. "Those thuds get louder as you gain in years. Go back to sleep, little girl, everything's fine."

"Goodnight, Pa."

Everything's fine, he'd said. I wanted to believe his words. But at sixteen, I knew the recurring dream meant approaching trouble in my life. This wasn't the first time I'd fallen in the middle of the night. Call my unease woman's intuition.

I shivered and crawled into bed—eyes wide open.

Pulling my coverlet to my chin, I recalled my first collision with the floor. Wasn't it twelve years ago, before Mama died giving birth to her stillborn son?

I remembered whispers from the midwives—exchanged glances and knowing nodding of heads—a strange quietness in my mother's demeanor. Several days later, more murmurs and instructions—no lifting, no bending. But she'd bent over and picked me up.

Since then a question had crept into my mind...was I the cause? What minor incidents had triggered tonight's dream? I went through the week's happenings. Nothing sprang to mind. "Mama." Two tears slid from my eyes. I didn't think of her often, yet I missed her tender ways—the few I could recall. Mama's memory remained vivid only in the dream. Her sudden leaving was the first deep hurt I experienced connected to my nightmares. Others were experienced when something I loved was ripped from me, leaving a hollow in my trusting, child's heart; to love meant hurt and loss.

The next morning, May 31, 1858

"Gracie, after dinner I'm takin' the buggy into Nashville. Gotta run errands and buy wire for the new barn lot. You've got chores to do."

I glanced at my father—the dream of the night before already an unclear memory.

Before I could open my mouth, Pa set his coffee cup down and rose from our kitchen table. He patted my shoulder harder than usual and stepped too quickly toward the back porch. "Have our food ready a little early," he slung over his shoulder. He hurried out the door.

"I will, Pa," I called, turning on my seat, draping my arm over its back as the screened door slammed shut. Raking his fingers through a full shock of straight brown hair and rubbing his clean-shaven face, he disappeared down the back porch steps.

My brow furrowed. Food early? Going to town on Monday? Except in an emergency, we always bought supplies Saturday afternoon. Chores kept us home during the week. And why did he not ask me to go? He always had.

His change of routine surprised me. I could have set our mantle clock by Pa's habits.

No matter. Chores needed to be done. I cleaned the breakfast dishes, wiping off the checkered, yellow-and-white oilcloth tablecloth.

Picking up a wicker basket of soiled clothes, I sorted them atop the table, turning pockets inside out. Something small and white fluttered to the floor. I reached down, amazed at the stiff piece of paper from Pa's pants. I never find paper in his pockets—maybe a tool or sawdust. I flipped the card over.

BUTTERFIELD OVERLAND MAIL
Mr. Samuel. A. Augustine
100 Broad Avenue,
St. Louis, Missouri
Taking mail and travelers from Coast to Coast.

"Overland Mail? St. Louis, Missouri? What business do you have with Pa?"

But the stark black words on the white business card looked strangely familiar. Where had I seen them before? Pa rarely kept things from me. Could there be a secret attached to the card? So many unanswered questions.

I placed the piece of paper on the kitchen table with my morning's work. The words continued to plague me.

Grabbing a dish drying cloth to hold the handle of the large iron kettle, I emptied scalding water into cooler water in my wash tub. Gathering my scrub board and a large bar of lye soap, I took one of Pa's dirty shirts—scrubbing the blue cloth on the ridged metal, making a rough but rhythmic bumping sound as I pushed the item up and down. With the shirt between my hands, I twisted the cloth tightly. A squish of escaping air meant the excess water was gone. Then I plopped the soapy, scrubbed article into a large, metal dish pan and reached for a dirty pair of pants.

The white card flashed. I stared at the words. They glared back at me. I dried my hands on my apron and pulled the card toward me, reading the words again.

"Oh, fishhooks!" My brain connected my thoughts. I remembered where I'd seen the words.

7

Through the open window over the low wooden counter, I could see my father. His lithe figure, dressed in his customary brown trousers and blue shirt, moved back and forth between the barn and a lean-to next to the chicken coop.

"Here chick, chick," he called. From an old, blue coffee can, he threw feed in an arcing motion to the hungry hens. "Chick, chick." They ran in his direction, clucking and pecking at the ground.

I had plenty of time. Monday mornings, Pa repaired harness and broken handles on his farm equipment. He'd placed three pieces on a bench outside the barn.

The walk from the kitchen through the front room to his tidy bedroom took only seconds.

Yes. The letter was there, exactly where it had rested for several days. Crossing the room, I stood in front of his clothes chest. The reflection of a blond, curly-haired image appeared in the mirror hung on a nail over the top surface. The likeness revealed a clear uneasiness in the blue eyes and square face.

I put my hand toward the letter but closed it into a fist.

Should I, or shouldn't I? I never messed with Pa's correspondence, but then he never kept anything from me—except when we talked about Mama.

Curiosity got the better of me. I seized the letter and headed to the kitchen. From the window, I saw Pa hauling another piece of harness from the barn. I'd be safe if...

Carefully, I slipped two pieces of folded paper from the white envelope and read the first business letter dated April 1858.

Mr. Tipton,

Per your letter earlier this month, our company would be pleased to sit down and discuss a position with the Butterfield Overland Stagecoach Lines.

Your experience with the military and familiarity with Texas and the Chihuahuan Desert is a definite plus for the employee we seek. Since I will be making an inspection of our intended Memphis headquarters, my train schedule permits me to be in the Nashville, Tennessee area on Monday, the thirty-first of May, at one o'clock. Please let me know if this day and time is acceptable to you.

Yours truly,
Samuel A. Augustine

I hurriedly read the second letter, dated the second week of May:

Mr. Tipton,
Thank you for confirming the date of our meeting. The company is pleased at your continuing interest in becoming an employee of Butterfield. I believe we have the exact position you seek. I will meet you at Harding Town Square, which I understand is an easy walk from the train depot. Thank you for the map. I look forward to discussing the particulars of your employment with us.

Yours truly,
Samuel A. Augustine

If someone had thrown a bucket of cold water in my face, I couldn't have been more shocked. Hurt from long ago rushed back. My chest constricted. The starch left my legs. I sat hard on a kitchen chair. What on earth did Pa intend to do? Move to the desert? Go to Texas? I knew he loved the state. He'd fought for the Republic of Texas.

Coming back to Tennessee after the war, he had married my mother, and I was born. Four years later, my mother died giving birth. And I lost my baby brother.

After Mama left me, Pa and I had done everything together. "Gracie, we're a team," he'd told me. Even as a five-year-old, we had worked together. Although I felt his pain at Mama's absence, I couldn't explain why nothing I did had banished his inner struggle.

Months after Mama passed, Pa went to fight the Mexican War, leaving me with his friends, the Watsens. "He's runnin' from the hurt," the Watsens whispered to each other, shaking their heads.

9

I remember his goodbye kiss, him smiling and waving as he left. The days turned into a week. Each morning I went to the road and looked in the direction he traveled. One day, my little legs churning, I ran down the road. He couldn't be far. I ran and ran. Seemed like forever. The Watsens found me under a bush. Lost. Crying my eyes out. I didn't find Pa.

Mr. Watsen picked me from the ground. I lay in his arms like a human dishrag. He gently patted my curly hair.

First, my Mama was gone, and now Pa. For two days, not a bite of food passed my lips. I curled into a ball next to the warm hearth. My two reasons for living had vanished.

Pa did return, but trusting him to be part of my life had taken years. Now, Pa had dredged up feelings I'd packed and put away. The hurt of that last leaving came back at me. Tears sprang to my eyes. The pain engulfed me again. I jumped from my chair and paced the kitchen, wiping the coursing water from my cheeks.

Texas, always *Texas*. I hated the word.

Why hadn't he told me about his intention? He'd been planning to do this for months. Did he mean to go without me? Leave me again?

"No, no!" Where he went, I went. The longer I thought about his plan, the angrier I became. He wouldn't hurt me by leaving me behind this time.

I stomped over to the calendar hanging by the porch door. Today was the thirty-first of May. Now I knew the reason for the trip into town, for not asking me to go, for going during the week. This explained the reason for last night's dream. Little changes in his routine had triggered it.

I shoved the two letters into the envelope, stalked back to his bedroom, and replaced the pieces of mail along with the card atop his chest. Returning to the kitchen, I picked out a skirt from the basket and took up the bar of lye soap. Rubbing the cloth against the corrugated wash board, I gave the helpless thing the scrubbing of its life.

Piece by piece the clothes entered the hot water. Finally, all were clean with the water rung from them.

By the time I went to the back porch to rinse the soapy clothes, I'd lost some of my anger and started to rationalize his actions. Going to the cistern pump, I pulled the long metal handle upward and pushed down hard. Several thrusts later, cool water splashed from the square metal mouth into my pan. I pumped, filling the container to the rim. Of course, Pa wanted to surprise me—to tell me after he took the job. I started rinsing the soapy clothes.

Maybe he was afraid I wouldn't want to go, wouldn't want to leave our comfortable home here on the outskirts of Nashville, and wouldn't want to leave Sarah or Paul, my best friends. My mind went to my school friend, Paul Peerson. A year ago, he'd brought me a book called *The Young Fur Traders*. A week later, riding home from Hume School, we'd talked about heading to Canada, making our living trapping beaver, mink, and other animals, much as Charlie Kennedy, the book's hero, had done at Red River. We'd canoe raging rivers and ride a sled with dogs pulling it. I could picture doing such a thing with Paul. Our relationship had grown slowly. I trusted him and liked the idea of seeing different places.

That day we were two friends daydreaming. Now, Texas was a real possibility.

I dipped my clean clothes in cool rinse water from the cistern, deciding right then not to be left behind. If Pa didn't intend to take me, I'd find a way. The morning slipped by. I hung the clothes to dry and worked at finishing my chores.

The thought of following Pa to Nashville hadn't entered my mind, but as soon as the rattling buggy rolled out of the driveway, I ran to the barn and started saddling Boone. "Come on, fella. We're headed to Nashville." Twenty minutes later, I rode hard after Pa, my horse's shod hooves throwing clods of dirt into the sky—the air whistling by my head.

After a rushed five-mile ride into Nashville, I sat concealed behind a thicket of green, clipped hedges, heart leaping in my chest. My apron fanned the air. I swiped sweat off my dripping forehead.

"Whew!" The muttered sigh escaped my lips. I closed my eyes, pushing the thick drooping curls off my forehead,

11

imagining bath time and the clear, flowing water of Deer Creek cool on my warm skin. "This year, June in Tennessee will be as hot as the firecrackers shot off on the Fourth of July," I mumbled.

Uneasy about spying on Pa, something I'd never done until today, made me feel sinful. But how else would I know what transpired?

Forty feet away, my father leaned forward, sleeves rolled up and elbows on the table, talking to a distinguished man in a brown frock coat. I couldn't see Pa's face.

Mr. Augustine's outfit fascinated me. The unbuttoned coat exposed a fancy gold, shawl-collared vest. His black cravat stood out against a starched, stiff white collar, and a gold ring flashed on his hand. He gestured in the hot, humid air. The man's scuffed leather briefcase with shiny gold buckle lay beside him on the bench.

A man of obvious wealth and importance, he spoke in earnest tones about a new venture opening in the West. I strained to catch some of the words he emphasized. "Stagecoach line," "Guadalupe Mountains," and "Pine Springs" were familiar phrases piquing my curiosity.

Fascinated, I edged closer. *Crack!* A twig snapped underneath my feet. I sucked in my breath and froze in position. Engrossed in their transaction, neither man turned to check out the sound.

"We've got a deal then," the gentleman said, smiling broadly. He reached across the table to end the discussion with a handshake and wiped his sweating brow with a white handkerchief.

"So, you agree the wild frontier of Texas is no place for Gracie?"

"I do, Jay. Life for a woman is tough. Wild Indians, hard riding men, disease, and the elements take their toll on the womanly best."

My jumping heart dropped into my feet.

Pa nodded. "She won't be happy about not goin'."

Pa's new boss pulled his mouth down into a thin line, raised his eyebrows, and gave a half-smile. "She can join you later after things settle down a bit."

Pa straightened his back. "I'll get ready and be headin' west in about three weeks. Sellin' the farm won't be hard. A neighbor's interested."

"July and August isn't the best time to travel. The heat will be oppressive. But you must be at The Pinery by September. If things progress as Mr. Butterfield has planned, the first stage is scheduled to arrive on the twenty-sixth of that month." Augustine pulled a small black case from his inside pocket, snapped it open, and took out a pen and small bottle of ink. I saw his long, skinny fingers move as he scribbled on a piece of white paper, which he handed to my father along with a sheaf of papers and booklets.

"You can count on me, Mr. Augustine." From the sound of Pa's voice, I knew my father was smiling as he looked at the man's signature. I pictured the crow's feet at the corners of his eyes and the half-dimples in his cheeks as he leaned forward and opened one of the printed pamphlets. He started leafing through its pages.

Unlike Mr. Augustine, Pa was underdressed in his rough britches and coarse, blue cotton shirt. His clothes were clean because I scrubbed them devotedly, but frayed cuffs and collars told of their countless days of usage. Where Mr. Augustine's hands looked smooth and white, my pa's were rough, calloused, and brown.

"Jay, I'll be in touch. If you run into any trouble, any at all, reach me at this address." Mr. Augustine stood and handed my father another card from his waistcoat pocket. He stripped off his loose-fitting frock coat, scooped up his black hat, and pulled out a gold timepiece. "I've got to catch the train back to St. Louis, Missouri."

He disappeared down the dusty street. His long legs carried him along at a fast pace. His heels whipped a beige powder in tiny circles with each step. The sun reflected off his gold vest, blinding in the sunlight.

Mesmerized by this sight, I'd lost track of time. I needed to leave—and fast. My pa hadn't moved from the spot where he sat. He put one pamphlet down and drew another toward him. I walked quietly, careful not to snap another twig, mounted Boone, and rode for home.

13

I stewed for days, watching Pa come and go on errands to Nashville and other nameless places near our farm home. On Monday, one week after I had followed him to his meeting with Mr. Augustine, Pa suggested eating our noon meal under the trees in the apple orchard. We used the shaded picnic area with a makeshift table and chairs for special occasions. Would he tell me of his plans as we ate?

When he returned from the barn for dinner, my washing rested on the back-porch table, waiting to be hung on the clothesline to dry.

"Whew! Today's going to be another scorcher," Pa said, pulling out his blue checkered handkerchief and mopping his brow. "I'll go get the milk from the springhouse."

I placed bread, butter, and cheese on the table—simple fare for a noon meal. Because of the afternoon's hard, hot work, Pa preferred not to eat a heavy dinner, although supper was more substantial with vegetables and meat.

I watched him return down the well-worn dirt path to the spring, carrying a gallon glass jar and whistling "Amazing Grace."

He poured the milk and sat down at the skinny table. Our knees touched underneath. Pa spoke a short blessing. Taking the kitchen knife, he sliced the cheese, placing the thin, yellow pieces on pieces of bread. I folded mine, took a bite, and chewed.

"Gracie, there's somethin' important I need to tell you. Do you remember me readin' to you the article from the Nashville paper about the government establishin' a new mail and travel route from Missouri to California?"

"Yes, Pa." My cheese and bread started to make a ball in my mouth. I grabbed my glass and gulped my milk. "That was months ago."

I looked into serious brown eyes.

"I don't know how to say this but just to say it." He drew a deep breath, and the words gushed out. "I'm goin' out West, daughter. I've been offered the position of station man at Pinery

Springs in the Guadalupe Mountains on the Texas, New Mexico territory border. I gotta be there before September."

He waited.

I tried to act surprised. "Isn't the Guadalupe Mountains where you stayed with William Boone after the Mexican War?"

"The one and the same. I'm amazed you remember. I'm headed back there."

I ignored the *I* in his statement. "When do we leave, Pa?"

"Here's the problem, little girl. I can't take you with me, but I'll send for you or come to get you after I'm established in the post and the area settles down."

"Pa, I want to go with you. I can carry my own weight. I won't be any trouble. None a'tall." My normally ravenous appetite began to diminish.

"The frontier is just too hard on women—not the place for a grown one, let alone a young girl. Too much can happen."

"I'm almost seventeen and of marriageable age, Pa. You know that. If you ask me, that's grown up." I sat straight until my eyes were on the same level as his.

"I guess I can't argue with your observation. I sometimes forget how old you are, but I still can't take you."

I jumped from the table and paced under the apple trees, my uneasiness mounting. "I thought you said we're a team. Teams stay together. They do their best together." What was so bad about me that every blooming thing I loved seemed to leave me alone and hurting?

"The western frontier is too wild. I won't risk you goin' at the present time. I can't see you gettin' hurt. Once the Butterfield route is established, you can come on the mail coach."

Raking in a long breath and controlling my frustration, I sat back down at the table and tried one last time to persuade him. "But Pa, pioneer women go West every day. I don't want to stay here without you. You left me once before. Don't do this to me again." My eyes filled with tears. I let one slide down my cheek. Maybe tears would help.

"I promise you, Gracie. I'll send for you. We won't be apart as long as last time. Maybe a year."

"A year," I echoed dully, thinking of the dreary days ahead with my life torn to pieces.

15

My father hadn't eaten a bite of his food, and what I'd eaten hadn't gone down easily. He reached across the table and wrapped his fingers around mine.

"We've done well here, Gracie, but there's no challenge left in working our farm. John Butterfield's started this grand adventure. He needs good men to help him make a success of the overland mail. This business is important to our country—gettin' mail safely from one side of America to the other. I'm goin' to Texas and settle the land I helped liberate. I'll send for you." He continued to hold my hand, looking into my eyes, trying to reassure me.

I looked back at him. For nine years, we'd worked hard to establish our farm outside Nashville. Was he ready to leave it all behind?

What else lured him West? I knew the reason; he'd told me many times before.

He might be sittin' here under an apple tree in Nashville, Tennessee, but he was in love...not with a woman...his heart belonged to Texas. I could see it in his eyes, a faraway look tuned to the shining face of El Capitan and the sparkling waters of Pine Spring. He was already there climbing the Guadalupe and drinking from the cool mountain stream.

I nodded. "I see." Didn't mean I exactly agreed with him. But he took my words this way.

"The Watsens want you to come and stay with them. I have the house sold, and some of the money will go for your upkeep. We need to be off the property in two weeks. The Watsens will come to get you the day before I leave."

"So soon?" I said shocked at how quickly my life would change.

"Yes."

"And you've sold all the equipment and furniture with the land and house?"

"Yes. All I'm takin' is my clothes, two teams of red mules I purchased from a farm toward Nashville, and some of the smaller items around here. In Memphis, I'll buy a wagon and more supplies for the trip west."

"I guess your decision is final."

Pa nodded. He looked intently at me. "I must say you're taking the news fairly well."

I looked down, not meeting his eyes. I wanted to yell. *No, no, don't mess up our ordinary lives.* I took another bite of my bread and cheese so I wouldn't have to answer. If he could only see how jumbled my insides were, how my heart hurt, he wouldn't have made such a statement.

"Maybe a year," Pa had said.

In my calculations, he might as well have said a lifetime.

Pa went back to the barn, cheese and bread in hand.

I carried our dinner items in to the kitchen, and looked at the familiar surroundings in the room.

The iron skillets, deep pans, and egg turners hung in neat rows behind the stove. I wandered over to the sink, a Christmas gift Pa had recently installed in my kitchen counter. How proud I was of my newfangled possession. A pipe running through the floor to the outside of the house let me use the dirty dishwater to soak a bed of zinnias nearby—my beautiful zinnias of pink, orange and gold.

The brown crock pitcher, sitting on the cupboard next to the wood-burning stove claimed my attention. Pa's mother brought the two-tone jug from Cades Cove in the Smoky Mountains. He'd said his grandmother had used it for honey at the kitchen table. Large stirring spoons, metal and wooden, stuck out the top. I removed the tallest one. Hand-whittled of walnut, the rough edges I fingered at the tip of its shallow bowl told of many uses. The utensil had belonged to a great-grandmother I never knew. Women were scarce in my life.

The enormity of leaving everything behind overwhelmed me. I went to my bedroom, flung myself down and sobbed. My jerking body shook the feather bed. I cried until the hurt was gone. When I stood, I felt better.

Leaving my home on Deer Creek would tug at my heart, but I resolved not to let anything hold me back from my intention to go west—not even my budding feelings for Paul Peerson.

The bright sunshine greeted me as I walked to the clothesline to hang my wet laundry with wooden pins. From the front of the house came the noisy rattle of a buggy as it rolled west down the dusty road. The driver headed in the same direction my pa would be taking shortly. I turned to watch its progress until it disappeared.

Pa continued with preparations to leave, and I was doing the same—not to the Watsens, but to join Pa on his trip west! My decision was made. Like a canoe caught in violent rapids, I became the sole captive of my plans with no one to help me. This was my choice, no matter the severity of future consequences.

❦ 2 ❦

On Saturday morning before we planned to leave on Monday, I packed a picnic basket and headed toward Sarah Cobb's home. She was my best friend in the world—and my first goodbye. I met her in the deep woods behind our homes. Her pet lamb, Wooly, scampered toward me to say hello.

"Gracie, you're late."

I waved off her comment. "Not by much."

We walked through a forest of ferns, dogwood and redbud trees to a bubbling spring oozing out of the hillside. The water flowed into larger Deer Creek nearby. Easing down on hollows well-made from previous visits, we ate our scrambled eggs on buttered, toasted bread—our favorite food on these woodland treks. Lazing back on the grass with the leaves smelling of deep decay, we spoke about the week's happenings. Today, our rendezvous took on a different, sad air.

"Gracie, it's hard to believe we've been out of school for a whole year." Sarah leaned on her elbow, picking at woodland violets blooming within our mossy retreat.

"We're a year older." I grinned, realizing my comment was small talk not pertaining to the real subject on both of our minds. Normally, we'd have talked of boys and marriage or chores on our fathers' farms. "Sarah, I don't know if we'll see each other again. Texas is a long way."

Wooly, her pet lamb, nudged my hand. Wooly's mother had rejected her offspring. The baby would have died except for Sarah's tender care.

Tears and pain showed plainly in Sarah's blue eyes—the color darker than mine. "You're my best friend in the entire world," she sniffed.

"Best friends don't ever forget each other." Sarah knew about my plans, and I'd sworn her to secrecy. "Sarah there's something you need to do for me." I pulled a letter from my pocket and handed the envelope to her. "Mail this on Monday. I've explained my decision to the Watsens. They need to know what I'm doing and that I'm safe. Can you do this?"

"Of course." Sarah tucked the note into her apron pocket. "Is it dangerous where you're going, Gracie?"

"Naw, it'll be a lark. One big adventure after another." I remembered Pa's statement to a neighboring farmer about the frontier being an easy place to die. Even though phrases like rough riding, dry and dusty desert, tornadoes, and marauding Indians were bandied about during the last two weeks, I'd put all this talk aside and decided the trip was going to be pleasurable.

"When did you start loving the unpredictable and exciting?" Sarah moved her head side to side and brushed away a tear that threatened to wash a pathway down her dusty cheek.

Nodding my head full of short blond curls tinged lighter by the sun, I put my arm around Sarah and gave her a quick hug. "Maybe you could ride the stage to Texas? Maybe you could come and see me. What an adventure that'd be."

Reaching up, I pulled my new wide-brimmed felt hat down firmly on my curls and tightened the leather string-pull under my chin. The salesman called it a Western sombrero, saying he sold many to people heading to the frontier. Pa had questioned this Saturday purchase, but being busy with his preparations to leave, he didn't dwell on the subject.

I pushed a wild curl behind the sweatband underneath the low crown.

Cut short, I could brush my hair. Otherwise, running a comb through the tangled, unruly mess of tats proved impossible. I envied Sarah's long brown hair which flowed down her back in beautiful waves.

"I already asked Daddy. He said it's too expensive and a long way for an unaccompanied girl to travel." Sarah pulled Wooly to her and gave the lamb a hug.

"Sarah, you shouldn't have told your father. He may see Pa and tell him. The cat might be out of the bag—another problem to worry about.

"No, Gracie, there's no chance. Daddy's gone north to Kentucky with our neighbor to purchase more cattle. He won't be back for several days."

"Thank goodness. I've got enough problems without Pa finding out my plans. He won't let me go if he does."

"Gracie, I want you to take Wooly, so you won't forget me. Daddy says I can give her to you." She pushed her white fluffy lamb in my direction.

Horrified at the prospect of removing Sarah's most precious possession, I exclaimed, "I can't do that. You love this little lamb, and you saved her life."

"But Gracie, when I think of Wooly, I'll think of you. And when you see her, you'll think of me. We won't forget each other." How could I argue with such an astute observation?

"*Baa-a,*" said Wooly, echoing her master's words.

A lamb with wanderlust. I smiled at the ridiculous thought. "Sarah, I really..."

"I won't take no for an answer." Sarah had made her decision. I knew better than to disagree with her. The only arguments we'd had in our years of friendship were over her stubbornness. She either won, or I walked away. I couldn't walk away today. Being angry was not the way to end our long friendship.

"You're goin' to miss the July Fourth fireworks."

"I know. We'll be halfway to Memphis by then. I can't wait to see the Mississippi. Oh, Sarah! There are so many new, excitin' places I'll be going." We sat and talked for several more minutes before I walked her home. The tears started flowing at our final hug. At the end of her driveway, I turned to wave goodbye.

When I left Sarah, I led Wooly on a rope beside me. What would my father say? A less than half-grown sheep wasn't on

21

Pa's list of necessary supplies. "Wooly, I'll tell Pa you'll be dropped off at Sarah's as I travel to the Watsens' home."

We were riding our horses to Memphis. At least, I hoped we were and leading four sturdy red mules Pa had bought to pull the wagon and supplies for the trip to Fort Smith, Arkansas and beyond.

A sudden stab of guilt at sneaking behind Pa's back rose from the depths of my soul. His patience would be stretched to the limits when he realized what I'd done. How many days might pass before he forgave me?

I'd been sleeping fitfully since making my decision to go with Pa, dreaming of holding onto a porch post with someone tugging at me, trying to strip me from my home. I strained to see who this person might be. The man turned out to be Pa. Then I'd dream of being transplanted to the high mountains, the desert spread out before me where I rode Boone faster than the wind. I tossed on my bed. My appetite came and went with my moods.

And what about God? He knew exactly what I intended to do. I'd involved Sarah in my scheme, and this sneaking, lying, and generally breaking the rules I'd been taught from the Holy Bible weighed heavily on my conscience. I struggled to maintain a happy demeanor and whispered into the night.

"Please God, forgive me."

"*Baa-a.*" Wooly echoed my words. She brought me back to the present.

The wind made tiny whorls of dust in the road as I walked toward home, kicking at loose rocks and sending them flying down the road. Tall oaks spread their branches over my walkway, and scrub pines emitted a nostril-opening, pungent smell which floated in the warm summer air. I took a deep breath and looked down at the white fuzzy animal walking beside me, "Wooly, you'll have to help me persuade Pa when we join him on the trail, and this may not be easy. Hurry, let's go home."

Home… Where was that? It wasn't the white frame house I'd lived in for eight years. Pa had sold it to our neighbor. My father was proud of the price he got out of it. He'd left the furniture, machinery, and livestock, because the buyer planned to move his son onto the property—an instant home he'd called it, for his offspring. He was right.

Tomorrow afternoon, the Watsens planned to come for me, but I intended to persuade Pa to let me spend another night with him. This couldn't be the last night I'd sleep in my bed.

After several minutes of walking, I came to the path leading to Hillside Cemetery. A movement in the area caught my eye.

"Wooly, I guess we're goin' to have that talk a little sooner than we planned."

My father's eyes were red, and I knew he'd come from visiting my mother's and brother's graves, saying goodbye.

Spying the lamb, he called, "Little girl, is that Wooly. Where do you think she's going?"

"Pa, Sarah gave her to me. I couldn't tell her no. I'll take Wooly home on my way to the Watsens'."

"Don't plan on takin' the lamb to the Watsens. You see she gets back to Sarah."

"I will Pa."

"We need to hurry on home and go into Nashville. I left several things off my list." I got the impression he didn't have time to argue, which worked in my favor.

I tried to stay abreast of his long steps. "Are you takin' the buggy?"

"No. The horses. The items are small."

My pa loved organization. He'd shown me a schedule of the whole trip to Texas with dates of arrival at important cities and forts. I realized this complete life change was taking its toll on his structured life. "Pa, you've been forgetful of late."

He didn't answer.

I rushed past the house to the barn and put Wooly in a stall. Passing bags of supplies ready to load on the red mules, I hastily saddled Boone. Pa appeared from the barnyard with his saddled ride. Taylor was named after a beloved commander in the Mexican War, General Zachary Taylor, who became president.

"Are you ready, Gracie?" He urged Taylor toward the road.

I nodded, put my foot in the stirrup, and slung my leg over the saddle. I caught him as he turned out onto the road.

On our two previous trips into town, I'd missed Paul Peerson. He didn't know I was leaving. I needed to tell him goodbye.

23

On Saturday afternoons, Pa and I always headed into Nashville in the buggy. He'd give me five dollars to trade at the local shops, while he checked out the mercantile and hardware stores. As I had for the past year, while Pa made purchases at the local hardware, I sat on the front oak boardwalk in a wooden chair. Paul came from his home across the street to join me.

I like boys. I didn't know this until a comely Paul came along the last year I went to Hume School where Paul still studied. He wanted to be a lawyer.

Paul was a year older than I, fairly tall, stocky, and a new arrival in the area. Every girl in school ran after him, but he preferred me. Sarah dubbed me lucky.

He liked history, numbers, and reading. So did I. During rides home after school let out, we discussed the day's studies.

Our English teacher required her students to memorize a favorite quote from a list she supplied, and Paul memorized one of Abraham Lincoln's. He often cited the passage to me, raising his arm and emphasizing the importance of being truthful. *I believe it is an established maxim in morals that he who makes an assertion without knowing whether it is true or false, is guilty of falsehood; and the accidental truth of the assertion, does not justify or excuse him.* As a lawyer, Paul intended to emulate Lincoln. And like his hero, Paul never lied. If he knew what I was doing, he would not be happy with me.

During the ride to Nashville, I kept trying to think of ways to soften the words I must speak. However I said them, he would be shocked and hurt.

I loved a short walk through the hardware store, but today I needed to do something more important. "Pa, I'll wait for you outside."

With a new brace and bits in his hands, Pa reached for a paper bag of sixteen penny nails and smiled. "I understand, Gracie."

Under the porch roof, I sat in my usual chair. The door of the Peerson house banged shut across the street. Eighteen-year-old Paul walked toward me. I loved his smooth distinctive stride. His long legs carried him well. "Gracie, I've been missin' you," he called, smiling as he approached.

Oh dear. This isn't going to go well. Misgivings swelled inside me. I arose from my chair, stepped down into the street, and walked away from the front of the busy hardware store. No use in taking the chance of Pa hearing what I intended to say. "You haven't been around when we've come to town."

"I've been here on Saturday," he argued. So, he'd watched for me. My womanly senses tingled at his admission.

"Pa needed some things. We came during the week," He was right. Coming to town during the week was not normal for us.

"Why? Why did you come during the week? Are you upset with me?"

"Oh no, Paul. You haven't done anything for me to be angry about." I drew a deep breath and plunged on. "Paul, I-uh, I'm goin' West with Pa." There, I'd said the dreaded words. I feared hurting Paul.

"West to where. When will you be back?" Interested, he didn't understand the finality of my words.

"The Guadalupe Mountains in Texas. I don't think I'll ever be back."

"What are you saying, Gracie? How will I see you? I thought we were best friends—no, more'n that." He looked at me intently, trying to grasp the meaning of the words I'd uttered. "Being a lawyer takes a long time, I, uh, we..."

I threw my hands in the air and shook my head, exclaiming, "Pa's goin' and I'm goin' with him. I can't stay here...alone." Why did I have to add the word alone? I mentally kicked myself, seeing the next statement in Paul's eyes.

He grabbed my hand, holding it tightly, "Gracie, I don't want you to go. Maybe, we-we could get hitched, and..."

Controlling new emotions surfacing in my heart, and shocked at his words, I cut him off. "Hitched, you've never mentioned gettin' married. And anyway, it's all arranged. Pa and I leave day after tomorrow."

"You should have told me sooner. I might have..."

"Paul, you should've asked me, but you didn't." I pulled my hand from his and crossed my arms on my chest. I couldn't look at him. The conversation had taken a turn I didn't want to discuss. Not now, anyway.

The creaking door of the hardware opened behind us. Paul and I turned around as Pa came out of the door with one of the store's employees following him. The employee carried a sack of animal feed. "Paul, it's good to see you." He walked over. They shook hands. "Are you telling Gracie goodbye."

"I guess so. I didn't know about her leaving." I wondered if Pa detected the hurt in Paul's voice, but I breathed a sigh of relief as Pa walked over to the horses. I saw him glance back in our direction.

Paul and I were at the end of our short but difficult conversation. I put my hand on his arm. "You'll always be my best friend."

"Gracie, I might come looking for you in the Guadalupe Mountains."

With nothing else to say, I nodded, smiled, and went to mount Boone.

"Are you ready to go, little girl?" Pa asked.

"I am, Pa."

I looked back once. Paul stood in the road where I left him, his head down and his arms hanging limply at his sides. Well, he should've said something sooner. The more I thought about his lack of backbone the more put out I got.

I don't know much about love. My pastor says God loves me, and I know I love Pa. I'd fight anybody about to hurt him. When Sarah and I discussed man-woman things, she said there's a different kind of attachment between a man and woman. She'd seen this bond between her mother and father. I'd never seen this between my parents.

Out of the blue, Pa said, "Paul Peerson's a hard worker, Gracie. He'll make someone a fine husband."

Pa suspected Paul's feelings. I felt a sudden twinge of distress at leaving him behind. I felt unhappy for him and me. Sorry, because he hadn't stepped forward and plainly declared his love. Given a little time to ponder his question, I might have said yes.

Now, going to Texas was more important than any feelings I had for Paul.

Then another thought occurred to me. If I stayed, maybe Pa's plan included Paul as my future husband. Sometimes, we ran into the Watsens in our hardware store. I shook my confused head. When Paul picked Lincoln's quote, I picked its companion. The words of Sir Walter Scott rolled around in my head. *Oh what a tangled web we weave, when first we practice to deceive.* I laughed out loud.

"Gracie, what's wrong with you?"

"Nothin', Pa. Nothing." I realized this was another lie. I should have said everything—everything's wrong. Something else I realized, I was tired of being angry and sad all the time. I was tired of alternating between hope and despair and of telling lies and being confused. I'd be glad when my life settled down to normal—whatever normal turned out to be.

Sunday was a day of rest. Pa and I rode to church for the last time.

After the service, he stood at the doorway talking to our pastor and church friends—telling them goodbye. I returned to the center aisle, scanning the unremarkable sanctuary—wooden benches, glass windows, and pulpit—a country church. My eyes found the small altar at the front of the building. There, I'd met my Savior on a snowy day four years past. One month later, after being baptized in Deer Creek, I almost froze to death on the way back home.

Today, Pa and I ate our noon meal at Aunt Maggie's Eatery, taking with us enough leftovers for supper.

When the Watsens arrived in the late afternoon, I'd already persuaded Pa to let me spend the night at home one last time. I'd head to their Nashville home tomorrow morning. They loaded the trunk containing my few possessions onto their wagon.

"Gracie, your trunk is awful light," observed my father, looking at the leather and wooden box with a curious eye and slight smile, but he didn't look inside.

Pa didn't know that my clothes and special belongings were stuffed helter-skelter in the bottom of the bulging bags he'd load on the mules in the morning. My late-night ramblings took care

27

of this. Boone's saddle bags were secreted under my bed along with a tow sack wrapped in my bedroll.

I intended to lead Wooly some of the way. When she tired, I meant to put her in the large bag, slinging it over my saddle. She and I'd practiced the tow sack issue. I found putting the lamb in the rough sack's black maw no easy matter—legs thrashed and her body contorted in all sorts of gyrations. Her head stuck out the mouth of the bag, and she looked at me with sorrowful eyes as I sat on Boone.

"Okay, I feel the same way too," I said, sweating after the struggle. Her warm body lay against my leg. "You can walk most of the way, and part of the time, you can lie across my saddle,"

I promised her. "Little Wooly, you'll get fat and sassy in Texas."

Being my father's daughter, I thought I'd covered everything. Without Pa seeing me, I needed to haul my saddle bags and bed roll out to the side of the road into a clump of bushes I'd deemed safe to hide them. I planned to stop and reclaim them when I headed west behind my father. The opportunity came when he went to milk the cow and feed the chickens the scraps from our last meal together.

Later that afternoon, I walked west down the road in front of my home. Turning around, I looked back at the picket fenced yard. My summer flowers, larkspur and bachelor buttons, stuck their fronds between the openings in the slats. The blue, lavender, and pink blossoms stood out in contrast to the white fence. It hurt to think the new owners might not tend these beauties with the tender care I'd lavished on them.

To the side of the house, our apple and peach orchard's summer bounty hung in smaller imitations of the final fruit. Behind that, the garden we planned to harvest was full of early corn, beans, and tomatoes. I couldn't help but think of the hard labor and profuse sweat Pa had heaped on his plants.

In the high branches of an oak tree, a robin chirped the end of the day. In the pasture a cow mooed, and a distant whippoorwill sang a mournful song of goodbye. Even though I would leave this place tomorrow, the serenity of nature calmed me. God willing, a home would be mine again in Texas.

I said goodbye. Tomorrow, I didn't intend to look back.

REBA RHYNE

3

The much anticipated and fateful day arrived. Pa and I left home on Monday, the first day of the week and the start of my new life. I hated leaving my friends and home, but during the days of preparation before our departure, the lure of adventure and the unknown I'd find in the west grew stronger, calling me there. Nothing in this world would keep me from Butterfield's station known as The Pinery in Texas—from the splendid home I pictured in my mind.

I stood beside my horse in the gray dawn. Pa fiddled with Wooly's rope. "Remember Gracie, I'll send for you, and I'll write and tell you how things are goin'. Don't be a bother to Mrs. Watsen and help her around the house."

I couldn't say anything. Afraid if I opened my mouth, I'd blurt out my intention to follow him.

He continued, "I'll miss you, daughter. I-I love you." He threw his arms around me, hugging me close.

"Pa, I..." Sobs, and more sobs. I found it strange to cry, knowing what would happen in the next few minutes.

Instead, I climbed on my horse. Pa handed me Wooly's rope. "Be sure and leave her at Sarah's." He slapped my horse's flank. Boone moved forward.

At the end of our driveway, I turned and waved. "Pa, I love you. Be careful."

I rode onto the main trail, heading east. At the first bend in the road, I pulled Boone off into a stand of pine trees and dismounted. Walking to the road's edge, I waited in the shadows. Wooly nudged me with her nose. I pulled her close, needing the assurance of the wee lamb's presence. Closing my eyes, I breathed a prayer, "Dear God, I don't know if I can ask You to bless me on this trip since I'm goin' against my pa's wishes. But at least, I can ask You to keep me and Wooly safe until I join Pa tonight. Thanks, amen."

I knew according to Pa's schedule, he couldn't afford losing three days' travel time to turn around and take me to the Watsens. At least, I hoped not.

Minutes later, Pa walked Taylor west leading the four packed red mules. He disappeared around a curve. I followed leading Wooly—heart pounding in my ears, breath coming in short gulps as I rode after him. I'd never felt so alone.

"Gracie, what have you done?" I wondered out loud, shaking my head. "No matter, you've cast your lot toward Texas, little girl. Ride on."

I stopped to get my saddle bags and bedroll, congratulating myself on how well my plans were going.

The eastern sun appeared over the red-hued horizon as we headed west to the Harpeth River. A slight, moist breeze hit my face. The light danced down the leaves on the trees and bounced off clouds in the west. In the misty dawn, I pulled my jacket around me. Within an hour, it would be tied around my waist. The sun's rays warmed the earth and humans alike.

At the Harpeth, the road narrowed, heading toward the distant city of Memphis. I stopped to let my horse water. Wooly skipped down the bank, plunging in to her belly.

"Just like a little-one," said an older man, holding a bucket he was filling in the river. His friendly eyes looked at me as he introduced himself. "My name's David Ormand. I'm headed to California." He tugged at his pants. They seemed too large for him. "Lost my suspenders," he explained. He ran his fingers through sparse, dark hair graying at the temples.

I shook hands with him. "I'm Gracie Tipton. Pleased to meet you."

"Gracie," he tested the word, "that's a pretty name."

"Thanks. My Ma said I was an amazing baby, and Pa's favorite song is "Amazing Grace." So they called me amazing Gracie. You're not going for gold, are you? In California, I mean." I watched two other riders walk their horses to the river's edge to be watered.

"Well, I don't know. My brother's been there for years. He sent for me. Guess he's gettin' a little old for the job—rheumatism, you know—and needs help." Mr. Ormand laughed easily.

"Are you goin' by way of Memphis?" I asked, thinking he might be too old for the job too. "I'm headed there."

"Yes. Are you travelin' by yourself?"

"No, Pa's just ahead of me. I plan to catch up."

"Don't mind a little bit of company, if you'll let me ride along."

"Don't mind a bit. This here's Wooly, my lamb."

"I'm driving a small wagon. Your lamb's welcome to ride with me." Mr. Ormand hefted the bucket of water for his wagon horse. I followed as he climbed the bank, thinking the good Lord does provide.

We forded the Harpeth River with Wooly riding in Mr. Ormand's wagon.

Eight hours later, we gained on my father who had stopped beside the road. The sun filtered between clouds piling together in the west, making light gray streaks from sky to earth and casting dark shadows underneath the trees.

"That's Pa," I said, shading my eyes against the sun, which sat on the tops of the oak trees, silhouetting his familiar form down the road. I pulled to the side of Mr. Ormand's wagon. "I guess he's stopped to find a place to eat and sleep."

As we approached, Pa strode to the middle of the road and stood with his hands on his hips. I dismounted. Setting my face in a gritty unwavering manner, I stepped toward him, stopping at arm's length.

"Gracie Tipton," he said. "This isn't the way to the Watsens. What do you think you're doing?"

"Pa, you can't leave me with them. Not again. I'm not goin' to let you. I'm goin' to Texas with you." My chin jutted out as I proclaimed my intention and stood my ground. I flicked my gaze toward Mr. Ormand. He looked amused. What was so funny?

"Gracie, you've disobeyed my orders." Pa tried to be firm in his words, but I could tell something was amiss. His mouth was twitching strangely.

Suddenly, Pa and Mr. Ormand burst out laughing. My mouth dropped open. "What's goin' on here?"

Pa clapped his hands on his knees. Between guffaws he explained, "I've—known—about—your scheme—for some days. Ever since I found—your extra shoes and nightgown—stuffed in the bottom of a sack I rearranged. I figured if you could pull off this stunt, you could go."

"O-oh!" I exclaimed, raising my fists to beat him on the chest. He held me at arm's length and my licks were more like tender whacks. "How could you do this to me?" The pressure was off. Tears started running down my cheeks.

Pa put out a finger and brushed one away. Then he pulled me to him. "Gracie, I didn't intend for you to go, because the trail ahead is a hard one. I needed to know if you had enough gumption to take whatever might befall us."

"And Mr. Ormand?"

"He's a friend of the Watsens, and he is headed to California. He agreed to be at the Harpeth River to escort you. I needed to be sure of your safety."

"The Watsens knew of your plan?"

"Yes." Pa pulled back so he could look at me.

"Pa, you don't know how I've agonized over my decision. How bad I felt at deceivin' you."

"Yes I do. I know you, little girl. Can you forgive me?"

"Yes, and can you forgive me for lying and sneakin' around behind your back?"

"If you promise never to do this again, I think I can."

I nodded, shaking two more tears loose.

"And now that's settled, we need a place to stay the night." He put his arm around me and looked west.

Ahead was a prosperous looking farmhouse. "I'll see if I can get permission to stay on their land. Gracie, you and David wait here." Pa rode off on Taylor.

Mr. Ormand approached with Wooly trotting beside him. "Gracie, I'm sorry I couldn't tell you I knew your father."

"Whew!" I pushed the sigh out between thin pursed lips. "Don't worry. I'm glad Pa wasn't mad as a nest of buzzin' hornets." I shook my head at this thought. The burden I'd carried for many days was lifted from my shoulders. My spirit soared on new wings. I felt light as a feather. But my body was not in as good of shape. Not used to riding eight hours with only stops for water and a trip behind a bush, my body ached, and my legs were stiff. I walked back and forth in the road, rubbing my abused back and hips.

"It's not much fun traveling long distances by horse if you're not conditioned to it," observed Mr. Ormand, a half-smile on his face. "If you get tired, I'll swap places with you. You can drive my farm wagon."

I walked over to him. He knelt beside his wagon, checking a hub for grease. His wide-brimmed hat bore sweat stains on its rounded crown. A pair of bleached-out blue eyes stared back at me from his weather-worn face, which sported four or five days of stubble.

"Thanks, I may do just that. My bottom is sore."

"Can't say that riding on a wagon bench will help your soreness, but at least it'll be a change." He stood and pulled at his pants.

"Pa wants to make thirty miles each day. We have to be in the Guadalupe Mountains by September first. He's got a job there with the new Butterfield Stagecoach Lines, but I guess you know this."

"Yes. You're headed for Texas and New Mexico Territory," Mr. Ormand said.

"I guess so." I noticed a hole in his wagon cover. Something inside caught my eye.

"I think Texas is mostly flat with plains, Indians, and buffalo."

"I don't know. I've never been there, but Pa's been twice, and he knows a lot about the state. Is that a box of books in your wagon?" I'm not usually nosy, but this man I found interesting.

"Yes."

"I love to read. My favorite book is *The Young Fur Traders*." I thought of Paul.

"By Ballantyne." Mr. Ormand nodded. "Yes, I've read the book. Ballantyne is an Englishman. I'll look through my collection and find one I think you'll like, something by an American author."

"Somethin' about the West?"

"Maybe... Here comes your pa. From the looks of him, he's found a place for us to spend the night."

We stood in silence watching my smiling father walk toward us. "There's a spring about two miles down the road. We'll find clean water and grazin' for our horses and mules. The owner will let us overnight at this spot."

The place where my father pulled off of the road had seen the feet of many travelers. Trodden down, the grass grew in tufts over the bare ground. I helped stake our animals, including Wooly, in the field nearby. In a pit, surrounded by rocks and covered by an iron grate, Mr. Ormand built a fire from brush he'd gathered in the dense forest. A couple of already well-placed oak logs provided seating for our weary bones in the fire's glow. Nearby, oft-used straw piled deep upon the ground formed a lumpy mattress for our bedrolls.

Supper consisted of bread, boiled eggs, and cooked cabbage with bacon crumbled in it. A piece of pound cake I'd baked yesterday, with strong coffee to wash it all down, topped off our meal. After my long, stressful day, I ate with enthusiasm, savoring every delicious bite.

Dark settled in as supper dishes were washed in spring water next to our horse's makeshift corral. I went to get my lamb from the field. "Pa, I'm tired. Wooly and I are goin' to bed."

"There's a sack of food for Wooly with our supplies."

Sure enough, the sack turned out to be the one Pa had carried from the hardware as I told Paul goodbye. I gave a chuckle, opened the sack, and pulled out a handful. Wooly stuck her nose into my hand and ate. "Little lamb there's no need to worry. My pa's takin' good care of us both."

Leaving the men by the fire, I carried my bedroll over to my new bedroom under the starry skies. Moonlight struggled through the trees as I knelt down and spread my bedding over the straw, which smelled faintly of musk and old dirt.

Until we got to Memphis, I intended to sleep in my clothes. When I slid into my bedroll, pulling Wooly down beside me, I felt a stab of homesickness. On this particular night, her comforting presence was needed, being my first night away from my picket-fenced home.

"Goodnight, everybody." Underneath my breath, I said, "Goodnight Sarah and goodnight Paul. And, thank you God."

"Sleep tight, little girl," I heard my pa's quiet chuckle. He continued to talk in low tones to our new friend. "She's done well today. This'll be a long trip for her, but she's got a lot of spunk, and...

I don't know when Pa and Mr. Ormand decided to go to sleep, but in the early morning Wooly woke me. I thought she might need to relieve herself. I knew I did. When I walked away from my roadside bedroom, the men were breathing deep and low nearby.

The pleasing smell of strong coffee and woodsmoke woke me the following morning.

"Gracie, come and eat." Bacon and eggs provided by Mr. Ormand made a stick-to-your-ribs breakfast. During the following days, this became his habit—cooking the first meal at sunrise.

"My mouth's waterin', and my stomach's grumbling," I told him, walking over to retrieve my full plate. An open Holy Bible lay beside him on the log where he sat.

I held a stick skewered with two thick slices of bread over the fire, toasting them for my meal.

"My Mom always said a good breakfast will hold you 'til supper. She sometimes had cinnamon-sugar cooked apples and sliced red tomatoes with our meal. Oh, and fried dried apple pies for supper." He stared into the glowing fire, remembering other times and places—a touch of sadness shadowing his face.

"Where'd you grow up, Mr. Ormand?"

"East of here, over the Smoky Mountains in Asheville, North Carolina. A beautiful place with lots of trees and runnin' water. I lived there all my life."

"Pa's family is from East Tennessee. The Smoky Mountains. I don't know any of them. Is your mother still there?" I said, digging into my eggs and bacon.

"No, I buried her last year. Bless her soul. She was a good mother. Always worked hard for her children. I miss her. This is her Bible." Mr. Ormand stroked the worn black book and poked at the fire with a stick. Flames and sparks flew upward. "Her passing made it easier for me to leave. There's nothing left to keep me near."

"What kind of work did you do in Asheville?"

"I was a parson and a teacher. I've often wondered if that's where the word preacher came from. Back in the hollers of the Blue Ridge and Smoky Mountains those two professions were frequently combined."

I wanted to ask him a hundred more questions, but our chat was interrupted by my father, who carried a shaving mirror under his arm. He wiped his face with a towel.

"Good morning, David. Gracie. Feels good to get the stubble off." He walked to his saddle bags, pulled out a small bag, and placed his shaving utensils inside.

"Your plate's over here, Jay." Mr. Ormand indicated a tin plate warming on one of the rocks by the gleaming coals he'd raked nearby. Pa rubbed his hands together and headed for his food. "Are you two travelers ready to go?"

"Might ought to hitch up my wagon and saddle the horses first," Mr. Ormand teased him—the sad expression on his face replaced by a sunshine smile.

Securing the warm plate, Pa sat down on one of the logs and dug in. Mr. Ormand took him a tin cup of coffee. "Cream and sugar?" he joked.

I liked our new friend. He didn't serve grouchiness with his menu, and besides the hot breakfast, his radiating smiles started my day off especially well.

"I'll go saddle the horses while you eat. Gracie, do you want to help?"

I sopped my tin plate with the last of the toast and jumped up. "Sure."

An hour later, we were on the road heading west. From now on, with the pressure relieved about sneaking and lying, I intended to really enjoy my trip.

For the first two hours, Wooly trotted behind my horse. Sometimes, she stopped to nibble at a tasty morsel she found in a clump of grass, but when she realized I'd foraged ahead, she flew on her long, wobbly legs to catch me. We laughed at her antics all day long.

On the third day, a slight drizzle accompanied our travels. My oilcloth raincoat and wide-brimmed hat kept me dry during the miserable, subdued ride.

Late in the afternoon, the Tennessee River blocked our progress. I sat looking down on the red and white ferry plowing through the dark-green water toward us. Oak, maple, and sweet gum trees lined the bank, and a couple of long-legged, blue-gray birds, startled at our approach, and flew from a marshy field in the lowland beside the stream.

"Pa, what kind of birds are those?"

"Great blue herons. We'll see them in Texas." Pa pointed his finger southward. "Look, over there." Another long-legged bird with snowy plumage stood still as a statue looking into the shallow water. "That's a white heron fishin'. Some people call her an egret."

We watched as the bird dipped her head into the water and pulled out a wriggling fish.

"Do we want to cross the Tennessee now or wait until tomorrow?" asked Pa, rain dripping off of his hat onto his brown saddle.

I voted for today and so did Mr. Ormand. We rode down the steep hill to the muddy bank where the ferry unloaded several passengers.

Pa started aboard the ferry with the pack mules. Big Red, Pa's gentle favorite, balked at stepping on the wooden, loading walkway. He stumbled around in the squishy wet dirt at the edge of the river, unwilling to board. Pa hurried back and a few soft-spoken words later, he led the red mule aboard. Mr. Ormand and Wooly followed. I rode behind.

Waiting for the others to load, I checked out the huge boat with its flat deck. The ferry had an enclosed tower with a metal ladder leading to a high platform. The Captain stood there with a skinny black instrument, sighting for objects in the river. While I gawked at the Captain in the tower, Boone tossed his head at the floating boat. My skittish horse pranced, making a misstep at the water's edge. Stumbling in the mud, he threw me from the bank into the deep darkness of the Tennessee River.

I struggled to the surface, gasping at the shock of the cool water, fighting to stay afloat—my heavy garments and shoes pulling me down toward the river's muddy bottom.

"Gracie!" yelled Pa and Mr. Ormand in unison. Pa ran to the side of the ferry, pulled off his boots, and prepared to jump overboard. Following Pa, people came from all directions and I watched from afar while I struggled to keep my head above water.

"Wait!" A tall member of the crew came running. He grabbed a wound rope hanging from the open rail and expertly tossed the length to me in the river. I managed to grasp the end and hang on as I was pulled to a side ladder. He hauled me over the bars, waterlogged and exhausted.

Pa pulled off my rain coat. "So much for staying dry during the day, little girl."

Embarrassed and dripping wet, I sat in a wet, cold heap on a chair, which appeared from nowhere. I wrung the water out of my full, limp skirt. It made a dark puddle on the wooden deck.

"My horse..."

"Your horse is fine and aboard," said someone I didn't know.

I wanted to crawl under a nearby wagon, but soon realized I'd become a sought-after celebrity. Most came by to talk and make sure I'd weathered my impromptu swim.

Even the Captain came to talk. "Nice day for a swim in the Tennessee," he observed, smiling. Then he shook my hand, "I'm glad you're okay."

Later, on the opposite side, we pulled off the road to make camp. The rain had stopped.

I stripped off my wet clothes and hung them to dry by the campfire. Putting on clean, dry clothes, I noticed Pa checking out

my drying duds and nodding. Many days later, I found out why
he nodded.

We traveled nine days to cover the two hundred and fifty miles
from Nashville to Memphis. The road got progressively rougher
and narrower. The land changed to shallow valleys and gently
sloping hills.

Sometimes, when I looked over my shoulder, I got the
feeling the road was rolling up behind me. The farther I went, the
bigger the roll, pushing me forward, quicker and quicker, farther
and farther.

As we approached Memphis, the land became flat and the
road widened. I noticed acres and acres of a different kind of
crop planted in the fields. When I asked Pa about it, he said, "It's
cotton. When time comes to harvest these fields, they'll be
almost solid white."

"There's a lot of work, harvestin' cotton, Gracie," said Mr.
Ormand. I rode horseback on one side of his wagon and Pa the
other.

"Have you worked cotton, David?"

"Yes. And tobacco in South Carolina. Most of the hard
work is done by slave labor. I don't know what the South would
be like without the black men."

"Are you for slavery?" asked my father. Pa was against
slavery, a topic that set him at naught with his fellow middle
Tennesseans. "The slave issue is rearing its ugly head, and I fear
it will tear the States apart."

"No, I'm not for slavery. I think all men should be free. I'm
not for seceding from the Union either. California should put
enough space between me and the troubles brewing here in the
East. I'm too old to fight."

I listened while the two continued to discuss the issue of
slavery. I'm sure I sided with Pa, but at sixteen it didn't seem as
important as their serious voices made it sound.

"When it comes to slavery," Pa said, "people in Tennessee
are about fifty-fifty but leaning toward secession. If Kentucky
goes Pro-union and Tennessee goes Pro-confederacy, then this

state will be a battleground. Both armies will strip the land of all food supplies and other usable products. Tennessee's water resources will become highways for both armies and unsafe for use by those producin' products to sell to the North or otherwise. You said you were too old to fight. I'm not too old, but I've fought in two wars. I'm not interested in killing another man on purpose."

"Is that the reason you're goin' West?"

Pa nodded. "One of them. I think it will be years before the ravaging of the South will be overcome. Texas may escape the brunt of the conflict."

"So, you really think there will be war."

"I don't want to be a naysayer, but only a miracle of God can prevent it."

"Jay, I hope you're wrong."

Pa nodded. "I do too."

I looked at Mr. Ormand. During our travel together, I'd found out this preacher and schoolteacher from Asheville had never married. He had sisters, but his only brother was in California.

By the time we got to Memphis, he and I were the best of friends. Could Pa and I persuade him to change his mind and continue with us on the Butterfield Trail?

4

"Price gouging!" exclaimed Pa. "Is everyone in America heading west?" I watched as he patted his hidden money belt making sure the money from the sale of our farm and cattle was secure around his waist. "Little girl, we gotta find a cheaper place to buy supplies." He walked over to an overall-clad man and started a short conversation.

In July 1858, I stood next to my horse fascinated by the hustle and bustle of the river port at Memphis, Tennessee. Standing on the Chickasaw Bluffs, above the river below, I looked dumbfounded as men rumbled past with Conestoga wagons—the huge prairie schooners of the West. I watched while eight horses pulling thousands of pounds of freight headed down the slope toward the ferry, which crossed the distant Mississippi River.

Nearby, an owner walked beside his four teams, cracking his whip and calling a loud "gee" or "haw," depending on which way he wanted them to go. His helper pulled at the brake chain, slowing the monster as it approached the river. I held my breath, watching as the horses and wagon rolled and slid down the wet, slimy bank while being loaded aboard. The operation went smoothly, and I realized these two men and those horses had performed the same operation many times before.

Pointing, I asked Pa, who'd returned, "Are we goin' to buy one of those?"

"No Gracie, ours will be a smaller version. We need to use our money for more important provisions than four teams of horses, and anyway we've got Big Red and the other mules."

The other wagons heading to the river were less impressive. Some were glorified farm wagons like Mr. Ormand's with wooden slats bowed in an upside-down U. The six inverted slats nailed or bolted to the wagon's sides held a tautly stretched canvas, making a roof above the wagons occupants and household goods, protecting them from the unrelenting sun or cold rain.

I saw women in colorful bonnets with wide brims—ribbons tied securely beneath their chins. A bit of air, relieving the noonday heat, stirred the few, moist curls escaping their tight bondage. They sat in bewildered wonder at the jostling crowd. Their shaded faces showed sorrow mingled with excitement at the recent disturbance of their well-orchestrated lives. Before us moved the quietly churning river, and only God knew what trials lay beyond. Were they wondering like me?

Children's shrieks of laughter caused me to turn around as they ran by me on both sides. A red-headed boy, around ten, stopped to grab a piece of flying paper driven by wind off the Mississippi Delta. Squealing and dirty, he and the others darted between the families milling about.

The smell of unwashed bodies, woodsmoke, leather, and horse's sweat mingled together with the dusty air and river smells. My nose rejected most of the stench and accepted the sweet perfume of stew cooking on a spit under a shed nearby.

"Pa, I'm hungry."

"Gracie Tipton, I swear you've got a tapeworm."

"What's a tapeworm, Pa?"

"I don't know, but you've got one." He was too aggravated to be sociable or helpful today. I shut up and told my growling stomach to wait. "Pa don't have time for you."

We followed him from the bluffs into the tightly packed city—one of the eastern ends of the Eighth Division of the new Butterfield Stagecoach Lines.

"Jay, where's the other end of Butterfield's Eighth Division?" Mr. Ormand looked over at Pa as he rode alongside his wagon. Pa stared at the leaflets he'd pulled from his vest pocket.

"At Tipton, Missouri."

"Do you think Tipton is as crowded and loud as Memphis?" Pa laughed. "No. I understand Tipton is a small, sleepy town west of the state's capital at Jefferson. Ah, here it is on the papers Mr. Augustine gave me."

Mr. Ormand and I watched Pa run his finger down the page. "Gracie and David, we need to find the new Butterfield Stage Headquarters. My papers say Commerce Street but there's no street number." My father knew nothing about Memphis. His two trips West bypassed the town.

Slow-growing Nashville was a quiet, genteel, literary metropolis compared to the raucous, bustling city we rode through today. Commerce Street continued to be an unknown address, and leading four red mules, plus a daughter on horseback, and including Mr. Ormand with his team and wagon through the dusty, dirty streets proved to be difficult. My father's temper didn't improve.

"How many people do you think live here, Jay?" asked Mr. Ormand after we'd stopped to ask directions two times.

"Only weeks ago, the Nashville paper ran an article on our state's growing cities. I knew I was coming here so I paid particular attention to Memphis." Pa stopped, wiped his sweating brow with a handkerchief he pulled out of his back pocket, and looked at the busy thoroughfare. "In 1850, Memphis's census showed an estimated population of about eight or nine thousand and it should have tripled in size since then."

"Twenty-four thousand. Land's sake! It's as big as or bigger than Nashville."

"Growing by leaps and bounds, the newspaper said." My father uttered this as we passed huge warehouses where freight haulers going West purchased goods to load aboard their wagons. The road ended at another bustling street. He turned in his saddle, squinting up and down the new street.

"Which way, now," I heard him mutter.

"This is Commerce Street, Pa." I pointed to a sign straight ahead over a clothing store where the latest men's fashions were displayed in a recently washed window. Puddles of water stood on the boardwalk in front. On a background of yellow, the black lettering stood out. *Bridger's Haberdashery*. The dark-green slogan underneath read, "*Where the fashionable purchase clothes.*" And the address in small, glittering gold lettering was 604 Commerce Street.

"Ah, then we're close," exclaimed my father, slapping his leg.

"Why don't you two wait here with the mules, and I'll find the office. Shouldn't be far down the road. I'll be back to get you as soon as I find the place." Before I could protest, he clucked to his horse and trotted off down the street.

Mr. Ormand climbed out of his wagon, and I dismounted Boone. "Guess we have the same idea, Gracie." He pointed to chairs on the shaded boardwalk in front of us. A couple of convenient, recently vacated, cane-bottomed chairs with slat backs would make us comfortable.

"You wait here. I have an errand to run." He jabbed his thumb toward the store across the street and uttered one word. "Suspenders."

He bought blue ones and wore them as he settled into the chair under the porch. "Looks like our herd is causing a problem with traffic."

"Yep, I've noticed a few dirty looks. Wooly's in your wagon. Didn't want her underfoot."

Leaning back against the storefront, we took stock of our position on the street corner.

"What's a clairvoyant?" I asked Mr. Ormand.

"Where do you see that?"

I pointed across the street to a shop five doors down from the clothing store. "There. The sign says, *Clairvoyant, Commerce Street Fortune Telling.*"

"A clairvoyant person. Well, they're supposed to be able to see into the future, connect you to the dead, or describe events from your past."

"Have you ever been to one?"

"No. I don't intend to."

"Why not?"

"Because, I don't want to know what's in the future. I prefer to let it sneak up on me," he teased. "And as far as connecting with the dead, let them lie in peace, I say."

I nodded, agreeing with him. His answers sounded reasonable. We sat in comfortable silence for several minutes.

"Wonder what's taking Pa so long?"

"Butterfield Station must be hidin' from him." Mr. Ormand chuckled.

"Sir, did I hear you say Butterfield Station?" A man's voice from within the store's interior responded. *Thud!* Both Mr. Ormand and I sat forward in our chairs. Our attention turned from the street to the porch.

A well-dressed man came from the doorway.

"Yes sir. Do you know where the headquarters are?" I asked. My, he was a handsome man with dark hair parted in the middle and a well-trimmed mustache under his nose. He sported the latest, fashionable pork-chop sideburns.

"Right here," the man laughed, and we laughed with him.

"But there's no sign over the door." Mr. Ormand hopped off the porch, walked back into the street, and looked at the storefront.

"No, we haven't had time to install one. Didn't intend to have a branch office here, but since the Charleston to Memphis Railroad was completed last year, Butterfield can carry the mail coming from South Carolina, Georgia, Alabama and Mississippi all the way to the west coast. Hard to imagine how sweeping our company's range can be."

I watched as he reached his finger and thumb into the watch pocket on his vest. He pulled out a timepiece.

Flipping open the face cover he continued, "Won't be long until dinner."

That reminded me of my growling stomach. Was that an hour ago?

Mr. Ormand went forward and held out his hand. "I'm David Ormand, and this here's Gracie Tipton. Her father went in search of your office. He's to be station man at The Pinery in Texas."

"Never heard of it, but I'm sure it's on the list Mr. Augustine left when he visited last month." He turned toward me, a distant train whistle authenticating his former statements. "Isn't your father getting a late start?"

"Here comes Pa." Riding down the street with his head down, the set of his shoulders told me all I needed to know. I started laughing as I ran out to meet him. "Pa, we found it." I indicated the place where Mr. Ormand and the soon-to-be ticket agent stood.

"What are you talkin' about Gracie?" He dismounted and stepped to the porch, looking at the nondescript building.

Our new acquaintance stepped forward. "Sir, Jeb Carson at your service. I hear you're to be a fellow employee of Butterfield."

"Jonathan Tipton. Call me Jay. Yes. I'm headed for Texas. Where's your sign?"

Pa shook Mr. Carson's hand, and Jeb Carson laughed. "Haven't had time to install one. And anyway our sign maker is behind on orders."

"I need your help."

"Why don't we discuss your problems over dinner? Let Mr. Butterfield pay for the meal."

"Oh, Pa that sounds great. I could eat a horse."

Pa rolled his eyes and gave me one of his, *Oh heavens! And please be quiet* kind of looks.

He turned to the ticket agent, "Thank you, Jeb. We'll take your offer."

"Then we've settled the question. Let me lock the door, and we'll go down the street to Bessie's. She has the best home cooking around. I'm sure you'll like it, Gracie." Mr. Carson gave me a slight bow and an eyeing, which made me fidget and straighten my dusty skirt.

"Where can we put our stock?"

Mr. Carson walked our group around to the back of the building. The corral, large watering trough, and patch of green grass were a welcome sight to the mules and horses. After a long swig of water, they immediately started grazing. Mr. Ormand unhitched his horse from his wagon and we headed for the front.

Mr. Carson secured the gate. "We've bought ten acres here and plan on building a rough cover for our stages and animals."

"You've got a long way to go," observed Pa.

"And so do you, Jay. I envy you going to Texas." Carson stopped. "By the way, a Tipton man organized Shelby County where Memphis is located. Any relation to you?"

"Probably, especially if he's from East Tennessee."

We continued down the street, and over lunch, Pa learned the information he desperately needed.

His afternoon purchases turned out to be to his liking. "We get our new wagon in the morning," he informed me. "After that, we'll need to purchase the items on the list I made."

Heading back to Commerce Street, we rode headlong into a square where at least two hundred noisy people were gathered. Shaded by a huge walnut tree and situated in the middle of the open area stood a raised wooden platform. On the stand a man in a black frock coat and black hat shouted, trying to be heard over the din below him.

"Come on, Gracie. We need to leave and quick." My pa grabbed the reins of my horse to lead me from the area.

"No, Pa. What's happening here?"

I jerked the reins out of his hand and moved my horse over to get a better view. A black child appeared out of the crowd. Hands pushed him to the center of the platform. The man on the stage said, "Here's a good'un. Open your mouth boy—good teeth, strong. I'm told runs like the wind. Turn around, so we can see your backside." The bewildered boy turned slowly, his head and eyes down. He was naked. "So how do you feel about this 'n? Do I hear an openin' bid for Joseph?"

"Gracie, what you're looking at is the dark side of growing cotton and tobacco. Plantation owners buy and sell humans to tend fields."

"Sold!" the auctioneer yelled and pointed to the buyer below him.

A shrill cry from the crowd by the stand caused me to rivet my attention on a young black woman.

"Joseph, son!" She attempted to climb the platform as her son stretched out his arms to her.

"Mama!" His anguished cry cut to the bottom of my heart. He struggled against the vise-like hands holding him. "Mama."

Another black man caught the boy around the waist and carried him off the platform directly opposite from his mother. She partially collapsed, but was then pulled to the stage and quickly sold to another buyer.

Her buyer and his black helper led the new purchase in our direction. Her hands were tied with a rope as they walked close to our horses. The sparse clothing she wore hung loosely on her thin body. Tears streaked her face, and she moved her feet, dragging them as if they were made of iron. For a brief moment her eyes met mine and looked through me. Loaded onto a wagon with three or four others, her head turned to catch a glimpse of her Joseph. He was nowhere to be found.

This was my first close look at the abuse of slavery. I grabbed at my waist with both hands. My insides pulled together into a knot. I had a sickening feeling in the bottom of my stomach. Was I going to vomit? Now I knew why my pa and Mr. Ormand were against slavery. It made you sick to your stomach.

Mr. Carson advised us on lodgings for the night. We left our horses in the corral behind the new office for the stage lines and headed down the street to our rooms. A boardwalk in front of the business buildings kept buyers' feet dry during rain but often left deep puddles at the end where foot traffic crossed from one street to another.

I was dawdling behind Pa and Mr. Ormand window shopping. At the end of one block, I almost stepped from the wooden walk into a mud puddle, but caught myself just in time to lose my balance. "O-oh!" I shrieked, knowing in two seconds I'd be a wet, muddy mess.

"Hurry, Jedediah! Help that lady."

I fell into the arms of a young man who looked at me in bewilderment. His eyes were the color of a robin's egg, and he wore a short, scruffy brown beard. His hair was cut to end at the bottom of his ears.

"What'do I do with her, Pa?" Jedediah exclaimed, looking stunned to find me in his arms.

"Gall durn. Carry her over the mud puddle and put her on dry ground," the older man said. The mustache under his nose twitched to the left and his cold, steely eyes bored into mine. I noticed his dirty clothes and the unkempt beard and hair.

I heard sloshing around Jedediah's feet as he walked through the water, and I felt the muscles of his arms move as he deposited me on the ground. "Sorry, ma'am," he said, a slight smile showed even white teeth in an angular face. "I'm not around women much."

I straightened my skirt and adjusted my out-of-kilter hat. "Don't be sorry. I thank you. The situation could have ended much worse."

"Come on, Jedediah. Don't have time to waste yapping."

"Yes, Pa." When Jedediah touched his hat, I saw in his blue eyes a flicker of fire at his father's harsh command. He strode to the boardwalk. His father grabbed him by the shoulder and pushed him ahead, making the young man stumble at the quick thrust of his hand.

Fresh from my encounter at the slave market, my emotions raged. With clenched fists, I watched the two men continue down the street and turn the corner, knowing I'd come face-to-face with another kind of abuse.

"Gracie," called my father, interrupting my thoughts. "Come on."

I walked to Pa.

"A man shouldn't treat his son like that," he said.

After a quick meal in the King Cotton Inn's dining room, I headed for bed. Pa and Mr. Ormand took another room together.

I found it hard to fall asleep that night. The sight of the young black boy reaching for his mother, and her shriek, kept me awake until past midnight. My eyes didn't shut until I was exhausted. I couldn't understand why any human being created by God could treat another one this way.

Our departure from Memphis depended on how fast we could complete our list, but we needed the wagon to haul our purchases. The following morning, we ate a quick breakfast.

"Gracie, before we head to pick up our wagon, there's one other stop we need to make."

I shot a puzzled look at Pa.

We crossed the street to Bridger's Haberdashery. Inside, I found every style of men's clothing and boots, including a rack of suspenders. Tucked in a back corner were sewing items. Buttons, pins, needles, and even some bolts of cloth arranged in neat displays on the shelves. I headed in that direction.

"No, Gracie, you need to come over here."

When we walked out of the store, Pa had purchased three pairs of brown cotton trousers and two pairs of boots to fit me. He said, "You can't go West and wear skirts. Save what you've got for special occasions and use these. They're practical and will wear longer." That's when I knew why my father nodded as my clothes dried over the campfire after I'd fallen into the Tennessee River. He'd determined to buy me more useful clothes after we reached Memphis.

On July 7, Pa and I rode our horses away from the crowd to the edge of the forest at Chickasaw Bluffs. Behind us Memphis stretched out in a dizzying maze. Down below, ferries, steamboats, and flatbeds plied the water, moving passengers, conveyances, and products on the massive river. Black and white workers busily loaded and unloaded boats. Mounds of square cotton bales, stacked neatly on the docks, were moving methodically a bundle at a time onto flatbeds for transport upriver to factories in the North. I shivered when I looked at the cotton—the slave market scene still fresh in my mind.

Where the docks ended on the riverbank, cottonwoods and willow trees crowded the shore of the Mississippi.

"Look there, Gracie." Pa pointed to a ferry leaving its dock. "That's the boat we take across the river in the morning."

We watched the boat churn toward the center of the river. A large paddle wheel to the side drove it steadily toward the distant shore.

"Let's return to Butterfield's Headquarters. We need to check our packing again. We should be at Fort Smith in fourteen days, little girl.

"I like our new wagon, Pa." Mr. Carson, Mr. Ormand, Pa, and I walked around the smaller imitation of the Conestoga. I tried to touch the wheel's hub with the toe of my shoe. Couldn't do it in my constricting skirt. Tomorrow, I planned to wear my new britches.

"A real beauty, I'd say." Mr. Carson stood looking down at me.

"Pa had the jockey box filled with tools and fastened to the side, and a full supported bench built on the front." My expertise on the Conestoga continued to develop.

"Do you plan on riding with your pa, Miss Tipton?" asked Mr. Carson.

"No sir, I plan on driving the teams."

Mr. Ormand laughed, and Pa said, "She can do it, Jeb."

I saw admiration in Mr. Carson's eyes.

"Anyone riding on the wagon seat will have one problem. They won't be able to pull the brake lever without breaking an arm." My father reached for the long, metal bar attached to the front wheel.

"Yes, Pa, but flat ground won't be a problem. The mules will stop the wagon."

"Gracie intends to sleep well on our trip. She's got a feather-stuffed mattress on top of our wooden cartons. She'll be in her bedroll underneath the canvas bonnet out of the weather." I jumped as Pa prodded me with his finger.

"Will you put pitch tar on the sideboards and bottom to make it watertight?"

My father nodded. "Yes. At Fort Smith before we cross into Indian Territory. I plan on staying two or three days while we refresh and restock our supplies. Catch a wagon train going west to Texas."

"Your Conestoga should pull very well with your four mules," observed Mr. Carson. "The overland road you've picked is well-established to Fort Smith."

"You think traveling down the Mississippi by steamer and up the Arkansas River to Little Rock isn't dependable?"

"Yep. Although it's faster by water, I think Butterfield will be changin' the route. Navigating the Arkansas is an iffy proposition. You worry about water depth and tree snags."

"Is the route shorter to go by land?" This from Mr. Ormand.

"Yes. By two hundred miles. I'll miss you gentlemen—and lady—when you leave." Mr. Carson bowed to me. "It's been a pleasure serving you. If you have trouble call on me for assistance. I might be able to lend a hand."

Pa thanked him and assured him he'd be the first to know if we needed help. "Jeb, you mentioned new maps of the trail from Fort Smith through to Texas. I'd like to have a set."

"Of course. Meant to give you copies." Mr. Carson turned to go.

"Gracie, will you get 'em?"

"Gracie, I'm curious." Mr. Carson rummaged through papers on a rolltop desk. I leaned against the front counter in Butterfield's office watching as he searched its cubbyholes. "Your pa's done a great deal of traveling from the East Tennessee Mountains where he was born."

"He has. His parents drove the rough road from East Tennessee. They resettled in Nashville. Yellow fever and pneumonia made him an orphan by fourteen. Friends of his parents raised him. Treated him well. Then he joined with Davy Crockett to fight for the Texas Republic."

"Really. Davy Crockett?"

"Yeah. The one and only. But Pa never made the trip to the Alamo. He came down with pneumonia at Nacogdoches in January 1836. Regaining his strength, he traveled on to Texas. Joined up with the fight clear into Mexico. He returned to Tennessee and married my mother."

"Mr. Ormand mentioned your pa's a widower."

"Yes. After Mama died, he headed back to Texas for the Mexican War and on to California's gold fields with his military friend, William Boone. He came back through Vicksburg, Mississippi. Traveled the Natchez Trace home."

"What happened to you while he was gone?"

"Stayed with Pa's friends, the Watsens."

He nodded. "I've been on the Trace as far as the monument where Meriwether Lewis, the famous explorer of the Louisiana Purchase died."

"Pa saw it too."

"Did he bring gold from California?"

"Enough. He bought land on the western side of Nashville, and we established our home—a good home for eight years. When the article announcing the Butterfield contract appeared in the paper, he wrote to Mr. Augustine and asked for a position. He sold our farm, and we headed here."

Mr. Carson nodded and handed me the maps. "Your pa will like these. The Butterfield crews have been working hard to update the ones available. Should be more correct. Gracie, I hope you like your new home."

"Thanks. I do too."

King Cotton Inn was a welcome sight after our long day. Supper that night was delicious but eaten in silence. I ordered a long hot bath. My nightgown felt heavenly after sleeping in my clothes for several days.

The eighth of July, we left Memphis. Pa drove the wagon with the four mules now in harness and attached to the wagon's yoke. I rode my horse and led my father's.

"Big Red's a natural at pulling the wagon," Pa called. Big Red was the first mule on the left just ahead of Pa. He was an instinctive leader and positioned as such in the two teams of mules.

At the ferry, Pa drove on first and locked the wagon's wheels. Mr. Ormand, with Wooly riding inside, did the same. They both came to the ferry ramp to watch me board. Sporting my new britches, I managed to ride onto the boat without falling into the mighty Mississippi.

"Whaaaa! Whaaa!"

I jerked my head around to see the same red-headed boy I'd seen on my first day in Memphis. He stood next to his mother on the deck of the steamer. His eyes were red and his face streaked with tears. He looked toward the riverbank from which we'd just embarked. His mother bent to console him.

"B-but I'll never see grandpa and grandma again," he bawled. "Oh, Mama!"

"My son, we don't know that. Come let's explore the boat. We'll send them a letter and you can tell them all about our ride." Mama gently pushed her son ahead to the bow of the boat.

We crossed to the Arkansas side, ahead of Pa's written schedule. Departing the boat, Pa maneuvered the incline from the river's edge and pulled to the side of the rutted path. Jumping off, he worked at adjustments in the harness, making sure the teams were comfortable for our future journey.

Normally, I would have helped him, but today I walked down to the riverside. Shading my eyes with my hand, I looked back at Tennessee's green trees. For two days, I'd managed to keep this leave-taking from my mind, but with the fervent cries from the young lad...my heart churned. Hot tears stung my eyes for my birth state. I never expected to see Memphis or Nashville again. Embarrassed at my sudden emotion, I quickly dashed the tears away before they ran down my cheeks.

The high-pitched whistle of the *Lively Lucie*, a steamboat heading north for St. Louis, announced a dreary goodbye.

"Makes me feel like another traveler thousands of years ago."

I jumped not realizing Mr. Ormand stood above me.

"Come, Gracie," he said, looking west toward the flatland of the Mississippi Delta in Arkansas.

"Who's that? The other traveler?" I asked, climbing the bank to join him, looking in the same direction.

"Abram, when God ordered him to leave Ur and head for Canaan. Do you think he was sad at leavin' the land where he was born? And do you think he felt excitement at headin' toward a new place where he would make a new home?"

I remained silent for a moment. Likening myself to Abram in the Bible never occurred to me. "Of course, he felt sad."

"And excited, Gracie?"

"Yes. Excited at the prospect of a different home and opportunities in a strange land called Canaan."

Mr. Ormand and I headed back to our horses. Pa waited on the wagon seat to start our trip.

"Going home to Texas will be no different, will it, Gracie?" I knew he was right. I mounted my horse. Mr. Ormand climbed onto his wagon, and Wooly looked over at me from her perch beside him. I fluffed her white, fuzzy nose.

Pa clutched the reins of our mule teams. "Come on Big Red," he called. "Let's go home."

That's exactly what I wanted to do—go home to West Texas, the Guadalupe Mountains, and whatever God had in store for me. Somewhere in the back of my mind, a thought arose. Abram might have been excited to travel to a new land but that didn't mean his troubles were over. What faced our trio ahead?

REBA RHYNE

❧ 5 ❧

The Arkansas-Mississippi River delta stretched for miles into the state. The road being smooth, Pa let me drive the mules the first day or two. Drive might be too descriptive, because our mules walked on their own without much guidance.

"I'm glad we brought these teams from Nashville. They work well together," Pa told me.

Our wagon traveled through thousands of acres of cotton, and cotton reminded me of the horrible scene I'd witnessed two days earlier. I wanted more information.

"Gracie, we were in Exchange Square in Memphis. It's not the only place where humans are bought and sold. You'll find slave auctions all over the South."

"Even in Nashville, Pa?"

"Yes, even in Nashville. I didn't take you around them at home. Couldn't see any reason to subject you to such an appalling scene."

I nodded. "Why or how did this come about?"

"Buying the black man for labor wasn't always practiced in America. Only when our growing population necessitated large industries, more commodities, and greater amounts of food did the white man deviate to putting men into bondage. At first, there were the indentured white people who worked at trades to learn jobs. Some of them came to America and worked seven years to pay for their passage on ships to our country. But they worked off their indenture and became free men. It would have been better if the Negroes were treated the same way—and they could have been."

"Did the black man come of their own free will to be slaves?"

"Heavens, no! Slavers forced them to leave their West African homes. Greed, Gracie! Men's greed was what enslaved the black man. Plantation owners could have paid the men, women and children to work for them. Instead, families were bought from slave traders and forced to work against their will.

"I can't believe Americans could do such a thing. Our land is a land of free men."

"Slavery has been practiced since the beginning of the human race. Even in Biblical times, there were slaves."

We rode for several miles as I digested this new information. Then, I thought of another question. "What will happen if the Northern states insist on the Southern states giving up their slaves?" I'd heard the talk before, but now I was ready to listen.

"It's a bad situation, Gracie, and it's called secession. The plantation owners are dependent on large amounts of free or slave labor to produce their products. The Northern industries are happy to get raw goods at a reduced price because the labor is inexpensive. I heard many of the business people I talked to in Memphis say they weren't for seceding from the union. It's that way across Tennessee—many are for and many are against. There are pros and cons depending on how freeing the slaves will affect you."

"What will happen, Pa?"

"I hate to think it, little girl, but the word war is looming behind us. I hope there's no fighting, but I don't see a way of avoiding a conflict."

Pa and I ended our conversation.

The flat land changed to rolling hills and low mountains as we continued due west, reminding me of the Harpeth River and Nashville. Pa took over the driving.

The stations of another overland stage line appeared as we traveled—rough hovels with bare necessities. I began to wonder what we'd find at The Pinery when we got there—glad the small Conestoga would provide sleeping quarters.

One day I tied my horse behind Mr. Ormand's wagon and rode with him. We discussed the possibilities of a new Texas home.

"Gracie, you may have to sleep with the rattlesnakes under the stars," he teased.

"I hope not. I'd like to think I'll see a five-room log home with plenty of windows," I gushed.

"I understand wood is scarce in the desert."

"Pa says there's plenty in the mountains."

"What else do you expect to find in Texas?"

I hesitated for a minute before baring my soul. "Besides a home, I hope to find a man who loves me, and I hope to have children."

Mr. Ormand shook his head. "Good goals, I must say. There's a chapter in Proverbs about a biblical wife. I understand the passage somewhat different than some of the notions in our churches today. You remind me of her, Gracie—independent, resourceful, and strong. When you have a chance, read it in your Bible."

"I don't have a Bible, Mr. Ormand."

"Just as I thought. Turn around and look in the top of my box of books."

I did as told. "What am I looking for?"

"A Bible, of course."

"Here it is." I held the black book out, expecting him to take it.

"No, Gracie, it's yours. Days ago, I dug through the box and found you one."

"Thank you, Mr. Ormand. I'll treasure your gift."

"Tonight, when there's still light, read the last chapter of Proverbs. I'd like to think you'll become a woman—a wife—like her. A good wife is a gift from God."

Mystified at his interest, I turned the Bible's pages. "I promise I'll read the chapter."

We rode on in silence, holding on to the wagon bench because rocks in the rough road sometimes jarred our teeth together. Before nightfall, Pa stopped at a small stream to make camp. I volunteered to take the stock to drink from the cool waters coming from the hills nearby. I carried my new Bible with me.

Turning to the designated chapter in Proverbs, I read the long passage at the tenth verse. *Who can find a virtuous woman? for her price is far above rubies. The heart of her husband doth safely trust in her, so that he shall have no need of spoil. She will do him good and not evil all the days of her life. She seeketh wool, and flax, and worketh willingly with her hands. She is like the merchants' ships; she bringeth her food from afar. She riseth also while it is yet night, and giveth meat to her household, and a portion to her maidens. She considereth a field, and buyeth it: with the fruit of her hands she planteth a vineyard. She girdeth her loins with strength, and strengtheneth her arms. She perceiveth that her merchandise is good: her candle goeth not out by night. She layeth her hands to the spindle, and her hands hold the distaff.*

This Bible woman never quits, I thought. She sews, cooks food, buys fields and plants them, and makes merchandise to sell. She has her own money from the products she makes.

I continued to read. *She stretcheth out her hand to the poor; yea, she reacheth forth her hands to the needy. She is not afraid of the snow for her household: for all her household are clothed with scarlet. She maketh herself coverings of tapestry; her clothing is silk and purple.*

She has plenty of food and beautiful clothes with enough left over to clothe and feed others. How wonderful to be in such a position. And then the verses said, *her husband is known in the gates, when he sitteth among the elders of the land.*

Could I expect to marry such a man? I couldn't help but giggle at such a wonderful thought.

She maketh fine linen, and selleth it; and delivereth girdles unto the merchant. Strength and honour are her clothing; and she shall rejoice in time to come. She openeth her mouth with wisdom; and in her tongue is the law of kindness.

I liked to think I was kind to everyone I met, but I realized wisdom came with age, and at sixteen—well, almost seventeen, I had a ways to go.

She looketh well to the ways of her household, and eateth not the bread of idleness. Her children arise up, and call her blessed; her husband also, and he praiseth her. Many daughters have done virtuously, but thou excellest them all. Favour is deceitful, and beauty is vain: but a woman that feareth the LORD, she shall be praised. Give her of the fruit of her hands; and let her own works praise her in the gates.

I sat and considered the passage I'd read. I couldn't imagine being one-tenth of this great lady, but in Mr. Ormand's honor I'd certainly try. Imagine, a man praising me for being his wife. The very idea filled me with determination. I wanted to be this kind of wife. I reread the passage.

Three fourths of the way across the state to Fort Smith, we came to Stinnett's Station, sitting between the Arkansas River and the Quachita Mountains.

Stinnett's Station was a log structure doing double duty as a home for the family and a swing station on the new stage line. In the future, around twenty well-maintained steeds would fill the corral at the back of the home.

The station man's duties at a swing station were to unhitch the tired teams of horses from the stagecoach and exchange them for a fresh set. The stop was a chance for the passengers to get out and stretch their legs for ten minutes while this took place.

Today was special for me. I wondered if Pa would remember.

The sun was setting when we arrived, and Pa decided to camp next to the small log house of the Stinnett family. Ronald, a red-headed, skinny child of thirteen, came to help us unhitch our mules.

He said shyly. "Mum, where ye frae? Uh—from."

"From Nashville by way of Memphis," I explained.

"Bonnie mules," he returned, rubbing the flank of the one nearest him. "Where ye goin'?"

"To the Guadalupe Mountains in Texas. My pa will be station man on the Butterfield Stage Line."

"My pa's station man here."

"Yes, I know."

"'Twill help with yer mules, mum."

I looked at him. He spoke funny. "Where're you from, Ronald?"

"Arkansas," he said innocently.

"No. No, I mean you've got a strange way of sayin' your words. You're not originally from Arkansas."

"Och. I ken yer meaning. Pa and Ma's hame is Scotland. My hame is here."

"That explains it." I found Ronald Stinnett charming, and I loved to hear him talk with his Scottish brogue.

"Donna ye wont to take your mules and horses to the corral—brush 'em down?"

"Yes. I'll get Wooly."

"Wooly?"

I laughed at him. "You sure ask a lot of questions. Come and I'll show you Wooly."

Ronald loved the little lamb as soon as he saw her. "Such a wee lamb."

Wooly scampered around us, trying out her unused legs. She'd ridden in the wagon most of the day.

Ronald and I walked the red mules to the corral and started brushing down each animal. One of the requirements of the stage line was keeping the horses and mules in superb condition. This was good practice for us both.

We worked for almost an hour before his mother called us to supper.

"I think we can quit, new friend Ronald. Bring Wooly, and we'll go eat. I've been hungry since I ate dinner."

"Am pure done in," he replied.

Mrs. Stinnett's husband was in Fort Smith fetching supplies for their station. "Twill be back day-after-tomorrow," she explained, looking at Wooly with a doubtful eye. Wooly and Ronald played on the wood floor. "Dinnae know it's an important hub in the stage line."

"I'm curious, Mrs. Stinnett. What's Fort Smith like?" Pa forked a bite of food off his plate into his mouth.

"A grand place—brick buildings, glass windows, and a parade ground jist bonnie with green grass. The bugles sound all day to help the soldiers stay on time and in the right place. The sound chills me when I hear it. The enlisted men's barracks and the commissary are large. The commissary supplies other forts to the west—all the way to Texas."

"Who's the commander of the fort," asked Pa.

"It's Captain Sackett, ye ken, since March."

"Do you know him?"

"Naw. I huvnae had the pleasure."

Mrs. Stinnett arose and started to clear the table. I stood to help.

As soon as we finished, Mrs. Stinnett told me to sit. She brought out a cake and placed it on the table. "I ken it's ye birthday, Gracie."

Pa hadn't forgotten. "Happy birthday," everyone said in unison.

"How auld are ye, Gracie?" asked Mrs. Stinnett.

"Seventeen."

"Going on twenty-five," added my father, chuckling.

Later, after eating a slice of Mrs. Stinnett's cake, I said to Pa as I prepared to climb into the wagon for the night, "Thanks, Pa. I was afraid you'd forgotten."

"How could I forget one of the most important days of my life, little girl?" He placed his arm around my shoulder and gave me a hug.

"Pa, don't you think calling me 'little girl' might not be appropriate since I'm seventeen now?" It was dark, and in the moonlight, I could barely see his face.

"Gracie, you'll always be my little girl. I'm not sure I want you to get any older 'cause one day soon you'll leave me." Pa headed for his bedroll in the back of the wagon.

I couldn't deny this fact. I did want to get married and have a family. This hadn't been important until recently—until Paul.

Something else I'd noticed the farther we went west. Women were scarce, but men were plentiful. If I never saw Paul again, finding a good man was in my favor.

Pa rummaged around in the back of the wagon.

"Pa, your bedroll's on the right-hand side," I called.

When he came forward, he carried a package wrapped in brown paper and handed the bundle to me. "You can't see this tonight so wait until it's light tomorrow," he said. "Happy birthday, Gracie."

"Thanks Pa." I squeezed the package. It was soft and pliable. When I crawled into bed, I placed it by my pillow.

July 18 had turned out to be a really special day, and I wondered what I'd find in the squishy package tomorrow.

❧ 6 ❧

$\mathbf{M}$y birthday package contained a beautiful, long, pale-green satin dress in the latest fashion, with ruffles in tiers down the full skirt, wholly impractical for the rough frontier.

"Pa, the gown's beautiful," I told him, holding it against me so he could see it.

"And totally frivolous," he said, smiling, "but I wanted you to have something special. Could be the last pretty dress you'll have for a long time." He reached over and pulled gently at a ruffle, and in his eyes, I was sure I saw another future reason for the dress.

"I'll cherish it." I folded it neatly, placed it back in the brown paper it had come in, and put it in a safe place in the wagon.

Ronald came from the house carrying Wooly.

"Traitor," I said to Wooly, scratching her fuzzy nose. She'd slept with Ronald in the Stinnett's warm home. "I wish you could come with us, Ronald. I'm going to miss brushin' the mules with you."

"Ah, mum, dinnae ye ken I'd better stay here and take care of Ma. Pa counts on me." He handed Wooly into Mr. Ormand's wagon. She poked her head out the open front, saying goodbye.

"Been nice meetin' ye, Miss Tipton."

"Same here, Ronald." He walked a bit too quickly into the corral and disappeared.

When Mr. Ormand appeared, he handed me another package. It was a round box with a string tied around and over it. "I hope you like it."

The box was lined with satin and inside was a bonnet with pink and green flowers that matched the dress Pa had given me.

"How'd you know?" I looked at him in wonder.

"I was with Jay when he bought the dress. I don't get many opportunities to buy pretty things for beautiful young ladies. Happy birthday."

"Do you think I'm beautiful, Mr. Ormand?"

"Yes, I do Gracie, and a lot of it comes from within. Some young man will be very fortunate to get you. Remember what we talked about."

I walked over and gave Mr. Ormand a hug, realizing in just a few days I'd never see him again.

"Let's go wagon train!" shouted Pa. He climbed onto the driver's seat, picked up the reins, and prepared to leave.

"Wait, Pa."

I ran around to the back of the Conestoga and placed my new hatbox inside next to my dress, then motioned to Pa to head out. The wagon rumbled ahead, and Mr. Ormand followed. A bit of wind stirred the oppressive, sticky heat of the July morning, and scattered clouds danced across the sky, giving us some relief as we left.

I mounted my horse and pressed my hat down firmly on my curls. After waving goodbye to Ronald, whose nose was stuck around the side of the cabin, I turned my horse to the west. Riding along, I thought about how fast I'd attached myself to the people I'd been meeting and how I seemed to be saying goodbye all the time. This was something I didn't often think about, nor the emotions that went with the leaving.

⬚ ⬚ ⬚ ⬚ ⬚

We pulled into Fort Smith on the fourteenth day after leaving Memphis. It was pouring rain and the streets were a quagmire of mud. My introduction to this last outpost on the edge of civilization was not a good one.

Mr. Ormand and my father went to look for dry lodging.

I sat under the overhang on the wagon with my oil slicker wrapped around me, watching the raindrops make pock marks in the puddles of dirty brown water on the muddy street. Light from lanterns hanging from rough porches reflected in the wet road. Hunched over and shivering from the cold dampness, I wished for a warm fire.

Several minutes after my father left, I heard voices coming from the back of the wagon. I drew back into the shadows of the canvas top as the sounds grew louder. Were the men drunk? One voice was especially loud.

"Jedediah, how can you be so stupid? Have I taught you nothing in your twenty-two years?"

I'd heard that voice before? Where...? Memphis! The mud puddle. The blue eyes. I peeked carefully around the edge of the bonnet.

"But Pa, I knew you wouldn't..."

The two men passed the wagon, and in the semi-darkness, I saw the older man pause and slap the younger one across the face. Jedediah reached his hand to his face. He rubbed the area, and stared straight ahead. In the dim light, I thought I glimpsed the other hand ball into a fist.

Without thought to life or limb, I jumped out of the wagon and headed for the arguing pair. "Don't you hit him," I said as I flew into the older man's face like an angry banty rooster—separating him from his son.

Jedediah's father drew back at my approach but quickly recovered from the shock of my words.

"Girl, this ain't none of your business. Git out'en the way." The stench of alcohol permeated the space between us. I waved my hand to clear the air.

"I'm standin' right here. You shouldn't hit him," I said, remembering Pa's words.

"You gotta lotta gall, gal, butting in."

When I didn't move, he caught my waving arm with his viselike fingers. I saw something akin to rage in his eyes as he clamped his hand on my arm. At that moment, I realized he might hit me as he'd done to his son.

Pa arrived as the man touched me.

"I wouldn't do that, Mister." I'd never seen Pa look so threatening. His eyes were dark as night, and he took a solid, unwavering stance.

The older man stared at Pa and Mr. Ormand and dropped his hand, but not before giving my arm a hard squeeze.

"Come on, Jedediah." He grabbed his son by the upper arm. They moved on down the street, and disappeared into the brightly-lit saloon at the corner.

"Gracie, are you crazy? That man would've hurt you. Have you no sense of danger?" My father was angry at me, and he had a good reason to be.

"I'm sorry, Pa. I acted on impulse." I stood shaking and rubbing my arm after the shock of my furious actions wore off.

"Use the brain God gave you the next time."

"I promise I will."

"Have we seen those two before?" he asked.

"Yes, Pa, at Memphis. Remember? The younger one kept me from falling into the mud." I recounted the exchange between the two men.

"I don't like to see anyone abused," said my pa who stood looking in the direction the men had gone.

"Did you find a place for us to stay?"

My father pulled in a ragged breath. "No, there seems to be no room at the inn, Gracie." I realized my father was tired. "Mr. Ormand and I did find a nice settler who offered the use of his barn."

"Yes, and we quickly accepted," Mr. Ormand said. "He's coming to show us the way."

The barn wasn't big enough to pull our wagon into, but we managed to build a fire under its overhang, and warm food from the farm family cheered us.

Pa and Mr. Ormand slept on the sweet-smelling hay in the barn's loft, while I bedded down in the wagon.

I soon realized sleeping in the wagon was a big mistake. The wind moaned and rain beat hard on the wagon's canvas, sending a mist through its woven threads. My bed became damp with the fine spray, and though I snuggled deeper into its feathers, my misery increased as the night wore on. Unable to sleep, my mind swirled with questions, and I couldn't help but wonder what lay ahead for us in the coming days.

Fort Smith was a developing frontier town compared to Nashville and Memphis. There was a long, single street with small businesses lining either side. Several warehouses sat on the back streets. To the west, I saw the United State's supply garrison of Fort Smith. Outside, a number of buildings supporting the fort's activities ran smack into the small town.

When I got dressed the next morning, there was a dark bruise on my arm left by Jedediah's father. Pa was right. He would have hurt me. I had no experience with someone who was abusive to others, especially one who was drunk. I resolved not to get between those two again.

I'd seen this duo twice, and Jedediah's actions made me realize how unhappy he was with his father. I was beginning to despise the older man.

While Pa and Mr. Ormand went to find the tar needed to waterproof our wagon's bottom side, I walked around town. The fort especially interested me.

It was a pentagon-shaped structure with high walls made of stone. Inside the three-foot thick walls, the buildings were arranged around a central flat area. I learned this was the parade ground, and the other three buildings were sleeping quarters for enlisted men and officers. The fort looked unfinished, because the walls weren't completed to the same height.

Following my nose, as usual, I walked into a bake house outside the fort's grounds. "Good morning, something smells good."

A young soldier and an older woman shaped loaves of bread from a mound of yeast dough on a flat table. They placed each one in a greased and floured rectangular pan. Behind them an oven sat against the wall ready to accept the product for baking.

"Maybe it's pecan pie?" suggested the elderly woman, nodding toward shelves behind the door I'd come through.

I looked where she indicated. Twenty pecan pies sat in a line on three shelves, and the aroma, oh!—the aroma made my mouth water and reminded me of Aunt Maggie's Eatery in Nashville. I felt a stab of homesickness.

Our grub on the road kept us alive but left a lot to be desired when it came to variety. "They look wonderful."

"We cook for the soldiers," the woman explained.

"Speaking of soldiers, the fort looks unfinished."

"It is, and it won't ever be. Fort Smith was started to keep the Cherokee and Osage from warring. But the building took so long, peace come about before they finished it. So Fort Smith become a supply depot for other forts farther west, dispensing food, medicine, and ammunition. Contrary to most forts, the stables, laundry and hospital are here on the outside of the main fort."

"How many people live in Fort Smith?"

She turned to the young man working beside her. "What do you think, Private, a thousand or two?"

Private nodded in agreement.

"We got a brewery in town also. It's a source of a lot of trouble, let me tell you. Friday and Saturday night ain't fit for a sober person to be out on the streets."

After last night's scrape, I could agree with that. "Where is the brewery?"

"On the other end of town about a half-mile. Are you passing through?"

"Yes, on the way to Texas. My pa's going to work for Butterfield—"

"John Butterfield! I met him," the woman said. "He's a grand lookin' man. Do you know where his office is here in Fort Smith?"

"No, but I'd like to."

"It's on past Knoble's Brewery. You can't miss it."

"Thanks for being so kind. Guess I'd better go. I need to find my pa. It's almost dinner."

I opened the door to leave. "Wait, Missy."

I stopped and watched as she went over to the pie shelves. "Here, take this'n with you. I can't stand that hungry look in your eyes." She laughed.

I took her offering, thanked her, and went out the door. She called after me, "Come by the day before you leave, and I'll give you a couple loaves of bread, and bring the pie plate back when you come. I can't afford to lose it."

"I'll be here," I told her and walked toward town with my prize, picking a few of the pecans off the top. Nobody would miss them.

When I got back to our wagon, Pa was complaining about not being able to find the Butterfield Stage Line headquarters.

"I can tell you where it is."

"You can? How come you know so much?"

I ignored his last question. "Yes, it's outside of town about a half-mile—past the brewery."

"I saw those buildings, Jay. You and Gracie can go there tomorrow."

"Aren't you coming, Mr. Ormand?"

"Gracie, Mr. Ormand is hooking up with a wagon train leaving tomorrow morning for California. This is his last day with us."

I looked down at my pie. Tonight, we would celebrate knowing this nice man, but the pastry wouldn't taste as sweet as usual, knowing we might never see him again.

REBA RHYNE

7

Another goodbye and tears this time, as Mr. Ormand waited his turn to join the wagon train. "I'll miss you, Gracie Tipton." He held out his hand to me.

"If you don't like it out West with your brother, come to Texas and stay with us," I told him, unsure of what I should do.

"I'll do that. You can count on it." He turned and shook hands with my father. "Jay, it's been a pleasure ridin' the trail with you."

"I echo Gracie's suggestion. We would welcome you."

"Gracie, my guess is, you think I've forgotten my promise to give you a book. But I haven't. Here's one I think you'll like. It's two different perspectives on today's ideas of America's native Indians."

I took the book just as the wagon master came by. "Mr. Ormand, you're next."

"I guess this is it." He turned to mount onto the wagon seat.

I rushed to him, grabbing his arm and flinging my other around his neck. So much for propriety or being unsure—I loved Mr. Ormand. "Don't forget us."

He gave me a hug and said, "Remember the verses in Proverbs, my dear."

"God go with you, David."

"And you too, Jay." He climbed onto the wagon seat and waved goodbye, and in his eyes, I saw tears.

They matched the ones in mine. I looked down at the scuffed copy of the *Last of the Mohicans*. Obviously, it was a book much loved by the previous owner.

Pa and I stood there until we could no longer pick out his wagon in the long line heading west. "He's a good friend."

"None better, little girl. Let's go find Butterfield's office and see if we need to pack anything else for our trip."

"Pa are we halfway there yet—to The Pinery, I mean?"

"Not quite, but don't get discouraged. Remember every curve, hill, or river brings something new to appreciate and brings us a step closer to our home." My pa was fascinated by the countryside and couldn't get enough of the original scenes rolling by us.

"I'm not discouraged, but I wish we could start housekeeping and get out of the wagon. I feel like my insides are scrambled like eggs."

Crossing a small stream, we left the muddy staging area where the westward heading wagons lined up. In a few short hours or days, we would be back in this flat field doing the same. Pa and I couldn't head west into Indian Territory and Texas without the accompaniment of fellow travelers. *Safety in Numbers* was a slogan heard in Fort Smith and other areas where overlanders bunched together, heading to new unknown lives in the West.

BUTTERFIELD OVERLAND MAIL
7TH DIVISION, FORT SMITH, ARKANSAS

Pa and I stood looking at the sign over the door.

"At least, the sign's on the building," he said.

"It's not like there's a lot of room to make a mistake out here on the vacant prairie." I said this, remembering our trouble at Memphis. Fort Smith headquarters proved easy to find.

"No, I reckon not," he said as we entered.

We stood before the counter in the new Division Headquarters. The smell of fresh-cut wood, crisp new curtains, and new signage greeted us as we entered the door. One particular sign—outside next to the entrance and now on the wall behind the counter—caught my eye. It said:

**YOU WILL BE TRAVELING THROUGH
INDIAN COUNTRY AND THE SAFETY
OF YOUR PERSON CANNOT BE
VOUCHSAFED BY ANYONE BUT GOD.**

I punched my elbow into Pa's arm and pointed at the sign. He glanced in the direction I indicated, shook his head slightly, and concentrated on the attendant before us. The man was riffling through a long list of names in a folder. "I'm sorry this is taking so long. Mr. Butterfield has around eight hundred new employees and one hundred thirty- nine relay stations scattered along the Southern Mail Route."

"I'm not in any hurry, sir."

Mr. Attendant continued to rummage in the folder. His movements were punctuated by brushing from his eyes straight brown hair, which fell in sticky clumps off his forehead. I wondered if he used bear grease on his hair. The thought caused me to giggle.

"Ah, here it is Mr. Tipton." He smiled, revealing a chipped front tooth. He held a smaller piece of paper, waving it in the air like a trophy. "You're one of the last to be hired."

"Guess they couldn't find a station man. The area's in Apache territory and isolated."

"Did Mr. Augustine give you some preliminary information about your new position?"

"Yes," and Pa pulled out the bunch of worn papers he kept in his vest pocket, pushing them across the counter to the attendant.

After leafing through the contents, the attendant looked at Pa. "I have a standard package of supplies for your station at The Pinery, and a list of suggested staples for you personally to consider buying. I see that your daughter is traveling with you?" He said this with a question in his voice while checking me out, top to bottom.

My father confirmed his statement. "Yes, this is my daughter, Gracie."

"You understand that Butterfield Stage Lines can't be responsible for her?" His eyes ran over me again.

"Yes, I do."

"I'll get your information, Mr. Tipton." Brushing the hair out of his eyes once more, the station attendant disappeared into the back room. At that moment, the door opened, and two men came into the office area. Jedediah and his father.

The older man took one look at us and immediately came over. The alcohol smell preceded him. "I think we got off on the wrong foot yesterday. My name's Hurricane Bailey and this here's my son, Jedediah Smith Bailey." He extended his hand to Pa.

"I'm Jay Tipton, and this is Gracie, my daughter, Mr. Bailey." Pa didn't say this in a warm, friendly voice.

"Jest call me Hurricane. Are you working fer Butterfield?"

I stood back while this conversation took place, looking at the young man whose attention-grabbing blue eyes darted once in my direction. Although I'd seen him twice and those moments were brief, I felt a draw—a tension between us.

Jedediah Smith Bailey was taller than his dad, as tall as my pa. His shapeless wide-brimmed hat shaded his face. I noticed a discoloration and swelling on his temple and wondered if his father's blow had caused the bruise. I put my hand on my arm and felt a sharp pang where Hurricane Bailey had squeezed it.

Jedediah was thin. He wore a blue shirt and brown britches, neatly patched at the knees. His boots were scuffed and well-worn. My eyes went back to the neat patches. They seemed out of place with his rumpled overall outfit. I thought him fine-looking in a rough sort-of-way.

"Mr. Tipton?" the station attendant returned with a large packet and handed it over the counter to my father. "You'll find a sign to place over the door, signs for visitors, and tickets for passengers. Various other necessities are included. I'm sure Mr. Augustine explained that your stop is a home station where passengers will expect to get fed. When you supply meals to passengers, you may charge what you wish and keep the money.

The fee shouldn't be excessive. We expect our suppliers to be fair."

"You can count on my pa being fair," I piped. Everyone turned to look at me. I felt hot blood rise to my cheeks.

The attendant ignored me and turned back to Pa. "Have you put your name on the list for a position on a wagon train headed to Texas?"

"Yes, I did yesterday. I think three others have signed to go."

"My advice is not to depart until at least ten wagons are going."

"How long do you think that will take?"

"It's hard to say. People arrive daily heading west, but you need to leave within a week. If you leave later than that, you can't make The Pinery and get ready by September twenty-six when the first stage is scheduled in your area. I'm here, if you need more assistance."

"Thank you, more than likely, something will happen."

"I'll say goodbye by using Butterfield's motto." Mr. Attendant drew himself up to his full, greasy-haired height and exclaimed, *"Remember, boys, nothing on God's earth must stop the mail!"*

As we left, I heard Mr. Bailey tell the agent he was head of one of the crews hired to keep the trail in shape. I was sure I heard Division 5. The Pinery was in this Division.

"Gracie, let's go buy some chickens." We were untying our reins and preparing to mount our horses.

"Chickens? What for?"

"Because, having fresh eggs at The Pinery would be nice, and the thought of fried chicken makes my mouth water." We mounted our horses and headed back toward Fort Smith.

Then I remembered the leftover pecan pie and Mr. Ormand.

"I guess Mr. Ormand is in Indian Territory by now."

"I should think so. I'll miss him."

We were passing Knobles Brewery when Pa stopped in the middle of the road. "Gracie, I need to go in here a minute."

"What for?" My father didn't drink. I couldn't imagine what business he had in a brewery.

"Be patient, I'll be right back."

"Can't I go? The sun's hot." I didn't hanker to sit on my unmoving horse in the hot prairie sun, and nosing around in a brewery sounded exciting.

"No. It's no place for a lady. Walk your horse up and down the road to keep cool."

Pa stayed for several minutes. When he reappeared, he held a piece of paper in his hand. "Gracie, don't let me forget to come by and get two used whiskey barrels before we leave Fort Smith."

"What do we need whiskey barrels for?"

"I don't know yet, but I bet they come in handy. We could use them as water barrels if nothing else."

"Pa, are you becoming a pat rat?"

He threw back his head and laughed heartily. "Daughter, I believe that's pack rat. Gracie, did I ever tell you the story of my ancestor, Jonathan Tipton? I'm sure I'm named for him although he lived several generations back."

"I don't think so, Pa." We walked our horses back toward town.

"The story goes that the first Jonathan Tipton was born in Jamaica. He was an Englishman whose father helped liberate the country from Spain."

"Do you know the time period?"

"Middle sixteen hundreds, I think."

"About two hundred years ago."

"Yes. Gracie, let me tell the story. Jonathan was a cooper—a barrel maker—as was his father. When his father and mother died, Jonathan wanted to come to the New World."

I smirked. "Goin' new places seems to be in the Tipton blood."

Pa ignored me. "Jonathan had money. Instead of paying passage, he made two large wooden barrels, one with an inside lock. With the help of his friend, a cook on the boat, the barrels were lashed to the deck as galley supplies—one with Jonathan inside. He made the trip across the Caribbean, around the tip of Florida, and sailed north along the east coast of our country. He landed in the Chesapeake Bay area."

"Didn't he run into pirates and storms in the Caribbean?"

"I think he did. Almost drowned during one storm. The sea kept rushing over the bow and covering his barrel, but he made it."

"If he had money, why didn't he pay for his passage?"

"Although the King of England would give him a patent on several acres of land, Jonathan wanted to buy more, and he needed to purchase materials to build a house and furnish it. As you see, a barrel can have many uses."

"Is that a big yarn, Pa?"

"No, the gospel truth, or it was told to me as if it were true."

"So, Jonathan Tipton was a real man?"

"As real as the horse you're riding."

"Did his descendants migrate to Missouri and settle in Tipton where the Butterfield Stage Line starts?"

"It's entirely possible, but there's no way I could know that. I'm sure there were many more Tiptons from England who traveled across the Atlantic and settled in the original colonies."

"You've got to admit, it's an interesting thought."

"Yes, it is. Now, let's go find those chickens."

"One other thing, Pa. Do you like Hurricane Bailey?"

"I'm not sure about that, daughter. We've both got three weeks to decide."

"Why three weeks?"

"I think he'll probably travel west with us, and it'll take that long to cross Indian Territory and Texas before arriving at Fort Chadbourne." He paused. "Gracie, I can't wait for you to see The Pinery."

I looked over at him, but he was far away, walking in the pine and oak tree forests of the Guadalupe Mountains.

8

We moved our wagon across a small stream to the staging area where the others going through Indian Territory to Texas were gathered. Six wagons made the contingent. Three days passed. My father was getting impatient.

The fourth night there was a meeting of the group around the central campfire.

Hurricane Bailey was the most vocal. "I think we should pack it in and head out tomorrow. I need to be working on the road west of Fort Chadbourne. The Indians in Oklahoma Territory ain't a problem and the Plains Indians of Texas are mostly quiet. We won't have any trouble a'tall. My old Hawken will assure us of that." Hurricane patted the slim rifle leaning against his shoulder. I wondered what one rifle would do against an Indian raiding party. "This is a mountain gun used by fur trappers and explorers of the West. I've shot a jack rabbit at five hundred feet," he boasted, his voice full of pride.

My experience with guns was inadequate. My father shot a gun when we needed meat for the table. I often heard him say, two wars were enough shooting for him. We did have a rifle, pistol, and plenty of ammunition in our wagon in case we needed them.

"I agree with Hurricane here," I heard my father say. "But I suggest we wait two more days. Someone else may drive in."

I heard several of the men and women agree with Pa.

Hurricane's unhappiness with the results of the meeting showed plainly in his face, but the majority turned against him. He was even unhappier with Pa's election as head of the wagon train. Mr. Bailey left the firelight. As wagon master, Pa would be calling the shots and speaking for everyone in our company. I wondered if Mr. Bailey would accept Pa's new authority.

Jedediah sat outside the main group as I did.

I decided to go over and speak with him. He jumped up as I approached.

"Good evening, Jedediah." This was the first time I'd said his name. It had a nice ring to it.

"Good evening, ma'am." Blue eyes turned in my direction.

"I believe we'll be riding the trail to Texas together. I hope we'll be friends."

"Yes, ma'am. I'd like that a lot." Did I see a hint of a smile?

"Gracie, let's go back to the wagon," Pa called, cutting short our conversation.

"I'll be right there, Pa," I answered. "See you tomorrow, Jedediah."

"Tomorrow, Gracie." I felt his eyes on me as I walked away. I raised my head, smoothed my skirt, and left as smartly as I could on the uneven, muddy ground.

Back at the wagon, I asked Pa, "Can you shoot a jack rabbit at five hundred feet? I doubt you can see a rabbit at that distance, much less shoot it."

"Hurricane does exaggerate, but that statement is possible. Hawken rifles are dependable and accurate.

"Will you teach me how to shoot, Pa?"

"That wouldn't be a bad idea. How about a little pistol practice in the morning? I'll need to go into Fort Smith and buy more ammo. I should have thought about your need to become familiar with firearms."

Since Mr. Ormand had left, Pa and I cooked our own breakfast. The smell of bacon and eggs made me think of him. After our second cup of coffee, Pa left for town.

Heating water in an iron kettle on a spit over the open fire, I decided to wash our dirty clothes. I scrubbed them with lye soap bought in Memphis. A small rope attached to a thin sapling and our wagon did duty as a clothes drying line. The tree was no more than a tall stick with a clump of leaves on top. The trunk picked bare by horses or mules in search of a delicate morsel. I expected my clothes to be dry by the time Pa came back from town.

Just before dinner, he returned from Fort Smith with more ammo. Following him were two more wagonloads of people. "They were signing their names, and I offered to show them the way," he explained as I pulled our dry clothes off the line. Now our number of wagons was eight.

"I think we can leave in the morning, little girl," he said. "I doubt anyone else will appear. Instead of target shooting tomorrow morning, we'll practice tomorrow night in Indian Territory. Right now, we need our barrels from Knobles and our chickens."

Pa hitched two of the mules to our wagon. I decided to ride my horse. "Pa, can you get the barrels and chickens? I have a pie plate to return."

He dug into his pocket and pulled out two dollars. "See if you can buy another pie. It'll taste good on the trail tomorrow."

He started toward the wagon. "Gracie," he called, "meet me at the hotel in Fort Smith. I think we can celebrate the next part of our journey with a store-bought meal."

"I can't sell you one of these, but walk down the street with me. I have some freshly made ones at home." The cook looked around her work area. "I'm through baking today." She took off her apron. "What is your name, child?"

"Gracie, ma'am." For the life of me, I couldn't understand why everyone insisted I was a child.

"Where did you get that head full of curls?" Maybe that was it.

"I don't know."

"Does your mother have curls?"

"No, ma'am. My mother is dead."

The lady stopped, turned, and looked at me with a sympathetic expression. "Did you know her?"

"No, I don't remember her—at least not much."

We walked out the door, down the street, and stepped across a field where a small house sat in a clump of woods. Unlike our home in Nashville, it had never seen a brushstroke of paint, and the grayness of the wood blended with the tree bark and gray-green grasses around it.

"When do you head west?" She asked as we went in the door. The furniture was sparse—a small table, two chairs, and a bed were in the front room. Curtains fluttered at the open windows.

We walked through it to the kitchen where a woodstove with stovetop oven sat next to a cupboard with a large tin pan for washing dishes. Hanging, open shelves held staples for cooking.

"We leave tomorrow morning—Pa says as soon as we can hitch the mules to the wagons and saddle our horses. I'm excited."

"My husband and I intended to go farther west. It turned out we could make a living here, so here we stayed."

"What does he do?"

"He drives freight to supply distant forts. I worry about him. Life on the trail is so uncertain." She opened a pie keeper and took out a perfect specimen. "Here Gracie is your pie and some pecans. I believe I promised you some loaves of bread. Do you have a sack to carry them?"

"In the saddle bags on my horse, and I brought one of my pie pans. We can transfer the pie into it."

"Good thinking. Let's go back to the bakery and get the loaves."

A while later, I met Pa at the hotel. He had the barrels lashed to the wagon's side, but I didn't see the chickens. "No one was home," he explained. I'll go after we eat and wait until they return. You head on back to our camp. I don't want you out after dark."

On the road back to the staging area, I heard a horse galloping behind me. I walked my horse, and Jedediah Bailey fell in beside me. "You've been into town, Gracie?"

"I went to the bakery for a pecan pie and bread for the start of our trip tomorrow. I'm looking forward to getting started again, but not to the bouncing journey on the wagon seat. My pa says I should drive the mules, at least for the first day. He wants to ride his horse and check on the progress of the other wagons."

"My pa's not happy with your father's position as wagon master."

"I thought he wasn't when he walked away from the meeting. Should my father expect trouble?"

"Pa loves trouble, and he always wins. Gracie, would you like me to drive the mules, and you can ride your horse. That is, if Pa approves."

"Thank you for your offer. I'll be all right. My father's planning on a meeting tonight. Will you be there?" We splashed through the creek near the staging area.

"If my father comes, I will."

Parting at the large flat area where the wagons sat in a rough circle, I called after him. "Come over tonight and have a piece of pie."

Jedediah didn't answer but raised his hand and rode on.

I got off my horse, took off the saddle, and staked him where the grass was green and high. Moving my father's horse and the two mules to join my mount, I sat on the ground nearby. Wooly came to nuzzle me.

What did Jedediah mean by "Pa loves trouble, and he always wins?" Could my pa be in danger? Or, was Hurricane Bailey an old windbag and rabble-rouser? Pa could take care of himself, but if someone had an intent to harm him, that might be a different matter.

REBA RHYNE

9

On Wednesday, July 27, one hour after sunup, my pa rode his horse from the staging area. Seven wagons followed in quick secession, and I followed at the rear. My heart was thumping so loud I could hear the beat in my ear. The seat on the wagon didn't seem so hard.

Behind me, two whiskey barrels with lids were roped to the wagon. Fastened securely to the side, a crate of chicks peeped their displeasure at being cooped together in such a small space. We wouldn't be eating one of them for some time, nor would we have eggs. In a separate box, a rooster viewed his future harem and occasionally squawked his pleasure. Twenty-five pounds of chicken feed added weight to our wagon.

My loaves of bread hung from one of the cross bows under the canvas top, and my pie rested in the top of an open wooden box underneath.

When we crossed the Poteau River and continued on into Indian Territory, I realized the truth of my travels. If I looked back now, I'd look at a strange land I hardly knew. Home was hundreds of miles east. And ahead was uncharted territory, full of new experiences and adventure. As a child of sixteen, I'd been on a lark. Now at seventeen, I was a woman, and my life, my home, my future was in the West. I leaned forward and urged the mules on.

The road in Indian Territory led over hills and through valleys. It was a well-traveled road and the Butterfield crew, working with the Choctaw Nation worked on the rougher sections as we went through.

The first impression I had of crossing this part of the Butterfield Stage road was the numerous toll roads, bridges, and ferries. The operators charged by the wheel, person, and animal. It was a good thing Pa still had money, because some of the people on the wagon train ran out. He paid their fare, and the families promised to reimburse him. He knew better than to expect repayment. He told me, "Gracie, if these people get to their homesteads and make a life for themselves that will be payment enough." We never saw any of the people again after our trip through Texas.

My pa was a really smart man. To keep from having friction between him and Mr. Bailey, he asked the mountain man to scout ahead and report back any hindrance or problems with our route. I saw the older man's face soften at Pa's suggestion. "Wagon train scout" had a good ring to it, and the post was one he was well qualified to handle. He and Pa called a truce and peace reigned for a few days.

Since Jedediah was out of sight most of the time, I didn't see him except in the morning or evening. We talked a little, but most of the time he didn't come to say hello or goodbye. It was as if we'd never met.

My father allowed sixteen to twenty days to Fort Chadbourne, Texas, and our group was making good time.

On the third day out, Pa was driving our teams of mules. We were the front wagon in our line of eight. In the distance, two wagons sat by the road with Mr. Bailey and Jedediah waiting on their horses.

"Hurricane, are these people in trouble?" Pa asked as we drew abreast. He looked at the wheels and axles on the wagons. One wasn't much more than a cart.

"Got a man sick inside." Mr. Bailey motioned to the back of the wagon where a woman sat fanning at something lying inside.

"What's wrong with him?"

"How do I know? I ain't a doctor. Might be the flu or yellow fever or the pox as far as I'm concerned." He waved his arm and announced loud enough for the people sitting in the wagon behind us to hear. When the feared terms, yellow fever and pox, were uttered, I heard exclamations from the couple.

Hurricane grinned slyly at the reaction to his statement. I looked at him. Why did he have to say those dreaded words? I wanted to fly at him and scratch his eyes out.

So much for the truce, I thought. I wondered how Pa would handle this situation.

My father put a calming hand on my arm. "Stay here, Gracie. I'll check this out."

Pa jumped down from the wagon and approached the woman, looking at the man inside. "Howdy ma'am. How's your husband feeling?"

"Not so good. I told Mr. Bailey his problem is pneumonia, but he wouldn't listen. My husband is so hot. Have you got any whiskey? I'd like to get some down him."

"No, but I know where we can get some."

Hurricane had ridden off some distance, waiting to see the results of his comments. Pa cupped his hand and called to him, "Got any whiskey on you?"

I knew this was a silly question. I'd never been close to the disgusting man without smelling alcohol on his sodden breath.

Mr. Bailey and Jedediah rode over. A bottle of the required medicine appeared from his saddlebag.

Pa handed it to the lady, "Just keep it," he told her, giving away Mr. Bailey's stash. I noticed the brief flash of a grin on Jedediah's face.

My father turned to Jedediah. "Will you ride down the line of wagons and see if anyone has any doctoring experience when it comes to pneumonia?"

"Sure, Mr. Tipton, if Pa says it's okay." He looked nervously at his father.

I wondered why he had to have his father's permission each time he was asked to do something. He was twenty-two—time to act like a man.

"Go on," said Hurricane brusquely, leering at my father. My father had nipped Mr. Bailey's intended discord in the bud. Everyone would know the man had pneumonia instead of something dreaded like the fever or pox.

I was proud of Pa.

Jedediah returned. "A lady's coming to help." As he rode by my wagon, I caught a glimpse of blue eyes and a brief recognition in them.

A middle-aged woman appeared, walking along the rutted path, wearing a long skirt and bonnet. She carried a black bag with her. "Mrs. Lawson, have you nursed people with pneumonia?"

"I know the sickness well. At least one of my children gets it each winter."

"Will you check out this lady's husband?"

I watched Mrs. Lawson climb into the wagon to look at the sick man. Pa handed her the black bag. She disappeared inside, and my father walked over to speak to the couple behind us. I knew he was explaining the situation.

My attention was drawn back to the sick man's wagon. The back board was let down, and five children jumped to the ground. The eldest appeared to be a girl about my age. She looked tired. After helping her siblings off, she smiled weakly in my direction. I noticed her dress to be the latest fashion with ruffles, layers of crinolines, and a parasol completing her outfit. She lifted her skirt in a dainty motion as she walked away from the wagon.

I looked down at my rough, brown britches just as Pa appeared around the corner of our wagon. He walked to the closest mule and absentmindedly patted it on the rear. Dust flew off its rump, and Pa sneezed.

"They need a good brushing, Gracie," he said, rubbing his nose.

"Pa, I think we could all use a good brushing."

He smiled at me.

"What will you do with this family?"

"We can't leave them here. I wonder where they're headed."

Mrs. Lawson stuck her head out the back of the wagon, "Mr. Tipton, will you come here?"

"I'll find out as soon as we know about the sick man," he said and walked over to discuss the situation with the two ladies.

I heard bits and pieces of the conversation; enough to know the man's name, Abraham Johnson. He was in very bad condition. They were headed to Fort Chadbourne where their officer son served with the Army.

"Lucy," called a woman's voice from within the wagon. The older girl swept over to the open back and took a dipper from her mother. She traipsed to a water barrel on the wagon's side and returned with a full container.

My pa walked over to his scouts. "Hurricane, Mrs. Lawson says Mr. Johnson won't be any better or worse if he continues with us. But Mrs. Johnson is worn out. She can't drive either wagon. I'll need Jedediah to drive the big wagon to Fort Chadbourne. Mrs. Johnson will ride in the smaller one with me."

"My boy's got other responsibilities."

"Maybe he does, but driving this wagon is more important at the moment. Can't you handle the scouting job by yourself?"

"Sure I can," exclaimed Hurricane indignantly, as if Pa was questioning his prowess. He continued, "Rode alone most of my life in the Rocky Mountains full of Injuns, grizzlies, and wolves. Won't be no trouble at all fer me."

When Mr. Bailey closed his mouth, he realized Pa had outsmarted him again. "Oh, heck," he said and rode off leaving Jedediah sitting on his horse.

Pa stepped over to the Johnson wagon. "Mrs. Lawson, do you mind ridin' in here with Mr. Johnson."

"Not a bit." She bent down and whispered something to my father and, "Will you tell my husband?"

"Jedediah…" Pa motioned to him.

But Jedediah had heard what Pa said and moved down the line of wagons.

"Mrs. Johnson, if you will get down and ride with me on the smaller cart, we'll proceed. Mrs. Lawson will spell you and tend to your husband."

Our wagon train headed west again. Jedediah sat by Lucy Johnson, whose crinoline's billowed in the breeze. I admitted they made a good-looking couple, and I had to admit this didn't make me happy. And Pa looked strange beside the Johnson woman. This day was not going well, and there was nothing I could do about it.

REBA RHYNE

❦ 10 ❦

Six days later we arrived at Colbert's Ferry on the Red River. The area bustled with activity as I drove in and stopped the Conestoga. I saw black men working acres of fields, operating the ferry, and digging at the steep red banks where we would drive our wagons to the water's edge. The operator of the ferry came to greet us. He introduced himself as Benjamin Colbert, a Chickasaw leader and supplier to Butterfield's stage line.

"We're working to reduce the steep banks. Make driving a wagon onto the ferry easier." He waved his arm toward the river bank.

While Pa talked to Mr. Colbert, I got down from our wagon and walked to the Red River. The muddy waters filled with red clay swirled at the bottom of the bank. On the other side, I saw Texas and the famous Texas Road. Only a few feet of water separated me from the weeks I'd dreamed of this state—the land my pa loved—and I couldn't wait to explore. I stared across at a confusion of mesquite, willow, and cactus crowding the steep edge. I hugged my arms to me as a thrill rippled down my body.

"I've been here before."

Jedediah's quiet statement caused me to jump. Enamored by the scene before me, I hadn't noticed his approach.

"I'm sorry, I didn't mean to scare you, but if I'd been an Indian, you'd be captured or dead."

He was right, of course, but after scaring the wits out of me I didn't want to hear it. I responded angrily. "Don't ever sneak up on me again, and I can take care of myself, thank you."

He raised his eyebrows. "Sure, you can," he said mockingly and walked off.

Jedediah had come to the river to share the moment with me. I'd hurt his feelings, and I was instantly sorry.

This was our last paid crossing in Indian Territory. When Mr. Colbert found out my pa worked for Butterfield, he didn't charge him, but the rest of our party doled out money to cross the Red River. Some of the people joined Pa and I at a sumptuous noon meal at the ferry owner's home. Of course, there was a charge. I had beef steak, corn, potatoes, and pie, washed down by real tea.

Before we crossed the river, Mr. Colbert gave Pa a short tour of his plantation. With the help of Negro slaves, he grew cotton and grazed cattle. He was a wealthy Chickasaw.

Our crossing of the Red River went smoothly—one wagon at a time. On the other side in the distance, there was a shack called The First and Last Chance. Being the head wagon, Pa and I pulled in front to wait.

"What does that sign mean, Pa?"

"It means you can purchase alcohol inside. Alcohol is illegal in Indian Territory, but cross the river and here's the place to buy it." He motioned with his hand.

"Oh."

Pa jumped down from the wagon and went to check on the others as they ferried across.

I looked at the ramshackle business before me. The wood door hung on its rusty hinges, and the windows—those not stuffed with cardboard—were dirty. Even though it was hot in the afternoon heat, smoke came out of a stovepipe sitting at a rakish angle on the roof. Two horses were tied to the poles of the porch roof, which threatened to cave in. I thought I recognized one of them.

Mr. Bailey came out of the shack, his pockets stuffed full. His eyes were watery, unfocused and he staggered when he walked. I wondered if he'd recognize me in the condition he was in. "Hello, Missy." Guess that answered my question and the way he said 'Missy' didn't mean he was being polite.

"I see you've been in a favorite place," I answered with the same attitude. I couldn't remember Mr. Bailey drinking in the daytime on the trail.

He pulled a bottle out of his pocket. "Homemade tarantula juice, Missy. Cures what ails you." He pulled out another bottle. "And here's some tanglefoot. It'll do the job if you drink enough."

"I'm sure you know all about that," I retorted, but wondered what did ail him to drink like he did.

I watched as he fumbled with his saddlebags and placed his treasures inside. The first time he tried to mount his horse he lost his balance and fell in the dirt. The second time he managed to get his stomach on the saddle. Finally, he eased his sodden body into the seat and rode off, slumped over on his horse, clutching the saddle horn.

It took two hours to ferry our wagons across the Red River. Jedediah continued to drive the Johnson wagon. When he and Lucy passed, Jedediah turned his head and ignored me. Mrs. Johnson drove the smaller cart alone.

Pa and I manned the rear of the train. Everyone was well-stocked with food and water, and our destination seemed closer at hand. We made camp for the night at a small stream where the horses and mules could water. I let Wooly out to explore the mesquite forest.

Pa lifted the chicks and rooster down from the side of the wagon. He made a makeshift pen of brush, and we turned the chicks loose inside. I gave them food and placed a tin full of water close by. The rooster had to stay in his pen. He would fly away if let out.

Pa and I had bought a supply of bread and some perishable staples from Mr. Colbert's well-stocked store. We sat down to fresh corn and potatoes boiled together in water over our campfire. Fresh butter melted atop and salt sprinkled over all meant a meal as delicious as Fort Smith pecan pie. I couldn't eat enough.

I had to take care of something else that had eaten at me all day. I went in search of Jedediah.

The Bailey's campfire was separate from our camp. Hurricane Bailey was a loner and preferred his separate existence, even to the comfort of a campfire. I kept thinking about our earlier encounter today. It was unusual to see him drunk in the daytime.

When he did wander into our camps at night in a drunken stupor, he kept us entertained with tall tales of his mountain experiences. By the next morning, the effects of the previous night's drink had worn off. I wondered how he lived in this fashion. I marveled that Jedediah stayed with him.

There was only one silhouette at their fire tonight. The elder Mr. Bailey was nowhere to be seen. Jedediah sat with his arms across his knees. The firelight flickered on his face, and strange shadows appeared to move in the dense mesquite behind him. I was sure he recognized my footsteps, but he didn't acknowledge me.

"Where's your pa?"

"Back in the woods, somewhere…drunk I suppose."

I nodded, but in the darkness, he couldn't see me. I stepped close to him. "Jedediah, I want to apologize for talkin' sharp to you today at Red River. I didn't mean to hurt you."

He didn't say anything, and I didn't like talking to the top of his head. I eased down next to him on the ground.

"I really am, truly am sorry."

He cleared his throat. "That's all right. I'm used to it."

His words stung. I'd acted exactly like his mean-mouthed father, and he was used to sharp, hurtful words. I wanted to be different. "I hope you'll forgive me. I want to be your friend."

"Gracie…" He turned to look at me, and in the flickering firelight I could see the sadness in his eyes. "You're the only friend I've ever had."

I stared at him. Was it possible to be in the world for twenty-two years and not have a friend? I couldn't believe it.

"Well you have one again now." I placed my hand on his. He curled his fingers around mine. Tenderness—a new emotion toward him I didn't expect—came over me.

Jedediah cleared his throat. "We're always on the move. Never in one place more'n a few days. It's like something's chasing Pa. He has to keep movin' 'cause the thing might catch him." Staring into the fire, I realized he was voicing thoughts he'd had many times before.

"Have you ever talked to him about it?"

"Drink does loosen his tongue. But he's a mean drunk. I don't ask anything when he's in that shape. Better to let him pass out from his misery. Sleep off whatever it is. Otherwise, he won't discuss the problem."

"Why do you stay with him?"

"How can I leave him? Who would take care of him?"

Exactly, I thought, who would take care of him? "I don't know."

I sat there at a loss for words. Jedediah was as tied up as that woman slave I'd seen at Market Square in Memphis. He couldn't leave his father even though his pa abused him and might do him bodily harm. This was a form of slavery I'd never thought about before—how one person is tied to another because of the other's weakness.

He broke into my thoughts. "Gracie, my pa saw Indian sign today. He hasn't told your pa. I guess he'll tell him in the morning."

"Is this bad news?"

"It could be."

We sat staring at the fire in a companionable silence, until noises from the woods meant his father was returning.

"You'd better go before Pa gets here."

I untangled my fingers. "I'll see you tomorrow, Jedediah."

"Yes. For sure."

Hurricane Bailey came early the next morning to talk to Pa. He carried his Hawken rifle with him. Eyeing me he said, "Tipton, can we speak in private?"

"Gracie's gonna know. We might as well talk here." Pa sat on a stool by the fire.

"You got coffee?" Mr. Bailey pulled a blue enameled cup out of his pocket. I'd seen him do this before at other wagons.

"Daughter, pour Hurricane the last coffee."

Getting close to the man made my skin crawl, but I walked over, got his cup, and filled it with the dark brew. I went back to the two men, thinking I knew what this conversation was about. Stretching out my arm, I handed it to him. "Thank ye, Missy."

"What did you want to talk about, Hurricane?"

Mr. Bailey squatted by the fire, took a sip of coffee, and plunged straight to the point. "I saw Indian sign not long after we crossed the Red River. About ten Comanche braves on ponies."

"What do you think they're doing in this neck of the woods?"

"They shouldn't be here. Over two months ago, Captain John S. Ford, with his Texas militia, drove them north into Indian Territory. What happened there has been talked about all over the plains—a massacre of men, women, and children. Killin' men in war is all right in my book. Women and children... I can't stomach that."

I couldn't help but think knocking his son around mustn't be a problem either.

"Captain John S. Ford," my father repeated. "I once met a Lieutenant Ford. He was a doctor when I fought in the Mexican War. "Rip" Ford they called him, because he had a habit of saying, 'Rest in Peace' after he read the names on the death list each day. He once treated me for an infection caused by a mesquite thorn." Pa rubbed the back of his arm. The scar from the thorn, I knew well. "I saw him later around Franklin near New Mexico. He and a man named Neighbors were scoutin' a trail from San Antonio."

"He's the one and the same Ford."

Pa moved his head in agreement and went back to the subject at hand. "Are you thinkin' the Comanche are on the warpath because of him?"

"Don't know. I ain't heard. But it wouldn't surprise me none."

"How long since they passed?"

"The trail's a little cold, but the question is where are they now?"

"Are we in danger?"

"Enough that I think we should bunch the wagons closer as we drive through this area. Sherman is a fairly big town within three or four miles. We'll stop when we get there and see what's goin' on in the area. Could be the Comanche are looking fer food."

"Your plan is fine with me. I'll alert the others."

Mr. Bailey started off toward his campsite but turned around. "By the way, Tipton, a Comanche can steal the beard off your face without you knowin' it, and they think mules are a delicacy. I'd tether them close to my wagon at night."

"Thanks for the advice. I'll do that." Pa headed for his horse, dragging his saddle from under the wagon.

"And Missy..." Mr. Bailey turned to me, his mustache twitching. "They capture women and children and sell them as slaves." He turned on his heel and walked away.

I shook my head and chuckled as I watched him go. I couldn't help but think he'd love for that to happen to me.

Why didn't he like me? Was it because I was a woman, or because I stood up to him? Did his drinking problem stem from a past problem with a female? My curiosity was aroused. Even though it might be dangerous, I determined that someday I'd find out.

I hadn't noticed it before, but this morning he walked away with a tiny limp.

REBA RHYNE

❦ 11 ❦

"**W**hat you need to worry about is the distance from Sherman to Fort Belknap." The man who spoke stood in front of the log courthouse in the small town. "We've heard of troubles along this route."

"Are Butterfield Stage Line stations built, or do you know?" My pa spoke to him from the seat of our wagon. Hurricane Bailey sat on his horse nearby. Jedediah was still driving the Johnson wagon until Mr. Johnson could get his strength back.

"I believe so, but wouldn't bet my life on it. Don't travel that far these days. Nobody in these parts does."

"I thank you for the information," said Pa. He started to move the wagon forward.

"Wait," said the man, waving his hand and walking closer. "There's something else you need to know. See that old gentleman smoking his pipe on the porch down yonder." He pointed down the street a couple hundred feet.

Pa shaded his eyes. "Yes."

"He's our weatherman. His bones and muscles tell him there's a bad storm a-brewing. He's almost always accurate, so keep a watch on the western horizon."

"I think I can handle that," said Pa, starting the wagons rolling again. "Thank you."

We waved at the elderly man who took his pipe out of his mouth and made eye contact until we'd passed.

"There isn't a cloud in the sky," I observed.

"Don't mean anything when your body tells you otherwise. Skies change quickly here in Texas."

Hurricane Bailey approached our wagon. "Tipton, I think we need to move the train faster today. Try to make Gainesville by nightfall."

"Whatever you say, Hurricane. Lead the way."

Gainesville wasn't any bigger than the log station built for the future stage line. We camped by the Trinity River, pulling our wagons into a tight circle.

The four men who would man the station came to sit by our central campfire. Hurricane and Jedediah soon appeared. I didn't know which set of men told the biggest yarn. I guessed Jedediah's Pa.

I seated myself behind Mr. Bailey, and Jedediah eyed the seat beside me. His obvious preference made me self-conscience. Since my apology after hurting him at Red River, he'd gone out of his way to recognize me.

Pa leaned on the Johnson wagon. He glanced in my direction as Jedediah sat down by me. Abraham Johnson had grown strong enough to sit on the wagon seat and listen to the yarns being spun by the fire.

Tomorrow, Mr. Johnson planned to drive the big wagon, and his wife, the little one. Pa told me driving the team of horses might be too hard on the recovering man, but didn't stand in the way of his trying. Jedediah stood ready to take over if need be.

"Yes," said Hurricane, "my fondest memory was on the Colorado River in Utah. Jedidiah Smith, the famous trapper and explorer was a good friend. My boy's named after him. Well, he aimed to go clear to California, and I aimed to go with him."

"Did you make California?" one of the men from the station asked.

"We sure did, and returned."

"That's obvious," another of the men said, slapping his pants. Everyone laughed, and Hurricane glared at the one with the smart mouth. Mr. Bailey wasn't drunk. Not yet.

"What happened on the Colorado?"

"Jedidiah wanted to float down the river to a place the Indians had told him about—where wind and water carved spectacular arches and lots of them. We got all excited at the prospect of seein' new country. All we had was two small boats, but we lit out in them. At first the water was smooth as glass. For several days, we used our oars to steer in the gentle current. What we didn't know was somewhere up river it had rained hard the day before. As we lazed along on the Colorado, it rose underneath us. We noticed the glassy surface turned to riffles, but by the time we realized what was happening, we were between the walls of two rose-colored cliffs and nowhere to git out. All we could do was ride out the roaring rapids we heard ahead."

Hurricane looked around at his audience and licked his lips. His mustache twitched to the left. Running his tongue around his mouth, he wiped off the last hint of alcohol. He didn't usually let those on the wagon train see him drink. Me—I was a different matter.

"Go on," urged the men. He had their full attention.

Hurricane used his hands with motions to describe the rest of the story. "The old Colorado kept gittin' deeper and swifter. We rowed to save our lives, but the white caps and rapids was too much for us. Finally, we jest hung on to the boats, expectin' them to capsize at any moment."

He grabbed the shoulder of the man next to him. The man let out a squawk. Everyone laughed, but soon we were back on the river with Hurricane in our minds.

"There was nothin' else we could do. Up and down we went in the angry, churnin' water. On one of the ups I saw something that scared the life out of me. A giant maelstrom as big as this circle we're sittin' in was smack in the middle of the thunderous river. There weren't no way to go around it. It swirled from one side of the canyon to the other. Imagine it, gigantic rose-colored cliffs on t'either side and a yawning, hungry whirlpool roaring right in the middle of the river—its maw open and inviting."

Hurricane could tell a good story, and everyone sitting around the fire knew it. "Jedidiah Smith and I looked at each other. I'm almost positive he said 'See you on the other side,' but the noise drowned out his words. I'm not a prayin' man, but jest as my boat was sucked down into that boisterous opening, I prayed for deliverance and took a deep breath. I'm certain sure I cleaned out the bed of the Colorado for a mile, bumping along the bottom and into rocks, but delivered I was. And so was Jedidiah. We were spit out into a calmer section where the river spread out over a wide plain. I've never been so glad to see anyone in my life."

"Did you find the arches?"

"Yep, back upriver a mile or two. We walked into the area and out again, headin' fer the Rocky Mountains. And then there's the bear story. Jedidiah bore the scars from that encounter for the rest of his natural life. We headed into the lower hills and..."

I didn't realize I'd tensed at the story. When Jedediah touched my arm, I jumped.

He held up his hand and shook his head, "Not again, Gracie."

Truth be told, I was about to say something not so nice. I relaxed and smiled at him. "Let's go for a short walk," he suggested.

We left the circle of firelight, walking an outside circuit of the wagons. The Texas moon shone through thin, wispy clouds, and the wind-blown grass on the prairie moved like white-capped waves in the glowing light.

"What's wrong with the moon?" I asked. An opaque circle surrounded it.

"The moon has a halo. Doesn't bode well for tomorrow."

"Why?"

"Means bad weather is coming," he answered matter-of-factly.

I remembered the man's warning in Sherman.

In the darkness, I felt him take my hand. "But this is a perfect night for a coyote to howl at the moon,"

We walked around the wagons and back to the campfire—our hands swinging with the rhythm of each step. Before we entered the circle of wagons, he dropped my hand. "Think I'll turn in, Gracie. See you tomorrow."

He took my heart with him when he left. We hadn't spoken a word of love, but I felt it there between us.

I was hard pressed to fall asleep that night. I tossed and turned in my feather bed thinking of Sarah and Paul—Paul who was my first special man friend. My heart was fickle and a traitor to him, but I couldn't help it. Jedediah was here. Paul was not. I'd left him in Tennessee and never expected to see him again.

Then I wondered why Jedediah had dropped my hand and left. The answer I thought was in keeping our attraction for each other from his father.

And what about my pa? How would he react to the news that his daughter liked another man? Now wasn't the time to let either parent know. At present, I wanted to enjoy the delicious secret I'd uncovered in my heart.

❧ 12 ❧

The elderly man at Sherman, Pa, and the moon had spoken rightly about the weather. The next morning, dark gray fingers emanated from ominous black clouds appearing on the horizon. All day long, we drove under the western wisps and toward the clouds until the edge reached over our wagons. Once over us, the bank of clouds headed east at a rapid pace.

The winds grew in velocity. The rain started pelting us in the afternoon. Stinging rain, running straight with the ground stung our eyes, and pea-sized hail rained from the skies.

"Gracie, I've seen this before," Pa yelled in my ear. "This is a bad storm, maybe a tornado. We need shelter now!" Pa ran the rumbling wagon beside a steep hill and stopped it. Jumping out, he yelled he was going to see about the other members of our train. "Dive under the wagon. You'll be safer there," were his parting words as the hail continued to fall.

I was scared. My body shook all over from the cold rain. Wondering if we were going to die, I leaped to the ground, dove under the wagon, and called for Wooly. All morning, she'd run merrily along beside the wagon, chasing leaves and bits of grass in the wind, kicking her heels in the rapidly approaching storm. Now she was nowhere to be seen.

"Gracie, you should have thought of her sooner." I scolded myself as I looked out from my safe position. "Where is she?"

A flash of lightning revealed her at the edge of the woods, fifty feet away. I called to her but she couldn't hear me over the howling wind. No doubt scared of the falling hail, she pushed into the woods. I scrambled out from under the wagon. This little lamb was my responsibility. She'd get lost in the woods.

And where was Pa? He couldn't help. I rushed into the forest. Thorns and branches grabbed at my shirt and scratched my arms. Between flashes of lightning, I stumbled over brush and cacti but kept my balance.

"Wooly, I'm here little lamb."

I kept calling her, squinting in the darkness for a flash of white. The rain poured out of my hair. I kept brushing water out of my eyes. "Wooly, where are you?"

A terrible roaring sound followed behind me. I had no idea what it was, but the sound was like a thousand freight trains rushing toward my position. The sky was almost as dark as night. In a flash of lightning, I saw my Wooly. She stood by a huge log lying across her path. The log had stopped her headlong flight, and she was confused. I hurried to her, just as someone grabbed me from the rear. "To the ground, Gracie," the urgent voice said.

I fell with Wooly, and Jedediah fell beside us, pushing us against the giant log.

"What is it?"

"Tornado…it's a bad one." His long arms were around me, holding me tight, and my cheek was against his rough shirt. His forehead was on mine, and I felt his warm breath against my cheek. I clung to him, closing my eyes. The world consisted of Jedediah, me, Wooly, and the storm. Being with him felt safe.

The wind bore down on us. When I did open my eyes, the trees bent in grotesque shapes, and faulty limbs snapped around the vicinity. The rain lashed at the ground, sending spray shooting back into the air. Wooly shivered and so did I. Jedediah hung onto me tighter.

We lay that way until the loud roar had passed away. I took a deep breath, and Wooly struggled from between us. Jedediah pulled his head back. Rain streaked his face as he searched mine. His eyes glowed with love and desire. His lips were on mine. My first kiss—warm with tender pressure. I found myself surrendering to his touch—yielding to this new pleasure. Again and again our lips met.

When his hand moved below my waist, I recoiled. "No," I said quietly. "No."

He stood and helped me to my feet, holding me closely in his arms. "You won't have to worry about me again, Gracie." His whisper brushed my ear.

"That kind of thing is for marriage, Jedediah."

"Yes, I know. I'm sorry." He cleaned the grass and dirt from my clothes.

After the mayhem at the forefront of the storm, the rain falling was light and gentle. Jedediah reached down and caught his hat, which had fallen to the ground. Without thinking, he pushed it down on his head. Rain water poured over his face and shoulders. "What the—"

I started laughing at his startled look. Lifting my hand, I wiped the rain off his face. He caught my hand in his. "Gracie, I think you're more than my best friend."

Was that the best he could do after our brief encounter with death and our subsequent intimacy? Friendship was a new world for Jedediah—being bound to his father had prevented it until now. How long would it take for him to realize that love happens next? Maybe never. I decided not to push it. At least, not for now.

I felt safe to say, "Yes, I am."

As we walked back to the Conestoga, another thought occurred to me. Was it possible for any man to tell me I love you? Could it be I attracted the weak man, one who couldn't articulate the three words I longed to hear? Paul hadn't been able to say those words.

Ah, Paul, he was so far away. Paul and Jedediah were two different people. Paul knew girls liked him, and he had lots of friends. Paul was stocky and good-looking.

Jedediah was thin and not ugly. His blue eyes were mesmerizing, beautiful, and the most interesting part of his face. I looked at Jedediah, sizing him up physically. The thinness of his body belied his strength. When he held me to him, I felt muscles ripple down his body, and the strength of his vise-like arms... I trembled at the thought.

My relationship with him was much deeper than my feelings for Paul. If there was any attachment left for Paul, I loosened it at that moment.

The rain showered the earth as we walked back to the wagons, rinsing off much of the leaves and dirt on our bodies. A chastened, wet Wooly followed along.

"Gracie," yelled Pa when he saw us. "I was worried sick when I came back and you weren't under the wagon." He came to me and hugged me. "What happened? Wooly's filthy."

"She ran into the woods. I went to find her, and Jedediah came after me. We huddled next to a log until the tornado passed, but the rain beat dirt and leaves onto us. Jedediah protected us from the tornado." I wondered if my face looked different after being kissed so well.

Pa looked at Jedediah. "Thank you, I don't know what I'd do if I lost my little girl." He shook hands with Jedediah and hugged me again.

"Where did the tornado hit?" Jedediah asked Pa.

"The funnel lifted off the ground and went right over us. We were lucky, but we need to see how everyone else fared. Do you mind helping?"

"Pa, I'll check the Johnson wagon." It was the closest to ours.

"Good. Jedediah and I will make sure the others coped well."

Mr. Johnson had almost pulled abreast of our wagon. It looked like theirs had come through the storm in fine shape, but Lucy Johnson was a mess. She lay beside the muddy road, her beautiful dress was ruined, and her hair as wet and stringy as mine. She sobbed, her body jerking with spasmodic movements, and her fine-looking face contorted into the most grotesque features imaginable. "I hate you," she screamed over and over at her mother.

I looked at Mrs. Johnson, standing at the front of the wagon. "What happened?"

Lucy's mother shook her head. "She's not been happy since we forced her to leave home. The hardest part was leaving a young man she liked very much. When the blast of wind hit our wagon broadside, she feared it would turn over, so she jumped off the wagon seat. The long fall sprained her ankle."

"I'll help her stand." I felt sorry for Lucy.

"Leave her be, Gracie. Let her cry it out."

I left Lucy in the middle of the muddy road and returned to my wagon. Lucy Johnson would never forgive her parents. I was sure of that.

When Pa came back from checking out the wagons, the rain had stopped, and we started moving again.

Jumping in a creek during our nightly stop later that evening washed my body and clothes clean. After dark, there was a meeting around the campfire, and Mr. Bailey cautioned everyone to be mindful of the Indians following our group.

Before the meeting ended, my pa said a prayer for the Lord's blessing of safe travel.

The second day out from Gainesville was uneventful, except for more Indian sign. Every moment of the day, I craned my neck, checking for strange objects or movement on the distant horizon. A couple of times when I looked in my father's direction, I noticed him smiling. "Pa, lookin' for Indians is like looking for a needle in a haystack."

"You might do better by looking for the haystack, little girl."

"Why?"

"Because that's where they're probably hiding—in the obvious place. Many people don't give the natives enough credit for being smart and knowin' the ways of huntin' and war. How do you think they've survived out here on the plains for hundreds of years? They're cunnin' and resourceful. Don't ever underestimate an inhabitant in his natural territory, animal or human."

"Pa is this southern route through Texas easier than one straight across the Rockies to California? I was thinking about what Mr. Bailey said about him and Jedediah Smith crossin' the mountains. Would his route be shorter?"

"That route is shorter. But according to the newspapers and Mr. Augustine, picking the southern route to California would mean less cold weather and snow, no steep mountains to climb, and reduced chance of diseases, such as cholera on the trail."

A bump in the road caused my teeth to jar together. "Nashville roads were smooth thoroughfares compared to the rough road we've been over since we left Memphis."

Pa threw back his head and laughed. "Oh, Gracie, there's no comparison, but Mr. Butterfield has done a lot to make driving the Texas Road easier."

"Did you ride on the Texas Road?"

"Oh, yes, but I rode horseback. Believe me, that's more pleasurable traveling than driving a wagon. If you think this is rough, the stage will be running pell-mell, day and night, for California. I'm thinking it will be a rutted and jerky ride most of the way."

Driving into Jacksboro was like sailing on a shimmering sea. The plain was flat and smooth. The rain of the previous afternoon had knocked the dust off the long, green grasses and now they glistened with diamonds of water in the bright sunlight. I imagined our Conestoga was a prairie schooner riding the glassy waves, heading for mysterious and exciting lands to the west, heading home.

Just outside the small settlement of houses, Pa circled the wagons. I jumped down from the seat and helped Pa make camp. We were almost finished when Jedediah and his father rode toward us and dismounted. Jedediah came to help me lift two camp stools to the ground.

Ignoring me, Mr. Bailey engaged my pa in an urgent conversation. "Tipton, we got a situation here. It seems there's been some Comanche activity around the area—a cow stolen and some pilfering in the outlying barns. Could be more dangerous as we continue toward Fort Belknap."

"Ford's raids only stirred the pot of skirmishes, huh?"

"Looks that way. The way I see it, we've got fifteen people who could probably shoot a rifle. We need to take stock of guns and ammo, and make sure these people know how to load the bullets and shoot their weapons."

"Then we'll have target practice after supper, if that's suitable for you, Hurricane."

"It is, and let's check each wagon fer the best place to keep the guns at the ready. Jedediah and I will be back to help."

"Why don't you and your son wash up and eat your supper with us?" said Pa.

"Thanks, but we were invited to eat in town. Come on, Jedediah."

Jedediah whispered to me, "Gracie, I'll teach you to shoot." Then he was gone.

The next morning's ride toward Fort Belknap gave me time to think about dying. It was a subject I hadn't thought about in many years. Not since my mother and brother had died. My whole attention to this time had been on living, loving, and having a future family and home.

Last night's shooting practice pushed the thought to the forefront. Jedediah was a good teacher, and Pa complimented me on my aim. But in a real fight they both agreed, I'd have a hard time hitting a moving target. One thing I knew for sure, I wasn't ready to die. Any human trying to kill me had better get ready for a good scratching, stomping, and screaming. I wouldn't go easy or quietly.

Pa estimated three days to Fort Belknap. These would be spent for the most part on the open prairie, riding through patches of trees, down gullies, and beside rivers.

❧ **13** ❧

Hurricane Bailey made it known that he was increasingly worried about the presence of Indians. He and Jedediah left at breakfast and scouted the area around our circled wagons.

"They're out there, jest out of sight. I know what they want. But why are they waitin' to get it. Makes my skin crawl."

For once, he and I were in agreement.

In the daytime, we were vulnerable on the prairie, but we could see for miles. We wouldn't be taken by surprise. We had little or no protection if they attacked at night. Without the moon overhead, the prairie was pitch-black.

The first night after we left Jacksboro, we crossed a small creek and camped at the bottom of a slight rise on the other side. Our wagon circle looked more like an elongated oval. Our wagon on the north end and the one opposite on the south being more exposed than the others.

"Gracie, we've been on the trail for forty-three days," Pa commented. He stood next to the wagon checking the calendar where he'd marked his estimation of the time it would take to travel between our stops.

I stood in the wagon watching six young boys as they made a game out of their job to pickup buffalo chips and brush surrounding the creek bank. These, they stacked in heaps next to the fire pits used for cooking our supper. They dared, laughed, and joked with each other as the stacks grew. Older men would start tonight's two fires—one at either end of our lopsided circle.

"Gracie, did you hear me?"

"I'm sorry, Pa. What did you say?" I'd heard his words, but they hadn't registered. I leaned over to look at the calendar he held in his hand. Large X's in each square meant the days were behind us.

"Forty-three days we've been on the trail," he repeated.

"Pa, you did well at figuring out our progress each day. It looks like we're right on schedule." Today was Monday. According to Pa's map, we would make Fort Belknap on Wednesday. That meant two more days of unprotected travel.

"Here, will you take this?" I handed him the iron skillet from inside the wagon, and a cup of feed for the chicks who roamed around in their small pen. He disappeared, and I called after him, "Come and get the small picnic basket as soon as you feed the chickens." I waited for him to return.

Looking out the back of our wagon, I watched the creek flow silently by. Three of our mules picked grass on the other side. One stood in the midst of the stream, drinking water.

Up the creek, two of the ladies filled wooden buckets for cooking and washing dishes. They weren't the only ones near the water.

A girl and a boy jumped in the stream fully clothed, splashing a fine spray into the hot air. A bar of soap from their bath left a thin milky streak in the water below them. Since we were moving all day long, washing clothes and bodies at the same time completed two tasks. Before it got dark, I intended to do the same. I'd hang my wet clothes from the wagon, and they would be dry by morning.

"Gracie, where is the basket?"

"Here, Pa." I handed the basket to him, and carrying the eggs and bacon we'd bought at Jacksboro, I followed our eating supplies to the ground.

When Hurricane Bailey appeared, his face was red and the mustache under his nose twitched with anger. He stormed after Pa who had gone for the mules and was securing them close to the wagon. "Tipton, have you lost your mind? What possessed you to camp here? Your wagon and the one on the other end will be impossible to defend if we're attacked."

One last time, Pa hit the stake he was driving into the ground and raised his body slowly. His face and manner seemed calm, but I knew he was stewing at being addressed with sarcasm. "I'm sorry, Mr. Bailey, if my choice of camp doesn't meet your specifications. But not knowin' if there was water down the trail and with the sun goin' down, I decided to stop here. Our animals need a respite from their labors, and the grass is plentiful and nourishing." Pa bent over to attach a tether to the first stake. "You should have returned earlier if you'd scouted out another choice."

Hurricane pulled his hat off, slammed it against his britches, and scratched his head. "Dadgummit! You should have waited."

"Well, we're here now. Let's make the best of it."

Hurricane stormed off, mumbling under his breath, "Best of it! Tarnation, a child could have picked a better spot."

Supper smelled so good, I ate every bit of mine and sopped the pan with my bread. "Gracie, I've never seen anyone enjoy food like you do." Pa stood at our folding table for washing dishes, the one he'd made with his forge and hammers in Tennessee. He carried two bowls of dirty dish water and threw them behind the wagon.

When he came back I replied, "After cookin' it, I don't believe in wastin' it." I was putting the clean utensils and plates back into the picnic basket.

"No one would ever accuse you of that." He pushed the table into its hanger under the wagon.

"Do you think our garden seeds will grow at Pine Springs?" We had a box full stashed away somewhere inside the wagon. Fresh vegetables meant more to me after the last weeks on the trail. Many kind people had shared their summer's bounty and we bought some when they were available. Thinking about fresh food made my mouth water even after I'd eaten my fill.

"If they don't, we can feed them to the chickens." Pa's big smile said he was kidding me. He walked back to the chickens and started placing them in their hanging cage. They squawked in protest. He called back. "We're gonna have to get to Pine Springs soon, or build a bigger cage. I declare girl, I believe they've developed your tapeworm."

I couldn't help but laugh. I walked back to watch the action. He'd secured all but one. We'd nicknamed that chick Li'l Scrambler because it was bigger than the others. Li'l Scrambler was flapping her wings, blowing dust everywhere and trying to climb the makeshift fence. The chicken's voice was changing, and I heard something between a cheep and a squawk.

I was laughing, Pa was yelling, and the chicken was squawking. The scene was hilarious—my pa running around the small pen and Scrambler neatly sidestepping him with mouth open and eyes bulging. Actually, I think they were both doing the same dance steps. Both were tuckered out when he finally secured her in the cage, and I'd laughed so hard my sides were hurting.

I climbed into the wagon, and he handed the skillet and basket to me. "Pa, I'm going to take a dip in the creek."

"Stay close by," was all he said. I watched him go to talk to another man down the line of wagons.

I pulled my soap and towel out of a basket and prepared to get out of the wagon. Glancing toward the other end of the camp, I saw Mr. Bailey and Jedediah moving the other offending wagon so it would be more protected. Something must have been said about us, because Jedediah looked my way. I waved at him.

I got my floppy shoes, hopped out of the wagon, and went toward the spot where the children had bathed earlier. Easing into the water, I squatted until it came to my neck. I put out my arms and swayed with the lazy current. The water wasn't the clearest I'd ever seen, but it was wet and somewhat cool. I dipped water with my hands to wet my hair and pulled the soap out of my shirt pocket.

Heaven. Running my fingers through my lathered curls, I closed my eyes and with my fingernails dug into my scalp, giving it a good raking. If there was one thing I liked as well as food, it was having clean hair.

Crack! The noise caused me to jump and look nervously toward the bank. Indians were not on my guest list.

Jedediah sat staring at me, two pieces of the stick he'd broken in his hand. "You scared the life out of me."

"Yeah, I can tell. If I'd been an Indian…"

I gave him a smirk. "Let me get this soap off my head." I don't know what he replied. I ducked into the water three times before I was satisfied the soap was gone.

"What're you doing here?"

"I'm guarding you since you don't use good sense at times. Don't you know better than to go off by yourself?" He scolded me. "I didn't save your life in the tornado only to let the Comanche have you."

"I told Pa where I was going. I don't have to tell anyone else." I tossed my wet head. Who was he to give me orders?

"Gracie, whether you like it or not, I'm goin' to stay here until you finish." I noticed his rifle rested against his knee.

"Then turn your back, Jedediah, and I'll get done."

I took my time in the water, making sure every part of me and my clothes were clean.

The sun went down behind the hill. Fingers of charcoal, red, and pink rested on the sky as if they'd been painted by some huge brush stroke. Dusky dark had set in. I stepped out onto the bank. "Jedediah will you hand me my towel?"

"Are you finished?"

"Yes, I'm ready to dry off."

"Then you come and get it. You can dry off as we walk back to the wagons."

"Well, I never saw such a stubborn man!" Irritation had flown away. Now, I was angry at him.

"Excuse me. Who're you callin' stubborn?"

"You! Get out of my way." Those were the last words I spoke to him that night as I huffed and traipsed to the wagon. He tried to help me climb in, but I rebuffed his efforts. After the long day's rough bouncing ride on the wagon seat and doing chores, I was tired. I excused my actions toward Jedediah as weariness. He should know better than to annoy a worn-out woman.

There was a pow-wow outside our wagon later that night. The group decided on a rotation of men on the train. All parts of the night would be patrolled. It was decided Mr. Bailey and

Jedediah would sleep inside the circle of wagons as a precaution—one on either end. Jedediah opted for the end away from our wagon.

Was Mr. Bailey telling everything he knew? I was jumpy, scared, and tired. I crawled back into the wagon and went to sleep as soon as my head hit the pillow.

❧ 14 ❧

A piercing scream from the other end of our circle woke me. It took me a second or two to shake off my sleepy daze and come to my senses. I threw back the quilt and started to get up. Two sets of rough hands grabbed my legs and pinned my arms. Now, the screams I heard were coming from me.

Guttural, incomprehensible sounds from the people around me meant the Comanche were raiding our camp. Where was Pa?

In the light of the moon, I saw several shadows securing our mules. One of them grabbed my horse and another pulled me from the wagon. I remembered Hurricane's words, "They take women and sell them as slaves." I screamed louder, kicking at those who were taking me, which wasn't easy in my long-tailed nightgown. My feet hit the ground.

Chaos all around me—screams, running feet, and shots being fired. Whining bullets zinged past moving shadows. The acrid smell of gun smoke—strong in my nostrils. I screamed for Pa, but my voice was lost in the commotion.

My hands were secured by rope, and I was flung upon Boone without a saddle. Grasping the reins with one hand and his mane with the other, I managed to stay on as we left at a fast trot. I heard horses running, lots of them. I couldn't tell how many braves were in the party. Others joined us as we left the camp. It seemed like a hundred.

After my first confused thoughts, I took stock of my situation. Surely Pa and the men back at camp would start after me, but what if the Comanche took all the horses? I hadn't stayed awake long enough to hear all the arrangements.

No, they couldn't take all of them, because Mr. Bailey and Jedediah had tethered theirs inside the compound—saddles on, ready to ride. And where was Pa's horse? Seemed like I remembered his beside the Baileys'. There were at least three horses left in camp. Our mules were gone, so Pa couldn't move our wagon. The train would stay where it was until this situation was resolved.

The Comanche party couldn't travel any faster than the mules could go. Our group maintained a fast trot until dawn. We stopped. There was a general discussion between the braves. The argument seemed to be over keeping the mules or me. The mules were slowing the raiding party down.

The braves kept motioning toward something behind me. I turned to look. Out of the corner of my eye, I saw another female on a horse. It was Lucy Johnson. The screams at the other end of the camp had been hers. Now, we were both captives of the marauders.

In the early light, I made a good head count. Twelve braves herded four mules, three horses, and us, and those with the mules were adamant about keeping them. I was glad of that. Horses traveled faster than mules. Anyone coming after us would gain ground on our moving group. Also, I realized several horses had been left behind—unless the Indians had run them off in the confusion surrounding the raid.

More discussion. Three men without animals or humans to attend left our company and rode back the way we'd come.

I knew, as a rear guard, their job was to ambush and kill anyone who attempted to rescue us, and I remembered Mr. Bailey saying the Comanche were good shots with a bow and arrow, especially on horseback. One of those leaving carried a rifle, the only gun in the raiding party. Anyone following us might die.

For the first time since I'd seen Mr. Bailey in Memphis, I appreciated his skill as a scout. If anyone could outwit this band of raiders, he could. I began to pray for the safety and skill of the men who were sure to follow us. "God protect them," I pleaded. "And God, protect Lucy and me."

The Indian in the lead headed forward, holding a rope attached to my horse. All day, we moved northeast in the Texas heat. Around noon, I heard popping sounds like gunshots a far piece behind us. Our column didn't stop to investigate.

No one ate the first day.

That night, the braves stopped for a few hours next to a flowing stream of water. Lucy and I weren't given food, but we were allowed to drink from the stream. She never said a word to me, seemingly oblivious to the circumstances around us. Urged on by her captor, she walked stiffly back to the Comanche camp, where I sat twenty feet from her on the other side. She was dirty and exhausted from riding the horse, something she wasn't used to doing. Her chin was on her chest. I knew she hated Texas soil, hated her mother and father, and I wondered if she cared to live. I started to worry she'd do something to rouse or antagonize our captors.

The second day, I was weak from hunger. This would have amused me, had my situation not been so grave. What was keeping Pa and the others? Weren't they coming? I couldn't give in to negative thoughts. Of course, they were coming. How could they not?

More solitary shots from behind our moving group.

That night, the three men of the rear guard came into camp with jack rabbits and a small antelope tied to their ponies. No doubt the shots I'd heard earlier in the day? Wasn't anyone looking for us?

Taking stock of the situation, I saw we were camped in a grove of hackberry and live oak trees. I sat braced against the trunk of one. My captor squatted several feet away next to a blazing fire, poking brush and wood onto the flames. He stood as two braves carried the dressed and gutted antelope on a limb toward him. The men busied themselves with positioning the animal to roast on a spit. My stomach—after not having food for over a day—growled at the smell of meat cooking. I wanted to crawl on hands and knees and rip a piece of half-raw flesh from their meal.

I turned my eyes away from the cooking meat. Tilting my head back, I pulled in a lungful of air.

Why? Why had they built a fire? The smoke and light would alert anyone in the area of their presence.

Then it hit me. No one had followed us. With an instant sinking feeling in the pit of my stomach—not caused by my hunger—I knew they felt safe in building the fire. Was Pa dead? What about Jedediah, Mr. Bailey and the other men on the wagon train? No! No. I couldn't believe they were all gone. I raised my hand and scraped curls off my forehead. I needed to think.

Since my capture, I'd thought my pa and others on the wagon train would rescue me and Lucy. If they weren't coming, this meant if I were to escape I'd have to come up with a plan—a good one and soon.

In the firelight, I sat staring at the Comanche brave who kept a tight rein on my rope during the day. Occasionally, he jerked the tether to let me know he was there. During the last two days, the other braves often conferred with him. He appeared to be someone with authority and respected by the others. His upper body and muscles were well rounded. Leather covered his lower torso and legs. Moccasins enclosed his feet. His black hair, parted in the middle and each side tied with long, leather thongs, showed a daubed-on yellow streak running down the exposed part at the center of his scalp.

Apparently feeling my eyes on him, he looked in my direction, and I quickly looked down. Rising, he went to the fire, bent over, and with a deadly looking knife, cut out a chunk of meat from the roasted antelope. He moved silently toward me and handed me the piece. I took it.

I looked into his eyes and searched his face, expecting to see hatred or a wild crazed light or anything to explain the last two days. But his eyes were calm—serene. This was his existence—hunting, killing, and raiding to survive on the western plains. He retaliated when insulted by another man and stood his ground. Death was another way of life to him.

My captor turned and walked away. But in that glance we'd come to an understanding. I would be dealt with in the Comanche way, which would be determined by the circumstance of the moment. Tonight, he might feel compassion and feed me. Tomorrow, he might kill and scalp me.

I looked down at the piece of warm meat in my hand. Being hungry, I wanted to gnaw at it like a dog. I didn't, but forced myself to eat slowly, savoring each bite.

Lucy sat across from me. The Indian controlling her followed the leader's actions. When she didn't respond to his outstretched hand, he roughly took her arm and placed the warm chunk in her palm. Her released arm fell to her lap, and the meat rolled onto her gown. She didn't touch it. Dark circles surrounded her closed eyes. Her long straight hair, which normally fell neatly on her shoulders, was matted from the wind, and I noticed her dress was torn at the hem. I didn't look much better. My nightgown was dirty, as were my hands, but the cloth wasn't torn.

Eating the meat, I continued to think. What would they do with me? My hand went to my curly hair. The scoundrels would never get my hair. Maybe there were times I didn't like taking care of it, but it was mine. I intended to keep it attached to my head.

Neither was I ready to be someone's slave. I thought again of Market Square in Memphis—the haunted look in the Negro woman's eyes.

Then I thought of the Guadalupe Mountains and Pine Springs. Suddenly, I wanted to get home more than anything else in the world. I yearned for the day. Pa had said we were within a month of getting there. Nothing was going to stop me, unless I died trying.

If Pa and the others weren't coming to help, I must think of a way to escape. I had too much to live for.

Calm down, Gracie. Think.

One thing was sure, I couldn't get away in the daylight. My escape must be at night. Try as I might nothing came to my exhausted mind. Tomorrow, during our ride, I'd think of...

It was around midnight. The moon had risen. I dozed off into a fitful sleep.

The hand over my mouth, and "Gracie, Gracie," whispered in my ear brought me fully awake. The whispers continued, "Move carefully backward, carefully. Don't make any noise. Don't say anything."

I inched backward, letting Jedediah guide my way while I kept an eye out for the Indians sprawled in every direction. Full of food and tired after our long ride, they slept around the fire.

I followed Jedediah's leading until he apparently felt it was safe enough to stand. I clutched at him, and he held me tight. "I didn't think you were coming."

"Gracie, I wouldn't let anything happen to you. I'd die first." He kissed me on the forehead and lips, gentle kisses full of meaning. "We must move quickly. Your pa's back in the woods with your horse, and my pa is trying to get Lucy. We aren't home free yet."

He walked in front of me, holding my hand, and guiding me along. I saw Pa and ran to him. He put his finger to his lips. We didn't say anything. He whispered something to Jedediah, turned, and helped me on Boone.

In the moonlight, I saw Jedediah grab his horse's reins. "You're comin' with us, aren't you?" I whispered loudly.

He shook his head and walked in the opposite direction, leading his mount.

"Pa?"

"Little girl," he whispered. "Jedediah can take care of himself. We're headin' back toward our camp."

We walked our horses for a while in the moonlight. I knew getting Lucy would be harder than rescuing me. In her shape, they might have to carry her out of camp. Not long after we left the area, we heard muffled shots behind us. I started crying.

"Come on, Gracie. Let's ride," said Pa. We urged our horses forward at a rapid pace.

At noon, we topped a ridge and turned our horses to look back. Riders were following us, and they weren't Comanche. Pa

decided to stop and let the group catch up. I couldn't tell if
Jedediah was among them. My heart ached just thinking about
him getting hurt.

Pa and I dismounted our horses. The excitement of the last
days caught up with me. My body rebelled at standing. My knees
gave way, and I sat on the ground.

"Sorry, Pa, it's hard to stand."

"I understand, daughter. Sit and rest. I'll keep watch on the
men."

"Is it Mr. Bailey and Jedediah?"

"Yes, I think so. Someone's slumped over on their saddle
horn. I can't tell who. Could be Hurricane. It looks like they got
the mules and horses back—plus some Indian ponies."

"What happened, Pa? Why didn't you come sooner?"

"Oh, we were on your trail, but always a little ahead of you.
Hurricane's plan was to make the Comanche think we weren't
following them. We hoped they'd feel comfortable, spend the
night, and not post a guard. We rode ahead and kept out of sight,
waitin' for the right conditions."

"And last night was perfect?"

"Yes, exactly perfect. Oddly enough the moon came out and
lit the area so we could see. Do you know what that bright
moonlight is called in Texas?"

"No."

"Comanche moon, because they love to raid by its light.
Gracie, two can play that game. We used their tactics to get
you."

"How far away are Mr. Bailey and the group?"

"About two hours, I'd say. They're not riding fast at all.
Take a nap, Gracie. I'll wake you when they get here."

"Thanks, Pa. I think I will."

I opened my eyes. Jedediah knelt beside me, shaking me.
"Gracie, are you all right?"

I threw my arms around his neck, impervious to the sudden
stares from several of those present, including my pa and Mr.
Bailey. "Yes, Jedediah, I'm completely safe with you here. You
always seem to be saving my life." I kissed him on the cheek and

pushed back to examine him, feeling his arms and chest. "Are you hurt? I was so worried about you when you stayed behind. And then Pa and I heard gunshots." I started crying, my emotions raw after the last two days of hardship.

Jedediah sat next to me, putting an arm around my shoulders. "I don't have a scratch, but Lucy's bad hurt."

This was the first time I'd noticed my fellow captive. Lucy lay in her father's arms—a dark stain on her clothes.

"Broke off arrow in the back," I heard one of the men say.

"Is she dead?"

"No."

"What happened?" I whispered to Jedediah

"Pa went in to get her like I got you. When he touched her she started screaming, jumped up and ran through the camp in a crazed dash. He grabbed her from behind attemptin' to calm her. She turned in his arms and fought him. That's when she got shot in the back. Another arrow grazed him in the arm."

"Your father's hurt?"

"He says it's nothing."

"How did your father manage to get Lucy out of the area?"

"Witherin' fire from the other men, cut down several of the braves, and the others ran into the woods. Pa carried Lucy out of the line of fire to where I stood with the horses. He broke the arrow off so she could ride with him. I helped him on his horse and raised Lucy to him. He left the area with her like your pa did with you."

"I'm going to check your father's arm." I wiped my wet cheeks on my nightgown sleeves and stood. Jedediah followed.

Mr. Bailey sat on the ground. He looked at me as I approached. "What're you doing here, Missy?" The old sarcasm gone from his voice, he looked haggard and tired. For once, he didn't reek of alcohol.

"Checking your arm." I knelt on the ground beside him.

He started to pull away but apparently thought better of it. I unbuttoned his cuff, rolled his shirt sleeve to where I could see the torn flesh. Grazed wasn't exactly the way I'd describe it. The arrow had gone straight through his upper arm, probably getting a piece of his muscle as it pierced the flesh.

"I broke the arrow in the middle and pulled the pieces out," said Jedediah.

"Yeah, and it hurt like blazes when he did it. A six-year-old coulda done as well," complained Mr. Bailey.

The ragged hole still oozed blood. Reaching down, I tore a piece of material from around the bottom of my nightgown and wrapped his arm in a makeshift bandage. "I'll fix it better after we get to camp." I promised him. "Do you have some liquor in your saddlebags? I'll need it to wash the wound."

After a brief discussion, the men decided to keep going until we made camp that night. When asked if the Comanche would follow us, Hurricane replied, "There's always that chance. But right now, they're trying to patch their wounds and take care of their dead. I wouldn't bet on them following today."

Mr. Johnson looked at him. He held his daughter in his arms—had been since she was lifted gently from his horse. "You'll try to get the arrow out tonight?" he said, looking at Hurricane.

Hurricane nodded again. "Tonight, I'll try." His words were gentler than any I'd ever heard him utter.

Mr. Johnson looked again at his daughter and I saw Pa and Mr. Bailey exchange glances. At that moment, I realized how grave Lucy's situation had become.

We mounted our horses and continued our journey toward camp.

REBA RHYNE

❦ 15 ❦

Saving Lucy Johnson turned out to be futile.

After Mr. Bailey took out the arrow and the shaft, she started to cough blood. "Pierced her lung," he explained to Pa. "Be a miracle if she lives." I listened as Pa and he discussed whether they should double back and see if the Indians were following us. At the end of the discussion, they mounted their horses and left. I paced back and forth for several minutes. Walking relieved the tension I'd felt all day. I was tired of worrying about Indians.

I looked over at Mr. Johnson who rested against his saddle with his daughter's head in his lap. It had gotten dark, and the firelight revealed deep furrows in his tired gaunt face. The pneumonia, his daughter's continuing antagonism, and her perilous wound proved almost too much to abide. He looked in pitiable shape. I went to sit with him.

"Gracie, I wish she could have been your friend, but my daughter didn't befriend people easily. She's always been a loner—played by herself, went to school by herself, even sat at church on the other end of the pew from the rest of the family. We bought her nice clothes, tried to include her in our games, and worried ourselves sick. Nothing we did helped."

"Some people prefer to be alone."

"Not this alone. It wasn't natural. Then Sonny Norbert came along. I didn't realize how much they felt for each other until two weeks after we left home. We were sitting around the campfire. Maw asked her to help with the dishes. Lucy jumped from the fire and started screaming about not doing the dishes, hating dirt and being dirty, and hating us for making her leave home—leave Sonny. The worst, saddest scene I've ever witnessed."

He needed to talk, needed to let his pent-up thoughts and emotions out to someone. I listened. "Gracie, she was old enough to get married, and I believe he wanted to marry her. But he never asked. We forced her to leave." He paused and I saw the tears in his eyes. Clearing his throat he went on. "This is all my fault for wanting something new and different for my family. For wanting a new start in the West. I thought I made the right decision."

"People settle in, Mr. Johnson," I said, reaching out and taking Lucy's hand. It was warm and soft. "I left a boy in Nashville, but never got bitter or resentful. Guess I wanted the adventure Pa wanted."

"Your pa is lucky to have you, Gracie. I've often told my wife that."

"Thank you."

He stroked his daughter's matted hair. "I hoped Lucy would reconcile to the change. Some people do, like you. Others don't. They give up. I believe my beautiful Lucy gave up." His mournful voice touched me. I didn't know what to say but continued to sit by him. Maybe my presence would comfort him somehow.

Almost one hour later, Mr. Bailey, Jedediah and Pa returned to camp, their horses lathered from a fast ride.

I went to Pa. Jedediah came and stood by me.

"There's no evidence the Comanche are following us, but we will continue our ride before daybreak in the morning. Put more land between us."

I nodded and looked at Mr. Bailey. "I need to look at your wound. No need in infection setting in if we can prevent it."

He looked at me rather timidly and walked to the fire where he squatted with the offending arm next to the firelight. "Jedediah, get a bottle from my saddle bag," he ordered.

I knew what I did to his arm must have hurt, but he never flinched—not one muscle. Stared straight ahead with a fixed gaze.

On Thursday, August thirteenth, after riding two hours under the Comanche moon, we'd stopped on a hill to get off and rest our animals a bit. I stood looking toward the east at the wonder before me. Deep darkness turned to gray-maroon. As the sun prepared to peek above the horizon, dark rose, rose and orange edged the sky. It was a proper display, knowing that Lucy would never see such a glorious sight again. I thought it fitting for her entrance into heaven. At seventeen, she was dead.

Only two days before, I'd thought I might die. Instead of me, Lucy had. Wrapped in her pa's bedroll and secured to one of our mules, she was on her last ride across the plains she despised.

We mounted our horses and moved out.

I'll always remember Fort Belknap. Escorted by soldiers we'd encountered on our last day's drive, we were a solemn group as we arrived. First, we went through the small town that had grown alongside the fort.

Passing the courthouse, the soldiers rode in front with their company flag flying high. Pa said they sat on the finest matching horses he'd ever seen. Hurricane and Jedediah came next, then our wagon, followed by the Johnsons'. The rest of the train ended the procession. We pulled to a stop in a level area beyond the fort.

The Johnson children, who'd ridden and slept in our wagon since Lucy occupied theirs, stood with heads stuck out in awe at the fine stone and frame buildings with multiple glass windows. Men dressed in soldiers' uniforms with sabers and pistols hanging from their hips hurried around the fort on company business. The bugle sounded, announcing fort activities.

Soon after we arrived, a wooden casket was brought and Lucy was laid gently inside. Her parents refused our efforts to bury her out on the plains where she'd died. "No," Mr. Johnson said. "Here, her grave would be lost and forgotten. We want to make her grave at Fort Belknap."

Mrs. Johnson carefully washed and prepared her daughter's body for burial. "We'll always be able to come back here and visit. It'll be a comfort to us."

Every soul in the wagon train attended Lucy's funeral. As a sign of respect, a delegation of the several soldiers stationed at the fort assembled around the family, along with a few townspeople. The local minister officiated, reading the traditional verse from Genesis 3:19. He opened his bible and in a loud voice proclaimed, "And God said to Adam, *In the sweat of thy face shalt thou eat bread, till thou return unto the ground; for out of it wast thou taken: for dust thou art, and unto dust shalt thou return.* " There was a moment of silence, and then he snapped his Bible shut. Standing close to him, I jumped at the sound. Mr. Johnson came forward and threw the customary handful of dirt symbolizing our bodies' return to dust. It was a sad, somber moment. I was glad when it was over.

Mr. Bailey, Pa, Jedediah, and I walked back to town. "Are we going to head out this afternoon, Tipton?"

"Hurricane, one of the officers mentioned a patrol leaving west toward Fort Chadbourne. They leave after sunup in the morning. I believe we'll go with them."

Hurricane nodded. "Guess Jedediah and I'll go into town and see what kind of trouble we can get into. We'll talk later this afternoon."

"See you later, Gracie." Jedediah hurried after his father's retreating back.

"Hurricane's mellowed out these last few days, Gracie," my father said as we continued back to the wagons.

"I noticed, Pa. What's caused it?"

"I don't know. He's an interesting man but hard to fathom and hard to live with at times."

"I've decided it has something to do with a woman. Maybe Jedediah's mother."

"I hope he doesn't get liquored up in town." My father stopped walking and turned to me. "Speaking of Jedediah are you and he forming an attachment?"

"I do like him, Pa, more than anyone else I've known."

"Be careful, daughter. He's been held tightly by his father. Cutting the string holding him to Hurricane may not be easy."

"I'll be careful." I was relieved that Pa knew I liked Jedediah. This made it easier to show my preference for him when Pa was around. But could my love for Jedediah cut the string Pa referred to?

REBA RHYNE

❧ 16 ❧

Being the largest settled area since our wagon train left Fort Smith, Fort Belknap turned out to be the hub of several area trails. Pa and I headed for town, which bustled with hard-riding men, farmers and soldiers on business. A contingent of Texas Rangers occupied space on the outskirts.

The local saloon emitted loud laugher and cursing as we passed. Surprisingly, we found several Indians living among the white people. "Scouts," Pa explained. "They help track down renegades."

After my recent brush with the Comanche, I wasn't interested in getting close to an Indian, including a friendly one.

Pa went into the tack store for new harness and ropes, and I walked across the street to the mercantile store. I browsed through rolls of bright-colored cloth, checked out the latest in china dishes, clothes, and rummaged through the spices available. But what caught my eye were fresh ears of corn in a basket by the dormant pot-bellied stove. My mouth watered. Within minutes, Pa joined me and laughed when he found out what I wanted to buy.

"Gracie, I have to say you're predictable when it comes to your stomach. How many do you want?" he said, reaching down and testing the freshness of the ears.

"A dozen, Pa."

"We can't eat a dozen in two days. After that the kernels will be hard as a rock."

I looked down at the basket. "Pa they're small ears," I pleaded.

The merchant sacked a dozen, a box of cinnamon, and some apples I hadn't seen at the end of the counter. I couldn't wait to sink my teeth into cooked apples with sugar and cinnamon. "Pa, ask if they have fresh butter and bread." They didn't, but a shop farther down the street could supply all we needed.

Pa insisted I buy some yards of cloth. "Gracie, after Fort Chadbourne, finding cloth, spices, and other staples will be impossible. Go ahead and buy here. Prices are probably cheaper."

His words made good sense. We carried several packages out of town. These we placed in an already packed wagon. I could barely get into my feather bed.

Later, when Hurricane and Jedediah appeared, we pulled the wagons outside the fort area and circled them.

The young boys scoured a nearby stand of oak and pecan trees, bringing back wood for our campfire.

I have to say my roasted ears of corn in the husks, with melted butter and salt, were the most delicious I'd ever eaten. Butter ran down my chin as I eagerly put away four ears.

I peeled the apples and cooked them, the fragrant smell of cinnamon drifting through the air. We had company when the apples were done. Jedediah and his father came by for a bowlful.

The next morning—reveille—the get-up hour for a soldier, was announced by a bugle. The fort soon became a beehive of activity. After the Saddle Call when the men fed their horses, we hitched the mules to our wagons and ate a quick breakfast. Before the bugle sounded Surgeon's Call we were following a contingent of cavalry toward Fort Chadbourne. They would escort us the first day, leaving us early the next morning. Their orders were to explore lands north and west of the Texas Road and to engage any hostile Indians they found there.

"Gracie, my papers say that mules will be used from Fort Belknap to Yuma, California."

140

"Why mules, Pa?"

"Because, you don't have to feed them as much." He punched me in the ribs with his elbow.

"So, you want to trade me off for a mule, huh."

Pa laughed. "It would be less expensive, daughter."

"Ah, you'd miss my mouth-waterin' cooking."

"Probably. Besides eatin' less, mules are sure-footed and have great strength. Butterfield has twenty-five days to take the mail from Tipton, Missouri to San Francisco. The teams will travel day and night. Even changed every ten, twenty, or thirty miles, a horse couldn't hold up goin' at breakneck speed across the prairie and hills of this arid route. Mules will fair much better. We'll see mules at The Pinery."

"Pa, I'm sorry we lost all that time because of the Comanche raid."

"Gracie, there wasn't anything you coulda done about it. I'd much rather have you than the four days. We'll still get to The Pinery in plenty of time for the first stagecoach to roll through."

"Do you think we'll come across more Comanche?"

"I certainly hope not. The farther we get south and west, and the time of year will keep them away. It's too dry, too hot for them to travel in the desert."

"How many days to Fort Chadbourne?"

"By my reckoning, about seven."

"Then, how many days to The Pinery?"

"Fourteen."

"I'll be glad to get there."

"So will I, daughter. So will I."

The following morning, I watched the Fort Belknap patrol ride off across the plains. I knew they must obey orders, but an escort to Fort Chadbourne would have been nice. Not many days passed without the tension of impending Indian attack. The patrol's presence the day before made my travel very pleasant.

At nightfall, we camped next to a river. "Clear Fork of the Brazos," Jedediah told me as we walked hand-in-hand along its banks. "The Brazos stretches for hundreds of miles throughout Texas. Pa and I have traveled much of it."

"Did you always ride with your father?"

"No, I lived with my maw until she died. Then Pa and I started scouting fer wagon trains and thrill seekers from the East. Pa's whole idea of livin' is having enough food to eat, a good gun and knife, and a bottle of whiskey."

"He's not drinkin' as much lately," I observed.

"He takes those spells. Somethin' will cause him to stop drinking, but I know him well enough to realize it'll start again. He's not bad when he quits chugging alcohol."

"Your mother... How did she die?"

"She just died, Gracie. I don't want to talk about it."

I pointed to a patch on his britches. "Did she teach you to patch holes in your pants?"

"Yes. She was known as a good seamstress. She coulda made a livin' sewing clothes for people back East, instead she married Pa and moved West with him."

"Where did they marry?"

"I swear, Gracie, you ask a lot of questions."

"When you like someone, you want to know about them."

"Do you like me, Gracie?"

"Yes, I do."

"I like you too." Jedediah stopped walking and turned to look at me. "Do you think we'll be together someday?"

"I hope so, but I guess that's up to you."

I wanted him to say more, and I waited for him to say it. But Jedediah continued to look at me while his free arm stole around my waist. He lifted his other hand, caressed my face and touched my hair as if touching something sacred. He pulled me to him and kissed me.

That was the last time we walked in the moonlight during the ride to Fort Chadbourne. His father scouted each day until dark and reported back at nightfall. Jedediah wasn't with him when he came to talk with Pa. And Mr. Bailey's scowl when I approached was enough to keep me from interfering or asking about him. He and Jedediah camped outside our wagon circle and didn't visit around the campfire. I wondered why Jedediah didn't come around, but couldn't guess the reason.

Around noon, five days out of Fort Chadbourne, a young man on horseback drew abreast of our wagon. His mount was the most beautiful black Kentucky mare I'd ever seen. When I finally took my eyes off the well-bred horse flesh, I noticed how striking he was. He wore his felt hat pulled down to shade his hazel eyes—a color I'd never seen before. His friendly face sported strong features with pointed chin, chiseled mouth that was quick to smile, and dark tanned skin. He wore a light-blue cotton shirt, sleeves rolled to the elbow, with striped vest of a darker blue and red, and a red bandana tied loosely around his neck. Brown britches covered the top of an expensive pair of cowboy boots, well-scuffed with wear.

He raised his hand in greeting. "Hello there. My name's Preston Stockton, Jr. My friends call me Press." He was looking at me and over me, from my curly hair down to my britches, a wide smile on his face. I'm sure he thought I was a radical woman since women didn't wear men's clothes. I gave him a short smile and averted my eyes.

"Glad to meet you, Mr. Stockton." My pa sat farther away from our new acquaintance. My name's Jay Tipton and this here's my daughter, Gracie."

I pulled my hat onto my head and looked down at him again.

"No, please, it's Press. Our group's ridin' behind your train. Do you mind if we join you?"

"Where you going, Press?"

"Fort Chadbourne and then home. My wranglers are coming back from driving a bunch of steers to Tipton, Missouri."

"That's a long road from these parts," observed my father. "What possessed you to make such a long trip?"

"Money and adventure, I suppose. The Missouri Pacific Railroad dead ends at Tipton. We wanted to get our steers to the eastern market in Philadelphia. Train's the fastest way."

"You're welcome to join. How many in your party?"

"Fourteen in all. We'll stay out of your way and act as your rear guard, if that's all right with you."

"Perfect," said my father. "We're glad to have you."

"I'll ride back to tell the others."

Press tipped his hat. "Miss Gracie."

During the afternoon's drive, I climbed onto Boone and rode ahead of our wagon as I often did when it was sunny, breaking the hour-by-hour monotony of jolting and bumping along on the stiff wagon seat or walking alongside. To be fair, some of the roads we were traveling weren't so bad. The Butterfield crews had been working hard to make the passengers on the stagecoach line's ride as comfortable as possible. I suppose the main reason I made the switch was the panoramic scenery and the freedom riding a horse provided.

I took off at a gallop. "Gracie, don't get too far out front," Pa called after me. I waved in response. My pesky hat blew off my head, hanging by its strings around my neck.

After living in the green hills surrounding Nashville, the vastness of the open plains never ceased to amaze me. A mile ahead of the wagons, I slowed Boone to a walk and hung the reins on my saddle horn.

I put my hat back on and paused to look around me.

Open spaces.

The wagon train was driving through an area of grassland—the land so flat I could see twenty miles in all directions—nothing to stop or hinder me. Ahead of me, a low range of hills waited to be crossed.

For several minutes I tried to understand the feeling I was having—hard to think it or express it.

But I felt it.

I sat breathing great gulps of unobstructed prairie air. I wanted to fly across the vast grassy plain until I came to its meeting with the blue sky above and shout to the wind, "I found you."

Instead, I raised my arms and my face to the sky and cried, "I love you, Texas!"

"You do, huh?" A man's voice teased behind me. "Too bad my name's not Texas."

Press Stockton, Jr. guided his horse to my side. "Don't you know better than to ride out from the safety of the wagon train, Gracie?"

He said my name like he'd known me for years. "I can take care of myself, Mr. Stockton, Jr. I think I've lived a second life since I left Tennessee."

"It's Press, and how so?" he asked, and I found myself telling him about my adventures on the trail, including the not as long ago run-in with the Comanche.

"I'm sure they were after your curly top. They're not used to seeing anyone with hair like yours." He looked at my hair and examined my face. I squirmed, uncomfortable.

"Is there something wrong with my face?" I asked, putting my hand on my face and rubbing my chin and forehead.

"No, you remind me of someone."

"Who's that?" Probably a long-lost girlfriend. With his looks, I could imagine there were plenty of broken hearts around. I assumed he was married.

"My mother, she was a beautiful lady, with blue eyes and great spirit."

Did he think I was beautiful? I believe he just told me so.

REBA RHYNE

❧ 17 ❧

Two days later, the five chimneys of Fort Phantom Hill stood out stark against the blue Texas sky. It was to be one of Butterfield's newly established stations, supplying water and horses.

"What happened to the fort?" I asked the station man standing in front of one of three stone buildings that remained—hulks of other buildings close-by.

"Burnt down by the Apache, or angry men, or maybe the phantom that roams around these parts." He laughed. "No one really knows. The fort was abandoned when it happened, and Butterfield has resurrected this part from the ruins."

I walked around the charcoaled remains as Pa drew water from the well and carried it to the mules. He talked softly, encouraging each big red animal while rubbing their dusty necks as they sipped from the wooden bucket.

"Gracie, come and water the horses."

"I'm coming Pa." Our stop took about thirty minutes, and then we were on our way again.

Most afternoons, Press came to our front wagon. If I didn't sit on my horse, he asked me to ride. On one of our visits he mentioned the name of his ranch—the Glory B. Our last day before arriving at Fort Chadbourne, I asked Press how his ranch got the name, Glory B. "The name is unusual."

He laughed as he told the story. "It's a long story, and I've heard it many times, but here goes. My grandfather wanted to come to Texas and homestead. He loaded my grandmother and their possessions, and they headed west from Louisiana. He was forty-five."

I interrupted. "My pa's thirty-nine."

"How old are you, Gracie?"

"Over seventeen."

"I see," Press looked at me and smiled. "You're a little younger than I thought."

"What age are you?"

"I'll be twenty-three at my next birthday."

"You're a little older than I thought."

"*Touché...* That means you got me back."

"What kind of language is that?"

"*Je parle le francais.* French, we speak it and Spanish around Louisiana and Texas—among other Indian dialects."

"So, you were born here in the West?"

"Yes. In East Texas."

"Are you married?"

"No," he said grinning at me.

"Oh. Why aren't you?"

"I've never found the right girl, someone as..." He didn't finish the sentence. "I thought you wanted to hear about the Glory B."

"I do. I'm sorry I interrupted."

"When grandpa arrived, he first settled in East Texas, around Nacogdoches. In case you didn't know, it's the oldest town in our state and established by the Spanish. My grandma told me he was restless living there. It wasn't far enough west to suit him. He wanted open spaces. They stayed in Nacogdoches ten years. Finally, my grandfather and my father cajoled, harassed, and threatened my grandma and my mother until they agreed to move. The plan included moving past Waterloo—or Austin as it's now called—since it was made the capital of the Republic of Texas."

"Ten families agreed to move with them, including a minister. Each family had a headright on 1,840 acres of land in the northern Glass Mountains, and this didn't include the single men who were eligible. I remember my mother asked my father what we would do with so much property. My Grandpa and Pa each had that amount. In all, our group would acquire over twenty thousand acres of land."

"And I thought one hundred and fifty acres a lot of land to tend!" I exclaimed, taken back by the enormity of thousands of acres of property to manage.

"That's what your father owned in Tennessee?"

"Yes, most of it hills with fertile valleys in between. We had a creek running through it. Pa had several head of cattle, and we made a huge garden. I hope we'll be able to raise some vegetables in the Guadalupes."

"You will, but you'll need to water them," Press continued, smiling as he looked at me.

"Go ahead. I'm sorry I stopped you again. Your story is fascinating. I'm learning lots."

"Five of the men rode west to explore and establish the land's boundaries and to decide on the best way to get there. There were trees—juniper, oak, willow, and madrone. Sparse grasses grew well enough to support several head of cattle, and Gracie, hundreds of thousands of cattle roamed free throughout the prairie. Water turned out to be the biggest problem with settling the land. Wells would need to be dug to have water for the cattle during the driest part of the summer."

"Three months passed and they returned to Nacogdoches. The men decided to go in early spring the following year, but my grandma put her foot down."

I laughed, "I think I would have liked her."

"She wasn't going, she told my grandfather, until the wells were dug and she had a roof over her head. I can hear her now. 'Press, you're not going to get me into a tent at my age. I demand a house with my piano installed in it, water wells and cistern, and a garden planted with food ready to harvest and eat.'"

"After a meeting of those who intended to go, the ones who had sons old enough to stay and help at home, loaded as many household goods as they could and headed west. Six months later they came home."

"'We leave in April,'" my grandpa told Grandma. She knew better than to argue. They left in April and Grandma loved every bit of the trip."

"Your mother, what about her?"

"I'm not sure she wanted to go, but she learned to love West Texas. She was a school teacher in Nacogdoches. So, she taught school in our Glass Mountain home—taught the children who went—including me. She's gone now—in heaven."

"You raise cattle?"

"Yes, free range cattle. We caught longhorns left behind when the Spanish missions closed."

"How many head did you take to Missouri?

"Over two thousand."

"Over two thousand!" I tried to imagine that many head of cattle in one herd.

"Did I hear an echo?" he teased. "We took that many, because grass isn't as plentiful on the Glory B Ranch, especially in the summer. You don't want them eating cactus and creosote bushes.

"How do you feed your cattle?"

"We rotate canyons in the area, and Pa built several small ponds in natural scooped-out areas that hold more water in the dry season."

"Back to my first question, how did your ranch get the name Glory B?"

"It's been the Glory B since my grandma laid eyes on it. My grandmother and mother rode west just like you did with many of the household goods we'd used in East Texas. We hauled machinery and equipment to till the land, along with our farm animals. They made quite a caravan driving through the hill country, past Comanche Springs, to the Glass Mountains. My grandfather drove their packed wagon along a draw until they came out the top. He turned left, drove the grassy flat land around a hillside for a mile—leaving the draw, the surrounding desert, and plains behind and out of sight. The land sloped upward toward the mountains. There were grasses on the lower slopes—pine and cedar on the mountainside."

I could almost picture it as Press continued. "My Grandfather pointed to a house sitting at the edge of the tree line. Grandmother got out of the wagon and looked around. 'Glory be, Pa. This is a beautiful spot, and that's a wonderful house.' The house sits there today, and now you know how the ranch became the Glory B."

"Your home sounds like a wonderful place."

"It is. Of course, the house has grown in size the last few years, and so has the ranch. We added more acreage as others left for greener pastures."

"My grandfather and father laid out a town with part of their property in a flat valley high in the mountains behind them, and invited any who would come from the East, to take free land and build businesses. We have about six different establishments at the center and a small church where Reverend Marshall preaches each Sunday. Five or six Mexican families live in town. Some work for us, wrangling cows mostly."

"Do you live there today?"

"Yes, Grandpa and Grandma are gone. My father and I live in the great house alone."

"How far is your ranch from The Pinery?"

Hmm. I'm guessing about one hundred fifty miles. On horseback, five or six days."

"I'd like to see it someday."

"I hope you will, Gracie."

That night as I lay in my feather bed, I thought about my conversation with Press. Was I a traitor to Jedediah for riding and talking with him? I didn't think so. I could appreciate another man's physical attractiveness and conversation without deserting Jedediah or ceasing to love my father.

And where was Jedediah? He hadn't been around in days. What was wrong with him? Our last meeting took place under the Comanche Moon after Fort Belknap. I trembled with expectation at the thought of seeing him again.

❦ 18 ❦

Fort Chadbourne reminded me of all the military outposts we'd been through.

Pa and I rode past a barbershop, mercantile store, and saloon before coming to the main military outpost. Someone plunked out the *Arkansas Traveler* on the saloon's out-of-tune piano. The jingling notes joined raucous laughter and the sound of boots hitting the wooden floor. Someone was dancing. Hurricane Bailey's horse was tied to the hitching posts in front of the watering hole.

"Gracie." Jedediah waved from where he sat on his horse just beyond the saloon. "I've been missing you."

Urging the animal forward, he joined me as we continued down the dusty street, passing the headquarters of the Butterfield Overland Stage—an impressive building of stacked stone like the rest of Fort Chadbourne—unlike the other stage buildings we'd been passing all day.

Pa stopped in front. "Gracie, I'm going to introduce myself to the station man. I'll be right back." He jumped from the wagon and disappeared through a door.

"Where have you been, Jedediah? I haven't seen you in days." I turned in the saddle to look at him.

"Gracie. Oh, Gracie. I couldn't see you. Pa's kept me busy."

The look in his eyes reminded me of Wooly when she wanted some loving. I couldn't scold him for not being around.

"Being busy is not a good excuse. Surely, you have a better one," I prodded.

"Gracie, Pa won't let me see you," he blurted out.

"What! Jedediah how—what happened? Why?" My eyes must have grown as big as walnuts at his impulsive comment.

"He happened to see us the last night we went walkin' on the Clear Fork of the Brazos, and he told me not to ever see you again. I think he's afraid I'll leave, and he'll be alone."

Now I was hopping mad. "Jedediah, if you like me and we're to be together, you gotta stand up to him and tell him." I'm sure my eyes were flashing fire.

"Gracie, will we be together? Like that?"

I pressed my lips together and shook my head. Gracie Tipton, I thought to myself, why can't you find a man who's willing to forsake all others, say I love you, and ask you to marry him? Why, here I was practically asking him to wed. I drew in a huge sigh and let it out in a loud rush. "Oh, fishhooks!"

He shot a look at me, "Now Gracie, don't get mad."

"Jedediah, you can't stay tied to your father's apron strings and have a life and family. Don't you see that?"

"Gracie, you don't understand." He looked behind us in the direction of the saloon.

"Yes, I do. I understand that we like each other. I understand I'd like to be with you. I understand that this isn't enough."

"Gracie, I'll come tonight, and we'll talk. Is that okay?"

"I guess it'll have to be. Pa and I are going into town on business. I'm sure we'll be back by dark."

"I'll see you then."

Jedediah rode back the way we'd come. I knew his ride would end at the saloon, playing nursemaid to his father.

"Jedediah going back to care for his father?" Pa asked as he returned to the wagon. Even he knew it.

"It looks that way, but he's coming over to talk tonight."

Pa nodded. He climbed onto the wagon seat. "The station man said there's a flat field about one-quarter mile down the road."

We circled the wagons west of Fort Chadbourne—three wagons less. For the Johnsons this was their intended destination, and the other wagons intended to go south toward San Antonio. Press and his cowboys circled with us.

"Gracie," Press called across the circle. "We're going to visit some friends at the fort. What time will your father pull out tomorrow?"

I turned to Pa who was examining a horseshoe on my horse's foot. "Tell him about noon," he said.

I turned around to yell the answer, and Press was standing by me. I caught myself, "I guess you heard."

"Yes, I did. I'll see you tomorrow." He reached out his hand and patted my arm, turned, and walked back to some of his waiting men. I saw them laugh, look at him, and then look at me. I felt a hot flush on my face as I watched them disappear in the direction of the fort.

Pa and I found a place where we could eat pinto beans, Texas onions, and cornbread baked in an iron skillet. Sliced, red ripe tomatoes with juice running from them sat in a blue bowl on the table between us. I dug in, savoring each bit. The food was delicious, and I didn't have to cook a thing.

"My, honey, has he been starving you," was the comment of the lady who graciously served us in a corner of the mercantile.

Pa shook his head. "No, she's always hungry. I'm planning on trading her in for another mule. They eat less."

"Pa!"

At his unexpected retort, the rotund woman threw back her head and laughed so hard her belly shook, and this made me laugh. Soon we were all three laughing to the stares of the other customers in the store. I hadn't guffawed in ages. I opened my mouth and let loose, relieving the stress of the last few weeks.

The sun was low on the horizon as I dressed and waited for Jedediah. Yellow rays streamed between distant clouds, coating the earth with a deep gold glow. Underneath the clouds, light-gray streaks blended with the dark-gray ground. Somewhere on the Texas plains the rain was falling, and every living thing was soaking up the cooling water until the next shower. Low hills to the west rose out of the flat plains. Only the bugle of Fort Chadbourne interrupted the quietness of prairie life. Military life depended on that bugle's notes.

I sat in front of the wagon on a high stool Pa had fetched for me, watching the spectacle of water giving life to the distant plains. The air was already hot and worse still because of the cooking fire burning several feet away. I decided Texas in August was best spent in the cooler mountains of the Guadalupe.

Tomorrow we started the last leg of our journey. Only two more weeks to go and I would see my new home. My heart beat faster just dreaming about seeing the place for the first time.

Across the campfire, one of our ladies busied herself cooking a meal for her family. She bustled around a wooden stand where a large iron skillet and a coffee pot waited to be used. I couldn't tell what she planned to cook but hoped she'd found fresh vegetables and meat in town. She looked in my direction and waved. I threw my hand up and acknowledged her. Going to her wagon, the woman called her daughter, who handed a smaller pan from the dark interior.

After coming back from Fort Chadbourne, I'd changed into a cooler skirt and loose blouse. Moving forward on the stool where I sat on my hands, I took my feet from its rungs and kicked my legs in sheer joy. They felt bare and free after wearing britches for weeks.

I moved to see where Pa had disappeared, and my skirt settled down around the stool. The light wind ruffled my hem. I smoothed out the wrinkles on my lap, looking at the dark rose flowers with green petals on a sea of light rose. The blouse was rose cotton with beige cotton lace on the bodice and around the collar. It had short, loose sleeves. Earlier, I'd picked the outfit out of my trunk. It was the coolest outfit I owned and the most handsome besides the one I'd gotten for my birthday.

Pa came around the corner of the wagon, wiping his hands from packing the wagon wheels with axle grease. He stopped and stared. "Gracie, you look very pretty in your pink outfit. I haven't seen you in a skirt in weeks."

"It's cooler, Pa. My legs are free. I'm surprised at how different I feel."

"Jedediah should be the one surprised and impressed to see you looking like a beautiful lady."

I grinned at Pa. "We'll see. I think I see him coming." I slid off the stool.

After greeting Jedediah, Pa hefted a reed basket sitting next to a wagon wheel. "I'm taking our washing into town, Gracie. I saw a sign saying Laundry."

"Thank you, Pa."

My father was gone, and I stood looking at Jedediah. He seemed tongue-tied.

"Gracie, you're..." He stood, apparently searching for the precise word he wanted to use. Except for our first meeting, he hadn't seen me in women's clothes. "Fine-looking," he finished, shaking his head.

Curtsying and flirting, I said, "I appreciate your kind words."

He looked around at the circled wagons. "Gracie, lets go for a walk. I think there's a good path out from the fort."

It didn't take five minutes to reach the well-beaten foot trail leading into the woods. Neither of us knew where it led. I walked ahead. When we were out of sight of the other wagons and the fort, he caught my hand and stopped me. Pulling me to him, he held me tightly in his arms. His cheek was against my forehead. He was trembling.

"What's wrong?"

He held me tighter. "Gracie, I don't want to lose you. Tomorrow you'll head west. I won't see you for a while."

"Aren't you going with us to The Pinery?"

"No. Pa and I will start work on the trail just west of town later this week. We won't be traveling with you."

"When did you find this out?" My thoughts jumbled together. He wasn't coming. We weren't getting married. He couldn't leave his father.

"After we got here this afternoon. Pa went by Butterfield Headquarters and checked in. They told us."

I thought about what Jedediah said. I guess I'd known this was going to happen, but I put it in the back of my mind. I didn't say another word.

He held me tightly around the waist as we walked slowly on until the trail ended at a small gorge. Across the cut were two distant summits. In the setting sun, they cast long dark shadows across the prairie. As the sun set, the shadowy silhouettes crept toward us. I shivered, leaned against Jedediah, and put my arm around his waist.

"Jedediah, what's going to happen to us?"

"Gracie, I'll come and get you."

"We can't live from place to place. I want a home. I want to be married."

"We'll get married here, tomorrow—tomorrow morning."

"Jedediah, you haven't heard me. I want a home."

"You can stay here. We'll make our home here, and I can continue to work with Pa. Our head office is at the fort."

Jedediah didn't understand. I wanted him away from Hurricane Bailey. Working with his father was unacceptable, and I needed to impress him with this fact—but how to do this without antagonizing him?

"Jedediah, I can't live here. For months, I've been anticipating living in the Guadalupe Mountains. I've got to complete my trip. That's my home." I pleaded, looking at him. I couldn't conceive of living any other place. Certainly not here in Fort Chadbourne with its ready brew, war attitude, and Hurricane Bailey. I'd be tending him as much as Jedediah. No, I wouldn't do it.

"But Gracie, I assured Pa I'd help with the trail crew. I can't go back on my word."

"You shouldn't have promised. Don't you understand? To be together as man and wife means not living with or around your father. I can't do that." I spoke frankly, plainly.

"But he's my pa—my only family."

So, it all came down to Hurricane Bailey. Hadn't Pa warned me about this? How people are tied to someone who physically controls them. I felt the tears come to my eyes. We were at a stalemate, and I could see plainly nothing would change it.

"I'm sorry Jedediah." I turned to go as the first wet drop of salty liquid slid down my face and touched my lips. It was followed by a flood of others.

Jedediah caught me. "No, Gracie. I'll come. Don't cry. I'll come to The Pinery for you. Let me complete this first section of road with Pa, and I'll tell him we're to be married, and I'll come. Don't cry. Please."

I stood looking at him as he brushed the tears from my face. "Do you want to marry me bad enough to promise me?"

"Yes, I do, and I promise you I will come to The Pinery." He moved to pull me to him, but I put my arms between us. I wanted to see his face as we talked. I scanned his countenance and smiled. I couldn't help myself. Jedediah would never tell a lie. He meant it when he promised to meet me in the Guadalupe Mountains—but when?

"Jedediah, when will you come?"

"I can't promise you a time, because I don't know. Don't ask me to." His eyes were pleading with me. "It's hard enough being apart from you."

I realized he couldn't agree to a specific day or month. "Okay," I responded softly. "I'll be waiting for you, Jedediah. I promise you that."

"Gracie, we could go ahead and be secretly married in the morning. There's a parson at the fort. Might be hard to find a minister where you're going."

"Jedediah, anything could happen. I prefer to wait. Things'll work out."

"I'll hurt for you since we're to be apart." His eyes showed plainly this was true already—a deep soulful sorrow new to him.

I stepped into his arms, and we kissed—a long, lingering goodbye. Why couldn't he say I love you? Why didn't I say it? Wasn't that what I felt? I turned my cheek toward the gorge. The shadows touched its edge. I shivered.

"Gracie, are you cold?"

"No, I'm happy—happy to be with you. Jedediah, I want to go back to the wagons." The shadow had crossed the gorge and started down the trail, rapidly approaching where we stood.

"We'll go, Gracie dear."

❧ 19 ❧

$\mathbf{P}$a made a madcap dash to get our laundry, and we left at noon on Monday, August 23, for The Pinery. According to his schedule, we would arrive on Sunday, September the fifth.

As we drove through Fort Chadbourne, our last semblance of civilization disappeared behind us. We continued through miles of cactus and creosote bushes. Cottonwood and other shade trees appeared only where water could be found. Every few miles a Butterfield outpost appeared, and we greeted the people manning the meager looking stations.

I sat on the wagon seat beside my father as I'd done so many days since we'd left Nashville. "Pa, your schedule has been nearly perfect since we left home—like a map of dependable days—reliable like you. I—I'm glad you're my pa."

"There's something nice about planning and the plans coming out okay." We rode a mile in silence before he said another word. He put his arm around me and gave me a hug. "Dependable or reliable are good words to have someone think of you, little girl. I thank you." Dropping his arm, he added, "Jedediah isn't going to The Pinery with us?" I recognized his words as a question and a statement.

"No, but he promised to come as soon as they complete the first set of repairs on the road west from Fort Chadbourne. His father is crew chief, and he gave his word to help. Jedediah won't break his word."

"He should keep his word. Will you get married?"

"That's the intention."

"I see. Where will you find a minister out on the desert?"

"I have no idea Pa, but things'll work out."

"I like your enthusiasm and optimism."

"After living with you, I find not being able to put a time on his coming very difficult, after all it's the most important part of my future and Jedediah's."

Pa nodded. "I'm here, Gracie, if you need me."

I gave him a hug, and we looked toward the western horizon. My mind and heart were a jumble of emotions.

Leaving my heart behind in Fort Chadbourne wasn't easy, and I felt heaviness in my body that I hadn't experienced before. I wasn't happy, and that wasn't like me. The relentless sun beating down on us didn't help, sapping my energy and spirit. Not long before we stopped for the night, Press came alongside.

"Mr. Tipton, I'd like to invite you and Gracie to take supper with us at the chuck wagon. Our cook, Jorge, is excellent. We have fresh venison, potatoes, and other vegetables for tonight—and Jorge's favorite skillet corn bread."

I noticed he was looking at me as he asked my father and gave the menu.

"Press, I think we'd like that. Wouldn't we, little girl?"

I nodded, conscious that my relationship with Press had changed since the last time I saw him. As a betrothed woman, I needed to restrict our involvement, and our afternoon rides. That thought added to my sadness, because I enjoyed our talks.

"What time should we come?"

"Sunset will be fine."

"How many days will you be ridin' along with us, Press?"

"We'll head south in six days."

"I'll be sorry to see you go. Our group is much smaller now. I've felt much safer with you and the other men around. We'll be entering Apache territory soon."

"Indians will be scarce on the desert—too hot and dry. I doubt you'll have any trouble. But if we see sign between here and when my group leaves, we may continue with you for your safety. I'd hate for anyone but Gracie to have that mop of curls."

He was smiling at me, and I couldn't help but smile back. I think this was the first time I'd smiled all day.

"I'd appreciate your continuing presence," Pa said.

"See you later, Gracie." He turned his horse and disappeared toward his company at the rear of the wagon train.

Pa was strangely quiet after Press left. I wondered what he was thinking about.

The meal was delicious. I walked over to the cook. "Would you like to have a job workin' for Butterfield Overland Stage Lines?"

"Miss Gracie, I have one." He laughed, throwing his head back in a deep chuckle. He pushed his hat back on his forehead, revealing a long, ragged scar. That was the only part of his face not covered with a beard.

"Do you cook for the Stocktons at the Glory B?"

"No, jest for the cowboys when they come in from the range. A Mexican woman cooks their meals. We have our own eatin' area and bunk house."

"The venison was great, really tender, and I loved the skillet cornbread. I've never fixed it that way."

"I beat the venison with a small hammer I keep for jest such an occasion. And as fer the cornbread, instead of baking it whole, I add onions and peppers and when I have fresh corn, I cut it off the cob and put some in. Hot grease and dropping a large serving spoonful at a time makes a tasty quick bread with your meal. My mother taught me, and I've done it this way for years."

"Pa taught me to make biscuits and cornbread. I don't remember my Mama."

"She died when you were young?"

"Yes, very young."

"Then your pa knows it's hard to bake a pone of cornbread in an iron skillet without an oven although my Ma used to do it on top of a wood stove. When the bottom got done she'd take an egg turner and flip it over in the skillet. She got to where she browned the bread as smooth as a baby's butt—on both sides."

"I'm goin' to try your suggestion as soon as we get to The Pinery—both of them."

"Jorge is she picking your brain for secrets?"

I turned as Press joined us. Behind him, Pa sat at the fire talking to the other wranglers about raising longhorns in Texas. The talk was animated and lively with loud laughter at times.

"Naw, we was jest talking, wasn't we, Miss Gracie?"

"That's right. New friends' talk."

"Gracie, I want to show you something in our gear wagon."

"Okay, I'll see you later, Jorge. Maybe we can share some recipes." I winked at him, and he grinned and winked back.

"Anytime, Miss Gracie. Better watch him, he's a lady's man."

"Really? Should I be scared?"

"Yes. They fall all over him, but he doesn't fall back. Seems to be waitin' for the right one to come along." Jorge winked again, and I heard him haw-hawing as we left.

I followed Press to a covered wagon parked to the side of the chuck wagon. The soft glow of the fire barely reached the back end, which was open.

"Gracie, I bought something in Tipton, Missouri. I want you to see it." He climbed into the back of the wagon, which was almost as full as ours. I heard him rummaging through a stack of boxes at the side. "Ah, here it is."

He came to the back with a rather large box, hammer, and a crowbar.

"What on earth are you going to do?"

"Take the lid off." He worked at doing that as he spoke.

The fire's flickering light danced on his face. Flecks of deep blue glittered in his gray eyes. No wonder women sought his company. He was handsome. I contrasted his smooth looks with Jedediah's rugged countenance. Each had their own magnetic appeal. One revealed the kempt looks of money and power—the other the unkempt but interesting look of hardship and toil. Not that Press didn't work, I knew he did.

What difference did I note? Press didn't carry the experiences that Jedediah's face revealed. His attraction included more than a handsome face and body. He was sure and relaxed in his actions. Even with money to back him, no hint of arrogance invaded his demeanor.

From my interaction with them, I'd come to the conclusion they were both honest young men.

"Gracie, are you here?" Press tilted his head at me and chuckled.

I smiled back and nodded, electing not to say anything.

He pried the nails loose from the oak boards of the crate. They made shrill squeaks as they left their tight holes.

"Here, Gracie, hold these while I get the others out." He grabbed my hand and laid the nails in it. "Don't lose them. I'll need to put the lid back on."

I curled my fingers around the warm fasteners.

Two more nails and the lid came off. "I had this packed in horsehair and cotton so it wouldn't break on our long journey home." He lifted the packing off the top and put his hand down beside whatever resided within.

Press carefully lifted out the most beautiful porcelain ewer I'd ever seen. The pear-shaped jug was white with blue scenes of flowers in tasteful arrangements on the surface. He handed it to me and reached again for its companion basin.

"It's beautiful, probably the most exquisite one I've ever seen."

He sat on another crate nearby and watched as I examined the twosome. "I want you to have it, Gracie."

I stood holding the pitcher and basin. "I can't take this. It's too expensive." I pushed it back at him.

"It's you, Gracie. The two belong with you. I won't take no for an answer, so there's no argument. You can use it to wash in the mornings at The Pinery."

"I don't have room in the wagon. Wooly just barely has enough room to stand now without worrying about things falling on her."

"I'll help you rearrange the Conestoga."

"But..."

"That's enough. I want you to have it."

I quit arguing. "I can't take it back tonight."

"I'll bring it tomorrow when we go riding in the afternoon." He took a deep breath and continued, satisfied that he had won. "You haven't seemed happy today, Gracie. Is something bothering you? Can I help?"

I kept my eyes down on the water jug and basin—my fingers running over its dimpled surface. When I looked up, his eyes bored into mine and went straight to my heart.

I opened my mouth and for seconds that seemed like an eternity, I didn't say anything. "Thanks, thanks for asking, but I guess not."

No use telling him I couldn't ride tomorrow, or any other day. I'd tell him about Jedediah and that would be it. So far, I hadn't mentioned a word about my intended.

All morning long I thought about how I would tell Press about Jedediah. I couldn't think of a way. In the end, I put it off until the next day. After the crate was stowed in the wagon, we rode off down the rough road that was to be used by the Butterfield Stage Lines with Wooly on our horse's heels. Jedediah, his father, and their crew had a lot of work to do on this section of the road. The land was rolling hills and rocky.

"Is it my imagination or is the road slowly rising?" I asked Press as we topped a low hill.

"The elevation rises as you travel west. You don't notice the change as much as you do when you come east and every hill is lower than the last one. Are you anxious to get to The Pinery, Gracie?"

"Yes, I am. I can't wait to unload the wagon and get into our new home. It will be nice to sleep in my own bed with an actual roof over it."

"Don't expect too much out here. Some of the Butterfield homes I've seen are adobe with little more than mud and sticks for a roof. You'll see several of those in the next few days."

"Thanks for encouraging me."

"Oh, I didn't mean to… I'm sorry, Gracie."

"You know what I'll miss the most?"

"No, what?"

"Milk, good old cow's milk lifted out of cool spring water. And all the things I can make with it like butter, buttermilk, and cakes…"

"And cornbread." Press was laughing at me.

"Yes, it takes milk to make good cornbread."

"Gracie, I'll see that you get a cow. I don't know how or when, but you will have a cow. I promise."

"I have a little money saved, and Pa says I can charge a dollar for meals served to the stage riders. So, I'll pay you for it."

"No Gracie, you don't have enough money to buy a cow from me."

"Press, what's that?" I pointed to a hill several miles in the distance where it looked like a cloud's shadow traversed the ground. The Texas sky remained clear.

Press stood in his stirrups. "It's a herd of buffalo. I wonder which way they're going?"

We stopped riding and watched the dark shadow as it continued to snake its way across the hill. "We'd better go back and tell your pa. If they cross the trail in front of us, we'll have to stop until the herd goes by. Sometimes it takes hours if they aren't in a hurry."

We turned our horses, causing Wooly to halt abruptly and look at us. "We're going back to the wagon, Wooly." Press and I set out with Wooly following close behind. When we got to the Conestoga, Press dismounted and lifted her to Pa, who put her behind the wagon seat.

"What's going on?"

"Herd of buffalo about twenty miles ahead."

"Could you tell what direction they're headed?"

"Not really."

"Do you guess we'd better step up our pace, try passing them should they turn north?"

"Yes, I'll ride back and tell the others."

"It'll take at least six hours until we reach the group," Pa called after him as he left.

"Gracie, tie your horse behind the wagon and get in."

I couldn't imagine what a herd of buffalo looked like that it might take several hours to pass across the trail in front of us. Later, I found out.

Two teams of mules in harness pulling a wagon make noise, but the ground shook and thousands of snorting buffalo drowned out any sounds coming from our rig. We pulled our wagon to a halt. They were already crossing the road in front of us. When I looked north from my wagon seat, I couldn't see a front end.

When I looked south the sea of coffee-colored, nodding heads and moving bodies was endless until they blended together in a mass, looking like boiling, moving chocolate syrup in a pot. Shaggy heads and bodies, fur-covered muscles, heads with horns, big and small moved in unison across the road.

Press came riding toward us. "Mr. Tipton, I think we need to circle the wagons and build our cook fire. If the herd widens out, they'll split around us and pass on by. Leave enough space to tether your horses and mules between each wagon out of their way. Do it quietly. We don't want to spook them."

"Okay, Press, please tell the others."

All night long, the snorting of buffalo told us the herd was passing. By daybreak they were gone. Pa laughed the next morning as he noted, "Lots of fresh buffalo chips to start fires, Gracie."

"Sure, Pa, you pick one up."

As we traveled forward, the tall grasses were gone in a large swath where the herd trampled them or took time to graze in passing. For miles, the earth looked like it had been plowed by their hooves.

❦ 20 ❦

During Thursday's drive the clouds piled up on each other on the horizon. I asked Press during our afternoon ride if those dark clouds meant stormy weather. When he answered, he seemed unusually serious and preoccupied. I looked at him.

"No, the rain will be gentle, maybe a little wind and a little cooler but there's not much chance of a bad storm."

"How do you know that?"

"I just do. I've watched the weather enough to know. You do that when you herd and drive cattle."

"I lived through a bad tornado not long after we crossed the Red River. The clouds looked a lot like those. A young man on the wagon train saved my life—and Wooly's."

"Really? Who was he? Is he still here?" Press's eyebrows rose. His interest was piqued, his eyes questioning.

"No, he left back at Fort Chadbourne. He and his father scouted for our wagon train." It was a perfect time to tell him of Jedediah, but I couldn't or didn't. Instead I related the stormy incident to him—almost all of it.

"I've never been close to a tornado, and if there's any way to prevent it from happening, I won't be close to one."

"You'll be leaving us on Sunday morning?"

"Yes, our group will head south on the old Comanche Trail." I heard his voice turn toward me and felt his warm glance.

"Comanche Trail...are the Comanche around here?" I hurried to ask, recognizing the mounting attraction between us.

"Not as much as they were. Sometime after we first moved here, my father said he saw several large raiding parties headed south through Texas. This was in the fall, and he was standing atop Moses' Mountain when he saw them."

"Moses' Mountain, that's a strange name—anything to do with Moses in the Bible?"

Press laughed. "The mountain wasn't always called by a name. The place got its handle when Reverend Marshall stopped on top during a heat storm. He said the lightnin' and thunder without rain reminded him of Moses on Mt. Sinai in the Bible. He expected a revelation any minute." Press laughed again. "You'd like Preacher Marshall. He's a good man."

"Aren't you afraid the Comanche will raid your home and kill you?"

"We try to do everything we can not to be noticeable. Before the fall season my father and mother stock supplies and don't go out of the mountains until winter. And all the other residents of our vicinity do the same. Our cattle and livestock are contained in areas where they are less apt to be found. That's not saying someday we might not be discovered. We'd be no match for a thousand raiding Indians."

"How many people live around you?"

"Counting children...I'd say ninety or so."

"Don't you have any military protecting you?"

"In the Davis Mountains, west of us there's Fort Davis— erected for that purpose and to protect the Jackass Mail route from San Antonio to San Diego, California. I think that's one reason the Comanche raids are much less, and then many treaties have been signed."

"Why do the Comanche go to Mexico to plunder and rob?"

"Because the northern Mexicans have no protection, and that makes them easy targets. The Comanche Trail, which runs from Oklahoma Territory into Texas is a straight route to Mexico. It splits at the Glass Mountains and some raiding parties go east or west of where I live, following a route through Persimmon Gap into the Big Bend. They ride past the Chisos

Mountains, and ford the Rio Grande River at Grand Indian Crossing into the Mexican state of Chihuahua."

"It must have been terrible for the people of Mexico, loosing their possessions."

"The Mexicans dreaded the fall of the year."

"Why the fall?"

"Because it was cooler and food was easy to find on the ride south. Fruit and nuts were ripe, and water more plentiful. The raiding parties took horses, cattle, and women and children for slaves, leaving a swath of blood and death far into Mexico. But as I said, raiding parties haven't been as pronounced these last few years." He added, "We have two Indian families living in our town at the Glory B."

"Comanche?"

"No, Lenape. Their tribe is famous for being guides and scouts for many of the first military and exploratory expeditions to the west. Ones like Fremont and Kit Carson made. Looking for a peaceful and permanent home, they came south to the Glass Mountains. We welcomed them."

"Should we worry about raids in the Guadalupe Mountains?" I kept rattling the questions off, trying to change his present solemn mood. And, I had to admit, trying to keep the subject from turning back to Jedediah.

"I haven't heard of any problems lately, but that doesn't mean a few renegades couldn't be in the mood to murder, or steal food or horses. Those riding the Butterfield stage will have to keep an eye peeled for any Indian sign as they travel." He turned in his saddle, "Gracie, I…"

"What do the Guadalupe Mountains look like?"

Press laughed. "Gracie, I feel like an encyclopedia on horseback."

"I'm sorry for so many questions, but you know everything about West Texas."

"And you're hungry for information." He nodded and smiled at me. "I like that facts are important to you. Gracie. They're important to me too. So many people aren't interested in details and history."

"I come by it honestly. Pa's fed me history for as long as I can remember. Lately, it's made me want to go places, see things, and soak up particulars about them, especially West Texas."

"To answer your question about the Guadalupes, they're not like anything you've seen. Your neck of the woods in Tennessee reminds me of the area around Nacogdoches—hilly with lots of trees."

"You've been there—to Nashville I mean?"

"Took the Natchez Trace to Northern Mississippi. Not all the way."

"You were close."

"Yes, I was, but there's a great difference in the two areas— from Nashville to the land of West Texas. The mountains of the Guadalupe look like several chunks of gray rock thrust into the sky by a big, angry fist hidden underneath. El Capitan's sheer cliff guards the end with the highest peak north of it. It's an awesome sight the way the whole area rises out of the flatland."

"But Pa said there are trees on the mountains."

"There are in the lower to mid elevations, lots of them. The mountaintops are solid rock."

"I'll be glad to get there. I'm tired of ridin' in the wagon. Sometimes when I get down off the wagon, my body feels like it's still going."

Press laughed again. "You become one with the wagon's movements, just like ridin' a horse or travelin' by boat." He was quiet for a while.

"Do you still remember Nacogdoches?" I asked. "I thought you were really young when you left?"

"I was. When my mother finished sharing what she could teach me, my parents sent me back to Nacogdoches University for two years. I stayed with some of their friends and went to school. I missed Texas and home." He was looking at me, running his eyes over my face and figure.

I hurried on. "Did you know that Nashville is known as the 'Athens of the South'? We had the first public school system in the Southern states."

"No, I didn't know that."

"It was in 1855 that Hume School was established. I went there for two years. Of course, I rode my horse in and out of Nashville every day. My friend Sarah went too. Sarah gave me

Wooly to remember her by. Come to think of it, I haven't thought of Sarah in several days."

"You'd better keep your word, Gracie." Press had stopped in the road and turned his horse toward mine, catching the reins of my horse at the same time. Our knees touched as we faced each other sitting in the saddle.

Dear Lord, here it comes.

"Gracie, I'm going to come to The Pinery to visit you and bring you the cow, but I'd like to stay a while and visit when I do. Our conversations have been a highlight of my coming back home to Texas. I'm going to miss them and you—especially that curly hair." He reached over and tweaked a stray curl. His face was close to mine.

"Come anytime, Press. Pa talks about climbing the trails on the mountain." I hurried on. "I'm sure he won't have time. Maybe we can discover some of them." He made me nervous, as he continued to lean toward me with his elbow on his knee.

He nodded as he smiled. "I'd like that, and I want you to visit the Glory B. I'm sure Pa would like to meet you, and Maria would like to have another female in the house."

"Who's Maria?"

"Our cook. She loves company. She'll fill your ears with stories of her life in Mexico. She's married with four grown, married children."

"She sounds like fun."

"She is." He turned serious. "I've depended on her since my mother died to be sympathetic, lend an ear to my ramblings, and give me a hug when I need one. She's special to me, just as you are, Gracie."

"Thank you, for considering me as your friend."

"I consider you much more than a friend."

"I-I can't be any more than that, Press."

"Then that'll have to be enough—for now." I caught his special meaning in the last words he spoke.

Why didn't I tell him the reason? I wanted to kick myself for not blurting out that I was soon to be married. I couldn't. The words wouldn't come.

"We'd better go back to the wagon train," I said, clutching at my reins. He caught hold of them.

173

"Gracie, I could use a hug now."

I thought my heart would jump out of my body as I looked into his eyes and they penetrated into my soul. I wondered briefly what he saw. I started to protest, but instead lifted my arms and gave him an awkward hug. His embrace was warm and safe. It was the soft kiss on the cheek that was totally unexpected. I drew away.

"Gracie, aren't you going to miss me at all?"

I replied truthfully, "Yes. I don't believe I know as much about any other human being except for Pa and my friend Sarah. I've enjoyed our rides and talking to you."

His eyes searched mine again. I believe he would have said more, but something he saw restrained him. He hugged me again and let me go.

"Instead of going back, let the wagons come to us. Do you see that hill yonder?" He pointed to one higher than the others closeby. It was covered with grass as high as the belly of our horses.

"Yes, I do."

"Let's ride there, we'll see them coming." Press started ahead, and I followed behind. The gathering clouds were more visible from the top of the hill, and the wagon train's progress could be seen without obstruction as it snaked its way along the rough path.

On Friday, the rain fell steadily, making those riding on horses and in the wagons miserable. When I crawled into bed after a day of bouncing on the wagon seat, the bedding was damp, and instead of getting a good night's rest, I tossed fitfully on my feathers, which smelled like wet chickens, making me wish I had a clothespin for my nose.

Saturday, the morning ride was cooler until the sun came out at noon. The earlier rain had cleaned the air of dust and smoke, causing me and Pa to pull our hats down over our eyes to protect them from its brightness. The distant horizon appeared vibrant with sharp lines against the clear sky. Pa explained that we were starting to cross the southern part of *Llano Estacado* or Staked Plains. "It's a high mesa, flat as far as the eye can see and part of the Chihuahuan Desert. We've been climbing toward it. We'll find little or no water as we cross. According to our maps, the Butterfield people have established places for watering our animals. But just in case, we'll fill our smaller vessels with water—where it's plentiful."

"But Pa, I see plenty of water—large lakes around us."

"They're called playas, Gracie."

"Won't the playas supply water on our trip?"

"Not for long. They consist of a low place or basin where water stands when it rains in the desert or on the plains. They're shallow, dry up quickly, and leave an alkaline salt flat. The bottoms appear white. You can't drink anything found in the area. When we get close to the Guadalupe Mountains, we'll drive along a large playa for several miles."

"I can't wait to get there."

"Yes, Gracie, when we get to Pine Springs we'll be home."

"Home," I repeated. "Do you think our house will be ready?"

"I hope so. It will be nice to get our chairs out of the wagon and eat at a real table. I'm tired of sitting on the ground or a stool."

"Yes, and it'll be good to cook on a real stove instead of over a campfire. Pa, you'll need to hang my shelves and put my bed frame together…" I gushed, excited at the prospect of reaching home.

"Daughter, slow down."

"Pa, I want a bedroom all my own like I had in Tennessee."

"I promise you, Gracie, you'll have one. Even, if we have to build it ourselves. Women on the frontier are scarce. You'll need your privacy."

"Thank you, Pa."

"Until we get your room done, the Conestoga will be your sleeping quarters. We'll secure it inside the compound that I hope is being built."

"Home," I thought. What a delicious word. "Pa, I'm ready to get there today."

"My estimate is three to four weeks, little girl. It'll pass fast enough. We'll ride through interesting territory before we arrive."

I'm not sure when I quit disliking Texas and started loving the state. But somewhere along the way, I had.

Periodically, we passed new stations for the Butterfield line. Some were no more than a couple of tents or rough one-room adobe huts with a single open window. All of the places were inhabited by men.

These posts were plunked down on the soil of the plains unlike most of those we'd seen on the rest of our trip. Pa and I looked at each other. What would our new home look like?

"Pa, didn't Mr. Augustine say our home would be a large one with a large corral?" I said this after checking out a particularly decrepit hut.

"Yes, Gracie, but I'm beginning to question what we'll find along with you. Surely the tents along our route are only temporary, and more permanent quarters will be built. But I can't promise you any different lodgings, although I understood we'd have some stone and wood construction involved. Could be the Conestoga will be our home for a while like we planned."

"I'm okay with that Pa. At least Wooly will have a place to run and play." I looked around into the front of the wagon. The lamb lay halfway under the iron stove, rocked into dreamland by her swaying ride.

Many times, we slowed down and spoke to the station man and his helpers who walked beside our moving wagons to talk. Pa was in a hurry. We stopped only if our animals needed water.

Wells, rain barrels, or larger water tanks were in place to supply the much-needed life-saving staple to man and animal alike. Where rivers or springs didn't flow, this was the only way to make sure of a constant source of liquid. That was one detail of traveling that we didn't have to solve the way settlers had on earlier trips. They carried full water barrels where it was scarce.

Corrals were built or being built. Some were already stocked with mules to change out the tired ones on future stages. I began to realize the large scope of the operation Mr. Butterfield had undertaken.

"Pa, it takes lots of money to start a stage line. Men, animals, stations, and stagecoaches have to cost plenty."

"Lots of money, Gracie. I hope Mr. Butterfield's enterprise pays off. We must do everything possible to make sure it does."

"It will help that we'll have several men working with us."

"Yes, there'll be a blacksmith and someone to handle the mules or horses. He'll be responsible for grooming, feeding, and doctoring our animals. With our stock of spare parts, the wagon repair shop will be able to fix broken pieces on site or travel to a broken-down stage on the trail."

"Will we have an extra stage just in case?"

"Someone will. Gotta keep the stage running according to John Butterfield. What's our motto?" He threw his hand in the air to start our chant.

"Remember, boys, nothing on God's earth must stop the mail!" We said it together and laughed at our lack of unison.

❦ 21 ❦

Press left the train on Sunday, but not without coming to tell Pa and me goodbye.

He rode along beside us as he talked. "Mr. Tipton, it's been a pleasure riding through Texas with you and Gracie. I hope to see you soon. I've promised your daughter a milk cow. I'll bring it as soon as possible and visit for a while."

"We'd like that Press. You're a fine young man, and anyone would be proud to call you a friend."

"Thank you, sir."

"Gracie and I will be praying for your safety."

I watched him go with mixed emotions. Was it possible to leave parts of your heart with more than one man?

"I really like Preston Stockton, Gracie."

"He's a good friend, Pa. I'm going to miss him."

Press turned his horse on a distant hill. I saw him wave his hat. I pulled mine off and waved back. When he disappeared out of sight, I realized I knew more about Press than I did about Jedediah.

The next day we had a funeral. The chicken crate broke off the wagon and Li'l Scrambler died in her cage. It was a subdued group that gathered around the grave of the popular chick. That was two deaths on our trip West. Didn't they say bad things happen in threes?

For miles, Pa drove our teams of mules on the flat plains—the worn trail visible straight ahead in the distance. Only the constant wind interrupted the blistering heat, which started at sunrise. Our vision blurred during daytime travel from heat waves radiating from the ground. To my amazement, the cool nights broke the hot temperatures of the day and provided a respite to be deliciously enjoyed.

Around us, the luscious purple-tinged prairie grasses with gray-green stems, matted in their abundance, appeared as waves with the wind's variable direction, blowing hither and yon to the purplish-blue horizon. This prairie hadn't seen a buffalo herd of several thousand for some days. Only a stray bush or an almost invisible draw interrupted the vast expanse of fields.

Anticipating a first glance at our new home, I rode my horse ahead of the wagons.

Finally, the top of the Guadalupe's rocky mounts peeked above the horizon, but we traveled another day before the whole range appeared in the distance.

I looked to my right at the gentle slope rising to the foothills of the peaks. The undulating draperies of the Guadalupe's rocky incline flowed gracefully from sky to earth. Their magnificence took my breath away as my eyes raked along the splendor before me. Sheer rock sides went up, up, and up. I recognized El Capitan from Press's description. The steep drop from the western end gave it away.

A cut to the right of the highest point, Guadalupe Peak, must be the valley where Pine Spring's clear waters flowed and where Pa and his friend, William Boone, spent many enjoyable days and evenings. I wondered how many people actually experienced someone else's most enjoyable travels. I couldn't wait to explore in the steps of my father. The Guadalupe Mountains didn't disappoint me. They were everything Pa and Press had described and more.

From the main road, a newly constructed pathway turned toward the lower hills. I hung back until Pa caught me and then urged Boone onto the trail. Pa followed. All around me were chunks of rocks, grass, and green bushes. The road made a loop, rejoining the main road farther west. I heard the rest of our train pull by and halt on the road behind us, knowing this was our stop, not theirs.

The sight of tents in the immediate vicinity didn't take away my exuberance at being home. I looked for the stone house. Instead, I saw a new corral built of aromatic pine trees brought from somewhere deep in the green mountains.

"Ahoy there," called a male voice as Pa pulled the Conestoga into the area. Pa helped Wooly down from the wagon. A man appeared from behind the wooden enclosure. He smiled, holding out his hand. "Might you be Jay Tipton?"

"Yes, all the way from Nashville, Tennessee. This here's my daughter, Gracie. Who are you?"

"I'm your station blacksmith, Caleb Carter from North Georgia. Cephas and I've been expectin' you. I see you brought fresh food." He laughed as my lamb went to greet him.

"No, Wooly's not food. She's my daughter's pet. Where is Cephas?"

"He's gone to get more mules. We tether them away from the corral during the day so they can eat. I was going to follow him and help bring our animals to the stockade. Our stock for the station is already here but we don't have any feed except the field grasses."

"Looks like you got plenty of those." I motioned back behind me.

"Yes ma'am, we do."

"Caleb, you go ahead and help with the mules. Where's the best place to park our wagon. Guess we'll have to use it as sleeping quarters for a few days."

"Sure, we cleared a place for a tent, but your wagon will sit there as well." He walked toward the base of the mountain about a hundred feet and indicated a spot cleared of rocks and shrubs.

"Very good. Gracie and I'll say goodbye to the others in our train and start our housekeeping on this site."

"That's a good-looking set of mules, you got there."

"They've done a great job of pulling our wagon from Memphis, Tennessee."

"I won't hold you up, Mr. Tipton." Caleb turned in the direction of a faint trail into the grass.

181

"No, please, it's Jay."

"Yes sir." Caleb left with a wave of his hand.

"Gracie, let's go wish our fellow travelers well."

Putting our wagon in the exact position Pa wanted it to rest, proved a little harder than I expected. Finally, it was perfect, and we unhitched the mules, taking them to the new corral through the swinging gate in the front to join eight others already inside.

"Caleb and Cephas must have been here several weeks to build such a grand structure. They've done a good job of it," observed Pa, running his hand over the large hinges with flat areas cut out in the pine to attach them.

"Pa, how're we going to feed people? We don't have any way of setting out our stove to cook. Or our supplies. Or our pots and pans. I can't imagine preparing food for passengers on the stage line in these conditions." Fixing grub over a campfire wasn't what I'd imagined for those who had enough money to ride the stage.

"We'll think of something, Gracie. Don't you worry, little girl." He raked his fingers through his hair.

We were standing outside the corral gates discussing these matters when Caleb appeared leading four mules.

"Here, let me help you, Caleb," said Pa heading toward him.

"Oh, I'm not Caleb. I'm Cephas."

"What. But—but you look just like Caleb." Pa took the tethers of two of the mules and stood looking at the young man.

"I should. I'm his twin brother. His *older* twin brother. By a whole ten minutes." Cephas's laughter surrounded us. It was obvious he and his brother enjoyed fooling people. He headed toward the corral.

Caleb arrived just as Pa and Cephas were closing the gate behind them. I looked from one to the other completely dumfounded. "How will we ever tell you apart?"

"I'll tell you a secret, Gracie."

"Aw, Caleb, whydaya have to do that?" his twin said. "You're takin' all the fun out of life."

"Gracie, come closer. You see a dark mole on the side of my brother's eye next to the hair line?" Caleb pointed to the spot. "If you see that, you're looking at Cephas."

"What's your occupation, Cephas?" asked Pa.

"I'm your repair man and builder, Mr. Tipton. And right now I'm also tending the animals. We haven't seen the person who's to take over that duty or any other fellow workers."

"Hopefully, they'll be along soon," said Caleb.

"We have plenty of stock to tend now that Gracie and I have arrived. Let's see, we have twenty mules, four horses, eleven chickens, plus a rooster, and one lamb."

"When he shows his face, that'll keep him busy."

"Have you looked for stone to build the station?"

"Yes, we have. And we think we've found some nearby. We'll take you there tomorrow. With any luck, the stonemasons will be here soon. My knowledge of quarrying stone isn't extensive," said Caleb, who seemed to be the spokesman for the twins.

"One of the first things we need to do in the morning after normal chores is build an area for our chicks to run. In a few months, we'll have fresh eggs for breakfast."

"Do you want to unload your wagon now?"

"No, we'll do that tomorrow. Right now, I want to walk Gracie to Pine Springs. She's heard enough about it. I want her to see it."

"Do you mind if we go along?"

"Not a bit. It'll be a pleasure to walk instead of riding in a wagon all day," I said.

I liked Caleb and Cephas from the start, especially their sunny attitude toward everything around them. I knew Pa was relieved. These two would be easy to work with, and so far, they followed his instructions.

Everything about the Guadalupe Mountain area was different from home. Tennessee was green with millions of tall oak, hickory, and pine trees. The mountains in West Texas were gray rock, swept clean of vegetation. Our hills were high and rolling. These protrusions were towering, skyscraping—jutting, raw projections thrusting their presence into the vast heavens above.

"What kind of trees are these?" I asked of the squatty bushes we walked by on our way to Pine Springs. I went over to examine the branches.

"That's a juniper tree, Gracie," Pa told me. "And the other is a Pinion Pine. See the short needles that sorta look like the field pines in the woods behind our house in Tennessee."

"This here's a maple, and that's an oak," said Cephas, pointing to two trees as we walked toward the spring. They were larger trees but not rivals of our Tennessee kind.

Boulders littered the hills beside the stream and occasionally we skirted a large rock in the trail.

"What's this ditch?" asked Pa of a new trench dug into the ground, leading south toward where we'd come from. Water ran down its bottom.

"Ah, we got tired of carrying water for the horses and mules," Cephas replied.

"That's the water supply for our corral. It runs almost to the stockade where we hollowed out a log, elevated the lower end, making the water run through a hole in the pine corral and empty into a galvanized tank. Our animals have a constant supply of fresh water within their shelter."

"I saw your water tank in the corral. Good thinking," Pa responded.

"When we get the stone fortress built, we'll do something similar and have gravity-fed water inside our quarters. That way, Gracie, you won't have to walk to the spring for water. Right now, you can catch all you need before it spills into the corral tank."

"I see we have a couple of people with good imaginations," said Pa.

"Naw, we're just lazy, so we come up with ideas to make our jobs easier."

"I can't imagine you two being lazy," I said.

Cephas laughed. "Ah, we're still trying to figure out some way of gittin' the mules and horses out to pasture without having to walk them."

"By the way, Gracie, be careful of snakes when you walk to the spring and in the desert, especially in early morning and evening. Cephas and I have seen several rattlesnakes since we've been here. We'll take you and show you where we usually see them."

Cephas added, "There are also mountain lions on the mountaintops. 'Course they don't come down here, and they're not sociable, so you'll never see one."

"Not true, Cephas. Remember the morning we decided to walk to Guadalupe Peak?" Caleb stopped in the middle of the trail and turned to Pa and me. "We took our bedrolls and food so we could stay all-night. It's different up there, Gracie." He looked upward to the left of where we walked. I followed his gaze, but seeing anything besides scrub brush was impossible from the depths of our deep canyon.

"Yeah, Caleb and I ate our supper and bedded down for the night. The next morning, not fifty feet away, we had company, and it was switching a very interested tail."

"Probably enjoying your snoring."

"Brother, your noise isn't exactly a purr."

"Good thing she wasn't hungry."

Cephas laughed, "How do you know the lion was a she?"

"Because she didn't eat two good-looking men like us."

"Ha, you'd have made a good steak."

"Better 'n eating your old tough hide."

"We get the idea, men," Pa said. "How long ago did you hike to the top?"

"Probably two months." Caleb replied.

"Have you seen any Indian sign in the area since you've been here?"

"No, not a bit," Caleb answered. "Scuttlebutt from one of the men helping us build the stockade is that several Apache families are over in McKittrick Canyon. Camped out, he said. That's several miles from here."

"Plenty of water there for watering animals," added Cephas. "We don't expect them here unless they ride over on a scouting mission."

Pa stopped in the middle of the path. "Here we are, Gracie. The place looks smaller than I remember."

He pointed to a stream of water coming from under some boulders on the far side of the trail, which continued to climb the canyon.

"You'll need to take a drink of the water, Gracie. It's cold coming out from under the mountain. Here, I'll help you across." Cephas took my arm, preparing to guide me over the stones and rough ground to the spring.

"I'll help too," said Caleb, grabbing my other arm.

Jerking my arms away was my first instinct, but that might be rude under the circumstances.

Instead, I looked to Pa for help. He stood laughing at the spectacle of his independent daughter being led by two obliging males to drink from Pine Springs. "Reminds me of leading a horse to water," he said, saying part of an old adage often quoted by farmers. "Are you going to drink?"

I did drink. And the water was cold like Cephas had said.

Pa and I learned much about our two helpers on the way back from the springs. They were born in Georgia and went to San Francisco after their parents emigrated there during the Gold Rush of '48.

"Pa and Ma never got rich, but we had food on the table and clothes on our backs. Pa taught me to blacksmith, and we both learned to work with wood. We build everything from chests and bookcases to wagon wheels encased with iron. Perfect training for jobs here at The Pinery. We even went to sea once. Frisco's a good place for that. Didn't care for the bounding main at all, but we made some good friends."

"And when we heard that Butterfield was looking for helpers on his new stage line, Caleb and I decided to apply. We always did like challenges and seein' new things."

"Pa and Ma followed us to Franklin. We'll visit them there."

"How far is Franklin from The Pinery?"

Both men's eyes turned toward me. "About two days by stagecoach, Gracie."

By the time we'd heard the condensed version of their lives, we were back at the station.

Although Pa had said we wouldn't unload the wagon, he did decide to take out enough so I could put my feather bed on its curved wooden floor.

Pa and the Carter twins grunted with the exertion of lifting my cast iron stove from its high perch to the ground. But the prospects of mouth-watering food caused Cephas to exclaim, "Shiver my timbers. Look, Caleb! Real food, brother." He danced a jig around the blackened wood-burner. "And we thought we'd be eatin' grub over a campfire."

"What did you say?" I asked. I'd never heard Cephas's expression before.

"Shiver my timbers? Aw, we say that all the time. It's like sayin' 'let my boat break into pieces.' An old salty dog taught us. He's a seafaring friend who lives in San Francisco," said Caleb.

"Salty dog? What's that?"

Cephas looked at me and laughed. "A salty dog is a seasoned sailor—someone who goes to sea. He's experienced in the ways of a ship and weathered from the elements," he explained.

"Yeah. Our mother didn't go for cussin'. She'd wash our mouths out with soap. But she doesn't quibble with our sailor words. Some may be a little strange to you."

We stretched a piece of oilcloth over the level stove and one over the table and chairs, which now sat on the ground. I piled the table high with staples we'd bought in Fort Chadbourne.

"Gracie, I can't locate the stove pipe," called Pa.

"Guess real food will have to wait until we get it out of the wagon. Maybe we'll have fresh cornbread tomorrow night. Won't be as good without milk," I told the brothers as they looked over our stash.

"Makes my mouth water," exclaimed Cephas. "I'm tired of stale bread and jerked venison."

Before the sun set, Pa and I walked down to the road. It would be our lifeline during our stay at The Pinery. We looked east from where we came and then west.

"Do you think I'll ever go to California, Pa?"

"I guess that's your call, Gracie. You're a grown woman, and you can make your own decisions. What do you think about your new home—or lack of one?"

"I love the mountains and learning about new things. I think I'm going to like being here, but I'll be glad when we've got a real roof over our heads, food on the table, and our station is running smoothly."

"Have you had enough excitement for a while?"

"Yeah, and enough riding on a horse and wagon seat. I'm ready to settle down to a daily routine. It's good to walk on solid ground."

"I have to admit I agree with you."

As we stood there, the sun went down and in the dusky dark our surroundings became silhouettes against the sky, details faded into one continuous plane. Somewhere a coyote howled at the moon. "Pa, look at the sunset."

El Capitan's dark face stood out in contrast against the deepening colors streaming from the west. Mixed in the clouds were streaks of yellow like long maiden's hair surrounded by flaming orange-coral, deepening to gray. It reminded me of another sunset when Jedediah and I watched together. I missed him.

"Gracie, I feel a chill in the air."

"I always find such change amazing after the sweltering heat of the day."

We walked back together, and I climbed into the Conestoga, thinking I'd need to make it my bedroom for a few more days. The glow of a lantern from outside the twins' tent meant they were close to calling it a day.

"Good night, little girl," said Pa softly.

I wondered if he thought of Mama and my little brother. The one I'd never known. Not long after, I heard him snoring underneath the wagon.

I didn't go right to sleep that night. The excitement of the day and my new home chased slumber away. I thought of Mr. Ormand. I missed his smile and advice. I remembered him talking of Abram and Canaan—the new land God sent Abram to.

How much time must pass before Jedediah would come to Pine Springs? And Hurricane Bailey... So many unanswered questions.

The following morning when I awoke, I realized that I'd been dreaming of Press and the Glory B. We were standing on Moses' Mountain, looking down on the sprawling ranch house below. Large herds of longhorn cattle crowded the verdant valleys to the west. I could hear their muted lowing and the soft sound of wind in the pungent pine trees below. To the east, the steeple of the town church poked its cross over a hilltop. A sense of peace and calm permeated the place along with trust in a man I hardly knew.

Why did I dream of him? Puzzling? I excused my dreams, thinking he was the last friend I'd left behind. It was only natural to think of him.

❧ 22 ❧

The days before the first stage arrived at our home station were busy ones. According to the schedule given to Pa at Fort Smith, the first stage to San Francisco would arrive in Fort Chadbourne on September 24 at three-fifteen in the morning. By Pa's calculations, we could expect it on September 26.

During this forty-minute stop at The Pinery, we would feed the stage passengers. How many or exactly what time of day they would arrive was anybody's guess. Also on this day, the stage going east from San Francisco to Tipton, Missouri would pull in for a change of mules and food. If the run remained true to the printed schedule, our station sat halfway on the long run—east or west.

The historic arrivals should occur around twenty to twenty-three days away. In fact, the first stage had already left Tipton and was headed our way.

The Pinery sat on the west end of the Fifth Division's four hundred and fourteen miles. The stage drivers who drove sixty mile segments had around four days to make the run from Ft. Chadbourne to Franklin. By Pa's figuring, they must make close to ten miles-per-hour.

His information said the stage coaches would travel day and night to make Butterfield's two thousand, eight hundred, and sixty-six-mile trip—generally, if nothing catastrophic happened—in twenty-two to twenty-five, bone-jarring days.

191

Our division agent, Mr. Coburn, arrived four days after we did. His responsibility extended two hundred fifty miles east from Franklin. His stature within the Butterfield ranks was such that no one ever called him by his first name. He was judge and jury in the overall operations of our section of the organization. Only John Butterfield was more important than him.

When Mr. Coburn introduced himself to Pa, I looked him over. His outfit consisted of a long yellow linen duster, knee-high leather boots and a flat, wide-brimmed hat called a "wide-awake" hat. Underneath his yellow outer garment, his stark white shirt didn't have a collar but buttoned at the neck. Over this a partially hidden linen waistcoat matched his suit coat and brown trousers.

I soon learned that most of the operation's people, division agents, conductors, and drivers wore the same company uniform. Mr. Coburn was no exception, and I never saw him without his suit coat, although he did take off the linen duster when we sat down to eat. He made a dashing figure in his set of clothes.

Our agent arrived with two wagonloads of supplies and two new employees plus the six stonemasons who were to construct the stone walls of our fortress home.

"Mr. Tipton, I plan on staying with you until tomorrow morning. There are tents to unload and assemble for me and your new men. The stonemasons have their own food and supplies. Their provisions are in a wagon coming behind us. Where do you want the men to go?"

Pa walked over to a spot several feet behind Cephas and Caleb's tent. "Here's a good spot."

"I see you've set your cook stove under a lean-to. In a few short weeks, I hope to have a more suitable place to install it. But that works for now." He looked over the stove and seating arrangements. "You'll be able to put your table and chairs in one of the extra tents. Depending on the number of passengers on the stage, your workmen may need to eat in shifts, at least until we get The Pinery's rock walls built."

"Gracie and I'd thought about that."

"Gracie?"

"My daughter," Pa motioned for me to come forward. I still wore the britches Pa had bought me in Memphis. Now was a good time to change back into a skirt.

Mr. Coburn turned around and looked me over. "So, she is. I'm sorry, Miss Tipton, I didn't realize...Uh you didn't appear..." Finally, he took a couple of steps forward and held out his hand to cover his awkward moment. I saw piercing green eyes as I looked at him. "Miss Tipton, I'm pleased to meet you," he said with a slight bow. There was a hint of a smile around his mouth as he again took in my baggy pants. "How do you like your new home in the Guadalupes?"

"I love it, sir. It's everything I dreamed of, especially the wide-open plains and the tall mountains and..."

"She'll go on and on, Mr. Coburn."

"Miss Tipton, are you cooking for this group?"

"Yes, sir."

"Then you're going to enjoy most of the items in the first wagon. Why don't you get the Carter boys and start unloading?"

"I will." I rushed off in search of Caleb and Cephas. Sounds coming beyond the stockade meant they were making something with hammers and nails. I already had rough shelves and a nice stand at my cook stove to ease the difficulty with fixing meals.

Now, a low table was taking shape. "What's that?"

"For washing clothes, Gracie. Your tub and scrub board should fit here nicely and you won't have to bend over so far."

I shook my head. "You're making my life too easy, or are you hinting?" I grinned at the sweating twins.

"Might be a lot of both." Cephas grinned.

"Ma always washed our clothes," said Caleb.

Commandeering them, we hurried back to the indicated wagon.

"It's mostly cooking supplies." I laughed with delight. "Look, potatoes, eggs, cured ham and bacon, and onions and cheese. Apples! We'll make an old-fashioned apple pie. Boys, we'll have a feast tonight." I didn't realize it, but Mr. Coburn had walked nearby to see my reaction.

"Miss Tipton..."

I threw up my hand and interrupted him, "Please, call me Gracie. I don't know any Miss Tipton."

"Gracie." He smiled, and I decided I was going to like him. "You have a new helper. Mr. Fulton?" He called to the bunch of men standing nearby. An older, gray-haired man with a bush-like silver beard separated from the others. "Ben Fulton, I'd like you to meet Gracie Tipton. She will be cooking with you."

I shook the hand offered to me. It was rough and calloused, not at all what I expected from my new cook-helper.

"Pleased to meet you, ma'am," he said bowing, grinning, and showing a missing front tooth.

"Mr. Tipton." Mr. Coburn always addressed my pa and his workers by their last names if he knew them. "I'd like to make an inspection of your facilities."

"Of course." Pa led him around the station, giving him a rundown of our activities.

While they were gone, Ben, Caleb, Cephas and I unloaded the wagon of cooking supplies. "I wonder how often we get a wagonload."

Ben answered, "Mr. Coburn told me every two weeks. We're to send a list by the conductor on the stage to division headquarters in Franklin, and they'll do their best to get supplies to us."

"Could we put milk on the list." I giggled, knowing this was impossible.

"Don't laugh, Gracie. Placed on the afternoon stage from Franklin, it jest might make it here. Actually, I saw a cow not two stations away. Why don't we ride over there and get some?"

Forty miles or two days for milk! Why not? We'd store it in the cold spring water in the canyon until the twins thought of a way to have a tank of free-flowing cold water coming nearby. They'd done it for the corral. Wouldn't that be nice? We could store the majority in the spring and what we were using under the trees at the mouth of the canyon. We'd cross that bridge when the milk or cow showed up. I could taste it now.

While we were discussing milk, Pa and Mr. Coburn finished with the tour.

"Who's to take over the feedin' and groomin' of the mules and horses?"

"Mr. Taylor will handle that chore, and he can start with my horse and the animals pulling the wagons."

A thirty-something man with a handlebar mustache and hair parted in the middle came swaggering forward and took the reins from our division agent.

"Cephas," called Pa. "Will you show Mr. Taylor where the rubdown supplies are for the animals, and while you're at it, take him out to the site where our mules and horses are tethered. He'll need to know our daily routine."

I figured Mr. Taylor for a dandy from the get-go with his slicked down hair and well-waxed mustache. I wondered if he knew how to work. He and Cephas disappeared into the corral.

Mr. Coburn continued. "Have your extra feed and hay arrived?"

"No, we've been expecting them any day, but they haven't been delivered yet."

"I'll check on that. We want to keep our animals well-fed if they're to do the hard job we demand of them—nothing but the best will do." Mr. Coburn pulled a notebook and pencil out of an inside coat pocket and made himself a note. From another pocket appeared a handkerchief, with which he wiped his brow where little beads of sweat stood out on his sun-tanned face.

"This heat'll calm down in two or three weeks, and I'll be glad."

"Would you like to take a walk to Pine Springs while we wait for supper? It's cooler in the mountains."

"Delighted, Mr. Tipton." Mr. Coburn walked over to the two remaining men. "If you gentlemen will unload the second wagon's provisions against the corral"—he pointed to the western end—"I would appreciate it. Oh, and you can help Mr. Taylor by unharnessing the horses and seeing they get to pasture."

"Gracie and Ben, I'll be waiting to see what you can stir up for supper. I'm hungry for real grub after that long ride from Franklin."

He and Pa headed out. As Pa passed me, he winked.

The stonemason's wagon arrived. I'd thought The Pinery was bustling with activity before. I was wrong. Men crowded the area.

Mr. Coburn pulled one of our cane chairs out of the new eating tent and lit a pipe he drew from another inside pocket. I'd seen Swiss cheese in Nashville, and I was beginning to believe his coat must have as many hidden holes inside.

Pa sat in another chair, and after seeing the supper dishes clean, I hauled a third one out. The air cooled rapidly as the setting sun cast El Capitan's long shadow across the grasses before us. A lone crow flew overhead in the dimming sunlight.

Caleb, Cephas, and the new Mr. Taylor disappeared on the other end of the stockade, heading out to walk the stock back into The Pinery. Crickets chirped, and a coyote howled in the distance.

"Gracie, if you feed our passengers the kind of meals you fixed tonight, they'll stop here and not keep going." He looked over his pipe at me, and made a circle of the smoke he blew from his mouth.

"Ben helped, but I'm thankful you enjoyed it, Mr. Coburn. Thanks for the provisions. We'll have more variety with the potatoes and onions. I told Ben venison stew is on the menu tomorrow night. All we need is carrots and celery to give it real flavor."

"How did you get the venison steaks we ate at supper so tender?"

"Pa made me a wooden hammer, and I beat the meat to loosen its sinews. It's much better that way—any meat for that matter."

"Carrots and celery, is there anything else you'd like?" He looked at me with raised eyebrows and a doubtful smile. His eyes twinkled so I knew he was teasing me.

"A cow would be nice." I saw Pa cringe on the other side of Mr. Coburn.

"Getting a slow-moving cow through a hundred and fifty miles of dry Chihuahuan desert might present a problem, but I'll see what I can do. Don't expect a miracle. You know thousands roam loose on these plains. You might run into one out there." He nodded at the flat expanse before us.

"She has the promise of one, but we don't know when it will arrive."

Mr. Coburn gave a few puffs of his pipe, making more little circlets with the smoke. I watched them float skyward and disappear into the air. I stretched out in my chair, crossed my legs now covered with a long skirt, and breathed in the clean night air. An off and on gentle breeze ruffled the curls on my head. This was heaven on earth.

Only Jedediah needed to be here for life to be perfect, but he still worked in the eastern section of Division Five. To come to The Pinery, he would be out of his territory. I wondered how he was going to manage this miracle. He had to break from Hurricane Bailey. I let my breath out in a ragged sigh.

Pa broke the silence.

"I'd like to thank you for the lanterns, coal oil, and candles. It'll be nice having dependable light when the stages roll in at night."

"We're supplying all our stations with the new fuel—realizing that half our team changes will be in the dark after the sun goes down. Five gallons should last about a month."

"Any problems with the Apache or Comanche?"

"Here and there. Nothing of substance. We have treaties with most of them. There's still some renegades running loose hereabouts. It's best to keep your eyes peeled for any sign of them. Our stations are reporting visits by nomadic bands, but they're friendly."

"We've heard there's an encampment in McKittrick Canyon."

"I hadn't heard that, but it's possible."

We chitchatted for another thirty minutes until Mr. Coburn said his goodnights and headed for bed.

"Pa, things are getting better."

"Yes, Gracie, we'll soon have a roof over our heads."

"How long do you think it will take?"

"I don't know anything about quarrying rock. Why don't you ask the head mason tomorrow?" Pa stood and stretched. "I think I'll turn in too. Good night, little girl."

"Good night, Pa."

Lingering on my chair, I wondered what Jedediah was doing. Could he see the same stars I saw from my new home? With a sigh, I got up and headed for my feather bed's warmth.

REBA RHYNE

❧ 23 ❧

One week after the division agent left for headquarters in Franklin, Texas, Pa and I set off down the main road to examine the complaint of one of our stop-in visitors about a boulder rolling into the middle of the path. The rock obstructed travel, causing wagon detours from the main route. The stone needed to be moved before the first stage arrived. From behind us the sound of construction meant the fortress building proceeded as scheduled.

It was early morning. Our walk was pleasant but uphill.

"I wonder how far you go before you top this rise and start down the other side."

"If my memory serves me right, not far."

"Can we walk there?"

"No, its best to ride. There's a steep downhill through a short valley then you climb another hill."

"I never dreamed America could have land like this within its borders. It's so...so different...isolated and lonely."

"Different is an understatement, Gracie. You've never seen the Pacific's rocky bluffs, or the peaks of the Rocky Mountains, or the Giant Sequoias of California, but I have."

"What's a Giant Sequoia look like?"

"Oh," he chuckled, "it's a kind of redwood tree two hundred feet tall, and so big around it sometimes takes ten men to circle its trunk."

Trying to grasp his statement, I walked along, putting out my arms, imagining ten men in a circle.

Pa's laugh was one of contentment as he continued. "Then there's a place in the Northern Rockies where hot geysers spout out of the ground for a hundred feet, and frying meat would be easy in one of the hot pools bubbling from the ground. Throw a piece in and seconds later you fish it out well-done."

"I can't imagine water that hot comin' from the ground."

"Just northwest of us, the Colorado River's made a deep, almost impregnable canyon in Nevada Territory rumored to be the largest in the United States. One man told me you can stand on the precipice and look straight down for a thousand feet. Far below where you stand, the faint sound of a roaring cascade rises to your ears. If I'd had time, I'd have visited those when I was out West, but I missed my little girl."

"I'm sorry you didn't get to go."

"I'm not. Seeing you grow into a young lady has been the most important event in my life. Now, you're able to be part of my adventures."

"Pa, do you think you'll ever get married again?"

"I don't plan to, Gracie. But life has its twists and turns. Who knows what God has in store for me...or you." He turned his head in my direction. "Daughter, you've matured since leaving Nashville."

"Life's experiences age a person, I suppose. Our trip wasn't humdrum. Look, there's the rock ahead." I pointed to a large boulder in the middle of the road.

Pa looked at the cliff above us. "There's where she came from." He indicated a hole in the rock face. "It rolled a long way to reach this spot."

We stood looking at the monster. He said, "I'm not sure we can move it. Might be easier to clear another road."

I stood by and watched him walk around the jagged chest-high rock. He bent down and put his shoulder to its edge. He laughed as he pushed against it, "Don't guess that's going to happen. Let's go back to the station. We'll plan on coming back before dark with the others. Maybe the stonemasons will have an idea."

We returned to the circle drive leading to The Pinery. "Gracie, it looks like we have another visitor," said Pa. An approaching horse and rider were distorted in the shimmering heat waves from the dirt road.

The stranger's back was to the sun so his face wasn't clear. Visitors weren't unusual at the station. I'd already fed Express riders and a mule pack train heading Southeast to San Antonio. Butterfield tank wagons filled up from our spring and headed out for dry stations on the trail. We were a central location for water. I couldn't remember a day when we hadn't had at least one visitor.

The rider walked beside his limping horse. His smooth stride caught my eye. I'd seen it before. Jedediah was my first thought, and I started running toward him. Halfway there I stopped in my tracks. It wasn't Jedediah. It was Paul!

"Gracie. Gracie, I can't believe it's you," he yelled, hurrying toward me.

He let go of his horse's reins and lifted me off the ground, swinging me around in his excitement. "You're light as a feather."

"Paul, w-what're you doing here?"

"I told you I'd follow you."

"I believe the exact sentence contained the word 'might' see you. I didn't expect you to come."

"Now, Gracie, let's don't quibble over words." He hugged me to him. "Aren't you glad to see me?"

"Of course, I'm glad to see anyone from home. How's Sarah?"

"I don't know. I didn't go to see her before I left. I was in a hurry to get here—to see you."

We stood looking at each other in the middle of the road.

Finally, I broke the glance, rolled my eyes, and shook my head. "Is this really happening?"

Paul laughed, "Aren't you going to invite me to see your new home?" I don't think I'd ever seen him so happy.

I had to laugh. "Sure, come on." I looked around for Pa. Coward. He'd disappeared from sight.

I walked Paul toward our compound, which was starting to take shape.

"What's wrong with your horse?"

"He threw a shoe, and I didn't know it, and there's a cut on the inside of the hoof. I've been leading him the last twenty miles."

"Let's see if we can find Mr. Taylor. He tends our animals and doctors them when they're sick."

I walked over to Caleb and Cephas. They were working on the door casing for the soon-to-be stone wall around our home. The hole was dug, posts in place and dirt tamped tightly around the eight-foot supports. They had straightened the door frame to the posts and were busy leveling it with a plumb string.

I watched as Paul looked from one to the other.

"Twins," I said, taking off my hat and brushing the curls off my forehead. If I closed my eyes would Paul become a mirage and disappear? *Oh, please God, let it be so.*

"Ah, that explains it."

"Paul Peerson, meet Caleb and Cephas Carter—two of Butterfield's finest stage workers."

Caleb and Cephas dusted their hands on their britches and each shook Paul's extended hand. "Pleased to meet you."

"Paul's from my home town in Tennessee. He's come to visit." I stood twisting my hat, knowing I'd need to explain his presence. "He said he might come, and here he is." I lowered my voice and repeated my last words. "Here he is."

"Gracie was surprised to see me." Paul put his arm around me. "Weren't you?"

I stiffened at his touch and pulled away. "Yes, I was. Caleb, have you seen Mr. Taylor? Paul's horse is lame, and I want him to look at his foot."

"He's probably out there somewhere sittin' on a rock, spitting his tobacco juice all over the place—the part that don't lodge on his mustache. Don't think he's struck a lick this whole morning," said Cephas.

"Brother," admonished Caleb. "Don't you remember our decision not to talk about the hired help?"

"Sorry, Caleb, it popped out."

"Well, close your mouth the next time somethin' like that wants to pop out."

"Which way did he go?" I asked, ignoring the sarcasm but wondering what the basis for the comment was.

Cephas pointed his finger down toward the grazing area.

"Have you seen Pa?"

"He headed in that direction too," added Caleb.

"Can Paul leave his horse here with you?"

"Sure, we'll watch her." Paul dropped his horse's reins nearby.

We hadn't taken too many steps into the grass before Paul and I heard angry words being spoken. My pa and Mr. Taylor were in a loud argument.

I ran toward the sounds with Paul following me. In the midst of the animals, the two men stood toe to toe.

"Pa!" My piercing yell stopped the possibility of blows and scattered the horses nearest to me. The men stepped apart. The veins on Mr. Taylor's neck stood out, and his usually pink face was redder than the comb on our rooster's head.

Pa released his balled fists and spoke first. "Go back to the station, Taylor. We'll settle this in a few minutes." He looked down at the ground after he spoke—his hands on his hips and his lips set in a determined thin line.

Caleb and Cephas appeared, flushed and breathing hard from running. Mr. Taylor hurried toward them. He roughly pushed Cephas aside and headed for the stockade. "Gracie, we heard you yell. You all right?"

"I'm okay, but I'm not so sure about Pa. What happened?"

Pa took a deep breath and walked over to one of our red mules. He stroked its back and spoke soothingly, "It's all right, Big Red. I'll see that he doesn't have another day to touch you." He gave the mule a reassuring pat on the shoulder and turned to us.

"Taylor—I won't honor him by calling him Mister—Taylor's been abusing the animals. I suspected this, but minutes ago, I saw him in action. Why Mr. Coburn hired him to tend animals, I can't understand."

I stood, stunned at his words. One thing my father and I didn't do was abuse our animals. "What was he doing, Pa?"

My father looked around the area and headed for a large stick, almost a club, which he picked up from the ground. He held the piece of wood out to us. "This is the instrument he used," he said with disdain in his voice. "No one hits any of our animals." With that he reached back and flung the offending piece of wood over the tops of the grass toward the sloping hill behind us. I heard it hit the ground with a sickening thud.

"Sorry excuse for a human," said Caleb, turning to look in the direction where he'd last seen Taylor. "What're you gonna do, Jay?"

"Send him packing," said my father. "Now." He took a few steps toward the trail back to the fortress. "You boys come with me. I don't want to do anything wrong—nothin' he could report back to division headquarters. I need witnesses. I'm still mad enough to thrash him."

Pa vanished down the trail with Caleb on his heels. Cephas lingered long enough to whisper to me. "Guess Handle-bar struck a lick but not the right one. Didn't last but a week," he said, not smiling. "Don't want to cause bad things to happen to anyone, but I hope your pa gets rid of him. I didn't like Taylor from the time I first set eyes on him."

I remembered thinking the same thing.

Cephas left, following his brother and my father.

"Whew, looks like I stepped into a hornet's nest."

During the exchange, I'd forgotten all about Paul. How would I deal with him? Of course, he couldn't stay. Jedediah might come any day. Best to tell him the truth and send him packing along with Mr. Taylor. I'd accomplish this right after supper. "Come on Paul, I'll show you how The Pinery will be built."

When we got back to the clearing, Pa, Caleb, and Cephas were standing in a huddle. "He's gone, Gracie. Packed his belongings and disappeared with his horse and saddle. Glad I didn't have to fire him. But now we'll have trouble keeping the stock fed and watered."

"We'll do double shifts, Jay," piped Cephas.

"Mr. Tipton, I'll be glad to fill in. Maybe become permanent if Gracie will have me. How about it, Gracie?" Paul turned to look at me.

My eyes got big as saucers and my mind cried, *No. He can't stay!*

Before I could open my mouth, Pa answered him, "Paul can you shoe horses and…"

What in the… Is Pa going to take him up on his offer? Didn't he know this would put me in a bad spot?

"I helped Pap with ours back in Nashville. I don't know much about mules, but I'm willin' to learn."

"You'd be a great help to me. This will be temporary, of course. Only Mr. Coburn, our division agent, can hire people for this station," he said, not considering my feelings at all.

"I appreciate your confidence, Mr. Tipton. It'll give me a chance to be close to Gracie. Do a little catching up."

"Yeah, sure will," said Pa shaking his head in amusement. "Cephas, show Paul his work area, and help him through his first day here?"

"I'd be glad to." The two headed for the corral but stopped at the large swinging door. Caleb joined them.

"Gracie, I'm going to check on the stonemasons. Don't get distracted and forget about dinner," Pa teased.

I watched him walk into the corral. Heard him sling his saddle over his horse. Soon he led Taylor out of the pine-walled area, mounted, and waved goodbye.

Angry enough to spit nails, I turned on my heels and strode determinedly toward the trail to Pine Springs.

"Gracie, I'll come with you…"

"No, Paul, stay there." I shouted at him.

As I reached the woods, I heard him ask Caleb and Cephas, "What'd I do wrong?"

"Nothing, at all. Let Gracie go. She'll be all right. Meanwhile, let's get the stock out to graze. Cephas can examine your horse's hoof."

"Yeah, you couldn't go anywhere with your horse's lame leg. Might as well get paid fer stayin' around here."

Pine Springs was a restful place for me. When I could squeeze in a few moments, I headed there to watch its cool waters flow from underneath the moss-covered rocks. Today was no different. The gurgle and movement soon cooled me off. I got over my mad spell. How could Pa put me in such a bad place and find the situation funny?

Ten minutes of peace and quiet started me thinking. Guess if this happened to someone else, I'd be amused too.

I couldn't let this state-of-affairs rest another day. Tonight, I'd tell Paul about Jedediah. I couldn't figure out another way I could exist under the present circumstances. I wondered how he'd take the news. I stood and headed back to The Pinery.

❧ 24 ❧

"**W**here's Paul?" I asked Caleb when I returned.

"He went to tend the animals. Said he'd be there most of the day. Cephas went with him." Caleb leaned on the handle of the shovel he'd been using to fill in dirt around the door posts.

I nodded. "Where's Ben?"

"He's using my blacksmith tools to make a stand and hooks for a stewpot to hang on. He said something about jackrabbit stew for supper tasting better over an open fire."

I stood shifting my weight from one foot to another. I noticed he was waiting for me to say something. "Caleb, Paul is just a good friend. There may have been a chance for us to…I mean we might have been more than…" I shook my head. The words wouldn't come.

Caleb finished my sentence. "Paul likes you. He may like you enough to be your husband. Is that the situation?"

"I think so. I—I might have agreed with him some months ago. Now, I don't feel the same way. He needs to know the truth. I plan on telling him tonight after supper." Caleb and I were friends, but I'd never confided in him before about personal matters. He didn't even know about Jedediah. No one but Pa knew.

"I think he'll appreciate you being honest with him. Most men would."

"I won't find telling him easy. In fact, I dread the thought of causing him pain. He's come a long way from Tennessee."

"All men love adventure and new things. You may be part of his travels—but there's a chance you're not all the reason he's here."

"Do you think so? I'd find telling him easier if that were true."

"He's made a few statements. I'll leave it at that."

I looked at him. "Thanks for easing the situation."

"I have faith you can do it, Gracie. Does this mean Cephas and I have a chance?" Was he serious? I caught a twinkle in Caleb's eye and a hint of serious lingering beyond.

I laughed, feeling sorry for all the single men on the frontier. "My future husband, Jedediah Bailey, is somewhere between here and Fort Chadbourne. He's working on maintainin' the roads for Butterfield Stage Lines with his father, Hurricane Bailey."

"I wondered. Sometimes I see wistfulness in your eyes—a deep longing. I told Cephas such was true—that there was a man in the mix."

"The story is long, Caleb. Maybe I'll share it with you someday."

"I'd like that, Gracie."

"I'm goin' to see Ben."

Finding out Caleb had a perceptive nature took me by surprise. It added new depth to my appraisal of him. Our developing friendship had found a new level.

"All right." He dug the shovel into the ground with a thud as I left.

After a supper of rabbit stew and potatoes, Ben offered to wash the dishes. I walked Paul over to the future station.

The stonemasons had laid out the level foundation, outlining the fortified enclosure that was forty feet wide by one hundred and ten feet long. The high, eleven-foot walls of Guadalupe limestone and adobe mortar would be thirty inches thick. A long, dirt courtyard ran the full southern length of the interior. The only entrance to the fortress showed plainly in the middle of this wall.

At the center of the northern wall, there were four distinct rooms all included in one long single row. Their rock walls were to be interwoven into the main structure. As soon as they reached the right height, the roofs of pine logs, adobe bricks, and adobe mortar would be placed atop.

At the western end, away from the corral, my stove, tables, and chairs would constitute the eating area. I stepped over the four-inch high foundation stones outlining the kitchen and Paul followed.

"This is where I'll spend most of my time," I explained to Paul. "The roof will be made of adobe to keep off the hot sun, rain, and frost. I asked the masons if the surface could be sloped so the water would run off at one spot. I plan to put one of Pa's whiskey barrels under the edge of the roof to catch rainwater."

"Sure, use the water for washin' dishes, or if for any reason your water supply is stopped, you can drink it. I don't see an inside wall into the courtyard. Won't you be cold cookin' out here in the winter?"

"The kitchen area will be open, but a rollup canvas will be used, if needed, to separate Ben and me from the elements, and if you will turn around, you'll see the outline of a double fireplace in the future eating area. With the canvas down, the heat from the fire should warm the area."

"Good thinking, Gracie. I always said you've got a good head—plus a curly one—on your shoulders." He pulled at a curl with a finger. I ignored his affectionate gesture. "I can tell you're excited over your new home. Will any other rooms be heated?"

"Only my bedroom, being closest to the kitchen. Part of the double fireplace will open into it."

Paul stepped over into my future bedroom. "Here's where you'll sleep?"

I nodded. "Spacious room," he observed. "You won't be bumpin' your elbows on the rock walls."

"All of the rooms are big." I put my arms out as if reaching from one wall to the other. "I can't wait to move in. Sleepin' in the Conestoga works fine, but havin' my things where I can get to them"—I shook my head—"Heaven is the best word I can think of to describe that future day."

We walked down the courtyard to the end away from the kitchen and past the sleeping rooms. "Here at the end closest to the pine corral is Caleb's blacksmith shop. The thick roof will be thatch." I turned around. "The forge and bellows will sit right here."

"The twins are takin' good care of my horse's lame foot."

"They're good at most everything they do."

Paul pointed to a break in the wall adjacent to the stockade. "What's that?"

"A small short door going into the corral—like a crawl space under a house. Havin' one door to escape in case of Apache attack or another problem wasn't to my liking. Course, we can go over the wall on ladders. Pa considered my suggestion and insisted on the escape openin' to where our animals are kept."

"Will you have windows?"

"Only small portholes to shoot from and see the outside area. They won't be large enough for a man to crawl in or out."

"Thirty inches is an extremely thick wall."

"Yes, you can't knock one over." I turned around to look at the layout before me.

The whole structure seemed appropriate for a fine home station on the overland stage line.

"Will you have overnight boarders?" Paul stood looking at me keenly.

His stare made me uneasy. I rushed on, "We've got that in mind, but our main plan is to have good food. Our table will be an excellent place for all travelers to eat."

"Gracie, I've missed you. Do you remember the plans we made to see the frontier? I'm ready to head farther west as soon as your pa finds help to take care of the horses. Will you go with me? Our lives will be filled with exploration and excitement."

"What happened to being a lawyer?"

"I can study when I return home—be anything I want to be." He held his hands forth, palms up.

"Paul, let's walk toward Pine Spring so we can talk."

He followed me, crossing over the first course of our stone foundation. I took quick steps toward the now well-used trail to the springs. Wooly followed us. Pa and Caleb waved as we passed, and I remained silent until we got to the edge of the scrub brush.

"Gracie, don't walk so fast."

I let him catch me on the trail and walk abreast of me.

"Paul, I have something to tell you."

"Now Gracie, I know I haven't spoken too well of my feelings for you, and I'm sorry for that," he started.

"Paul, don't." I shook my head. Did he know what was coming? I watched him out of the corner of my eye, thinking he'd had time to consider my greeting and words. I hadn't thrown myself at him when he arrived.

"I want you to know how much I've thought about you, and what's happened here today is perfect. We can ride to Franklin and get married. Don't you want to experience the beauty and danger of the Rockies? Camp by wild mountain streams and live off the land. Gracie let's go West."

I drew a deep breath and plunged in. "Paul, I am West, and I've had enough trail life on the road to Pine Springs. Texas is where I'll put down roots and live. I don't want to leave. My life's changed since I left Nashville. I can't marry you, because there's someone else—someone I met on the wagon train. His name's Jedediah Bailey, and we're to be married."

Paul stopped walking. I turned around to watch him. He went to a nearby rock, sat down, and put his head in his hands. I went to him and put my hand on his shoulder. He reached to put one of his hands atop mine.

"I sorta expected you to say this. Something about you was different—different before you left for Texas."

"I'm sorry Paul. We liked each other, but not enough for a commitment, isn't that it?" I asked him.

He nodded. "You're right, Gracie. I hate to say that. I do think we would have made a good marriage. We liked the same things."

I didn't answer him, but I agreed we did have a lot in common, and yes, we could have been happy. But what about love? Deep, abiding, trusting love? The kind that lasts a lifetime? I wasn't even sure I had it with Jedediah. I wondered if you ever knew.

Paul stood. "Gracie, I won't make this an issue while I'm here. Tomorrow, I'll tell your pa I'm not staying. I'll be here until a replacement can be hired."

"You're going to move on?"

"Yes, I want to see California. I could stay there or go on to Oregon Territory. I hear it's full of trees, rivers, and mountains. Sounds a bit like Tennessee, doesn't it? I know some people who moved to the area. I'll try to find them."

"What about being a lawyer?" I asked for the second time.

"I haven't stopped my schooling. I'll go home and start again. You know, Gracie, when I left Nashville you were the reason, but the farther I traveled west, I found an instinctive need to be a part of the expanding frontier—to become a part of its discovery."

"We've always been good friends. I hope you'll send me letters telling me about your adventures. You know the mail will pass right by here."

"I'll try, Gracie. I'm not much of a letter writer."

"Let's go back to the station."

I think both of us were breathing easier as we returned to The Pinery. Paul had changed as I had. In growing up, we'd grown apart. He'd pulled up roots and headed west with no intention of putting those roots in solid ground at present. Me, I knew Texas was my home...nowhere else would I find contentment.

No one was in sight when we returned. "I forgot, Paul. Everyone's probably out lookin' at a huge boulder blocking travel on the road. Pa and I were checkin' on the rock when I saw you this morning."

"I think I'll mosey out there and see for myself." I watched him walk down the road with his familiar smooth stride.

That night I slept fitfully, dreaming of a huge rock keeping me from reaching Jedediah, Paul shaking his finger at me, and Press sitting on his horse, telling me goodbye. When I woke the next morning, I was tired from wrestling with the issues associated with my nightmare, but I forgot the dream as chores for the day kept me busy.

❦ 25 ❦

Late in the afternoon on Tuesday, September 28, the first transcontinental mail service on the Oxbow Route across America pulled into our home station at The Pinery. The stage was two days late. If it hadn't been for express riders alerting us to troubles along the new route, we would not have been prepared.

My heart beat with excitement as only ten minutes earlier I'd heard the distant bugle announcing the stage's impending arrival. This sound meant get the teams and food ready. The noble bugle sounded again as the stage pulled into our front entrance.

Although the men of The Pinery had worked to make this stop as easy and unhurried as possible, the actuality of seeing the celerity wagon arrive with its two teams of mules caused a flurry of excitement. I laughed as everyone, including my pa, hurried to their assignments.

One of the rules of the Butterfield Company demanded the mail never be left alone. Cephas was placed as guard over the stage.

From my position in my outdoor kitchen, I saw Caleb and Paul rush to unhitch the tired animals and herd them into our corral. Four fresh mules with harness attached were put in place, two by two.

Within fifteen minutes the stage sat ready to go.

I prepared to feed the conductor, driver, and one passenger with venison steak, baked beans, and fried potatoes with onions. Ben's biscuits baked in my stovetop oven, and gravy made with flour and water topped off the sumptuous meal. I thought the meal was a supper fit for a king.

"Ben, I'll fill the plates and take them to our customers. Why don't you pour the coffee?"

I carried heaping plates of food to the wooden table where I'd already placed my mother's metal eating utensils brought from Tennessee. Pa had taken them and my dishes out of my packed trunk. No wonder it was so light when he hefted the wooden box into the Watsens' wagon.

Missing from the table were the linen napkins my pa and I frequently used at home. I refused to let them be misused by my visitors, and I already had enough laundry to wash without adding anything else.

"Ben's bringin' coffee, unless any of you gentlemen would like spring water."

As I tended the table, I listened to the men talk over their supper.

"Waterman, this is certainly the best food we've eaten in several miles," said the conductor running his tongue over his lips. He sat by the driver who was darker-skinned and appeared to be a Mexican. Pa had told me a driver on the line was known as a Jehu.

Waterman, the man to whom the comment was addressed, nodded. "A far cry from the wormy bread and rejected Army bacon we ate after we left Fort Chadbourne. It's the best meal I've had since Fort Smith or maybe New York."

Returning to my cook stove, I had a chance to observe this young man. He had a thick mustache under his nose. It ran down each side of his mouth, but he was clean shaven except for this furry intrusion on his face. His chin was remarkably pointed. Dark, twinkling eyes sat under bushy eyebrows, and hair hung over the top of his ears. He sat in a blue flannel shirt and britches, eating with the fork and knife I'd placed on the table. The other men shoveled in the grub with their spoons, occasionally using their knives to cut the tender venison steak.

I could tell Waterman was a city man because he wore a pair of congress gaiters on his feet. I'd often seen these elasticized, pull-on leather boots worn by suited men in downtown Nashville. They weren't exactly western boots.

"Miss," he said, "could I have some of the spring water you were talking about. The coffee is very good, but I've been craving water most of the day. And could you fill my canteen?"

I took the canteen he held out and hurried to the outlet coming from the spring, grateful for Caleb and Cephas's resourcefulness.

While bustling around and serving my customers, I checked out the conductor and Jehu. Like Mr. Coburn, they were dressed in the Butterfield Company's employee attire. A long, flowing yellow linen duster down to their knees added another layer of protection from rain, wind, and dust alike. Black, knee-high leather boots—pant's legs tucked inside and low-crowned, felt "wide-awake" hat completed the outfit. In addition, the driver had taken off long gauntlet gloves, for holding the reins, and placed them beside his whip on the table. The long leather strap wasn't used to hit the mules or horses, but its loud crack got their attention.

The conductor left the other men at the table.

My customer's needs satisfied, I followed him as he walked to the stagecoach. He checked the connections of the harness to the wagon, the wheel axles, and then stood making notes in his company log. He was responsible for everything but driving the mules.

"Thank you, young man, for guardin' the mail. I'll take over," he said, dismissing Cephas for other duties.

Cephas disappeared into the corral. He soon appeared with two of the newly arrived mules, heading for the area where we normally tethered our animals to graze. Paul had already taken the others.

I followed the conductor around the stage. "Who is he?" I asked, nodding toward the noteworthy passenger still sitting at the table conversing with my father.

"Waterman L. Ormsby, a reporter for the New York Herald. He's ridin' straight through to San Francisco and reportin' back for his newspaper. Told me he rode with John Butterfield from

St. Louis on the Missouri Pacific Railroad and transferred to the stage at Tipton, Missouri."

Knowing how the roads were between here and Fort Smith, I couldn't help but ask, "How's he makin' out?"

The conductor laughed, "I think he's had some ups and downs." The man laughed harder, slapping his thigh. "The road gets pretty rough in places, and sleepin' on a board bench isn't my idea of a feather bed. From the looks of him, I'd say he has an expensive bed at home."

I agreed, checking out the boots again. "The road is rough in places. Pa drove slowly to reduce the jostlin' when we came through."

"Ormsby said he finally got so tired it didn't matter if his head was hittin' the ceiling or the side of the coach. He took off his boots, stripped down to his longhandles, put his coat under his head, and covered his body with a traveling shawl. I'm sure he slept like a baby on a rocky horse." The conductor laughed at his own joke.

Mr. Ormsby appeared at that moment, stopping the conversation. "Young lady, I understand you are responsible for that sumptuous repast. Here's your dollar and an extra one for serving the most excellent food I've encountered on the stage line."

"Thank you, sir. How do you like our Guadalupe Mountains?"

"Lovely," he said, rubbing one of his hips, grimacing, and looking west at El Capitan. "I think the sunset will be spectacular."

I looked with him. "Yes, we have beautiful hues of coral, pink, and orange, especially when there are clouds in the sky."

"What's your name, young lady?"

"It's Gracie, Gracie Tipton. My father is station man here."

He held out his hand. "Pleased to meet you."

Before he could continue our conversation the conductor broke in, "Mr. Ormsby we're ready to go. Have to stay on schedule." He tapped his logbook with his finger.

"You and that confounded logbook," exclaimed Ormsby. "Butterfield's bible! If you don't slow that three-seated contraption down, it'll be the death of me." He rubbed his hip again. "I think the rides already killed my hip." But he was smiling.

"Nothing can stop the mail," said the conductor, looking at me and grinning. "Isn't that right, young lady?"

I grinned back but didn't say anything.

"Gracie, if you are ever in New York please look me up at the Herald." Mr. Ormsby pulled a white card from his pocket and handed it to me. "I'll treat you to a meal in Manhattan." He winked. "Can't promise it'll be as good as the one I just ate."

I took the card. "Thanks for the offer."

He stepped into the coach with a loud groan while looking out of the corner of his eye at the efficient conductor. The Mexican Jehu came from the fortress wiping his mouth on the back of his hand.

I watched as the conductor and driver mounted to the driver's seat. "Come on," yelled the driver to his fresh mules. He raised his whip and cracked the leather thong over the new teams. At the sharp noise, I jumped in my tracks and so did the mules, then dug their hooves into the hard ground. The stage advanced slowly.

Pa came forward from the corral as the stage moved out. "Gracie, we did well," he said looking at his watch. He snapped the cover closed.

"We did?"

"Yes, the whole stop lasted forty-two minutes. John Butterfield should be proud."

"Was that all? It seemed like an hour," I said pushing a curl off my forehead, realizing the pressure was off. Pa and I were joined by all our employees at The Pinery.

"Did we make it?" asked Cephas.

"Sure did. Outstanding job, everyone." Pa turned around and shook hands with the rest of his crew.

"How long until they get to Franklin?" asked Paul.

"Hmm—two days, I think. There's some rough riding until you get out of our mountains. After that, its smooth sailing and making good time most of the way."

We stood watching until the creaking, jangling stage turned the corner onto the main road.

"Better get ready for the next one," called Pa as we headed back to our respective jobs. "It'll be here sometime before midnight."

When the eastern stage left, the rays of the setting sun began to disappear behind El Capitan. Not two hours later, we heard the bugle of the western stage coming from San Francisco.

The next morning I rode out with Pa to check on the stonemasons' progress in getting the material for our shelter. Piles of chiseled stone in neat heaps surrounded their work area.

"Don't interrupt their work, Gracie. I think you can see how they get the stone loose."

Pa was right. I watched, fascinated by the amazing progress the four men were making. The limestone cliff was in layers of different thicknesses. Each man inserted a flat chisel into a seam between the layers and hit the chisel with a metal hammer. This broke the stone loose, letting the workers pull the chunk of rock out of its resting place. The stones were like snowflakes, no two were alike.

Another man grabbed the stone and placed it on a wooden pallet ready to be pulled by horse to The Pinery where our walls were already one foot high. It looked like another foot was cut and ready to be transported and installed.

"You're making good progress," stated Pa to the head man of the masonry team. He walked over and felt the limestone and the seams between each row.

"This stone is easy to get loose. At the rate we're going, you'll have a nice place to live and work within the space of two months or less. Our plan is to cut one day and lay the stone the next. That'll give the adobe a chance to set up since the walls are so thick. When we get to eight feet, we'll put the roofs on the inside rooms and Gracie's lean-to roof over her cooking area."

"You should be finished before the worst cold weather sets in."

"That's the plan. I'm not sure where we go from here, but I think we have two or three more jobs toward Arizona. We're hoping they're in warm weather west of here."

I stood watching him use his hammer and chisel, expertly lifting and hitting the cutting instrument. Forgetting my father's advice I asked, "Could I try that?"

"Sure." He handed the tools over to me.

The hammer quickly pulled my hand toward the ground. The blunt end narrowly missed my toes as it whacked the earth. Pa and the mason laughed at my clumsiness.

"Wow, that's heavy," I said, trying to lift the heavy tool with one hand.

"It's a three-pound hammer. Doesn't look heavy, but it is. The chisel's heavy too. Try lifting it."

I hefted the chisel and agreed.

"Gracie's always been curious about the workings of most anything. How about it, little girl? Do you want to stay out here and help today? I'm sure Ben can handle the cooking."

"I hate to admit it, but I wouldn't last long using that hammer. Guess I'll stay with my iron skillet. It's heavy enough."

Both men laughed again as I retreated to the safety of my horse. My curiosity concerning stone cutting was completely satisfied.

REBA RHYNE

❦ 26 ❦

Early in October, the stage arrived from Franklin with a letter from Press. My pa handed the sealed envelope to me. I felt the hot flush of blood at my temples as he looked at me. Instead of standing at the cook stove to read his note, I headed for the intimacy of Pine Springs, placing my treasure in my apron pocket.

Press's handwriting was remarkably good, flowing, and easy to read.

September 29, 1858

Dear Gracie,

I hope this letter finds you well. I have been tolerable since I returned to the ranch. I find it hard to believe over a month has passed since I parted your company and headed for the Glory B in the Glass Mountains.

We arrived in good fashion, although one of the wheels came off the chuck wagon. No wonder, since the roads we traveled were very rough. We repaired it as best we could and continued on. You should have heard Jorge moan over his precious wagon and cargo. You would have thought his best friend had died. We laughed at him over the campfire that night. He finally got up, mad as a wet hen, and blessed us with his absence. We were tired of his complaining. I fixed his confounded wagon good as new when we got home.

My father was glad to see me safe and sound. I am sure being gone several weeks is a worry for him since so much bad can happen on the trail. Of course, some good things happen as well—like meeting you. I miss our conversations and afternoon rides. Father has heard all about you and is anxious to meet you. Maria keeps asking when you may come and mentions you often. You see, I haven't forgotten you.

Neither have I forgotten your cow and have one all picked out. Pa thinks I can get away around the first of November. If such happens, I will try to see you around this time.

Please write and tell me the news of The Pinery.

Affectionately yours,
Preston Stockton, Jr.

My heart thumped loudly as I read his warm letter, and my mind jumbled with mixed emotions as I finished. I hugged the letter to me and looked into the unreadable, swirling waters of Pine Springs. I wasn't going to marry Press, but he'd taken time to write me. I hadn't heard from Jedediah.

"Where are you?" The words squeezed out of my aching heart.

I led a hectic life at The Pinery except for the weekends. Then my thoughts were continually about Jedediah. The lack of his presence overshadowed everything I did. I found relief in being so busy.

My frustrations regarding Jedediah were expressed on trips to Pine Springs. I picked up rocks and sent them flying through the forest. Yes, I cried—the tears flowing freely down my cheeks. Then I remembered our last night together, his kiss, and his promise to come. Hurricane—he was the problem. I had to blame someone.

❧ 27 ❧

My days and weeks slipped into a familiar routine. Once, for three days, a patrol from Fort Davis camped close to the rapidly rising stone fortress.

By the middle of October, the walls of The Pinery were at a point where the roofs of the inside rooms needed to be woven into the overall structure.

I saw large wooden vigas or ceiling beams installed, laid side by side, over my bedroom, visitors' sleeping rooms, Pa's bedroom, and my open kitchen. The next step involved coating the rooftop with a layer of adobe blocks and mud mortar to keep out the rain.

One hundred feet from the stockade, I watched as the workers stirred wooden vats of sand, clay, and straw to form the rectangular squares.

"The blocks aren't going to be easy to get out of your molds," I observed to the head stonemason as the first ones were poured into the wooden frames by the laborers.

"We'll let them bake in the sun until they get more solid and then remove them to completely dry." He walked over to give advice to the crew making the adobe blocks, and I walked to the rising fortress walls. Two men were setting rocks onto the top using almost the same mud mixture as the roof blocks. They stood on a riser made from wood and planks.

The overseer joined me. "Gracie, this clay cement will be holding these fortifications together a hundred years from now."

"Imagine dried dirt lasting that long."

Earlier, the stonemasons had laid the flat rocks and adobe mortar around the posts holding the large door frame, making them an integral part of the door. Today, they hefted the heavy lintel so it rested across the top of the free-standing door. These long pieces of rock reinforced the top of the openings, holding the rock walls taking shape over five feet above them. With eight-foot-high walls firmly in place, it became necessary to open the front entrance to walk into the inside courtyard. Caleb installed an inside lock on the four-foot-wide door.

Portholes appeared in the walls at six feet. I could look out of the openings on tiptoe.

As soon as the adobe roof over my kitchen area was installed, Caleb and Cephas moved my stove inside to the corner with the wall and installed the stove pipe to allow smoke from the cooking fire to escape outside. Being in the corner meant storms would not hinder Ben's and my cooking. They hung the roll-up canvas and moved my table and chairs.

"Gracie, we're going to stack most of your stove wood on the southern wall. Where do you want the wood for the fireplace?"

I looked around my kitchen area. "It seems reasonable to put it down the wall next to the fireplace, and you can put a little in my bedroom."

Pa joined the twins in cutting the winter wood, and soon there were generous stacks in both areas.

"Gracie, I'm glad we're getting close to moving into our new home. The morning air has a sharp nip in it."

"When do you think I can move into my room?"

"The head mason said Monday. That'll give the adobe a chance to dry a little."

"Really? That soon?"

"Yes, I need to tell the twins to make a frame for your feather bed."

"Where will you pull the Conestoga, Pa?"

"Right close to the back of the building, next to the extra stagecoach. It'll be safer from storms and thievery. We can start moving your boxes into your room on Sunday."

Without warning, tears flowed down my cheeks. "I'm sorry, Gracie. Did I say something to offend you?"

"No Pa. It's just that… It doesn't seem possible that our home is almost finished." He came over and put his arm around my shaking shoulders. I tried to hold back the tears but couldn't. I sobbed uncontrollably and put my head on his shoulder. He let me cry for some minutes, rubbing softly on my back.

"Gracie, is the fact that Jedediah hasn't come part of the reason for your tears?"

"I can't deny it. It's in the back of my mind every waking minute. Where can he be?" I pulled my apron to my face and wiped away the tears.

"I wish I knew. Maybe you should send a letter to Fort Chadbourne and ask him when he's coming. You could send it on the stage next Tuesday."

"Pa, that's a great idea. I'll write one Monday. I don't know why I didn't think of that before."

"We've been busy." He started to walk away but stopped. "Gracie, I'm real proud of the way you've taken to our station. I want you to know that."

"Thank you, Pa. It means a good deal to hear you say it." My tears were quiet as I went back to my stove. I felt better now that I had a plan of action. The next stages were due in the afternoon. I'd better get cooking.

There was no way of knowing how many people might be joining me for supper each night. One day, the western bound stage had six, and the eastern bound three. There could be as many as eighteen passing through The Pinery. I couldn't imagine having that many passengers in one day in such primitive conditions.

The riders were mostly men. Women and children were in short supply here on the edge of civilization. Travel was especially hard with children.

Butterfield's celerity wagons weren't very comfortable— not like the sporty Concord stage coaches. The Concords had cushioned seats and padded sides. The plush stages were for smoother roads and greater traffic. The sturdy-built celerity wagon was for rough frontier paths.

The middle seat on the celerity faced forward with a canvas strap for a back. The front seat faced backward. The knees of the passengers on the middle and front seats interlocked, making movement of any kind almost impossible. I decided I'd grab a back seat if there was an opportunity to ride to Franklin. Pa and I had talked about going there.

Pa was authorized to act as agent and sell tickets, not that anyone lived in our area to buy them. The charge was fifteen cents a mile. The through ticket for Mr. Ormsby, our first supper customer and the reporter for the New York Herald, was two hundred dollars.

"Gracie, the westbound stage is here," Pa called the following Tuesday as the bugle sounded. The coach rattled, and the snort of the mules loudly proclaimed its presence outside.

I had my letter safely tucked in my apron pocket as I stirred the stew pot with its dried beans cooking inside. This wasn't the stage I intended to put my note on. That stage was the second one going east to Fort Chadbourne.

I heard low muffled voices, but since I couldn't see out of the rock-walled Pinery unless I left my stove, I never knew who was on the stage until they walked through the front door.

More spoken words just outside the open door that led to the inside courtyard caught my attention. "Mr. Tipton," someone said. "Where's Gracie."

As Pa answered, I ran toward the door. "Jedediah," was the only word I got out before he appeared, rushing toward me. Being embraced by his strong arms and smothered in kisses meant I didn't have to pinch myself. He was here.

"Gracie, Gracie," he whispered in my ear.

"I've been so worried. I didn't know what happened to you. I was afraid…" I jabbered as he stroked my hair and smiled.

"I'm here, Gracie, and I brought the preacher. He's traveling on the stage and staying over. He'll marry us tomorrow. Then he'll head on west on the next stage."

"A preacher? Married tomorrow." I gasped in wonder. Somehow getting hitched on the morrow was far from entering into my plans. Yet, wasn't this what I wanted?

"Yes, I've found a preacher to marry us? We needn't wait any longer," Jedediah repeated, thinking I didn't understand.

"Jedediah, we need to discuss several things before we..."

"Okay, let's discuss them."

"I can't right now. The passengers need to be fed. After that, we'll talk." The prospect of impending marriage had caught me completely off guard.

"Gracie, there are only three passengers. I'll help you feed them, but first, I need to leave my horse with the man who tends your animals."

"That would be Paul. He should be in the corral or bringing the animals in from pasture." Paul and I had gotten along famously since our little talk at Pine Springs. Would that change now that Jedediah was here? He would know who Jedediah was the minute he introduced himself.

Jedediah put his arms around me and gave me another excited hug. "I can't believe I'm here with you. I've missed you so much." He left to see to his horse.

I watched him leave. Five minutes had elapsed during our conversation. Ben came forward. "That's Jedediah?"

"Yes, Ben." I didn't have time to elaborate, for just then, the conductor, Mexican driver, and passengers came through the open doorway. "Guess we'd better feed them."

My hands shook as I dipped bowlfuls of pinto beans seasoned with bacon. Ben placed a plate of fried cornbread on the table and another of sliced onion. We were out of potatoes but expected a sack on the stage from Franklin.

"Gracie, I tell the paying customers this is the best grub on this section of the Butterfield trail. I look forward to getting here and hate leaving," the Jehu explained as he sat down to eat. He always rode the stage coming from Fort Chadbourne. I saw him twice a week.

"Thanks, Juan." He was part Mexican with a dark, swarthy appearance. The yellow linen duster stood out in sharp contrast to his brown skin. He smiled a lot, flashing white teeth.

"Your future husband came with us, no?"

"Yes."

"I assume you're Gracie?" A tall man with graying hair at his temples looked at me with probing dark eyes. His spoon full of beans was suspended in the air. On the table beside his plate lay a folded newspaper. "I should have known. You're all he talked about in Fort Chadbourne and on the road here."

Jedediah came in at that moment with my father. "I see you've met Preacher Dixon." He beamed at me and the reverend.

The reverend rose from the table. "No, we haven't met yet." He took the necessary steps to walk around the table, extended his hand, and said in a booming voice, "Reverend Anthony Dixon, a former resident of Providence, Rhode Island, graduate of Brown University, and proud progeny of Francis Wayland its President—chosen by God to be a missionary from the American Baptists to the Indians of the Southwest—at your service." He bowed deeply.

His reverberating voice startled me. Every living thing within a thousand feet now knew his claim to fame, including the mules in their pasture. I shook his hand. He squeezed mine with steady, hard pressure.

"Gracie Tipton of Nashville, Tennessee," was all I could manage.

Reverend Anthony Dixon went back to his spoon and pinto beans, and the conversation turned to slavery in the East—the favorite subject of most talks at our supper table. Texas was no different than the eastern states. It was divided over the question of slavery.

I motioned for Pa and Jedediah to sit down and brought them their food. Every time I passed him, Jedediah reached out to touch me. I'm sure he was making sure I wasn't a mirage, like some people fancied when lost in the desert.

I jumped again as the preacher's voice boomed. It commanded attention. "I have it here," he tapped the newspaper beside his plate. Pushing back his chair from the table he opened the newspaper. "The question of slavery will not be settled peacefully," he insisted. "Here's what Abraham Lincoln said in the Charleston Debate with Stephen Douglas on September 18 in Illinois – '*it perhaps would require more time than I have now to set forth these reasons in detail; but let me ask you a few questions. Have we ever had any peace on this slavery question? When are we to have peace upon it if it is kept in the position it now occupies? How are we ever to have peace upon it? That is an important question. To be sure, if we will all stop and allow Judge Douglas and his friends to march on in their present career until they plant the institution all over the nation, here and wherever else our flag waves, and we acquiesce in it, there will be peace. But let me ask Judge Douglas how he is going to get the people to do that? They have been wrangling over this question for at least forty years.'* Isn't that true?" exclaimed the pastor.

"Do you think Lincoln will be elected senator from Illinois?" Pa asked him.

"It's doubtful. Douglas is the incumbent and very well known, but I do think this will position Mr. Lincoln for a run at the presidency next year. His speeches have been published in the East and in the territories west of the Mississippi. By all accounts, they've been well received."

"Yes, I've read some of them in newspapers brought here from Fort Smith. Will he run as a Whig or Republican?"

"Republican, of course. The Whig Party is permanently split because of slavery."

"I wanted to get away from the issue of slavery. Seems it's followed me here to Texas." Pa sat staring off into space.

"Are you for or against slavery?" asked Reverend Dixon.

"Against," said Pa. "The black man has a soul just like you or me. I'm firmly convinced the Bible backs me on this issue."

"I agree with you," said the minister.

The rest of the meal was eaten in relative quiet, except when the question of marauding Indians arose.

The conductor mentioned seeing a large band east of The Pinery, "At least three to four days away, toward the Pecos River. They were camped in the desert next to the river. From the looks of them, they weren't planning to move for a while."

"As long as they stay there," I exclaimed.

"Gracie's seen enough of Indians." Jedediah grinned at me as he said this.

"Well, boys," said the conductor. "It's time to leave." He got up from the table and headed toward the door. Stopping, he turned around and asked, "Reverend, you're staying here to perform a marriage?"

"I think so." Reverend Dixon looked from Jedediah to me.

"You'll resume your trip on the Friday stage to Franklin?"

"Yes, that's the plan."

The conductor disappeared through the door. I collected the price for the food, and the others followed.

❧ **28** ❧

Three mornings later, a strange sound woke me. On my wedding day, the sky dropped water. I remembered the old wive's tale of rain being a bad omen on this special day. Phooey, I didn't believe those old adages by women who had nothing better to do than dream up bad sayings for people to worry about. But why had rain poured down today? We'd only had one other rainfall since coming to the mountains.

I threw back my covers, stood, and lit the coal oil lantern that sat on a low table beside the door to my room. In its warm glow, I made out the articles in the room. My bed with its feather mattress and comforter was on the back wall. To the right side my rocking chair, and on top of my bureau, the blue ewer with basin that Press had given me.

I walked over to my rocking chair, the one I'd made Pa bring all the way from Memphis, Tennessee. The night before, I'd draped my beautiful birthday dress across it, the dress I'd been given at Stinnett's Station. The matching bonnet from Mr. Ormand hung on the chair top. I felt its silky smoothness. I'd planned to wear the lovely dress for the ceremony today, but now, with the rain and mud outside my door, I had no intention of putting it on.

Instead, I opened the trunk at the foot of my bed and carefully placed my treasure back inside. The hat with its coral ribbons I returned to the hatbox on the shelf over my bed. Going

231

to the pegs on my rock wall to the left, I pulled down my next best outfit and put it where the coral one had rested.

Drawing aside the cloth curtain that served as a door, I stood in my nightgown looking out at the falling rain. In the dark, I could make out the entrance door, and I could hear Ben in the kitchen, digging out the pans. His preparations for cooking this morning's breakfast were already underway. The rattle and clang of pots being shoved together served as an alarm clock to our station workers. I knew they were getting out of bed, shaving, and dressing.

Ben offered to cook all the meals on my special day, wanting me to enjoy its moments. I intended to relish each part. My bed looked inviting. I walked back over the worn rug covering the dirt floor, deciding to hop back into bed. I hadn't done this in months, not since we left Nashville. Snuggling into its warmth, I thought of Jedediah.

I didn't intend to get married without an extended conversation with my intended. I'd waited several weeks for him to come, a few days more wouldn't matter.

Two nights ago, we'd talked about Hurricane Bailey. Jedediah's father still directed the work crew at Fort Chadbourne. He hadn't changed his habits, working hard during the day and getting roaring drunk at night.

"Gracie, I won't go back. I'll never work on his crew again."

"You promise?"

"Yes." His words were simple and good enough for me. Jedediah's concern was finding work after we got married. He'd thought about this problem and made plans to travel to Franklin to talk to the division superintendent. Getting onto one of the work crews west of The Pinery but close to home seemed to be the best plan.

The rain lulled me back into dreamland. When I awoke, it was light outside. The hard rain had turned to a cold drizzle. I pulled on my work dress and headed for the cook stove, welcoming its warmth.

"Gracie, I wondered if you were goin' to sleep your wedding day away." Ben stood at our utility table, pouring hot water into a basin to wash the breakfast dishes.

"I thought about it, but decided to get up." Even the talk over breakfast hadn't aroused me from my slumber.

"Your breakfast is sittin' inside the warming oven."

"Thank you, Ben. The food will taste good this morning." I walked over and pulled the plate out of the oven. Ben handed me a fork. "Have we got more hot water? I want to take a bath."

"I only used a little from the hot water reservoir on the stove. I'll put the large pots on the cook top. You'll have enough to take a long, hot one."

My one failing, if you can call it that, was loving a hot bath every chance I got. We had plenty of water from Pine Springs, which we didn't have to carry, thanks to the Carter twins. I'd ripped an old cotton sheet into two pieces and managed to make a drape at the edge of the kitchen area. Behind it was a half-way decent tub of porcelain with claw's feet. Mr. Coburn had sent it from division headquarters at Franklin with a note:

Gracie,
*   Besides my wife, you're the only lady in our division. I thought you might enjoy this extra tub that I found here at the division house. I'm sending it for your use at The Pinery.*
*   Coburn*

Packed in the tub, along with other supplies, were carrots for my stews, apples, and grapes. They didn't last long, because the workers and I gobbled the unexpected treats. Why was I thinking about carrots? This was my wedding day.

I finished my breakfast and started for my room just as Jedediah came through the entrance door. "Eek! Jedediah, you're not supposed to see me before the weddin'. It's bad luck."

"Too late," he said, hurrying forward, embracing me, and pushing me back under the overhang of the kitchen area out of the drizzle. He bent his head to kiss me.

"No, really, you're not supposed to see me until the wedding." I pushed him away. "Get out, now."

"Do you really believe that old tale?"

"No. Leave anyway!"

"Okay, Gracie." He walked down toward Caleb's blacksmith area and peeked around the stone wall at me.

"No, don't do that."

I heard him laughing as he greeted Caleb.

Stepping into my bedroom, I thought of his change from the reserved, quiet young man I'd first known. Could this Jedediah be an imposter? His fetters broken, a new man emerged away from Hurricane Bailey—someone I could admire as well as love.

The wedding took place just before dinner with everyone crowded under the overhang in the dry kitchen area. New smelling straw covered the dirt floor. Its smell permeated the air, blending with the smell coming from Ben's food cooking on the stove.

The stonemason's crew in their work clothes, Cephas and Caleb, Paul and Pa, and the Reverend Dixon in a black suit stood or sat in the chairs used at the eating table. The whole scene had a surreal quality—not at all as I imagined my wedding would be—in a church, filled with flowers and women and men in their finery.

Pa came to meet me as I walked out in the midst of the manly crowd in my favorite skirt and blouse. The outfit was the one I'd worn the last time I'd seen Jedediah in Fort Chadbourne. I looked down, touching the soft folds, smoothing out imperceptible wrinkles as we stepped forward.

In a blur, I saw the dark rose flowers with green petals on a sea of light rose and the blouse of rose cotton with beige cotton lace on the bodice and around the collar. The sight of this familiar and loved set of clothes steadied me. I looked up.

Jedediah came forward to meet me.

Leaving Pa, my future husband and I joined hands. We stood before the reverend in front of the fire crackling in the fireplace.

I jumped again when the reverend's large voice boomed out. Jedediah put his arm around me and held on tighter.

"Dearly beloved, we are gathered here in the sight of God to join this man and woman in the holy bonds of matrimony." I know I heard his words, but I didn't hear them either. When he got to the place where it was necessary to say "I do," my response was mechanical and Jedediah's was enthusiastic. "I now pronounce you man and wife. Jedediah, kiss your bride."

Bride? Did the reverend proclaim me a married woman?

The men came crowding around, clapping Jedediah on the back and claiming a kiss from me. It was true. I was married, something I'd waited and looked for all my life. I remembered Sarah's words. "Gracie. Women are born to be married, have a home, and children. That's what Mama tells me all the time." Sarah wanted to be a doctor.

I was married, but as for a home, the Guadalupe Mountains and The Pinery would have to serve as such. And children, they would come.

Ben placed dinner on the table. I noticed Pa trying to get my attention. "Gracie, I want to talk to you and Jedediah."

"Okay, Pa." I got Jedediah by the arm, and we followed my father out into the misty air and into the blacksmithing area.

"Here's my weddin' gift to you." I recognized tickets for the stage. "Why don't you go into Franklin and celebrate your marriage. I think you'll be more comfortable out of the stares of the men here."

"Mr. Tipton, I wondered how we'd get through that. We'll be glad to, won't we Gracie?"

"Thank you, Pa. You're the most thoughtful man I know."

"Gracie, I'll sleep on the extra cot in your father's tent until we leave on the next stage." I realized Jedediah could make decisions.

Later in the afternoon, Pa and I were alone when he confided that Paul had decided to move on. "He's headin' to California sometime after you and Jedediah leave on the stage. He said to give his job to your husband." Pa paused and shook his head. "Husband. Gracie, it seems so strange to use that word about you. Guess I'll have to quit calling you little girl."

"Pa, I thought you should have quit years ago. Now I don't care. I feel like an old married woman already." I stood smiling at him, knowing he wouldn't be number one in my life now that I was married. I loved my pa.

He hesitated before asking the next question. "Gracie, are you scared about your weddin' night?"

His unexpected query shocked me. Since he'd been a good father and aided me in every situation, I should have expected it. Was he going to tell me about the birds and bees? Suddenly embarrassed, I truthfully answered. "Guess I am a little bit."

"I'll talk to Jedediah. I don't feel easy talkin' to you about such things. If your Mama was here…"

"Thanks, Pa. Talking to Jedediah will be enough," I said, anxious to get this part of the tête-à-tête over.

The reverend left on the afternoon stage. That night, Jedediah and I slept apart. The next morning the sun was shining brightly as I cleaned the breakfast dishes.

"Gracie, don't do that. Celebrate your marriage and take it easy," Ben insisted.

"I hate to leave you with the cookin' and fire buildin', but I thank you for takin' over so Jedediah and I can visit Franklin."

"Are you packed for your stay?"

"Almost finished."

"Ben, you've been to Franklin. What's the place like?"

"You'll like it, Gracie. It's a green oasis in the dry, dusty desert." Ben held up his finger as he cautioned, "Let me remind you, the town is still a rough frontier town. Everyone carries a gun. Street fights are common, so be careful."

☙ 29 ❧

I'd seen many people get on the stage during the past weeks. My boarding afforded the different and exciting experience of becoming a passenger. The sun headed behind El Capitan as Jedediah and I entered.

Since the celerity wagon was empty except for mail bags piled on the front seat, we sat on the backseat, exactly where Pa and I had decided to ride should we go to Franklin. After eating a community goodbye supper prepared by Ben, the stonemasons and the station employees piled out the fortress door. They gathered to catcall us as the mules strained to pull the heavy stage forward.

"Don't do anythin' I wouldn't do," called Cephas. The stage moved forward.

"Brother, you are so confounded…" The rest of Caleb's chastisement blended with the rumble of the wagons' wheels.

"The twins never change," I said, looking at Jedediah's face. A faint red color showed at his cheeks. As we rounded the bend and pulled onto the main road, I looked back. Pa stood waving at the departing stage—a lonely figure in the midst of the crowd.

I snuggled against Jedediah as he pulled me to him, willing to put my future in his hands. We bumped along the road, traveling the hills and ravines of the Guadalupes, laughing at the way we bounced off the seat with the wagon's swaying and jolting passage. The evening sun disappeared behind the hills with a brilliant orange glow, leaving the cactus, grass, and mesquite with a strange, glowing expectant blush.

With the mountains behind us, the roadway leveled out, and in the darkness, we heard the conductor call out the approach of the other stage. A brief stop to hear the road conditions ahead, and we were off again.

The dark night continued full of stopping and starting, bugle blowing, and the pawing of countless mules as they were exchanged for fresh teams. By morning, after a sleepless night, both Jedediah and I were exhausted. Our valises had bounced under the middle seat and rested close to the front one. The United States mail rested atop them.

The morning sun revealed a dry, miserable, hot road with the wind kicking whirls of dust from our animals' hooves. There was no way of keeping the fine powder off our clothes or out of our eyes and mouth. The last thing Pa had given me were two canteens of cool water from Pine Springs. I blew the dust off a cap, unscrewed the lid, and pulled the woolen-covered metal container to my lips. I drank deeply and handed the liquid to Jedediah.

At nine o'clock, the conductor blew his bugle to announce our next station. "We'll eat breakfast here."

Our teams pulled to a walled area with four or five adobe huts…a small pueblo here in the desert. A mesquite tree grew at the side of the mud-plastered walls, and three clumps of green, prickly-pear cactus flourished under its filmy branches. Several ragged Mexican children greeted us on our arrival. Chickens and pigs ran in numerous directions as three men led the new teams of fresh but wild mules toward us.

Jedediah and I dismounted the stage. I started rubbing my hip and suddenly burst out laughing.

"What's so funny," asked my new husband, startled at my outburst.

"I remember my first passenger to come to The Pinery. He left rubbing his hip. Now I know how he felt."

"Oh, I see. I thought maybe the jolting had addled your brain. Come on, Gracie, let's see what the cook at the station has for breakfast."

"One guess," I said.

"Eggs," we exclaimed together as the clucking chickens pecked at the sand nearby.

Strange noises interrupted our progress toward breakfast. Before we could enter the station house, the mules already attached to their harness and led to the coach cut loose. Everyone present witnessed such bucking, snorting, kicking, and braying as to send them into gales of laughter. Dust, rocks, and dirt flew in all directions. The Mexican handlers jumped and danced, evading the angry mules.

"Wild, loco mules—from prairie." Juan, our Jehu told Jedediah. He stood with us watching the episode taking place.

The conductor explained, "Butterfield couldn't purchase enough mules for the stage lines so wild 'uns was captured from the desert and prairie. Dad-blame creatures ain't broke in to the harness. Don't understand the importance of pulling the US Mail from coast to coast." He laughed, but then admonished, "Watch it, boys," as the mules' antics threatened to overturn the coach to which they were now attached.

"Come on, Gracie. We'd better get breakfast."

Jedediah held my hand, and we ducked as we entered the nearest door. He and I guessed right. We had salty eggs, fried with onions and peppers, and wrapped in tortillas with rain water to wash them down.

"Mexican food," explained Jedediah. "They pound fresh corn until its very fine to make this thin flat wrapping and cook it over a fire."

"Umn," was my comment. I couldn't say anything else because my mouth was full.

"How do you like it?"

"I do like the taste except for a bit of sand now and then. Corn, onions, peppers and eggs—the flavors are interesting."

After eating my fill, we walked outside to stretch our legs. The stage stood ready to carry us on the last leg of the journey. "Not having to prepare the stage for leaving is a different experience, isn't it Gracie."

"I feel like a rich woman," was my comment to my new husband.

"You are a rich woman, Gracie."

After Jedediah made the comment I thought about its import. He was right. I had everything I wanted or needed in life. I couldn't ask for more.

"Come aboard," the conductor called, mounting to the driver's seat.

The mules set off at a ragged pace but soon settled down into a constant rhythm. We endured several more hours of interesting travel through the desert. I amused myself by asking questions about the plants passing by our coach.

"What's the tall spindly plant with smooth limbs and red berries as large as grapes?"

"Which one?" asked Jedediah.

I pointed the next one out as the stage went by.

"Oh, that's Christmas cholla cactus."

"The spines look deadly."

Jedediah laughed. "They're even more deadly if you run into one hidden within a bush as I found out on a nightly bathroom trip as a young boy. Pa picked several out of my hide." He rolled his pant's leg almost to the knee and rubbed a slight indention on his leg. "There's the result of one." We hadn't mention Hurricane Bailey in days. We both fell silent.

For several miles we drove parallel to a deep ravine that grew shallower and shallower until it smoothed out and disappeared into the desert.

"That's a tree cholla, Gracie." He pointed to a tall, fuzzy cactus growing on the side of a ravine we were passing.

Jedediah cleared his throat and started giving me a running description of what I was seeing. When he didn't talk about the vegetation or some incident which happened along the road, I spent the rest of the time imagining grotesque figures in the wind beaten and twisted limbs of the roadside mesquite trees. Some of the time I napped—putting my head on my traveling shawl in his lap—my feet on the bench. Jedediah could sleep sitting up straight—a habit he learned sitting in saloon corners waiting for Mr. Bailey to head home.

Once we saw a distant herd of several thousand buffalo and another time two young antelope danced around each other on the prairie as the rest of the herd grazed nearby. Jedediah explained that the buffalo were heading to their winter pastures.

"There'll be myriads coming by here in the next few weeks. These are early arrivals. You should have plenty of fresh buffalo meat for the winter."

The following day as we came into Franklin, acres and acres of cultivated and irrigated vegetables appeared on both sides of the stage. Running water ran through adobe tiles under the road.

"Where does the water come from?" I asked my husband.

"The Rio Grande, Gracie. There's a dam and a grist mill on its banks. This area is warm enough to grow food all year around."

"The grist mill, that's where The Pinery's flour comes from," I exclaimed.

Large pecan trees, vineyards and groves of fruit trees with ripe fruit waited to be picked. The Mexican owners bent to cultivate and harvest the open fields. Their heads shielded by large sombreros.

"Ben said Franklin was an oasis in the desert. I believe him."

The sun hung low in the sky before our bumpy ride ended at division headquarters in Franklin. I craned my neck from the window as we came into town, watching as we passed several pueblos with separate smaller frame or log homes scattered between.

"Jedediah, there's a two-story building in front of us. It looks brand new."

Within seconds we pulled to the front of the edifice. The sign said, BUTTERFIELD OVERLAND STAGE LINES. I watched as Mr. Coburn came to open the stage door and greet the passengers. My pa did the same as station man at The Pinery. Mr. Coburn wasn't in his normal Butterfield duds. Today he was hatless.

"Gracie," he exclaimed as I alighted from the stage with Jedediah following. "You're the last person I anticipated on the coach."

"Well, sir, I didn't expect the division headquarters to be this handsome."

"We had our local surveyor, Anson Mills, build one worthy of the Butterfield Overland Mail. I'll show you around. Who's this young man?"

"This is Jedediah Bailey. He's my husband."

"What! Gracie, what have you done?" Shocked, Mr. Coburn stuck out his hand. "Jedediah pleased to meet you. You've got a fine lady here." He was beaming at us both.

"Thank you, sir. I'm well aware of that."

"There must be a story behind your marriage. Come on in. We'll find some refreshin' lemonade. When did this happen?"

"Before we do come in, Mr. Coburn I need to get rooms at the hotel for Gracie and me. It's gettin' awful late."

The district supervisor clapped Jedediah on the back. "We can take care of that right here, Jedediah. Our rooms are new, and I can assure you they're clean."

He led us through the front door, poured us a glass of very sweet lemonade, and walked us around the front of the headquarters, showing off his new office with its desk, high-backed chair, and wire baskets of important looking papers. Going through a side door and down an open breezeway, we were shown two rooms with large beds, chests with many drawers, and wash basins. Glass windows were open and curtains fluttered in the late afternoon breeze. Each had an outside door and shared a common wall.

"For important supervisors and passengers on the stage line," Mr. Coburn explained. "Which room do you want?"

"You mean we can have one of these?"

"Of course you can, Gracie. Free of charge. You're a fellow employee and very important."

"Jedediah is too, or he was."

"Really. What does 'too' and 'was' mean?"

"It means I worked on the road crew out of Fort Chadbourne with my father."

"Hurricane Bailey?"

"Yes. I came to The Pinery with Reverend Dixon to marry Gracie."

"The reverend passed through here a few days ago on his way to Apache Territory in Arizona. The Indians won't have a hard time hearing him." Mr. Coburn chuckled and put his hands to his ears. We walked back to the office.

"I'd like to get on the road crew out of Franklin, if there's an opening."

"Jedediah, I intended to tell you. Pa said there's a position at The Pinery. Paul's headin' for California...if, if Mr. Coburn approves."

"I didn't think Paul was a long-timer. He had that look in his eyes." The supervisor went to the open window to look out. He turned around. "The job's yours, Jedediah, if you want it."

"I do, sir, and we'll take the room. Is that okay, Gracie?"

I nodded. "Is there a place to eat in town?"

Jedediah bent over laughing, slapping his knees a little too hard. "I swear, Gracie. All you think about is food."

He didn't know it, but there were other things on my mind at present, and thinking about them made me nervous. I wondered if the same thoughts caused his rambunctious smacking of the knees.

"Here's the key to your room, and food's this way," said Mr. Coburn. He pulled his Cordoba hat off a peg on the wall, led the way out of the building, and strode down the street. "Amora feeds the passengers on the stage. Eat there any time on the company's money. If you tell her when you'll be present, she'll fix you special food or a picnic. I always eat dinner with her. Sometimes my wife joins me, Gracie."

The last rays of the sun tucked themselves into the horizon as we walked to the door of a nondescript building with a dim interior. "Amora," he called. "You have customers."

A plump Mexican lady appeared from behind a brightly-woven blanket at the back of the room. She carried a lantern. "Si, Señor Coburn. Please sit." She motioned with a wave of her hands, and we sat at a table under a window at the front. Mr. Coburn remained standing.

"Oh, I'm not staying. I'm going home to eat, but Gracie and Jedediah will stay." He started out the door. "They're newlyweds," he winked knowingly at the older lady, explaining further in Spanish. Her eyes grew wide. She smiled and clapped her hands as if she'd been told a great secret.

"Jedediah, I'll take you and Gracie on a buggy tour of the area if you wish. Just let me know when." He disappeared into the twilight.

Although Amora tried hard to make our supper interesting and merry, both of us were preoccupied. We got up to leave. "No stay on streets after dark. Es dangerous…many drunk hombres with pistola."

Jedediah attempted to pay her, but she wouldn't take his money.

"Mr. Coburn, he pay bill," she explained.

We walked out the door. Darkness disappeared in the bright moonlight illuminating the road. There was a noticeable chill in the air as we left Amora's. I wanted to walk fast, and I didn't want to walk fast.

A glowing lantern hung on a peg outside our room. Jedediah pulled it off. He fumbled with the key furnished by the division agent, and finally the door opened. We walked in and found our valises sitting on the corner bed.

Mr. Coburn's rapid departure from Amora's meant rooms ready for our occupancy. Sitting on the dresser, a yellow rose brightened the room.

Jedediah and I washed in the basin as best we could, using clean towels and fresh water in a large metal pitcher placed on a nearby cupboard. What I'd give for a hot bath.

I turned my back on my husband to unbutton my blouse. Out of the corner of my eye, I saw him pull off his clothes and crawl into bed. I tried brushing my curly hair and fiddled around in my packed toiletries. Somehow, I got my nightgown on. I couldn't delay the inevitable any longer.

With a huge drawn chunk of breath, I crawled in beside my husband who pulled the covers aside so I could slide in easily. His white naked skin was a total shock to me, but he was warm and smelled of soap as I touched him.

Jedediah blew out the lantern, turned, and embraced me. The pale light of the moon came through the window where the cool night wind stirred the curtains. His face looked ghostly in the moonlight as he kissed me. Nothing was unsure about his performance.

❦ 30 ❦

"Your wedding gift, si?" Amora explained the next morning as we ate our breakfast of fresh pork, eggs and biscuits. Outside in a pen not far from the house, a large sow provided milk for several small piglets soon to become food for the woman's table. "We want to do something to help you celebrate your new lives together."

Her husband, Hernando, looked like the other Mexican men we saw in Franklin. He wore white pants, white shirt with multicolored trim, and his head was covered with a large sombrero. The hat, made of straw, contained a kaleidoscope of colors. He stood inside the room, grinning from ear to ear, showing perfect white teeth. "He no speak English," Amora explained. "But he give you ride in his canoe on Rio Grande before he work fields."

"Amora, Jedediah and I would be delighted to take a boat ride on the river. Could we visit his fields? Would that be all right?"

She turned to her husband and spoke several sentences in Spanish. "Si, is okay. Take ride first. Then walk fields."

We followed Hernando down the street past the hotel, saloon, and sutler's store, which supplied the people's basic needs. The heels of our boots made thumping sounds on the boardwalk. As I stepped off the end, Jedediah caught my hand, reminding me of a misstep several months ago—the first time I saw him. My eyes met his.

He whispered and my heart jumped in response. "The first time I held you in my arms."

He kept amazing me at his delightful emergence from his father's web of abuse.

We continued behind our Mexican guide, down the steep bank to a docking area where several boats of every description were drawn to the bank. Hernando went to one with yellow sunflowers painted on the side and motioned for us to get in. We headed out into the main stream of water—our captain rowing upriver. The Rio Grande's swirling waters flowed by, and the day passed in its enjoyable clutches. Looking across to the Mexican side, Jedediah informed me more people lived in *El Paso del Norte* than in Franklin.

Hernando pulled on the oars, rowing past thick, water-logged canebrakes where leaving the small craft and climbing on the river bank to explore seemed impossible. Here and there large banks of sand attested to the river's power as it meandered through the desert and riverside brush. Several huge cottonwood trees brought relief from the steaming sun as their branches overshadowed the water.

I almost didn't see the lone scraggly coyote—his head bent lapping water from the bank. He blended in perfectly with the scrub brush, sand, and brown-tinged tufts of grass living on the river's edge. Our intrusion caused him to run back a few feet, where he stopped atop a sand bank, and gawked at us as we floated by him. Sometime later we heard his haunting howl with yips and a distant answer.

"I wondered where his friends were," said Jedediah. "Most of the time the coyote hunts and lives alone, but in fall and winter food is scarce, and they hunt in packs."

The river disappeared behind us as Hernando dug his oars below the surface of the water. A small man, his arm muscles were well-developed from rowing and tending his fields.

"Look above you, Gracie." Jedediah pointed out the conical nests of cliff swallows that clung to the undersides of low-lying cliffs beside the water. "The nests are made out of round daubs of mud. See how uneven they are. When the mud dries, the attachment to the rock is permanent. Each year the bird returns to the same mud home and lays her eggs."

I shaded my eyes and looked at the sky, expecting to see a chattering colony. "Where are the birds now?"

"Gone south into Mexico or South America to winter." Jedediah might not have a lot of book learning, but his practical knowledge of the West and Western things turned out to be extensive.

"How do you know all this?"

"Pa taught me." This was the second mention of Hurricane Bailey.

The sun stood straight overhead when we left the river. It beat down on our heads in the muggy air. I regretted asking to see Hernando's fields, wishing to get out of the heat, but he motioned for us to follow him.

He grew tomato plants, rows and rows of them. Their red ripe fruit stood out against the green leaves and stems. We walked through a field of corn ready to harvest, eggplant, carrots, and onions. Vines with ripening melons made my mouth water.

"Jedediah, do you think we could take some fresh vegetables back on the stage?"

"I think we'd have mush by the time we got back to The Pinery, but we can try. Maybe Mr. Coburn has some extra crates we can pack with straw. Are you ready to head back to town? I want to get out of the sun. There's not a breath of air stirring."

We shook hands and waved goodbye to Hernando.

Walking back toward Franklin, we passed an outdoor market where one could purchase sombreros, food, and Mexican crafts. At the sutler's store I went inside to browse the merchandise.

"Jedediah, I want to buy a hoe."

"A hoe. What for?"

"I brought seeds from Tennessee. Next year I intend to see if they'll grow. Pa said the biggest problem is getting water to the plants. I think I know how. The twins will help me. I'll make adobe tiles and irrigate like they do here at the Rio Grande. At least, I want to try."

"A hoe it is." Jedediah picked one out and paid for it. "Gracie, would you like to take the ferry across to the Mexican side. We could explore the pueblos."

"Maybe tomorrow. I'm ready for some of Mr. Coburn's cold lemonade."

Loud voices came from the saloon as we passed. A sign outside advertised beer, whiskey, and billiards.

At division headquarters, we passed a distinguished man with a mustache and goatee coming from the two-story building.

Mr. Coburn welcomed us at the front door as he bade his visitor goodbye. "Come on in you two. It's too hot to stand around in the afternoon sun. I'll bet you'd like another glass of cool lemonade." He busied himself with providing the named refreshment while a dark-skinned Mexican *Señora* hovered in the background.

"Who is that important looking gentlemen? The one we passed as we entered." I asked as I received the tall glass of sweet, pale-yellow liquid.

"Anson Mills," came the reply. "He built this building, and he is currently surveying our town, laying out more streets. We think our village will be a crossroads to Mexico and the Western states, especially since Fort Bliss and her soldiers are stationed north of here. Mills intends to suggest changing the name to El Paso...El Paso, Texas. Has a nice sound to it, I think. We have a hotel, various stores, post office, and our mail route extends from one end of America to the other, thanks to John Butterfield. If our community doesn't prosper, the fault won't be ours."

I watched as Mr. Coburn poured himself a glass and sat down. "Are you enjoying our town, Gracie?"

"It's the closest thing to civilization I've encountered in the West, after Fort Smith, Arkansas."

"How are the stonemasons doing? Is The Pinery almost finished?"

"Yes sir. By the time Jedediah and I arrive back in the Guadalupes it should be almost complete. Ben and I love our new kitchen under the adobe roof. We moved the stove as soon as the roof covered the area. It's cool even in the noonday heat and the fireplace will take off the chill in the winter."

"Now, when are we going to take that buggy ride?" Mr. Coburn took a long sip on his refreshment.

Jedediah answered, "In the morning, Mr. Coburn, if that's all right with you."

"Morning it is, young people. Say around nine o'clock?"

I nodded. "We're going to sit in the breezeway and let the afternoon wind off the river keep us cool."

"I'll treat you to supper at Amora's at six. Gracie, I want you to meet my wife."

Mr. Coburn had mentioned his wife before. "I'd be delighted to meet her."

Two days later, Jedediah and I headed to the market to purchase the supplies I wished to take back to The Pinery. Mr. Coburn went with us. "Gracie, it's time for another supply trip to your station. Get what you need. Any overload we'll store at headquarters and put on the wagon's regular run."

"Mr. Coburn you'll be sorry you said that. Food is Gracie's biggest downfall."

He laughed. "She's a first-rate cook, Jedediah. She deserves a good stock of staples."

I did just as Mr. Coburn said, walking down the aisles and picking out fresh vegetables, dried fruit, and a beautiful Mexican wool blanket. I whispered to Jedediah, "The blanket will keep us warm this winter when it snows."

I bought a large straw bag and piled it full of my purchases. "Do you think my bag will pad the food and keep it from crushing?"

"I think it will help."

"Remember, Gracie, I have three crates to pack supplies for your trip back on the stage." Mr. Coburn picked out another blanket and added it to the growing pile.

"For your father."

Two tightly woven straw mats caught my eye. I bought two colorful ones to cover the dirt floor in my bedroom at The Pinery. They would brighten my rock room, replace the worn rug, and feel great on cold mornings in the coming winter.

I stood looking over some pottery, especially a large platter with matching bowl, when something made a streak between my feet. Thinking it was a large rat or other varmint, I squealed.

Jedediah, Mr. Coburn, and the Mexican running the stall laughed. Jedediah picked up a kitten and held on tightly for me to see. "Gracie, it's just a cat and a yellow one at that."

He patted its head and the poor little thing meowed. I reached for it.

"You're an itsy-bitsy thing." I stroked the kitten's short fur. "You'll get stepped on and break a leg if you don't watch where you're going." I felt a lump underneath its neck as I rubbed its fuzzy face against mine. "Jedediah, I think there's a tick here." I knew about ticks, because Wooly got them.

My husband pulled the offending insect off the little one's body.

"Do you think…?"

"A cat at The Pinery. I know what you're thinking."

"A perfect idea. We won't miss one here in this town," said Mr. Coburn who spoke words of Spanish to the stall owner. The vendor smiled and eagerly nodded. "It's yours…a gift for the newly married couple."

"*Gracias, Señor.*" I could speak two words of Spanish, I thought proudly.

"What are you going to name her?" asked Jedediah.

"How do you know it's a her?"

"Trust me, the kitten is a her."

"Well, just in case you are wrong, Mr. Bailey, I think I'll call her Ticksy…itsy-bitsy, Ticksy."

"I hope Wooly likes her."

I put my new kitten over my head and looked at her. "You'll be the best of friends, won't you Ticksy?"

We walked back toward town, bade Mr. Coburn goodbye, and took the ferry ride to the large pueblo across the river. That afternoon we ate a leisurely meal at Amora's. Later, we found Caleb and Cephas's parents' home. We visited with them until we almost missed the stage home.

The time for leaving on the stage arrived too soon. The stage pulled into headquarters in the afternoon as two men exited the local saloon yelling loudly. We ducked for cover as bullets flew above our heads. The conductor and driver jumped from the stage, as did the two occupants. One man from the saloon was wounded. He fell in the street, and the other one, obviously drunk, staggered back into the business.

"Guess that's our goodbye from Franklin, Gracie," Jedediah observed, heading for the man who lay in the street. "You stay here."

Mr. Coburn came from his office. "Jedediah, I'll tend to the wounded. You and Gracie load your supplies on the stage. I'll send the supply wagon on tomorrow. Have a good trip home." He headed down the street toward the saloon. Others came from the sutler's store.

The prone man was moving as we passed him. The drunken man's aim hadn't been good. "It's only a surface wound," Mr. Coburn shouted. Franklin or El Paso had lived up to its reputation.

The following afternoon, we were stopped by a mounted patrol from Fort Davis. Captain Tom Stevens explained to our conductor that they were searching for a rogue band of Apache. "Been stealing livestock and killed a New Mexico homesteader in the process."

When he found out we were heading to The Pinery, he told of another incident at Apache Pass. "Butterfield's stone fortress held off a raiding party at the springs, but a wagon train lost two men not far away. It's time for the Indians to make camp in the area. Guess they don't want to share."

"Is this raiding activity escalating?" asked the conductor.

"Could be. We'll ride along behind you for part of the way."

A crack of the driver's whip and the rattling stage went east toward home

I looked at Jedediah and whispered so our fellow passengers couldn't hear, "I'm glad you've got a new job with Pa, and you're not on the road crew. Sounds like trouble in New Mexico, and our end of Texas isn't out of raidin' territory."

We headed on to The Pinery, stopping to pick up a gallon jar of milk for use in cooking. Jedediah and I took turns holding the glass jug during the night and next day.

Two days after leaving El Paso we passed the westward bound coach and arrived home after dark.

❧ 31 ❧

Relief meant my shoes on the ground. I couldn't imagine anyone riding the stage from Tipton, Missouri to San Francisco. I wondered if the reporter for the New York Herald survived.

"Gracie." Ben hurried toward me. "How was your trip?" He looked ridiculous as he came running, waving a large stirring spoon in the air.

I laughed at him. "Franklin—or El Paso—was very interestin'. I'll tell you all about it, but right now I'm starving." Jedediah headed for my room with several parcels he'd carried from the stage. He reappeared to take mine.

"She hasn't changed a bit." My father came through the fortress door. "Married or unmarried she's hungry twenty-four hours a day." He gave me a bear hug and shook Jedediah's hand. "Here let me take some of your packages." He grabbed at one of my covered baskets. Ticksy meowed. "What's in here?"

"A needed addition to our family—somethin' to catch desert rats."

"It's a cat?" asked Ben, coming to take the basket from my pa and opening the top. Ticksy's yellow head appeared above the rim. Seeing so many curious eyes, she ducked back out of sight.

"You mean it's another mouth to feed," Pa complained. But he was smiling.

Everyone came to stare into the cat's hiding place. I took her out and placed her on the ground. She immediately ran behind the stove. Cephas and Caleb appeared as she darted across the floor.

"Whoops, what was that? Did we hear someone say cat—to eat rats?"

"Yes, she ran behind the stove. We've scared her terribly."

The twins went over to look at the kitten. "She's going to have to grow a bit. Most apt, the rats will run off with her," observed Cephas, calling the little one like a chicken. "Here cat...cat...cat." He snapped his fingers. "Come on out. I won't hurt you."

"So what's her name?" asked Caleb.

"It's Ticksy."

Pa laughed. "That's a strange name for a cat."

"Itsy-bitsy Ticksy," I replied.

Caleb tried to coax the kitten from her hole behind the stove. "All right, I give up. I think that's a good place for her to live. We'll see she has a box for a home." He stood and left for his forge area.

In all the excitement over Ticksy, feeding the stage occupants had taken a back seat. They stood in the open fortress doorway. "Come in," called Ben. Our two traveling companions followed him to the eating area.

I gave Jedediah a quick hug, went into my bedroom to pull off my traveling clothes, and joined Ben in serving our guests. Jedediah, Pa, and the other workers hurried to harness fresh mules for the stage.

After hitching the new animals for the trip to Fort Chadbourne, they joined the others at the table. I listened to the banter of the men as Ben and I served them. Conditions on the stage route remained the favorite topic.

"Ben, I love being back to my normal life here at The Pinery," I whispered.

"There's a difference, Gracie. Now you're a married lady."

I looked over at Jedediah. Away from Hurricane, he'd changed so much from the young man who'd kept me from falling in the mud puddle in Memphis.

Ah, Memphis, that seemed years ago. Paul and Press were forgotten in the rush of my deepening love for Jedediah. I looked forward to our future lives together.

❀ 32 ❀

Floating, white puffy clouds blocked the sun as Wooly, Ticksy, and I ran outside to pour soapy water out of a bucket after washing the dirty laundry in the kitchen area. They played amongst the rocks nearby, scratching at a frog hopping to avoid them.

"You two pranksters better leave the frog alone, or you'll be sick to your stomach."

I laughed as they jumped higher than the frog. Wooly and Ticksy had become inseparable in the weeks since I returned home from El Paso.

Noises from the road caused both of my pets to stop and look in the direction of a horse walking toward the fortress. This allowed the poor frog to escape. I often heard sounds at the front of my home so I did not hurry to check out the steps behind me.

When I straightened to look, Hurricane Bailey dismounted his horse, tying his reins to the hitching post in front of the stockade. At first, I couldn't believe my eyes. He looked my way and gave me one of his leering grins. I couldn't mistake that smile.

"Mr. Bailey, we weren't expectin' you," I managed to say.

"Missy Tipton, I'm lookin' for Jedediah. Do you know where he is?" He came straight to the point with exactly the question I hoped he wouldn't ask.

"He's out with the stock at the grazin' area."

"Where's that?"

What could I do but tell him? I walked over and pointed at the other side of The Pinery to an obvious trail leading into the bushes. "Follow the trampled grass and you will find him with the stock."

Without so much as a thank you, he turned on his heel and headed in the direction I indicated.

I stood and watched his disappearing back, wondering what changes his coming would bring to The Pinery. Would the peace Jedediah and I had experienced since our return from El Paso be broken by this old scheming man?

The clouds passed on and the noonday sun beat down. A sudden cold chill made goose bumps on my arms. Walking back inside to the kitchen area, I absentmindedly wrung extra water out of the drying clothes hanging on my clothesline. I wanted to go to Jedediah and stick my nose squarely into the conversation I knew he and his father were having. I couldn't. My husband needed to stand strong against whatever his father wanted. Their meeting would be the first test of his promise to me.

"Ben, I'm goin' to the spring. I won't be gone long." I needed some space to think. As I walked to the spring, I barely noticed the coming colors of autumn around me, and the tumbling waters didn't soothe me as usual. I remembered Pa's words earlier. He'd said it might be hard to get Jedediah away from his father. Was I naïve enough to think I'd done it? No. Jedediah had promised, and I believed him. Working with his father couldn't be a choice. As usual, I talked to the spring. "Gracie's makin' a mountain out of a molehill." The water gurgled in reply.

Jedediah and his father didn't appear until supper. My father's shocked expression informed everyone of his surprise at seeing the elder Bailey, but Pa welcomed him graciously. After all, Hurricane Bailey had become my father-in-law when I married his son.

"I hear my son is married." Mr. Bailey said after coming over to the stove to see what was cooking in the pots.

"Almost three weeks ago," I replied. For some reason I couldn't think of another thing to say. He stalked off in my embarrassing silence.

Thank goodness my father broke the quietness. "Hurricane, what are you doin' here?" I wanted to know the answer to that question myself. Pa's directness caused Hurricane to answer sharply.

"Well, it's not fer socializin', that's fer sure."

"Pa's goin' to work west of here," volunteered Jedediah, looking at me. He didn't smile like he always did.

"That's sure true. Some sections of road through New Mexico into Arizona need extra work, and my division superintendent asked fer volunteers to help. Injuns and stuff make the area dangerous. They'll pay extra. I said I'd help. I knew Jedediah had come here, and my boss agreed we'd be a good team to get the work done."

I found my tongue. "Jedediah's not going. He has a job at The Pinery, and he promised." I met my husband's eyes and read there the awful truth I didn't want to see. He quickly dropped his eyes to his plate.

"Missy, you may be married to him, but he's still my son. He still does what I tell him. Mark my words."

I held my tongue. I didn't plan on having an argument here at the supper table. Jedediah and I would talk later.

I turned my back on the group at the table and on Mr. Bailey's smirk. He took my silence as submission. The only time I turned around, I noticed my father looking at me. His face showed his concern for my problem.

After the dishes were washed, I headed for my room. I thought Jedediah would follow me. He didn't. He didn't appear until it was dark outside. By that time I was so angry, I couldn't speak. I stared at him, sputtering.

"Gracie, don't be mad. I jest couldn't refuse."

"What do you mean? You promised me! That was a condition of our marriage. You know that."

"I tried to refuse. He needs me to help him."

"Jedediah, he's a grown man. He can fend for himself. You have a job here. What about it?"

"Cephas will help until I get back. I promise I won't be gone long."

"How long is long?"

"I'm not sure, but I promise to come—"

"Your promises don't mean anything. Not any more. Not to me." I started to cry.

"Don't cry, Gracie."

"I will cry, if I want to," I said between sobs.

Jedediah came over to put his arms around me.

"Don't touch me! Get out! I don't want you in here."

"But Gracie…"

"Get out." I heard his footsteps leave the fortress. If he'd made any progress to break away from his father, the steps forward were gone. I threw my aching body on my bed and cried myself to sleep.

I don't know where he went, but he didn't come back to my room that night. The next morning, he and Hurricane were gone.

If someone had dropped me in a bottomless pit, I couldn't have been more lost. My perfect, happy life had disappeared, destroyed with Mr. Bailey's appearance.

Ben took over the cooking duties the following day. Later, I found out my pa had asked him to help out.

"Thanks, Pa, for lettin' Ben cook today."

"Gracie, did Jedediah tell you when he'll be back?"

"No, we had a big argument and didn't talk before he left."

"I don't like the idea of him being with Hurricane. All the news I've heard from New Mexico and Arizona Territory says the work area isn't safe, although I'm sure Bailey will head a crew of several workers."

"He promised he'd not work with Hurricane again," I cried.

"Blood is thicker than water, Gracie."

"You don't have to rub it in, Pa."

"I wasn't trying to."

"It seemed like you were."

He held up his hands. "Gracie, I know you're upset, so I'm goin' to walk off. Don't say anymore. Let's leave this alone for a while."

Pa walked away. I sat down at the kitchen table, banged my fists on its top, and put my head in my heads. What was wrong with me, fightin' with Pa? We never argued.

"Gracie, is there anythin' I can do?" asked timid Ben.

"No," I answered, my voice muffled as I spoke. "Only time will take care of my problem."

"You don't like your new father-in-law."

"No, he drinks a lot, and he's a mean drunk."

The weary days struggled on and I with them—my emotions as tangled as my hair. I'd never had to depend on the honesty or trustworthiness of another human being except Pa. After coming home from the war, he'd never let me down again—unless I counted his plans for the job with Butterfield.

For the first time in my life, I couldn't or wouldn't turn to Pa. I was alone without my familiar anchor.

Just when I'd started to trust and love him completely, Jedediah had hurt me terribly.

Trips to Pine Springs didn't lessen my heartache. Even Wooly and Ticksy didn't understand. I needed another person to talk to—one I could trust.

REBA RHYNE

❧ 33 ❧

I didn't expect my life to be normal again, and I didn't know what kind of reception I'd give Jedediah when he came home.

On November ninth, Ben and I finished with the dinner dishes, and I walked outside to look at the clouds appearing behind El Capitan. I stood there, arms crossed in the cool morning air, looking toward its enormous rock face. We would have rain tonight. I was sure of that, although I remembered Pa saying there'd be snow on top of Guadalupe Peak—and soon. Behind me, I heard the men taking the stock to graze.

Pa and I had arrived at Pine Springs a little over two months ago, and so much had happened since then. Behind me there was no sound of stone being laid. The stonemasons had finished their work over the weekend and left for another job on Sunday morning. The sound of the mud hoes scraping in their wooden mud boxes and men working, jarring stone on stone as they laid The Pinery's walls was gone. It was strange to hear so much silence.

Moo-ooo... The sound in the desert was no more expected than church bells. I turned to see where it came from.

"Press!" I cried, shocked to see him, running to tell him hello.

He dismounted his horse and hurried to meet me, giving me a big hug and kiss on the forehead. "Gracie, you're a welcome sight for my eyes. I've missed you so much."

He would have continued to hold me, but I disengaged from his arms. I smiled at him. "What took you so long?"

"My father and I were buildin' onto our home, and then we needed to move the cattle to another pasture. I couldn't get away until last week."

"I see you brought the cow as promised."

"Yes, with Bossy you'll have all the milk you need."

To cover my confusion and feelings at his coming, I went over to pet the cow, putting my head on the soft hair of her forehead, and looking into her liquid brown eyes.

"She's very gentle and should have a calf in the spring." Press came close to me. I could feel the heat off his body.

"Press!" My father, coming from the pasture trail, interrupted the intense moment between us. He came forward and warmly shook Press's hand. "I've been expecting you for several weeks."

"And I've been busy at the Glory B." Press said this to my father, but he kept looking at me.

My father noticed. "Come. Let me show you The Pinery." Pa took Press in tow, and I didn't see him again until supper.

By that time, Ben had milked the cow and prepared a cake for dessert. "Thank you for the cow," he told Press.

"I promised Gracie, and I keep my promises," Press told Ben, shaking his hand. He turned in my direction. I was hurrying around the kitchen area, trying to stay busy. I wondered if his comment about promises meant Pa had told him I was married—and that my husband hadn't kept his promises.

"Sit down. Ben and I have food ready to eat." I met his eyes briefly. I thought I saw reproach and sorrow in them. I didn't look at him again as the crew at the fortress ate their night meal. Tonight they ate early, because they intended to go hunting when the sun went down.

"Do you think it'll rain on us?" asked Caleb.

"Might," returned Pa. "But if we don't see any game, we'll come back early. No use in gettin' soaked to the bone."

"It's goin' to be cold," Cephas added. "I'm taking my heavy coat."

"Ah, you're just a baby anyway." Caleb chided his younger brother.

"You think so, *little* brother." Sitting on the kitchen chair, Cephas straightened himself to his full height. He might have been younger, but he was taller than his brother.

"Yeah, I think so. Guess that's why Ma said to take care of you."

"Don't—"

But Pa interrupted them at that moment. "Okay boys. I believe we'll never establish which one of you is the strongest, tallest, oldest or whatever. It doesn't really matter to me or anyone else here. What's important is you're both hard, capable workers. I appreciate you both."

"Aw, we was only joshing each other," said Caleb. "Makes us realize we're both still alive. We've actually quit some of our foolishness since coming here to work. Haven't we, little brother?"

"There he goes again." Cephas threw up his hands, stood, and left the table.

Everyone laughed as he disappeared into the twilight. His abrupt departure signaled an end to supper. My table soon emptied.

Press came over. "Gracie, you promised me a walk in the woods when I came. I'm goin' to claim that trip in the morning." He spoke in a low tone full of pathos, turned without my response, and left behind the others. Where was he going? I guessed he must be sleeping in Pa's tent tonight. Although we had rooms for visitors within the fortress, could it be Press didn't feel comfortable sleeping in such close quarters to me?

I dawdled after breakfast, hoping Press didn't remember his claim on my morning. He reappeared while Ben and I dried the dishes. "Are you ready, Gracie?"

I wasn't ready, but his tone of voice meant this walk and talk was inevitable. "Yes, let me get a light jacket." I went into my bedroom and put on the navy blue coat I'd hung over my rocker the night before.

We walked out of the fortress, and I led the way toward Pine Springs. The night rain brought cool air with it. The trail was wet, and leaves and pine needles stuck to the bottom of our shoes.

Press broke the awkward silence. "Gracie, I remember the talks about establishin' your home here at The Pinery. You couldn't wait to get here. Has your home at The Pinery been all you hoped it would be?"

The direct question and opening meant I could tell him of my love of the area and my great disappointment in Jedediah. I decided not to mention my husband but talk of the Guadalupe Mountains. It was less hurtful.

"Press, the minute I saw the Guadalupes I loved them. No matter where I am, I can look and see El Capitan. He's an anchor for these high hills and for me."

The trail widened so he could walk abreast of me.

"I thought you would. You have a capacity to become endeared to your surroundings, and you like nature—animals, trees and flowers. Have you noticed the changing colors around you? Yesterday, I saw the yellow leaves of the aspens as I approached your home. They make ragged golden streaks down the mountain hollows."

"Oh, I haven't seen them. I've been so busy working." If I told the truth, my despair and pitying my circumstances had colored my life for several days, blinding me to the earth's changing beauty or anything else of importance.

"Tomorrow, we'll take a ride into the desert, and I'll show you. It'll be like old times on the wagon train."

"I've missed our rides. I've missed a lot of things. Guess I haven't taken the time to enjoy God's beauties around me for a while."

"We'll do that the next few days. I'm staying 'til Saturday, and then I'll head back for the Glory B."

"How's Jorge?"

"He's great. He said to tell you hello and to ask if you've made skillet cornbread. I think the food we ate last night answered that question."

"It was much better with Bossy's milk in it. Now I can make fresh butter and buttermilk. Ben's a great help with cooking our food. Without him, I'd never get out of the fortress for walks."

"I saw Wooly. She's really growing."

"She and Ticksy are constant companions."

"Where'd you get the cat—not out here in the desert?"

"From Franklin. Or El Paso…whichever name you want to call it."

"It's turning into quite a town, isn't it? Why did you go there?"

It seemed every word we'd spoken was pointing to this question. I was sure he already knew the answer.

"Press, I'm married." I felt tears sting my eyes.

"Your father told me. Why?" Press stopped walking and looked at me. His eyes bored into mine, trying to retrieve the answer to his question. He reached to catch my tears before they ran down my face.

I wanted to rush into his arms—sure he would comfort me, but I heard the hurt in his voice, and my heart answered by jumping in my chest.

We reached the springs, and I delayed my answer. "The water's cool. Let's have a drink and then we'll talk." I took the copper cup I'd carried with me, knelt down, and filled it with water. I pushed it in his direction. Press drank deeply of its contents as he checked the surroundings by the gurgling stream of water. He handed the cup back to me.

Dipping more cool water from the spring, I took a few sips and threw the rest into the woods. I walked away and sat on the pine needles around the spring. "Do you remember me telling you about the young man who saved my life on the wagon train?"

"Yes, you didn't supply much information about him when I asked."

"I married him."

"You didn't tell me you loved him. Do you?"

"Yes, I think I do, but one condition of my marryin' him was for him to stay away from his drunken father. I wouldn't have married him if he hadn't vowed to do that. No one can compete with Mr. Bailey."

"Hurricane Bailey? Is that right? The wagon train scout?"

"Yes. Jedediah's father came last week, and he went with him to help on his pa's road crew for the stage lines. He had a job workin' right here at The Pinery. He left it and me to follow his pa. Jedediah's job is to make sure Hurricane Bailey doesn't drink himself to death. I think that's why his pa wants him around—or maybe it's to bury him if he does." I sat on a rock with my elbows on my knees, resting my forehead on my open palms.

"I would have come to you, Gracie," Press said gently. I heard the intensity, the passion in his voice. "I wish you weren't married."

"But I am."

I looked at Press. He would have said more, but he didn't. He came over and sat near me. "Life has many strange twists and turns, Gracie." He seemed defeated and tired.

"My only hope is that someday Jedediah will be strong enough to pull away from his father. I thought he might be headed in that direction when Mr. Bailey showed up. I hoped he'd become—"

Suddenly Press clutched my arm. "Gracie, I hear someone coming down the canyon. Maybe several horses." Press looked around. "Hurry! Up here!"

He pulled me up the hillside behind the spring into the middle of some scrub brush. "Be quiet. Don't say a word and don't move."

"Who—"

Press put his finger to his lips. "Shssh." He put his arm tightly around me.

We sat there completely silent, our eyes riveted on the trail below us. I heard the unmistakable sound of horses' footsteps and rocks falling up the canyon. I smelled the horses before I saw them.

Whoever headed in our direction had followed the trail down from Guadalupe Peak. I wondered if you could see the rock walls of The Pinery from there. We didn't wait long before we found out the sounds came from a party of Indians.

"Mescalero Apache," mouthed Press silently.

The party paused to let their horses drink but didn't dismount.

One pointed to water still drying on a rock. This caused a brief stir, but they didn't investigate the sign of a recent spring visitor. If they had, I feared they would discover Press and me, so violently were my knees shaking.

One of the Indians gave a command, and the others followed him toward The Pinery.

When they were out of sight, I asked Press, "What were they doing here?"

"I don't know. They might be checking out your station, or it could be a hunting party. Gracie, you're shaking." He tightened his arm around my shoulder.

He sat so close with his eyes on mine. His face moved toward me. He would have kissed me, but at the last moment, I turned my lips away, brushing his cheek in the process.

"I'm a married woman, Press. I don't want you to lose respect for me."

"My fault, Gracie. Forgive me."

He stood and pulled me to my feet. "We'll wait another few minutes and follow along the hillside. We can't take the trail. They might come back this way."

Press and I picked our way gingerly along the mountainside. This was no small matter because the land was steep and rocky. We grabbed at bushes to steady our progress, trying not to make a lot of noise.

When we were perched on the hillside above my home, we found the Indians were not in sight, but the stock from the stockade could be clearly seen grazing in the distance.

"We'll wait and see if they reappear," said Press.

They did—to the west, following a rough, little-used path under the face of El Capitan. The scouting party was leaving the area.

"Do you think they'll come back?"

"Depends on what they were looking for?"

"We need to go tell Pa." I urged my companion off the hill. We hurried down, slipping and sliding on the wet hillside.

Until Press left on Saturday, we spent time riding each morning or hiking the mountain trails of the Guadalupe. He pointed out the maple trees whose leaves turned from yellow to orange in the fall. We passed ash and oak trees on the slopes, and I commented that the oaks needed to grow up. They were babies compared to the ones in Tennessee. We both laughed. Laughing felt good.

One day we started before sunrise and rode our horses all the way to Guadalupe Peak, passing a stand of Douglas fir on the way to the barren, rocky top. Press led the way. I could trust him, and this made me acutely aware of his presence. The confidence I had in him did much to calm my fears and lifted my spirits.

As we sat side by side on the mountaintop, he pointed in the direction of the Glass Mountains. "I wish we could see them from here, but the Apache and Davis Mountains rise before them."

"Where is Fort Davis?"

"East and south of the Apache. Why do you ask?"

"Because Captain Tom Stephens and the Mounted Riflemen often visit The Pinery."

"I know Captain Stephens. He's a good soldier."

"Do you want to eat our picnic here?"

"Yes." We dismounted and sat in the cold blowing wind, eating the snack Ben had prepared.

When Press got ready to leave, I was sorry to see him go, but he indicated a cattle drive was possible in late winter to the new gold fields in Kansas Territory. "Did you know about the Pike's Peak gold rush?" He asked me. "Someone discovered a mother lode last summer."

"I heard rumors. Why don't you go and find your fortune hunting gold?"

"No, I'll stick with cattle. They bring plenty of cash in the panning fields, and I'll travel new territory. Pa and I intend to get a head start on other drivers. Money isn't everything, Gracie. I'll come by The Pinery on the way north to check on you."

He mounted his horse to leave.

"Gracie, if you need me, write a letter. I'll come to you." He spurred his horse and rode to the intersection of the main road. Turning in his saddle, he waved goodbye and blew me a kiss. Then he disappeared down the road.

❦ 34 ❦

Three weeks passed with no word from Jedediah. Why would he even bother after my last words to him? The air was colder and the days were shorter. The stage from the east arrived at dark and the one from the west much later than sundown. The month of December came without notoriety and with it cold, windy nights.

Since their tents didn't provide protection from the cold, Pa, Ben, Caleb, and Cephas moved inside the compound and slept on cots near the fireplace, keeping a warm, toasty fire burning during the night. The men took their canvas shelters down and stored them in the blacksmith area along with smaller pieces of the same material used to keep the sun from baking their heads when they relaxed outside the tents in the fall. Other than this move inside the fortress, everything else remained the same around my home.

For some reason, I was more exhausted than usual. Each night when my head hit the pillow, I fell immediately into a deep sleep. After one particularly grueling day, I sat in my rocking chair in my bedroom. I was too tired to even get up and wash my face as I usually did by splashing cold water from the ewer and basin Press had given me. I fell asleep in the rocker. Jolted awake by the noise of someone putting wood into the fireplace, I crept into bed fully clothed.

The terrifying dream did not come often, but it came tonight. I sat on the top of our barn in Nashville. I could feel the locking grooves in the new metal rooftop. A horrible blackness surrounded me, and I couldn't see the ground below. How I got there, I had no idea. Neither did I know how to get down, but get down I must. Alone, scared and shaking, I searched for handholds in the darkness, touching the cold, slick metal and reaching blindly for anything to steady me as I descended.

My fingers slipped and with their failure, the sickening realization of sliding, sliding downward faster and faster. The friction of the metal made my skin warm to the touch as I bumped along. Then I plunged into the air, falling, screaming loudly, and coming down with a thud against the cold hard ground.

"Gracie, Gracie..." A woman's comforting voice came to me in the black darkness. "You're all right, sweetheart." Her arms surrounded me, holding me tight. She rocked me back and forth and I clung to her, needing her presence, wanting her nearby.

"Mama, I'm scared. I dreamed of falling."

"And you were falling." She laughed softly, her warm breath brushing the side of my face. "Right out of bed." Although her belly was round with another child, she gently picked me up, and placed me back beneath my warm covers.

"Gracie?" Pa's concerned voice broke through the semi-darkness, jarring me awake in my stone bedroom. "Gracie, it's Pa. Are you all right?"

From my position on the cold floor, I could see his figure in the moonlit frame of the doorway. He had pushed aside the curtain flap that served as a door.

"Yes, Pa, I fell out of bed again, but not as far as usual."

"Go back to sleep. Everything's fine."

"Goodnight, Pa."

Everything's fine, he'd said. How could I believe his words?

During the night, I'd made a warm hollow in my bed. I shivered as I climbed back into it. I lay there restless, tossing and turning, trying to find a more comfortable spot amongst the feathers.

Hoping to relieve the anxiety the nightmare stirred in my thoughts, I said a quick prayer for Jedediah's safety and let the dream jog my memory of Mama—her soft skin, her voice. Thoughts of her helped soothe my unease. I turned over and cried into my pillow—for her...and for Jedediah.

I hoped my husband would be back soon. I worried about his presence with Mr. Bailey on the road. In his father's drunken stupor, there'd be only Jedediah and the rest of the crew to help if an emergency occurred.

An hour passed before sleep finally returned.

During the next day, the dream haunted me as I went about my chores, making my steps even heavier. When I looked in my bedroom mirror, I saw bags under my eyes.

Last night's weird screams had scared the living daylights out of Ben, Caleb, and Cephas. Each of them showed concern for me.

"Gracie, are you all right?" asked Caleb. "I heard you scream."

"Yes, I have a bad nightmare on occasion. You'd think I'm too old to fall out of bed. I'm all right."

He went away not quite reassured.

I didn't sit in my rocker that night, but climbed straight into bed. The dream didn't reoccur.

❦ 35 ❦

The following Monday, I heard a wagon pull up to the front of The Pinery, but I didn't go to greet it. After breakfast, I put on my heavy coat to take my customary morning walk. Instead of going to Pine Springs, I decided to try out a new path along the base of the mountain.

Later, when Pa came in from jackrabbit hunting just in time for dinner, I couldn't believe my eyes. David Ormand was with him!

"Mr. Ormand, why are you here?" I gave him a big hug and kiss of welcome. "I thought you'd be in California with your brother."

"Gracie, I went to California, but when I got there I couldn't find him." He turned to look at Pa. "He must not have gotten my letter saying I was comin'. I searched for several days, but I couldn't find one bit of information as to his whereabouts. I recalled your invitation to come here, and here I am. You look pale, Gracie."

"Aw, I'm all right."

"Are you sure? I see bags under your eyes. That's not like the Gracie I know."

"She's been through a lot lately, David."

"What's happened?"

"We'll talk over dinner. I believe Ben and Gracie are ready for us to eat."

273

"What route did you take from California?" I asked as they seated themselves at my table. I had an ulterior motive for asking.

"South through Los Angeles to San Diego, and then I drove east through Arizona and New Mexico territory, ending here. The road is clearly recognizable, and there are crews workin' on the rougher places."

"Gracie's husband, Jedediah Bailey, is on one of those crews."

"Husband! Why Gracie, what have you done? Who is he, and when did you get married?

"Do you remember the young man who kept me from falling in the mud puddle in Memphis?"

"Vaguely." Mr. Ormand snapped his fingers, recognition coming to his eyes. "So that's where I'd seen the two men I passed on the road comin' here. In Memphis and again in Fort Smith. The young man's drunken father was the one threatenin' you with harm when you took up for his son."

"The father's name is Hurricane Bailey. Gracie married his son, Jedediah."

"I didn't gain a good impression of the older man on the two occasions I saw him."

"You were right in your notion. Hurricane became our scout for the wagon train. He stayed mostly to himself, because he got drunk each night. He exercises complete control over Jedediah by threatenin' and abusin' him. Jedediah's love for Gracie enabled him to break free of his pa. Or so we thought."

"It's hard to break an abuser's control. That's been my experience more 'n once."

"We left Jedediah at Fort Chadbourne. He vowed he'd come to The Pinery and marry Gracie. When he did come with Reverend Dixon, she made him promise not to work with Hurricane again."

"He promised and Gracie married him," guessed Mr. Ormand.

"Yes, and he broke his promise," Pa replied.

"Mr. Ormand, I was adamant about Jedediah breaking all ties with his pa, or I wouldn't have married him."

"I'm sorry, Gracie."

"Where did you see Jedediah and his pa?"

"In New Mexico close to the Arizona border. The men were stretching tents and cutting firewood getting ready to start work with their crew."

I saw the look Mr. Ormand gave my father and wanted to ask more questions.

"Gracie, David has agreed to take on Jedediah's work load until he returns."

"I'm glad you're staying Mr. Ormand. The twins will be relieved to have someone to help."

The conversation at the table turned to tending the animals. Ben and I served dessert. We placed on the table slices of the pound cake Mr. Ormand had eaten with us the first day he'd joined us on the trail months ago.

"It's still good, Gracie," he complimented me, obviously remembering that day.

I was glad Mr. Ormand had joined us at The Pinery. I could share with him, knowing my concerns would be kept private.

The following morning I awoke to the smell of fresh coffee and frying bacon. I smiled in spite of my troubles. Mr. Ormand hadn't changed. Breakfast would be ready as soon as I washed my face, cleaned my teeth, and stepped into the morning twilight.

"Good morning, Gracie. Us old-timers are cooking breakfast from now on. You can sleep in and get a few more minutes rest. Maybe those bags under your eyes will go away."

I walked over to the fireplace and warmed my cold hands. "I'll put the dishes and silverware on the table."

"No, no," said Ben. He rushed to the shelf where the items were stored. "You're our guest. Sit down and enjoy your break from work. We insist."

My days of preparing breakfast were over as long as Mr. Ormand remained at The Pinery. I took advantage of their offer, sleeping later and pulling my breakfast plate out of the oven warmer.

I kept wondering about Jedediah. Being anxious about him every waking moment hadn't changed except for a brief few days after we were married. He needed me to help him be strong. My distress became a heavy weight I lugged around day after day.

Five weeks after my husband left, I decided to tell Mr. Ormand of my frustrations.

In the early afternoon, I headed for the pasture where the stock spent most of the day. Three months of trampling by our animal's hooves clearly defined the path where I walked. Tall grasses beside the trail were vast and thick. Pa said they'd never be exhausted if we kept moving the stock from one grazing area to another. The distance from the fortress kept increasing each week. We would have worried about Indian attacks but our station was in the open. For any attackers, a day raid offered no surprise.

Mr. Ormand took Bossy and Wooly with the mules to feed with the other animals. Ordinarily, if Ticksy wasn't with me or sleeping behind the stove, she followed Wooly, hiding under bushes, and scratching at bugs and lizards in the tall prairie grass. She still had a lot of growing to complete before tackling one of the prairie rats. Fortunately, we hadn't seen many.

I heard my friend before I saw him, singing in a clear tenor voice, "*I once was lost, but now I'm found. Was blind but now I see.*" The words were from "Amazing Grace," a song often sung at my former church in Nashville. My name had come from this old hymn. Amazing Gracie. I laughed. I didn't feel so amazing today.

Wooly heard me and came running toward me, expecting a lump of sugar. I disappointed her. Today I had none. Other things crowded my mind. I gave her a matter-of-fact pat on the head.

"Mr. Ormand, where are you?"

"Over here, Gracie," he called. "I'm checking on a mule's hoof." He kept humming bars of his favorite song. "The animal seems to be limping."

"Do you have time to talk to me?"

"I always have time for you." He stood where I could see him. "Come where I am. There's a large flat rock at the edge of the desert." When I came close to him, he asked, "Can you guess how this boulder got here?" He motioned for me to sit.

"Not really."

"Me either. Sit down." He patted the gray boulder and waited until I settled beside him. I saw his mother's Bible and a brush for grooming the animals on the rock behind. "I think I can guess what you want to talk about. Since arriving, I've become increasingly concerned for your health. Your pa and I have had several talks about this subject."

I paused before saying with passion, "How could I be so stupid?"

"Now Gracie, don't blame yourself. You felt a need to help this young man."

"Pa warned me, and I didn't listen. I thought Jedediah would change. I'm so hurt."

"And he may yet change. Don't give up on him."

"It's been five weeks since he left. I haven't received a word. I don't know if I'm more miserable or annoyed at him. You'd think I'd be over him breaking his promise by now, but I'm not."

"You won't be over this trouble until you resolve it, and this won't happen until Jedediah comes back. You need to talk to him face to face. You say you haven't heard from Jedediah, have you written to him? Someone has to give first."

"I've been thinking about doing that."

"Then write the letter. Clear the air as much as you can, and tell him how you feel. But also, tell him that you love him. You do love him?"

"Yes, I do. That's another question I want to ask you. Does love always hurt?"

Mr. Ormand laughed. "I'll tell you what I think, and you form your own opinion. Is that all right?"

"Sure, I trust your judgment and view."

"Pure love doesn't hurt, Gracie. But this earth doesn't know pure love, not since Adam and Eve sinned in the Garden of Eden. They were the only ones to know pure, non-hurting love. That is, until they made the wrong decision. I've often wondered what a true give-and-take relationship—similar to theirs—was like in a perfect world. You and I both know the other kind. To find sacrificial love on the part of both parties would be an astonishing discovery. Maybe shocking is a better word. Human pride stands in our way."

"Human pride? What do you mean?"

"It's not humbling ourselves and instead, accepting the fact that even though we may be right, that's not what's important."

"What is important?"

"Why, it's your love for each other. This love helps you to work through your problems—give and take. Even those we think are insurmountable, like Hurricane Bailey."

I put my arms around my knees, drawing them off the ground and rocking on my backside. I felt better already. "Hurricane Bailey is a mountain of a problem."

Mr. Ormand smiled. "Yes, he is. But God can move—or remove—mountains, Gracie. Why don't you ask Him to help?"

"I have...sort of. I'll try harder. Surely Jedediah will be home by Christmas."

Mr. Ormand didn't answer but cocked his ear toward the main road. The sound indicated several people were approaching.

"Listen Gracie, I think it's horses, and they've turned into The Pinery. I don't hear the sound of wagon wheels. We'd better check on our visitors since the others are cutting firewood."

"The animals..."

"They're okay. I've staked them out to eat."

I followed Mr. Ormand back to the fortress. We soon learned the racket was from mounted infantry—Captain Tom Stevens and his troop from Fort Davis.

I walked forward. "Captain Stevens, it's good to see you."

He dismounted his horse, a fine-looking animal with graceful lines and dark brown color, taking off his gloves as he approached. I noticed his boots were dusty. "Mrs. Bailey, we meet again."

We shook hands.

"May I introduce you to Mr. David Ormand? He tends our stock here at The Pinery."

"Mr. Ormand," the Captain said in a deep voice, bowing slightly at the waist, "you're just the man I need to talk to. Is your father here, Mrs. Bailey?"

"No, he's cutting firewood on the mountain."

"Tell me where, and I'll send men to fetch him."

After the directions were given, I invited the soldiers inside the fortress. "We have plenty of cold water, cow's milk, or hot coffee." At least thirty soldiers made themselves at home inside the kitchen—some sat in chairs or on benches made by Caleb and Cephas. Others stood or squatted in the area, which became a sea of blue uniforms speckled with yellow insignia. Each had a government issued tin cup to be filled.

Pa arrived by the time I was serving the men. He walked over and shook hands with the Captain.

"Jay, it's good to see you. I have some news you need to know."

"Captain, please sit down."

"Jay, I'd like for my men to bivouac here at The Pinery. Will you suggest a site?"

"Of course. The stonemasons are gone. The area has been cleared of brush. You can camp there." Pa provided the Captain with directions.

The officer arose, walked over to his second in command, and gave him instructions on establishing their temporary home. After the men left, the officer sat back down.

"I came to warn you. We've had a rash of incidents with the Apache lately, regarding the stealing of stock from settlers and from some of the Butterfield Stations. You need to be careful where you place your stock, and guard them carefully while they're out to pasture."

"Where are the Apache raiding?"

"Not so much east toward Fort Chadbourne. We rode here from the fort and everything seemed quiet. There haven't been problems around you, but the activity is moving in this direction. Most of the problems are sporadic, so the where or when can never be determined for certain."

"Have our people had trouble around Franklin?"

"West of there, and one incident occurred at Hueco Tanks. They're hitting the most affluent settlers and stations. Yours certainly qualifies."

"Is anyone getting hurt?"

"Two people at Hueco Tanks were shot with arrows. One eventually died from the infection caused by the wound. Mostly, they just take what's in the stockade and ride."

Pa's questions kept coming. "When do the attacks happen?"

"Early morning before sunrise or late night are the preferred times, but some have occurred in broad daylight."

"The only Indians we've seen around here are a few stragglers. None of them would cause us harm. We use a large area for our animals to graze. We'll have a hard time protectin' our stock."

"I plan to stay in the region two or three days and move on. Maybe our being here will deter anyone from bothering you."

"Are you headed back to Fort Davis?"

"Yes, we're headed home for a breather and Christmas."

"Your presence will be welcomed. Maybe you can give us some advice on how to better protect ourselves here at The Pinery. I'd be grateful."

"How about in the morning?" The Captain stood to leave.

"We have sleeping quarters inside the fortress, Captain Stevens, if you'd like to take advantage of them."

"Thank you, Jay, but my men will have my tent assembled. I'll stay with them."

"Come and eat some of Gracie and Ben's cookin' for supper. I understand we have fresh buffalo on the menu, supplied by another Butterfield station."

"Now that, I'll be happy to do."

After he left, I asked Pa, "Do you think we'll have trouble with the Apache?" Except for the incident at Pine Springs when Press and I hid from the scouting party, we never saw more than one or two at a time.

"I hope not, little girl, but we must always prepare for the worst. Tomorrow we'll have target practice with everyone living here at The Pinery. I'll also assign fight stations for those inside our walls. Best to be organized if an attack happens."

❦ 36 ❧

Three days after Captain Stevens and his troop rode south for Fort Davis and the stages had come through, all was quiet within the rock fortress. I put on my nightgown and went to bed, snuggling deep into the feathers because it was cold outside.

The first indication I had of trouble was Caleb's yell and a loud gunshot. I immediately climbed out of bed. Running footsteps sounded past my doorway, and men's voices indicated that everyone was awake and headed toward their designated portholes in the fortress with guns in hand.

I grabbed Pa's revolver and some ammunition. Throwing my long overcoat over my shoulders, I went outside into partially moonlit darkness and frosty air. Glancing upward, I noticed spotty clouds floating in the sky as I headed toward my assigned hole in the wall of my rock home.

"Caleb," Pa's voice boomed. "What's goin' on?" For several nights, Caleb and Cephas had bedded down on sweet smelling hay in separate corners of the stockade, guarding the animals inside.

"I shot one over here—Apache, I guess—trying to open the stockade door from the inside. Musta crawled over the wall. He's dead."

"Have you been able to tell if there are others and how many?"

Caleb didn't have to answer. A loud yell followed by several whoops outside in the darkness solved the question. We were being attacked by a raiding party.

"Everyone spread out at the portholes and shoot anythin' that moves," shouted my excited father. I did as he ordered, continuing on to my station at the opposite end from the stockade, wondering if I could shoot another human if I had to.

Several minutes of riding the cleared space in front of our building didn't get the results the Indians wanted. We had guns and slits in our rock walls. They had bows and arrows that couldn't penetrate the holes. We were snug in the fortress. They were exposed on their swift moving ponies.

"I don't think we've shot another." I heard Mr. Ormand tell Pa and Ben.

"No," Pa said. "Aiming through our deep portholes is almost impossible. We're in a standoff. If they're to take our stock, another strategy will have to be worked out."

I knew Pa was right.

"They'll surely figure something to help their situation. Everyone, keep your eyes and ears open," yelled Pa over the racket.

"Don't we have two ladders the stonemasons left behind?" asked Ben.

"Sure," responded Mr. Ormand. "If we get them, we can see over the top of the walls—maybe we'll be able to check on their activities."

The two men hurried for the ladders.

The air around me filled with acrid gun smoke as loud reports from our Sharps rifles rang out in the air. Coupled with hollering Indians, horse's hooves beating the ground, and yelling men within the fortress, the racket filled my ears.

That's when I noticed a different smell. I sniffed the air just as Ben returned with the ladder. He raised it against the front wall.

I stopped him. "Ben wait."

"What is it, Gracie."

"The smell…"

Besides having a stomach that liked copious amounts of food, my sense of smell was acute. The stench wasn't the oak or maple we burned in our fireplace.

"What is that, Ben?" I called as the different aroma tickled my nose.

"Pine smoke!" yelled Ben.

"Caleb," shouted Pa. "Is the stockade on fire?"

"Yes, outside on the east end."

Fire burned outside the stockade. Wooly, Bossy, and Ticksy were inside! I knew my little lamb and cat must be frantic at the noise and smoke. I had no idea what a cow would think.

"Pa, I'm goin' to check on Wooly and Ticksy," I yelled. I didn't wait for his reply as I ran across the courtyard. I headed for the low door into the stockade, thinking Wooly would be burned to a crisp with her long hair. What could I do to protect her?

Stumbling around the blacksmith area, I brushed the stack of canvas from the tents and overhead sun screens. Grabbing one of the smaller pieces, which had a length of rope attached, I fell down on all fours and crawled under the fortress wall into the pine-lined stockade. Choking smoke met me on the other side, and flames licked through the wood walls.

I called for Wooly—not loudly but softly, thinking my screaming voice wouldn't help her situation.

"Gracie," I heard Caleb say. "Go back on the other side. We're trying to calm the stock and put out the fire."

I could barely see the twins as they beat at the fire with their blankets. Through the tears, now running from my smoke-filled eyes, they looked like they were dancing in the flickering firelight. I lurched into the watering trough and wondered why they didn't use it to quench the fire. "Use the water," I called. I pulled a headscarf from the pocket of my coat, dipped it in the cold water and placed the cloth over my nose and mouth.

Heaven knows I wanted to do exactly like Caleb ordered and return to the fortress. If the fire burned a good portion of the stockade wall, we'd be good targets for the people riding their horses outside, and they rarely missed with their bow and arrows.

"I've got to find Wooly," I replied.

"She's with us and she's all right."

I turned around to crawl under the wall as two flaming arrows imbedded themselves into the ground with a sickening thud, igniting the dry hay strewn over the dirt. Immediately, sparks and burning hay shards flew skyward. Gut-wrenching fear rose in me, and like a mama hen protecting her chicks I needed my babies safe within my arms.

"Wooly, Ticksy," I cried. I needed to get the canvas on Wooly. I batted at a burning piece of hay that lit on the arm of my coat.

"Wooly," I yelled again. She was standing at my feet. She looked ghostly in the flickering fire, her black nose and eyes a blank against her thick, white wool.

I knelt down and did the best I could at tying the rope around her neck. The smoke and flying hay filled the air. I figured if the smoke didn't get you, the flames would. There had to be a way out of our present danger.

I looked around. Across the way, I saw Cephas and Caleb trying to calm the stock. They'd quit trying to put out the fire. How much longer would they be able to stay inside? They couldn't let our animals burn up. When the gate was opened, we would play into the Indian's hands. They'd have our stock, and that was the last we'd see of the riders or the animals.

Ten feet from me on the back wall of the stockade and away from the fire, I saw something that might keep Wooly and I safe from flying sparks. I herded Wooly in the direction of Pa's large whiskey barrel. Throwing the heavy barrel on its side, I climbed in. From its mouth, I watched Caleb throw the stockade door wide open. We'd lost the battle. Our assailants were getting the horses, mules, and Bossy. The animals started out the door into the night.

I tried to pull Wooly in behind me. I tugged at her, but she took one look at the dark hole where I'd disappeared, planted her feet in the dirt, and decided she wanted nothing to do with it. She kicked at the barrel and me. I loosened my grip on the rope around her neck. Only wanting to escape from chaos, she saw the open stockade door and ran toward safety from the fire behind her.

"Wooly!" She headed toward certain capture or death. "Come back!"

The stockade floor slanted toward the front walls. I struggled to get out of the barrel. In my haste, I caused the barrel to start rolling toward the door. I would be following her into danger. Realizing this, I covered my head with my arms and opened my mouth. High pitched, terrible screaming came forth. Wooly heard the horrible sound pursuing her and dug her heels into the ground, flying out the door of the stockade, with the white canvas flapping around her. To make matters worse as the lamb exited the door, Ticksy jumped on the back of her friend. She often did this, but today it caused Wooly to go wild. She ran erratically into the center of the wild, superstitious bunch outside.

The white canvas waved around Wooly in the semi-darkness as she raced into the midst of the riding Apache. Ticksy hissed and arched her back like a mad, crazed wildcat. A haunted, screeching barrel followed on the heels of both of them—all was pandemonium.

As we rolled into the heart of the Indians, their frightened ponies reared, kicking their legs high in the air. With yells rivaling mine, the terrified Apache took one look at the white apparition and the weird screaming barrel and vanished into the night. I heard the thud of the ponies' hooves as they rode off.

My barrel met a cactus plant and came to a sudden stop. I lay there too exhausted and disoriented to move. I called to my pet lamb, but my voice was hoarse from yelling—the sound came forth as a squeak. Tears rolled out of my eyes. I lay inside a charred whiskey barrel—sobbing, exhausted and weak.

Caleb reached the barrel first. "Gracie, are you all right? We couldn't find you."

I couldn't see his expression of concern through my tears and the darkness outside, but I heard it in his voice. "I don't know." I whispered, "Wooly?"

"Wooly's being taken care of. The others are gathering the stock and putting out the fire. Let me help you out." He tugged hard, pulling the heavy barrel from the patch of cactus thorns. I felt his hand on my head, and between my crawling and his pulling, I made it out of the barrel. He helped me stand, but my shaking knees wouldn't hold me. He caught me and kept me from falling. Sweeping me into his arms, he carried me toward the fortress.

"What happened?" asked Pa, looking at me, then in the direction the Apache had taken.

"It's a long story," said Caleb, giving me over to my father. Pa took me straight to my room. After I stripped off my ruined coat and cleaned up, he tucked me into bed.

"Don't you even think about getting out of bed, little girl." He pointed a finger of authority at me.

He left, and I heard Caleb tell Pa what happened.

Several minutes later, the others joined them. "The stock is safe, and the fire is out. We tethered the animals in the field out front. Cephas, Ben, and I will take turns making sure nothing bothers them the rest of the night."

"After what happened, I doubt we'll see another Apache." Pa laughed. "They probably think they saw a white spirit animal."

"What happened?" Ben asked.

The whole story was repeated for the new arrivals. I even grinned in the darkness of my room thinking of the sight Wooly and I must have made.

"White is a mystical color to the Apache, or for that matter, to all tribes. Their lore contains stories of unusual white animals—buffalo or wolves—to be respected and honored.

"I'd sure like to know what kind of story they'll tell about this incident," Mr. Ormand commented.

"Could you tell Wooly was a sheep?" asked Cephas.

"Probably not."

"I can see it now," I heard Cephas say. "The story goes of a low-flying, solid-white eagle with flapping wings and a yellow cat—no, baby mountain lion—riding its back."

From where I lay, I knew Cephas was waving his arm in the familiar sweeping motion he used when relating a tale.

"Brother, there you go again, daydreaming."

"No, I'm just relating a possibility, Caleb." Cephas's hackles started to rise.

"Okay, you twins. Take your sleeping bags with you on guard duty. Let's see if we can get some sleep. This has been a long night, and I'm worn out."

"We'll need to repair the stockade tomorrow," said Mr. Ormand.

"Everyone will pitch in to help," replied Pa. I heard his cot squeak as he sat down on it. Not long after, I went to dreamland.

After the incident when the Apache failed to steal our stock, the tale spread through the local Indians that our Butterfield Station was inhabited by a strange apparition—a white animal with wings. No, it wasn't an eagle, but a strange, screaming spirit that skimmed just above the ground—its rider a yellow catlike animal, screeching and hissing. After that, they gave our station a wide berth, keeping a sharp lookout as they passed.

REBA RHYNE

❧ 37 ❧

My letter to Jedediah had brought no response. I didn't know what to think about his continued silence. Mr. Ormand kept encouraging me not to give up—to keep praying for a resolution to my dilemma. He and Pa kept my spirits elevated.

Christmas loomed six days away. I persuaded Caleb and Cephas to cut down a tree to decorate for the season, and each night I busied myself and them with making ornaments for the tree. We popped corn, and between eating and stringing the white kernels, we placed ropes of it on the branches. Cephas found enough red berries to make a single chain for the tree. Newspaper strips, twisted into ovals and pasted together with flour, added another chain to our decorations. I used scraps of various colored cloth from my sewing, bunching them into odd shapes and tying them with string to place on the tree as ornaments.

We decided to have a contest to see who could make the nicest tree ornament with the prize being their favorite home-cooked meal. Sitting in front of the fireplace with our work hidden from prying eyes, we sang of that first night long ago when the virgin gave birth to the baby Christ. *"Silent night, holy night, all is calm. All is bright."* I was beginning to think I might be as she was—with child.

On Christmas Eve the ornaments were placed on the tree, and we took a vote. Cephas had made a wooden gingerbread man, using dyes from the forest and desert plants. It had eyes, mouth, and detailed body parts. We voted him the winner.

"What do you want Ben and me to cook for you?" I asked, standing in front of our beautiful tree.

"Turkey and dressing, sweet potatoes with brown sugar and cinnamon, spiced apples with nutmeg, and biscuits washed down with real tea," he responded.

"You'll have to go kill the turkey if you want to eat one," Ben replied. "The sweet potatoes might be a problem too."

"We'll get the turkey in the morning. You can surprise me with the rest." Cephas was agreeable to our menu.

Mr. Ormand stood. Since he'd come to the fortress, he'd conducted a Sunday service each week. "Do you mind if I read from Luke and say a few words about the first Christmas?"

We all agreed it was the perfect thing to do. I sat listening to him tell the most important birthday story known to man. Looking around the room, I realized I had a family, and I wouldn't be alone like Jesus and his family at the first Christmas. I caught Pa's eye. I'm sure he was thinking the same thing.

Cephas and Caleb's mother and father arrived without notice from El Paso bearing groceries, so Cephas got his sweet potatoes with brown sugar and cinnamon. The spicy smell of cinnamon and nutmeg, mixed with laughter, permeated the air of The Pinery for Christmas, and we all sipped on sweetened iced tea.

New Year's Eve, Hurricane Bailey rode back into my life— alone. My heart sank into my shoes. No one had to tell me. The worst had happened. My knees are the weakest part of my body. Pa caught me as they gave way.

Ben ran to get a glass of water, and Pa half-led and half-carried me to the kitchen table. He went and stoked the fireplace, putting on more wood. I needed its warmth.

Hurricane sat down across from me, resting his arms on the table. He looked like a beaten man, and for once in his life, he didn't smell of alcohol. He didn't speak, but stared at a crack in the table's wood, tracing it with one fingernail. He reeked of sadness.

Finally, Pa spoke. "Where's Jedediah?"

Hurricane shook his head and didn't open his mouth.

"Man," exclaimed my father, coming to the table and bending over the old man. "Speak. What's happened?"

Hurricane looked straight at me. "He's dead. I killed him!"

With that the old scout and trapper buried his head on his folded arms and let out a sob I hoped I would soon forget. He continued to sob—the force of his crying shaking his whole body and the table. "I killed Jedediah, jest like I killed my wife."

I sat there alarmed at his terse statement. What did he mean? Had he actually killed his own son? With his bare hands or some other method? Perhaps if I'd ever held any respect for this broken old human, I'd have gone over to comfort him, knowing he couldn't have purposefully harmed his son. Instead, I sat glued to my seat. He needed to explain his statement and soon.

Ben came from the kitchen and poured cups of strong coffee.. We numbered four, sitting around the table, including Pa and Mr. Ormand. I curled my cold fingers around my cup to warm them. Ben hovered in the background. The others tended to various jobs around the fortress.

When Hurricane could finally speak, he told of working on the new road into Arizona territory. "I pushed the crew hard, and we worked long hours. I guess that's what caused all the drinkin' among the group. Course I always did hire men like me—hard drinkers and hard livin' men. After work, we'd sit around the campfire, drink ourselves into a stupor, and pile into our sleeping bags to sleep it off. All but Jedediah, he didn't drink with us, although he might have"—he glared at me—"after the send off you gave him."

Mr. Bailey looked directly at me. I saw a spark of the old Hurricane. He had a nerve accusing me of anything. "I wrote a letter and apologized to him. Did he get it?" I don't think the truth had sunk in yet—my husband was dead. I felt numb.

"I don't know. He didn't share much with me."

In a harsh voice my father demanded, "How did Jedediah die?" I could tell any respect he'd had for Hurricane's abilities had disappeared.

Mr. Bailey looked at him. "Jest like most people in the territory, we heard the Apache were pullin' their old tricks and raidin' in the area. Two weeks ago, after our usual drinkin', they raided our camp jest before sundown. Jedediah was the only one sober enough to defend against'em. I knew I should help, but my eyes were blurry and my hands unsteady. I couldn't have shot a tin cup three feet in front of me with a pistol."

Rubbing my brow, I mentally counted back. The raid happened the same night the fortress had been attacked. While we were fightin' off our attackers, my husband had been dying in a similar raid two hundred miles away.

"Jedediah took cover behind our stack of provisions. The Apache started circlin' our camp. It was jest a matter of time before he got hit. The arrow slammed into his back. When I reached him, it was over." Mr. Bailey sobbed anew.

We sat silent until he continued his story.

"I gladly let the Indians take our horses. I wanted the raiders gone. They left the mules. When the stage into Franklin came through, we boarded it and went back to headquarters. I quit my job and hung around there for several days before decidin' to come here. I figured you had a right to know since you married him." Mr. Bailey looked at me. The earlier flash of belligerence had disappeared. He was a broken man and alone.

A tiny part of my heart ached for him, but I couldn't bring myself to touch him.

I stood. "Pa, I'm goin' to walk to Pine Springs." I went to get my coat, hat and gloves. I had to get away from Hurricane Bailey and the fortress. I needed to be alone.

"I'm goin' with you, Gracie." Pa headed for his coat hanging on a peg protruding from the rock wall.

"No, please let me go alone. I need to think."

"I'll go halfway."

"That's acceptable."

It was late afternoon. The sun's warmth still permeated the air and the forest. Pa and I walked hand-in-hand on the path beneath the bare limbs of the winter forest. I felt as barren as they.

"Pa, I don't understand anything at all. I was prayin' for Hurricane to be removed as an obstacle. Why did He take Jedediah instead?"

"Gracie, if I knew the answer to your question, I'd be in high demand. Who can know the mind of God?"

I drew in a deep breath and let it out in a gush of air. "Yes, indeed."

"Here's where I need to stop. Are you sure you don't want me to go on with you?"

"I'll be all right but wait here on me."

He nodded and I turned and continued along the path.

With each step, the fallen autumn leaves crunched beneath my feet. I took little notice of this sound or the birds singing around me.

Dry-eyed, drained of all emotion by the shock of what I'd just heard, I sat and watched the water bubble out of the earth at the springs and run down a creek bed it had used for centuries.

"Pine Springs, what message do you have for me? How can you comfort me in the terrible reality of Jedediah's death?" I said the words softly to the flowing water.

I considered the water running southward toward The Pinery. There was a promise in the flowing water. The message became clearer as I sat there. Nothing stopped it—nothing. How many years had it run like this, day and night? Life would go on. I would go on.

I smiled when I considered these words. Life—the one that secretly grew inside me—would survive this horrible happening. I drew a deep breath at the thought.

The whirlwind of my marriage had turned into widowhood. Soon I would experience motherhood, and I hadn't yet turned eighteen. This remained the saddest fact on the rough frontier. Young women and men experienced a rapid growth into adulthood because of unexpected circumstances in their lives.

"Add Gracie Tipton Bailey to those numbers," I thought out loud as I walked the trail back to The Pinery. When I got to the place where I'd left Pa, Hurricane Bailey stood there instead as I approached.

"Missy, I wanted to talk to you a bit more," he said as we continued on down the trail. "I've been a drunk as long as I can remember. I don't drink now. But I didn't stop soon enough to save my son or my wife."

His wife—I hadn't thought about her. "What happened to your wife?" We continued to walk slowly down the pathway as I contemplated the new Hurricane Bailey.

"The only life I knew was taught to me by my father, a rough and tumble frontiersman, a hard drinker, and a scout for anyone who hired him. He settled down only briefly when he met my mother—long enough to have me. For years, he came and went, not stayin' fer any length of time. He didn't want to get used to the 'soft life in the East' as he called it."

"Where did you live?"

"St. Louis, Missouri, on the Mississippi River. When my mother died at thirty-five, he took me away over the protests of my grandparents. We hit the trail West. I was thirteen years old, and my father's life seemed excitin', wild, and free. We crossed the Rockies with wagon trains to Oregon. Traveled south around the mountains through Texas and the Arizona territory to the gold fields in California."

"The years passed, and I was jest as bad a drinker as he. I was twenty-six when he died as a seasoned old hand—a wanderer on the plains. I'd learned well, shunned money, and lived from one scoutin' job to another. After his death, I settled for a time in Independence, Missouri where most of the wagon trains left for California. There I met my wife."

"What was her name?"

"Ruby Eliza Linkford—one of the most beautiful women I'd seen in my life. What she saw in me I'll never know. After we were married, I moved her south of Fort Leavenworth, Kansas where a small town sprang up in support of the garrison recently located there, and because the Oregon and Santa Fe trails passed close by. Ruby birthed our boy, Jedediah, in this town."

"My guess is you were gone most of the time—like your father."

"Your guess would be right. I treated her jest like my pa treated my ma. I never stayed more'n a month. I had to be on the trail. It was in my blood."

"Doesn't sound like much of a life for your wife."

"No. I'm sure in my long absences she ran out of money. On one unexpected trip home, I found another man in my house—a soldier from the fort. I thrashed him pretty good, and after I got my belly full of alcohol, me and Ruby got into a terrible fight. I don't hold to hittin' a woman, but I was so mad at her. My temper got the best of me. We were standin' on the front porch when I slapped her across the face. She fell to the ground hittin' her head on a rock. She didn't move. In the house, Jedediah looked out the window. At eleven, he saw all that transpired."

We stopped in the trail. I stood looking at him. Disgust must have shone in my face. He said, "I'm not proud of my life. Now that I'm sober, it disgusts me as much as it must disgust you."

"You make me sick." I couldn't help but spill out my true feelings.

"I understand." Mr. Bailey said, and then continued with his story. "At eleven, Jedediah and I hit the many trails found over the west. He sure had Bailey blood when it came to scoutin'— silent and intensive, soaking up everythin' I told him, includin' astonishing tracking skills. Always scared he'd leave me, I made him afraid and dependent on me. Made him think I'd drink myself to death if'n he wasn't around."

"Gracie…" This was the first-time Mr. Bailey had used my name. "You were the best thing to happen to him. He loved you even though I tried to take him away from you. The first time he went against me was when he left Fort Chadbourne with the Reverend Dixon to marry you. I was losin' him, and I had to stop it from happening."

"That's the reason you came to The Pinery. You wanted to get him back?"

"Yes, I knew what to say and how to say it. You didn't stand a chance."

"And now, Jedediah's dead."

He nodded. "I buried him on a hill overlookin' the Butterfield Trail, facin' toward the Guadalupe Mountains."

Up to then I hadn't shed a tear. But now, I started to cry.

"I'm sorry, Gracie. I was wrong. I'll carry the awful fact that I killed my own son wherever I go. It'll be a heavy burden."

I didn't cry uncontrollably but softly. I'd lost two special and sacred things, my husband and marriage. There was something I needed to share with Hurricane Bailey. "Mr. Bailey, this is the first time I've been around you when you didn't reek of alcohol. I want to believe you've changed, but I must reserve my opinion until I see several days of results. I forgive you for your part in Jedediah's death. Be sure I hold nothin' against you. I agree your burden will be a great one to carry. What do you plan on doin' now that you are free from your position with Butterfield Overland Stage?"

"I haven't decided. I will soon."

Without speaking, we walked the rest of the way to The Pinery. Pa waited at the end of the trail.

During the night, I decided to tell Mr. Bailey of the coming child.

I never got the chance to do it. The next morning, he didn't show for breakfast. Pa went to look for him. His horse was gone. He'd left without saying goodbye. I felt sorry for him, but with such bad memories, I didn't care if he ever came back.

The day passed slowly, as I struggled through my chores in total numbness. I noticed furtive, wondering glances in my direction, but there was limited conversation. What was there to say?

At the end of the day, I pulled open the curtain, and walked with leaden feet into the semi-darkness of the bedroom I'd shared with my husband. The kerosene lantern I carried, revealed a previously unseen package, just inside the door of the room. When I examined the bundle, I noticed one of Jedediah's shirts was wrapped neatly around the bundle. It was tied with a couple of strings. I went to my rocking chair.

Clipping the twine with my sewing scissors, the bundle fell open to reveal Jedediah's felt hat and britches. The flood gates opened when I touched the neatly sewn patches on the knees.

❧ 38 ❧

After Hurricane Bailey's departure, sadness descended on me like a mantle of snow on the high peaks of the Guadalupe's. I spent much of the time exploring new trails in the desert and mountains with Wooly keeping me company. Wooly understood my tears as we trudged along.

"I'm sorry if my tears are depressin', little lamb." I sat with her white, fuzzy face in my hands, and she would look at me with her black eyes. I believe she understood my hurt. "I'm so glad Sarah gave you to me. I wonder how your former mistress is doing." I didn't sit long in the chilly air, and we would continue on.

My tears fell like cold, glistening raindrops on the slopes of the Guadalupe Mountains above me.

Pa, Ben, and the others gave me a wide berth so I could mourn the death of Jedediah. After several days, I began to seek the comfort of my friends.

David Ormand understood my need to be alone. We discussed the unexpected twist in my life when I volunteered to help him take the stock to pasture.

"Gracie, I know how you feel. I walked many miles in the foothills of Asheville's Blue Ridge. Seein' new places and different wildlife kept my mind off the heartbreak of my mother's passing."

"That's exactly my experience."

"Later, when I decided to disrupt my life completely and move to California, walkin' helped me make that decision. Walkin' is serious medicine for the soul and a good place to say quiet prayers to God."

I wanted to ask a specific question that was on my heart, but it came out as a completely different statement. "Mr. Ormand, I didn't expect to lose Jedediah."

"I know. We were prayin' for God to solve the problem of Hurricane Bailey."

"You were prayin' also?" I said, astonished at his avowal. The morning sun glistened, and I squinted to see.

"Of course. I wanted you to be happy."

"I needed my husband to grow to his full potential. With Mr. Bailey around, Jedediah would always take his orders and abuse."

"You felt he wouldn't become the man he was destined to be under his father's thumb."

I nodded, and tears came to my eyes. "I saw some of the transformation during the brief weeks we were married, and I loved him better because of this short time of change. Jedediah would have become the husband I needed and a great father."

Turning his head, Mr. Ormand gave me an intense scrutiny but didn't ask the question my comment had no doubt brought to his mind. We walked on.

"Do you think Hurricane will return?" I asked.

"No, I doubt we'll ever hear from him again. The man is a drifter and..." Mr. Ormand reached out his hand and stopped me. Excitement came to his voice. "Gracie, wouldn't it be wonderful if his change meant somethin' different—a turning point in his life. Maybe we should pray for God to use Mr. Bailey's experiences to help others. He could certainly advise those he met about a certain pathway not to follow. Could it be this is the reason Jedediah is gone?"

I carefully followed his line of reasoning. "Then at least Jedediah's death would have a purpose, wouldn't it?"

"Yes, of course."

I wondered how Mr. Ormand managed to stay a step ahead of me. "The question I came to ask you goes along with your last statement. Why did Jedediah die?"

He smiled. "I thought so, and I didn't have an answer until it came to me just a minute ago. Gracie, will you help me pray for Hurricane? Let's pray God will use his life to help others."

"That will be a switch. I've spent much of my time prayin' for him to be removed as a stumblin' block in my marriage." Could I pray for Mr. Bailey? I struggled with a response.

Mr. Ormand went on, "We'll pray that Hurricane will gracefully intervene in broken lives, helpin' those he meets not to make the mistakes he made. Will you join me?"

The question hung in the air between us as we started to stake the mules and horses out to pasture. When we were finished, I had an answer. "Mr. Ormand, I'll try to pray with you. It will be hard, knowin' the trouble he caused in my life."

"Tryin' is all that I ask," he said.

"Mr. Ormand, something else's been botherin' me." We were walking back toward The Pinery. He stopped and looked inquiringly at me. "It's a question that's hung in the back of my mind for many years. Is it my fault that everyone I love seems to die or leave me? What's wrong with me?" Tears started in earnest.

"Gracie— Gracie, there's nothing wrong with you. What prompted you to ask such a question?"

"Because, Mama died after picking me up from the floor. She wasn't supposed to lift heavy items. And my brother—I heard his heart beat. Pa left shortly after. He came back—years later. And now, Jedediah's gone. I don't know if I can trust love—trust my heart to love again."

"You've had more than enough hurt for a girl of eighteen— that's true, but these problems don't follow you, Gracie. They just happen. Don't blame yourself. Think about our Savior. He did wonderful miracles, but he had his hands and feet nailed to the wooden boards of the cross. Don't you think he hurt hideously? Why should he continue to love us? Our sin sent him there, but He loves us today, thank God." He paused, seemingly to ponder what to say next. "If it's any consolation to you, I'd be proud to have you as a daughter, and I'm not the least bit afraid to love you." He put his arm around my shoulder, pulled out his handkerchief and wiped my wet cheeks.

I sniffed as my tears dried. "Thank you, Mr. Ormand. You always say the right thing. God gives you much wisdom."

"Put a few more years behind you, Gracie. Most wisdom comes with age—not sayin' God isn't involved now," he explained, using his free arm to punctuate his sentence. "Come, let's go to the fortress so I can pack my dinner. I'm goin' to eat tending the animals today."

During my third month of being with child, I threw up some mornings. By the end of January, I knew for sure a baby would be born. I needed to tell Pa. I wrapped my long coat around me and went to find him. As I left the front entrance, the strong wind off the desert threatened to blow dirt in my eyes. It cut through my coat to my skin. I ran quickly to the back of the building where the walls provided protection from the wind's strong presence, and where I heard noises of someone working.

Pa wielded an axe, splitting wood for the fireplace. "It's a cold morning, Gracie," he observed. I noticed his coat lay on the stack of wood behind him.

"You're goin' to catch your death of cold. Put your coat on, Pa." His shirt was wet with sweat.

"I'll soon be finished, and then I'll come in by the fire to dry out."

I looked at the gray skies full of clouds. "Will we have snow tonight?"

He stopped swinging his axe at the wedge lodged in the chunk of wood. Placing the axe's head on top of the large piece, he rested his arms atop the handle. "Sometime before nightfall is my guess," he said, sweeping the sky with his eyes. "Did you come out here to discuss the weather?"

"No, Pa, I have some news that should excite you." I sucked in a lungful of air and continued. "I don't know how to tell you except to say it. I'm goin' to have a baby."

Pa's mouth flew open and his face was etched with astonishment. "Are you sure?"

"I won't be sure until I see the child, but I'm as sure as I can be without my belly swellin' and the actual birth." I couldn't help but laugh at his surprise.

He threw down the axe and came around to me, giving me a big hug. "Am I the first one you've told?" His laughter rippled around us.

"Yes." Although I had mentioned Jedediah as a good father to Mr. Ormand.

"This is amazing. When do you think the little one will be born?"

"My nine months will be up at the end of July."

"Not long after your eighteenth birthday?"

"I think so."

"It's hard to carry a baby through the hot summer." I knew he thought of another time and another place. "Gracie, we'll have to consider where you'll have your child. There are only two possibilities. Fort Chadbourne or El Paso."

"I think I prefer El Paso. Surely Mexican midwives live there."

"I'll see that Mr. Coburn knows your situation. He can advise us on midwifery in the town. Are you excited?"

"I am excited—and thinking about all the things my baby will need. Could we order patterns from the sutler's store in El Paso so I can start making clothes? And I'll need more material with baby designs on it. My crochetin' will come in handy to make booties and hats and..."

"Okay, okay, I get it. Do you want to return to El Paso for your supplies?"

"No, I'll trust Mr. Coburn's wife to get them for me."

"Now, if you want to go, we could take David's wagon, or I'm sure he might drive you."

"I'll think about it, Pa."

"O-o, I'm getting' cold. Gotta get back to work, little girl. I'm proud of you. And having a grandchild will be incredible."

I turned around to go back into the building. He called after me, "When will you tell the others?"

"Soon."

REBA RHYNE

❧ 39 ❧

I did inform the others a few days after telling Pa. There was so much excitement over the prospect of a new baby in our midst, you would have thought each man was having a child of his own. They fell all over themselves making me comfortable.

Secretly, I laughed and welcomed the unexpected attention.

February passed quickly, followed by March. At five months, my growing abdomen announced my coming child. My loose clothing did not conceal it. Mornings continued to be chilly, but the afternoons were warm and trips to Pine Springs comfortable without my long coat. I looked around me at the wakening forest. The new leaves on the trees were a bright green, and the sky a lovely blue. Spring had sprung, but the skies had closed up. We lacked rain.

On April first, eighteen fifty-nine, Press Stockton, Jr. appeared with the cattle he was taking to the gold strike at Pike's Peak. It had been five months since I'd seen him.

"Gracie," he said, heading toward me.

My heart pounded quickly as I turned to greet him. "Press, I'm happy to see you."

"I told you I'd stop by on my way north. Remember, I keep my promises." He smiled that handsome smile I'd learned to love on the trip to The Pinery. "How are you?"

I saw him glance quickly at my stomach. "With child," I said, smiling back at him. We both started laughing—me with embarrassment, and he at my boldness.

"Congratulations, Gracie. I know you and your husband will be very excited when the baby gets here."

"Press, please sit down. Do you have a few minutes to talk?"

"We're going to camp here overnight and move out tomorrow. I was hopin' to meet Jedediah."

I waited until Press sat comfortably at the kitchen table. "Would you like some coffee? I've made a fresh pot."

"Yes, I would, and I want to invite you, your husband, and Jay to eat at our chuck wagon tonight. Jorge is excited at the prospect of feedin' you again."

I poured two cups of strong black brew, replaced the pot on the stove, and sat opposite him at the table. Wrapping my fingers around my hot cup, I plunged into the news Press needed to know. "A lot has happened since you were here last year. Obviously, I am going to have a baby..."

Press interrupted me. "When?" he asked.

"At the end of July."

"Are you excited?" His smile disarmed me.

"Yes, I've been makin' clothes and booties and..."

Press reached across the table to touch my hand. "I am happy for you, Gracie."

I shook my head as I read the same message of affection in his eyes. Press never changed. "Thank you. There's something you need to know."

"Go on." He kept smiling at me.

I dropped my eyes to look at the black coffee in my tin cup. The emotions surrounding Jedediah's death rushed over me again. I felt tears burn in my eyes. It would be easier to say the words without looking at Press. Drawing a deep breath I continued. "My husband was killed in an Apache raid at a work camp in New Mexico territory in December."

I dashed the tears from my eyes with my hand and looked to see what effect my words had had on him. His frozen smile told of his shock. "Killed, in December? I don't understand."

"Yes, there was a night raid, and everyone was drunk except Jedediah."

"That figures from what you've told me about his father," Press said angrily. "What happened?"

"Single-handedly, Jedediah fought the Indians. His Pa said he died from an arrow in the back. Mr. Bailey buried him on a hill near where he was killed." I gushed, looking down again. I wanted to get the information out quickly. Two more tears rolled down my face.

"You've seen Hurricane Bailey?"

"He came by here to tell me the news. For once in his life, he was sober. Said he intended to stay that way."

"Where is he now?" From Press's voice, I felt he might do Hurricane physical harm. Amazingly, he'd taken up for Jedediah. Why would he do that?

"I don't know. He left without a goodbye."

Press stood from the table and paced in front of the fireplace. "I don't know what to say." He stopped and looked at me. "I'm in shock at the news."

"You can't imagine how I felt when I found out."

Press came to my side, sat at the table, and put his arms around me. He started to say something when Pa walked through the door of the fortress.

"Press, I knew you were here when I saw the milling cattle down by the main road. Are you headed for the gold strike?"

"In the morning, Jay." Press arose and met my father with a warm handshake.

"Aren't you afraid the snow will be too deep to get through?"

"From all accounts it's been a mild winter so I'm hoping our trip won't be hard. We'll follow the well-defined *El Camino Real* north. The Rio Grande will run along our route so there'll be plenty of water, and the grass is starting to grow."

"How long will it take to get there?"

"Seven weeks with the cattle, but we may have a buyer waiting for us just inside Kansas Territory. If that pans out, we don't have to go all the way to the gold fields on Clear Creek but only across New Mexico territory. Our trip back won't take as long."

"I wish I were going with you."

"Come along. We could use another good hand."

"Thanks for the offer. I'd better stay here. Did Gracie tell you I'm to have a grandchild in July?"

Press looked at me. "She sure did. What a surprise. I'm sorry to hear about the passin' of her husband."

Pa nodded. "We were all shocked when Hurricane rode in here with the news. We hadn't heard of the raid. Had one here ourselves after you left to go back to the Glory B last year."

"I didn't hear."

"Come along and I'll tell you about it. I'd like to look over your herd."

"I've invited you and Gracie for supper at the chuck wagon tonight. I hope you can come. Jorge says we'll have skillet cornbread and venison."

"Sounds good to me. Are you okay with that, Gracie?"

"Yes, I can't wait to eat someone else's cookin' besides mine and Ben's."

"Gracie, I'll see you then." Press went out the door with Pa.

Sitting around the campfire with Press reminded me of our former supper around the chuck wagon. This time he did not leave my side until it was necessary for him to help Jorge hand out the plates of food. I got the feeling he thought I'd disappear in a puff of air if he left for a second.

"Gracie, I think you've been eating too much skillet cornbread," said Jorge, kidding me about the bump at my stomach as he approached.

"I'm sure that's not the problem, Jorge." I took the cup of steaming hot coffee from his hands.

"I'm sorry about your husband. Press told me the circumstances around his death."

"A terrible shock to us all. I don't want to go through these last few months again. I want to look ahead, raise my child, and enjoy my home here in Texas. I never thought I'd love anyplace like I did Tennessee, but this land is so different from my former home. I'll be glad when it's a settled safe land."

Press came to sit by me and said, "The future holds that promise, but storm clouds continue to brew in the East over the slave issue."

"Yes," Pa said, looking at Press as he sat down. "And the Kansas-Nebraska Act has had the opposite effect it was supposed to have. According to the newspapers, there's already civil war in Bleeding Kansas. Voting to establish a free or slave state has brought both factions to the area to fight it out."

"Will it be dangerous to travel there, Press?" I asked, concerned for his safety.

"I doubt it. I'd more likely be run over by a stampede than shot by the fanatics on both sides." Those sitting around us laughed.

We ate our supper talking about the political situation in the nation and about droving cattle. I listened quietly to the discussion, content to relax to the drone of their different voices.

"Gracie, I hear you had a screeching white eagle with a mountain lion on its back at The Pinery not long ago." Jorge had joined us as we finished off our wonderful meal with his pecan pie turnover for dessert.

I laughed. "Whatever it was, the thing scared the marauding Indians into leaving. They didn't get our stock although they did burn a part of the stockade."

"I wish I'd been there." Jorge slapped his knee. "It must have been a wild night."

"We weren't laughing when it happened, but now the idea of timid Wooly scaring the Apache into flight is funny," I answered.

Pa added, "Gracie's high-pitched screaming even made my blood curdle."

When it was time for Pa and I to leave, Press walked back to the fortress with us. Pa said goodnight and disappeared inside. I stood outside for a moment.

"Gracie, I'll miss bein' with you until I get back. I promise you I will come as soon as possible. Don't forget that." His determined voice affirmed his vow.

"I look forward to seein' you."

I turned to go inside, but his hand on my arm stopped me. Turning me toward him, he held me in a tight hug. I felt his lips brush my forehead, but he made no other attempt to kiss me. "Goodnight, Gracie." Press let me go and disappeared into the darkness.

❧ **40** ❧

As my little one grew inside me, I became more awkward. Mr. Coburn sent another person to help Ben with the cooking, and I spent more time tending to the needs of my future child. Somewhere, the division superintendent found an extra upholstered couch. When it came on the supply wagon, I had it placed in front of the fireplace. I napped in front of the warm fire, resting on the soft horsehair cushions.

No one sat on the couch but me. If anyone tried, Caleb or Cephas or Ben shooed them off, explaining the sofa could only be used by a woman expecting a child.

"You mean there's a lady expecting a baby here in the desert?"

"Yes," came the reply.

When Press returned exactly five weeks later, that's where he found me. When I awoke, he sat in a chair next to the couch.

"Are you watchin' me sleep?"

"And you were sleepin' very peacefully I might add, except for a grimace now and then."

"That's when the baby probably kicked me." I managed to sit. "How come you're here? I didn't expect you back until almost June."

"We found a buyer in Santa Fe who agreed to take the cattle on to Kansas Territory. Gracie, I don't have much time. I need to get back home to the Glory B. I only wanted to tell you hello. I'll see you again soon."

Press stood and without so much as a handshake, he left me still reclining on the couch.

I wondered at his abrupt departure, but later Ben told me Press and Pa had already had a lengthy conversation while I was sleeping.

"Do you know what they talked about?" I asked Ben.

"No, Gracie, I couldn't hear."

Later I asked Pa, and he said they discussed the cattle drive to Kansas Territory and how long it would take Press to get home.

"He's concerned at the water shortage brought on by the lack of rain." It seemed as if Pa fished desperately for part of his answer. I wondered if he hadn't left out some important details.

In my seventh month, a letter came by stage from Mr. Coburn. He urged me to leave and come to El Paso since the two-day stage ride would be rough on me and my unborn child. I had progressed in size to large and aching.

I showed the letter to Pa. "Gracie, you're not riding the bouncing stage to El Paso. David and I'll take you when the time comes."

"The longer we wait, the harder the ride will be on me."

"Yes, I know," he said, looking down the path to the main road, drawing in his breath and blowing it out in a rush of air. "We'll need to go soon." Why did I get the feeling he was looking for someone?

Four days later Press appeared with four horsemen and a large stock wagon. He and Pa came into the fortress to talk to me. I didn't rise from the couch to greet him. Managing my lumpy body out of a sitting position wasn't easy. Press violated the rules and came to sit beside me on my couch. Pa pulled a chair from the table.

Pa started first. "Gracie, when Press was here last, we talked about the birth of your child. We decided it would be best for you to travel to the Glory B. Press says he's built a new wing onto the old farmhouse, and you're welcome to come there and use it."

"Really? Thanks for discussing this with…"

Press held up his hand to stop the tirade he must have known would issue forth from me. "Now Gracie, don't get mad. It's the perfect solution. You'll feel at home, and you'll know people that you can trust."

"I won't know anyone but you and Jorge. Are you and he going to deliver my baby?" All along I'd been thinking about El Paso.

"Gracie, you don't know any more people than that in El Paso," pleaded my father. "Be reasonable. I'd feel better knowin' you were with Press at the Glory B."

"Within an hour, you'll be Maria's best friend. She's waiting to meet you. Please come with me, Gracie. We'll take good care of you."

"What about deliverin' the baby?"

"Maria and Pastor Marshall's wife will attend you. I've already asked Julia, and she's agreed to help. Everything's ready. All we need is you."

I looked at my father, "Pa, will you come?"

"I'll certainly try, but I can't promise. Someone has to take care of the station."

Press looked relieved. He knew when he'd won.

"I'll need to pack my things. That'll take a while in the shape I'm in."

"Take all the time you want. I'm not on a timetable like the Butterfield stages. I brought my largest farm wagon so we can haul anything you need. I don't intend to leave a minute before you're ready to go."

"Did you two hatch this plan when Press came by before?"

The two conspirators exchanged glances and apparently decided to tell the truth. "We talked about it. We're both concerned about yours and the baby's health."

"What else did you talk about?"

"I-uh... Nothing," said Pa.

There was something else, but a branding iron wouldn't get them to talk.

I needed to tell The Pinery goodbye. While the men loaded the wagon with my possessions, I walked to Pine Springs. The trip took longer than usual because of the extra weight I carried. I checked out every familiar tree, stone, and flower along the way. I felt sad, as if I'd never see them again.

When I got to the springs, I decided not to cross to the other side. It was too dangerous, and I didn't want to risk falling on the moss-slick rocks. Because of the drought, the spring's flow had slowed.

I didn't stay long. On the trail back, I thought about those who'd walked with me on this path. Pa, the twins, Jedediah, Press, Ben, Mr. Ormand, and Hurricane Bailey all came to mind. Some of the time I was happy—some I was sad. Today, I was both.

A newly loaded wagon greeted me when I returned. Barrels, heavy with fresh water from the springs, were carefully stowed to balance the wagon. We couldn't take chances on not finding a waterhole.

My rocking chair appeared, carefully roped at the back of the wagon. No rocker, no baby, I'd told Press when he balked at loading my possession. He laughed at my statement.

"Gracie, my dear, I don't think you have much to say about having or not having a baby these days." He loaded the rocker and didn't say another word.

My chest of clothes sat behind the driver's seat. It was padded with a blanket. Press said we'd use it as part of the backrest, and if we got tired of sitting forward on the wooden seat we could lean back against it. The blue basin and ewer were packed carefully in wooden crates along with the baby clothes and other items from the shelves in my room. Press insisted on taking the couch, although loading it turned out to be a bigger problem than the rocker. Finally, everything was in place.

My feather bed stayed behind. Press said there was a nice bed with a mattress at the Glory B, and I made Pa promise to use mine. A feather bed for the station man seemed appropriate. My room looked bare when I walked out.

Everyone gathered for the send-off the following morning.

"If it's a boy, you've gotta name it Cephas after me. I'm your best friend."

"What do you mean? Aren't you being a little forward, brother?"

"I just figured I'd say it afore you did."

"What makes you think I'd ask?"

"You two," exclaimed Pa. "She's already said she'd name the baby after me." I hadn't, but his statement settled the question between the twins. He stepped to Press's side of the wagon. "Take care of my little girl. Let me know if the baby's a boy or girl."

"You don't have to worry about me taking care of her," Press answered. "And, I will send you a letter via the Jackass Mail and the Butterfield Overland Stage as soon as the baby's born."

I'd already hugged my pa before climbing onto the passenger seat—no small accomplishment in my condition. A box the twins had made helped the situation. "Bye, Pa. I'll see you after the baby's born."

"Now Gracie, don't come back until its safe for you and the baby to travel."

"I'll see to that, Jay." Press chirped to the horse, and we started slowly down the trail with the other four horsemen following. This leaving seemed eerily like my last one from The Pinery, except we turned east, following the stage road to the turnoff for the Glory B.

Pa stood waving as we rounded the corner to the main road. I waved back until I could no longer see him standing in front of the stone fortress. I looked at Press as I turned around. He was smiling.

"What are you smilin' about?"

"I didn't expect you would see the Glory B because you were expectin' a child."

"How did you expect me to see it?" I said indignantly.

"As my wife, Gracie," he answered gently, still smiling.

That took the wind out of my sails, and I remained silent with nothing to say in return. For some time, I'd realized that he loved me. There. I'd actually thought it—the word *love*, pertaining to Press. But I remained in mourning, because Jedediah's death wasn't far behind me. And the question of trusting had not been totally dismissed from my mind.

After his statement, I knew what Press wanted during this trip to the Glory B. He wanted to marry me. Was that the other part of his discussion with Pa? The one neither would confide to me when I asked?

I was quiet, but the wind wasn't. I adjusted my hat to shield my eyes from the blowing debris. "The wind is fierce," I observed.

"Did you smell the smoke earlier?"

"No, I didn't."

"There's fire somewhere on the prairie. I hope we don't run into it when we turn south to the Glory B."

I looked around but couldn't see evidence of either. "Why do you think we haven't had much rain this year?"

"It all depends on the winds, Gracie. They seem to be going north of us. They bring the rain."

"They aren't blowing north today."

"No. Maybe this one will bring rain."

"How long until we get to your ranch?'

"We'll take it easy. I'm guessing two weeks."

Every few hours, I'd turn around to see if El Capitan was still visible. At the end of the day, I could no longer see the mountain's dark face against the horizon.

The next day it poured rain for a short time, slowing us down as it pounded us.

Press cautioned his men as we moved forward. "We'll need to take care in the low places and watch for rushing water in the arroyos. Getting swept away by a flood isn't my idea of excitement." He gave orders for two of the cowboys to ride ahead of us and two behind. The rain stopped. No evidence of its downpour appeared the following day.

Uncomfortable and hot was the way I'd describe my trip, but the days flew by. Press worried when we drove through several miles of burned over scrub brush.

"We didn't come through this on our way to Pine Springs," he told me. "Lightning, probably. Guess the rain put the fire out."

At the start of the second week, Press decided to drive longer hours. "We're not making as much progress as I want. If you feel the need to rest, tell me, and we'll stop earlier in the day."

At the end of the fourth day, exhaustion took hold of me, and I rocked back and forward, side to side on the hard seat. "Gracie!" Press caught me, putting his right arm around me on one of my more violent swings. "Here, rest your head on my shoulder."

It was sweltering hot as the afternoon sun beat down on us. We crossed the Comanche Trail heading into the Glass Mountains. "We'll have more shade in the mountains, and it'll be a little cooler," he said quietly as I gratefully cradled my head against his neck.

There were times when I dozed off only to be brought back to the real world by his admonition of the danger of sleeping on the moving wagon. "Gracie, I can't keep you from falling from the wagon." On one of my trips into the world of sleep, I'm sure I heard him say, "I love your spirit, and I love you, Gracie." No one had ever said that to me except Pa. Not even Jedediah.

I opened my eyes for a brief moment, wondering if it was only the wind in my ears.

That night after I went to sleep, Press completely rearranged the back of the wagon so I could rest on my couch while we traveled. The clothes chest was pushed against the open cushion side, making a secure bed for me to rest upon. The crates were at the back of the couch.

Weariness had settled on me like a layer of Texas dust. I couldn't shake it.

The next day as I approached the wagon, I didn't notice the different arrangement. Before I knew what was happening, Press swung me into his arms and deposited me into the back of the wagon. "Can you make it from there?" he asked me, gesturing toward my makeshift bed.

I looked around the newly arranged area. "I need a pillow," I told him.

"Where will I find one?"

"In the chest—the bottom drawer."

Press leaned over the wagon side and pulled out the lowest drawer. After retrieving the pillow, he handed it to me. "Rest today, Gracie. In two days we'll see the Glory B."

"Press," I said. He'd started to mount to the wagon seat but stopped to listen. "Thank you."

I slept fitfully in the bouncing wagon with my hat pulled over my head.

❧ 41 ❧

About noon two days later, Press stopped the wagon. I struggled to a sitting position as he pointed to a ditch in the plains heading east. The gully sloped away from our position, growing deeper and deeper.

Press pointed. "That's the draw my parents and grandparents traveled when they came west to claim their land."

"Then we're not far from the ranch?" I turned on the couch and surveyed the horizon before us. There was no hint of a house.

"No, not far at all."

Press called to the men riding behind us. "Head on to the house. Warn Maria and my father that we'll be there for supper."

The four disappeared in a cloud of dust.

"Help me to the driver's seat. I'll ride with you the rest of the way." Somehow, I managed to swing my legs over the seat back. We laughed together at my awkwardness.

Press started the wagon forward, staying parallel to the side of the draw until the road turned away and the elevation started rising. We left the desert and plains behind as we climbed through grasses and trees. I noticed the air being cooler but not much.

"We're driving on the Stockton ranch now, Gracie."

One hour later, Press stopped and pointed to a house positioned in the tree line above us. "That's the Glory B ranch house."

I looked in the direction he pointed. The splendid, sprawling home sat almost on top of the hill in the edge of the trees. Made with rock and sawn logs and sitting in this desolate desert, the dwelling rivaled many of the homes in Nashville for beauty. Numerous glass windows graced its walls, and the dark, red-tile roof stood out against the evergreen forest. "How did you get sawn wood here in West Texas?"

"We have a sawmill in town. It's run by steam. More than one home is frame."

I thought about what he'd said. "You could sell lumber in El Paso."

"We don't want to call attention to our presence in the Glass Mountains, and anyway I don't own the sawing operation."

I looked down the barely perceptible road. "I'm glad you know where you're going. I can't tell our path from the undergrowth around us.

Press laughed. "Good, but I can assure you the worst Indian trackers can find the trail. I don't normally drive here, but I wanted you to see the house like my folks saw it the first time."

I looked at the structure again.

"Remember, I told you we've added on to our original home. Behind the new entrance, the old log house remains, and I built on another wing last year in the fall. You can't see it from here, because it goes into the pine and cedar forest behind the house. That's where you will stay, waiting for your baby's birth."

"Your home is beautiful. I can see why your grandmother loved it."

"Do you like it, Gracie?"

"Yes, of course. Where's the town?"

"Look in that direction." He pointed to the left of the ranch house. "A road leads around the hill to a short flat valley about one mile away from the Glory B."

"Come on, girl..." Press flicked the reins and urged our horse forward.

A short, rotund Mexican woman hurried from the house to greet us. Her whole face lit when she smiled. The long dress she wore swished back and forth above the ground as she walked.

Press jumped down from the wagon and called to her. "Maria, you sweetheart, we're here."

"Yes, I see *Señor* Press."

Press hurried to meet her, and they danced a short unskilled flamenco, hands clapping with stamping of feet. I shook my head and laughed at them as he grabbed her in a bear hug. Maria pushed him away.

"This is Gracie." Maria walked to the wagon and reached her hands to me.

"Whoa there, Maria. Gracie is a handful. Let me help her down."

I ignored Press's statement, and let him lift me from the wagon.

"Come *Señora* Gracie. You are tired, si?"

I opened my mouth to respond, but Press answered. "Yes, the *Señora* is tired. Will you put her to bed? I'll bring her belongings for you to unpack."

Maria put her arm around my shoulders, and steering me between the log posts holding the door, she ushered me into the front room, past the kitchen area, down a hall to rooms at the rear of the large ranch house. As I passed through, I caught a glimpse of comfortable but not lavish surroundings with lace curtains at the windows.

"This is your room, *Señora*."

Maria led me through a small sitting room into a large bedroom beyond. A beautiful quilt with the colors of a Texas sunset covered the immense, elegant four-poster bed. Yellow cotton curtains fluttered at the two open windows with a built-in bookcase full of books between. A green rug covered the wooden floor from the bed to the door.

"Maria, what a beautiful quilt," I said, walking over to gently touch the multiple star design on a field of white.

"*Señora* Stockton, *Señor* Press's mother, made it for him. It's a wedding gift for his bride."

319

"You must take it off the bed, Maria, and hold it for his future wife."

She looked at me and smiled. "Si, *Señora* Gracie."

"Is this Press's bedroom?"

"*Si*, but now the room is yours." Maria turned down the bed, making no attempt to remove the quilt. I watched her with raised eyebrows. I didn't say another word but decided I'd handle it tomorrow when she wasn't around.

"Hey ladies, here's one of the packed crates and Gracie's chest," Press announced, coming into the room. Jorge helped him carry the heavy items.

"Mrs. Gracie, I'm glad you've decided to visit the Glory B." Jorge smiled from ear-to-ear. "I hurried to the ranch house when I saw the wagon pull in front. Press finally managed to get you here."

"It's beautiful just as I've been told. Are you fixing supper tonight?"

"No, Maria will keep you well fed. She's a great cook."

"My mother taught her well."

"*Señora* Stockton was a good *profesor*," said Maria.

"And she was wonderful at quilting." I touched the edge of a star where Maria had turned the beautiful creation down.

"Gracie, we'll get your rocking chair and place it here in the bedroom. The rest of your things we'll put in the sitting room. I'd like you to rest until Maria gets supper ready. She'll help you unpack and get dressed for bed. Jorge will bring the rocker. I've got to ride out to see my father this afternoon. He's with the cattle to the west of the ranch house. I'll see you at supper."

After organizing my life, he left the room.

I was too tired to protest. I opened a drawer on the chest the men had brought in and pulled out a nightgown. Maria rushed over to help me out of my clothes.

I held up my hand, "Wait until Jorge comes with the rocker, and you can help me get ready for bed."

"*Si, Señora.*" She opened the wooden crate and removed the blue flowered basin and ewer Press had given me.

"You finally made it home," I mumbled to myself when I saw the pieces. To Maria I said, "Could you please get some water so I can freshen up."

"*Si, Señora.*" Maria placed the basin atop the chest and left the room with the pitcher as Jorge arrived.

"Jorge the trip from the Guadalupe's took the starch out of me. I'm so tired. Restin' this afternoon should revive me."

Jorge nodded. "Where do you want the chair?"

"By the window, I think."

Jorge placed the chair where I indicated. "We'll get together and trade recipes while you are here," he said.

"Good. I need some different ones. I'm tired of eatin' the same things."

Maria entered the room, "Shoo, shoo, Jorge. *Señora* Gracie needs her rest." Maria made as if to flog Jorge like a rooster might flog an intruder. Jorge backed out of the room with his arms over his head, pretending to protect his body from the Mexican woman. I giggled at their antics.

Laughing, Maria shut the door. She brought my gown and helped me undress. She shook her finger and became serious. "Jorge...I have to be very, very hard on him."

My buttons were soon undone, gown on, and I sat on the edge of the large four-poster bed ready for my afternoon rest. "Every day is good to take a nap after dinner," Maria ordered. "Your baby will be born soon, *si?*"

"Yes, at the end of July, I think. I've never had a baby before so I could be wrong." The way I felt at this moment, the baby might arrive now. The closer the time came for the baby to be born, the more I thought of my own mother...and how she'd died.

"Gracie, Gracie," Press whispered through the cracked door. Maria hadn't closed it completely because a slight breeze blew through.

I jerked the covers to my chin, my afternoon nap over. "Yes, what is it?"

"You've slept three hours, and Maria will have supper ready in a few minutes. I want to introduce you to my father before we eat. Do you feel rested enough to come to the front room?"

I stretched my arms above my head. I felt great except for a twinge here and there from the rough jolts of the buggy. "I'll get ready."

"We'll wait for you. The room is at the end of the hall."

I didn't know much about Press's father. I hoped I would like him.

Several minutes later I walked into the first room I'd entered upon arrival. Press stood, and an older copy of him unwound from a large armchair next to a small table. On the stand sat a lamp and an open book. The chair was positioned in front of a window where light streamed in, chasing the darkness away and illuminating the occupant's activities. An older upright piano took up most of the wall to my right.

The distinguished looking older gentleman strode toward me with an easy style reminiscent of one who was an inexhaustible horseman. His gray hair and skin showed the wear of sun, wind, and age. "Gracie, you're even prettier than Preston described you. I hope you rested well." He took my hand and looked deeply into my eyes as if he could know my whole life in a glance. "Welcome to the Glory B."

"Yes sir, I didn't realize today's travels would exhaust me so."

"I trust Preston drove carefully bringing you here." He looked over at Press. "There are times he reminds me of one of those Roman soldiers, driving a chariot or riding a horse at breakneck speeds on the Roman roads." Mr. Stockton laughed heartily.

"I've never seen him do anything so rash," I said, shocked at his statement.

"Then maybe you've settled him down."

"I didn't do anything. He's always been respectful of my wishes." He was poking fun at his son, but I bristled at his comments, ready to defend Press.

"We've been expecting you to visit the Glory B for several months."

"Months?"

"Yes, my son has been promising to bring you back each time he heads for the Guadalupe Mountains. I was beginning to doubt you existed."

I opened my mouth to answer his comment—to tell him I didn't know of his son's plans. My words were interrupted when Maria came through the door and announced our meal.

"Gracie," he said offering his arm. "Shall we go to supper?"

I resisted my urge to utter more words, took his arm, and walked into the dining room. Why did I feel the need to defend Press to his father? I heard Press chuckle behind me. My irritation turned toward him.

Mr. Stockton seated me—another unexpected happening and a first in my life.

"Thank you."

"A beautiful lady deserves to be treated as one." I instantly forgot my irritation with Mr. Stockton and his son. He went to the head of the table and seated himself. Press sat to his left and I to his right.

Bowing his gray head, Mr. Stockton asked a blessing on our food. When he finished, Maria entered through the kitchen door and served bowls full of soup.

The conversation turned to the summer drought. While Press and his father discussed measures needed to water their cattle, I looked around at my surroundings.

The dining room enchanted me, reminding me of the more expensive homes I'd visited in Nashville. From the tall windows, I looked over the pine and cedar trees to the valley below. The vista of open spaces stretched out before me, disappearing into the distant mists of Texas.

Inside the room, a large, beautiful painting of horses grazing on green grass by a smooth flowing river hung above a cherry wood buffet. On top of the buffet I saw a handsome tea service.

"The painting came from New York," said Mr. Stockton, noticing my gaze. "My wife fell in love with it and with me. She was born there."

"I love the peaceful setting. Do you know the location?"

"No, I think the site could be anywhere in the North. The silver tea service was her grandmother's and a wedding gift."

"You've been to New York?"

"Not in many years."

"I can't imagine anyone movin' from the comforts of the big city to the grit and dirt of the desert."

"My wife grew to love Texas. Didn't you move here?"

"Yes, but that's different. My pa has talked about Texas since I can remember. It's like we were destined to come here. He fought twice to liberate this state."

"Today, Texas is raw and rough, Gracie." He paused, thinking. "But our state has the potential to be the biggest and wealthiest in the union. You may live to see its glory."

Maria interrupted our conversation. She removed the soup bowls and brought plates of food for the main course.

"Father, when do you think we'll need to start hauling water for the stock?"

"We'll start before our ponds go dry, filling..."

When the conversation reverted to managing the drought, I glanced at the rest of the room, noticing the painting's reflection in a large gilt-framed mirror, dwarfing a small, portable serving cart underneath. A spinning wheel sat in one corner, and a majestic corner cabinet filled with china dishes sat next to the entrance.

This stately home left no question that in the Glass Mountains, the Stockton's were powerful and wealthy.

❧ 42 ❧

"**G**racie, we have visitors," Press said on my first Saturday at the Glory B.

I sat on a couch in the small drawing room next to my bedroom reading one of the books I'd pulled from the bookcase inside. Open windows allowed a good breeze to move the room's hot and heavy air.

Press led a distinguished looking man in a black suit down the hallway, accompanied by a woman I assumed to be his wife.

"Gracie, this is Pastor Marshall and his wife, Julia."

I made motions to rise from the sofa, but Julia Marshall hurried to me, gently pushing me down. She sat beside me. "Don't bother. In your condition we don't expect you to stand to greet us. How are you getting along?"

Mrs. Marshall leaned toward me and patted my hand. The soft waves of her dark hair were pulled into a bun at the back of her head. I looked into warm eyes the color of sweetened iced tea. A hint of rouge touched her high cheekbones and a tint of red lined her lips.

"Maria and Press are takin' good care of me."

Press hurried to bring another chair close to the sofa. "Please sit down, Pastor Marshall."

"Gracie, I've heard so much about you, I feel I already know you," said the Pastor.

I shook my head, sneaking a brief glance at Press. He'd never looked more handsome or happy. Was there any person on earth he hadn't told about me? "I've heard about you too," I managed.

I made use of the small talk about the dry weather to examine the reverend. He wore wire-rimmed glasses over his twinkling eyes and a string-tie. His over-the-ear hair was salt-and-pepper gray. He had a powerful voice, but unlike Reverend Dixon's, his wasn't loud and booming but strong and assuring. I almost expected to see a Bible under his arm. He sported an infectious grin.

He directed a comment toward me. "My wife and I wanted to meet you. I hope you'll be able to come to church tomorrow." He quickly added, "Although I understand your condition may hinder you."

"I intend to try. At least until travelin' might harm the baby."

"Have you had trouble carrying your child?" asked Julia.

"Not a bit. Not even much morning sickness."

"Then you're going to have a little girl."

I laughed. "How do you know my baby is a girl?"

"Because boys make you sick."

"Julia!" exclaimed Pastor Marshall, staring at his wife.

"No, that didn't come out right." Mrs. Marshall shook her head and hurried on to explain morning sickness is worse with boys. "During the early months, a woman is sick to their stomach more often."

"But this isn't always true, is it?" asked the Pastor, prodding his wife for clarity.

"Well, not always, but as a general rule..." Julia shrugged and waved her hands.

I glanced over at Press to see his happy expression had changed to one of horror that we would speak of such things so openly.

Pastor Marshall seemed not to notice. "Julia and I wanted to meet you since she will help deliver the baby, and we wanted to express our sorrow in the loss of your husband."

"Such a terrible tragedy for you to endure," murmured Julia, "especially in your condition."

"If we can make your stay here at the Glory B more comfortable, don't hesitate to request our help."

"I've asked Julia to come during the week to check on your progress," Press said. "She's agreed, and suggested using this time to make clothes for yourself and the baby. She's an excellent seamstress, and my mother left several bolts of cloth in her sewing room. You could put this time to good use and increase your wardrobe, Gracie."

Before I could protest or agree, Julia answered him. "I can't wait. I'll have an excuse to come several days each week. I've found my soon-to-be mothers fare better if we stay busy together."

I wanted new dresses, but I didn't need Press telling me when or where. I smiled at Julia. "Please do come and help me sew. My wardrobe is thin on clothes. I've spent most of my extra time making baby clothes."

"May I see them? Your baby's clothes, I mean."

Press jumped up. With Julia's help I arose from the couch. She followed me into my bedroom and pushed the door almost shut. Once inside, Julia whispered. "I'm glad we got away from the men. They don't understand birthing babies." From the other room, I heard the low sound of 'the men's' voices.

I opened the top drawer of my chest and started pulling out the baby clothes I'd worked on with such tender care. "This is the gown I plan on the baby wearing after its birth." I held the white cotton dress with embroidered cross-stitch on the sleeves and around the neck. We went through the others. With Julia watching, my heart sank at the stack's smallness.

She praised my efforts. "You've done a good job, Gracie, but we'll increase your quantity. Do you have enough diapers?"

"Not enough I'm sure."

"Maria and I keep a stash at the church for new mothers with babies. I'll bring them down with some bleaching lime and..." Julia dug into her pocket and pulled out something I'd never seen before.

"Safety pins," she explained. "You fold your diaper in half, create a triangle, and use the pin in front of your baby's bellybutton to hold it in place. This little metal contraption is a miracle sent from God to help America's women." She put four of them in my hand.

"You'll have to show me how to use them."

"No problem. Have you been taking an afternoon nap?" she asked as we replaced my baby clothes.

"Yes, Maria demands one."

"Maria's a sweetheart. We've delivered lots of babies together. You're in good hands."

We kept talking until Pastor Marshall called his wife to go.

"Julia, don't forget we need to run by the Spiels' and pickup your ironing."

"Yes, dear, I'm coming. I don't mind ironing, but he likes to support those in the community," she confided, giving me a hug. "We'll start our sewing on Monday."

As we walked into the sitting room, I whispered to her, "I'll make sure Press shows me the cloth materials his mother left." Julia smiled and patted my shoulder.

"Gracie, I've enjoyed meeting you." Pastor Marshall walked to me and extended his hand. His grip was firm.

"The pleasure is mine. And thank you for lendin' your wife to help with my coming child."

"Julia's very capable within the labor room. She's brought many babies into this world, along with Maria's help, of course."

"We couldn't have found anyone more skilled," said Press, looking at me, then turning to lead the pastor and his wife from the room.

"I'm hoping to be of further service in the future," Pastor Marshall called back with a wink. Press urged him down the hall.

I didn't get a chance to ask the pastor what he meant.

❧ 43 ☙

Julia Marshall turned out to be another godsend—the mother I needed to help me through the birth of my baby. She encouraged me to keep walking, brought me special food to eat, and gave me hugs when I needed them. Most of all, she told me what to expect. And after I told her about Mama, she tried her best to relieve my apprehension.

Driving the Marshall buggy on early mornings, Julia came three days each week. We often sat on the veranda attached to my small drawing room. The surrounding tall trees shaded us as we worked on my new wardrobe and baby clothes.

Press walked me to his mother's sewing room, showing me her treadle operated Singer sewing machine. "I'll show you how to sew." He did and moved the machine toward the light coming through the windows in my drawing room.

"Not many men are able to do a woman's work," I kidded him.

He didn't take offense. "How will I fix a broken machine if I don't know how it operates? I know the mechanics of every machine on the Glory B."

Julia helped me arrange a corner in my bedroom full of everything my little newcomer would need. We called the area the Baby Corner and invited those on the Glory B Ranch to help fill the space.

"Gracie, I'm going to go," Julia said one afternoon, standing and gathering her sewing supplies.

"It's early." I looked at the clock on the mantle, startled by her seemingly sudden decision.

"Pastor Marshall needs the buggy to call on one of his parishioners who's sick." She walked to the couch, bent down, and gave me a hug and kiss.

I heard her footsteps echo down the hallway. The sound barely died away, before Mr. Stockton appeared with a cradle. I watched as he tenderly carried his precious treasure into the room, placing the wooden piece in front of me. "I put Press in this cradle for the first time after he was born. My wife kept him by her side for two days before she felt comfortable enough to let him go." He sat on the edge of a chair.

"Why was she so afraid?"

"I never found out," he said, putting out a finger to rock the cradle. "I'm guessing she held on because of the mother instinct all women have."

"The mother instinct?"

"Yes, the natural urge a mother has to take care of a baby. I see this in cattle all the time, Gracie. The minute the little one is born, a mother will take her nose and nudge the baby until it's strong enough to stand and nurse. The baby understands this touch and an instant bond is made. Human mothers coo over their infants, suckle and cuddle them."

"It's interesting you apply an animal bond to a human bond."

"They're one and the same."

I sat watching the cradle's movement, thinking Wooly and her mother didn't make this bond. "How long does a baby remain in a cradle? It doesn't look very big."

"Not too long. You'll need a crib by six months. Your baby will be a laughing, chubby, bundle of joy. I love babies, especially babies on the Glory B. They speak of continuing life in the hectic world around us."

"Six months? I'll be back at The Pinery by then."

Mr. Stockton looked at me, smiled knowingly, but didn't say anything. This morning, he was approachable, not the sometimes-stiff owner of the Glory B.

I decided to ask him more questions. "How long has your wife been gone?"

He stopped the cradle from rocking and leaned back in the chair. "She's been gone eight years."

"You miss her?"

"Yes, I do," he confided. "I wish she were still here. She loved children and would've been a great help to you."

"You loved her very much."

"Gracie, if you find a love like we had, my advice to you is to go after it. Rush to it and don't tarry. For God's sake don't lose it."

I found myself surprised at his openness and responded in kind. "Thanks for your wise counsel. I want to find God's choice for my future husband—someone I can respect and love with all my heart and someone who loves me the same way. I thought I'd found this with Jedediah, but his weakness caused his death." This was true, and I'd been dwelling on these thoughts for months but hadn't approached Mr. Ormand with them. I'd begun to doubt my ability to choose any man. "I ached terribly for weeks. If I marry—and I'm not saying I will—my future husband will exercise the courage of his convictions, knowing exactly what he wants."

"I almost made the same mistake. I thought I loved another woman before I met my wife, but circumstances sent me to New York before our wedding. There I met Mrs. Stockton. My marriage to the other lady would have been a terrible mistake. I realize this now—a whim of a young man not mature enough to make a good decision."

I felt the pathos in his voice. The passion he felt for his wife. I felt no embarrassment as this affluent man shared his heart with me.

"I've had a hard time admitting I didn't make a good decision. I keep wondering what I did wrong."

"Think about it, Gracie. I've seen many young women and young men marry because they mistake the need to nurture someone who was needy for love. I almost did the same thing with the first lady to whom I was engaged. Neediness and love are not the same thing."

"Will you tell me what happened?" The more he said, the more I realized he was talking about me. Maybe he had the answer I needed.

"The lady couldn't stand her mother. They were always fighting over her dress, speech, or actions. To make matters worse, she had a perfect sister who couldn't do any wrong. She needed a way out. I turned out to be her escape, or so she intended. She cried on my shoulder, and I rushed in to help her. Notice I said help her. Helping a needy person is not the kind of love a marriage is built on." He slapped his hands on his knees. "Heavens, Gracie, I've got to check on the cattle." He stood, took a few steps toward the hallway, and turned.

"I believe the best marriages happen when you love someone who's secure and established as a person and visa versa. Find someone like this and you'll be happy."

"I appreciate your advice. I'll have time to think about what you've said."

"Have a good afternoon, Gracie." He turned and walked down the hall.

What had I done? Jedediah needed me to help him. Had I mistaken needing, wanting to help him, for love. Still, I think he might have changed. With this thought, I realized the idea of change became the expectation everyone had in such a marriage. I wondered if many who hoped for a miracle saw such a life transformation. Mr. Stockton's words gave me something to mull over.

I remembered thinking, after reading about the Proverbs woman, that wisdom comes with age. Mr. Stockton had said, "a whim of a young man not mature enough to make a good decision." Hadn't Mr. Ormand said almost the same thing? Being no longer an innocent girl of sixteen, my thoughts were maturing. I still didn't have a full understanding of my brief marriage to Jedediah. But I had made progress.

I congratulated myself. "Gracie, I believe you might be growing up." I looked down at my stomach. "Or out," I added, rubbing the bulge and grinning.

My Baby Corner soon held toys whittled by Jorge and the other ranch hands, including a rocky horse of pinion pine. Maria gave me a baby blanket and rattle. Julia added more baby clothes and baby toys. Press's offering was mysteriously missing.

By July, I waddled like a duck and could no longer see my feet to tie my shoes. This didn't matter because they swelled in the muggy heat and pushing them inside the leather openings created enough struggle.

From the town church, Julia brought me a paper fan with a wooden handle to move the hot air. I felt like sitting most of the time to relieve the pressure of my stomach. Maria brought most of my daytime meals to the drawing room. She served them on a portable tray.

I remembered Pa talking about carrying a baby in the summer being hard. I could agree with him. I wondered what he was doing—if my friends at The Pinery missed me—and Wooly, Ticksy... A pang of homesickness for the Guadalupe Mountains made me cry.

On July 2, Press came to tell me he intended to travel to Fort Stockton, a new fort established at Comanche Springs to protect the mushrooming flow of western pioneers. "I'll not be gone long, Gracie. My father feels we need to start filling our water tanks. We can't let the levels get too low. We'll lose the garden, plus our stock. It's a good thing we made the drive to Kansas Territory. We don't have as many cattle to water."

Every frontier family grew their own food. Maria's expansive basement cellar contained rows of canned foods in glass jars or crocks and store-bought canned goods. Potatoes, apples, and onions covered with lime supplied these foods for eating all year long.

The Glory B garden produced food for the family, ranch hands, and those in town needing assistance. I hadn't seen the cultivated area. Press had told me the large plot was in the vicinity of the bunkhouse.

"Is Fort Stockton named after you and your family?"

"No, the name is a coincidence." He came close, holding out his hands. "Take care of yourself and the baby. I should be back in ten days."

Hugging me proved to be uncomfortable, but he managed to give me an awkward embrace.

✵ 44 ✵

Six days before my eighteenth birthday, Press returned from Fort Stockton with his ranch hands. The long caravan included other residents in the area needing to replenish their water supply.

The wind blew dust from the moving wagon wheels, announcing their presence long before the wagons appeared. I saw them arrive, driving the long road from the northeast, getting close to the bunkhouse below. The wagons stopped. A brief discussion ensued. Several split apart from the group and headed for town. Each wagon contained several full water barrels.

I recognized Press, driving the lead wagon and Jorge managing the chuck wagon behind him. I couldn't identify the other drivers from where I sat.

Spread out before me, the peaceful hills and valleys of the Glass Mountains appeared hazy in the late afternoon sun—my normal range of sight shortened by the clouded nature of the air. Somewhere in West Texas, raging prairie fires burned.

Jorge pointed in the direction of the ranch house. Press turned, saw me sitting in the wooden rocker on the wraparound porch and waved excitedly. I waved back, my heart light at the sight of Press.

My afternoon nap over, I'd been waiting for Maria to announce supper. I'd expected to dine alone. Press's father would not be present for the meal. After dinner, he'd announced he must travel to the farthest part of the Glory B to check on their stock. Maria packed a meal for him in a tin bucket, and he left, saying he'd be back after dark. I'd watched as he rode out alone.

But now, Press would be here. I leaned back in the wooden rocking chair, marveling at how perfectly my back curved into the chair. I relaxed, closed my eyes, and set the chair in motion, dreaming of rocking my baby in the rocker sitting in my bedroom.

"Gracie, supper's ready," Maria called from the dark interior of the house.

I sighed, thinking of the coming struggle to get up. Leaning dangerously forward, I grasped the arms of the rocking chair, knowing that a sudden change of balance would put me on the porch floor. I couldn't make it.

"Maria come and help me." I waited, but Maria didn't come.

"Maria," I shouted. "I can't get out of the chair."

I might as well have shouted at Julia a mile away. Maria couldn't hear me. How could I have been so stupid as to get into a chair that caused so much trouble?

I pushed forward, and the rocker went backward.

Two arms caught me. "Gracie, be careful," admonished Press, keeping me from falling hard on the porch floor. He strained to stay erect, but finally managed to help me stand. "Goodness, you weigh a ton."

"Thanks for reminding me," I said with sarcasm. Usually, Press dismissed my sharp words with laughter. Today, he didn't.

"Aren't you glad to see me? I missed you." There was hurt in his voice.

Did he think, after calling me fat, that I'd actually admit how hard my heart beat at his arrival? "Really? I can't imagine why you'd want to come back to an overweight cow."

I started to cry. What on earth was the matter with me? I'd been crying off and on for the last month. Besides being fat, now my eyes were red, and my nose threatened to run. I needed to ask Julia if women bawled more during the last month of carrying a baby.

Press wrapped his arms around me—no small accomplishment. "I'm sorry, sweetheart, if I hurt you. I didn't mean to. Will you forgive me?" I saw the look of affection in his eyes—heard love in his voice.

He meant every word he said. Why couldn't I simply say, "you're forgiven?" Instead, I pushed his arms away and stalked or waddled toward the dining room, feeling like the fat cow I'd called myself.

Maria saw us coming. She smiled broadly at her boss. "*Señor* Press, you're home. I'll set another plate."

"Well, at least someone is glad to see me."

We made quiet, polite small-talk during our meal. I didn't eat much. Finally, I arose and went to the small drawing room outside my bedroom. Press didn't appear as he usually did. He was angry, and he had a right to be. I needed to apologize for my actions—and soon.

I didn't see him for four days. He didn't come to my wing of the house, and he didn't eat his meals in the ranch house.

On the fourth day, during Maria's usual chatter, she mentioned Mr. Stockton's return to Comanche Springs for water, and that Press had ridden out to watch the stock during his absence, taking Jorge and other ranch hands with him. "I see him early this morning. He came to tell his plans."

"I wonder why he didn't come and tell me?" I said this out loud without thinking.

"You were asleep, *Señora* Gracie. He said to tell you he's sleeping and eating in the bunkhouse with the ranch hands until his father gets back. He and the others check the waterholes. Some are dangerously low."

"Does he often sleep in the bunkhouse?"

"No, *Señora*. But we have no rain. The cattle die without water. They've lost several head. He's very concerned."

After Maria left, I shook my head. How could I have been so unfeeling? Press had enough to worry about without my petulant attitude adding to his worries over the water shortage and cattle loss.

But I knew better. His reluctance to stay in the house meant he didn't want to see me.

After supper on the fifth day after his return, I went to find him, walking the long road down to the bunkhouse. The dusty pathway curved in and out of the woods, ending in a field hidden from the road below. Each step was painful on my swollen feet. Beads of sweat stood out on my forehead as I approached the long, wooden structure.

I'd never been in the cowhands' sleeping quarters before. I paused as I heard men's laughter inside. Should I knock on the door?

I didn't want to surprise the men inside by entering unannounced. I knocked, and the laughter stopped. I heard the thump of cowboy boots on the wooden floor. The door opened and a ranch hand I recognized but didn't know by name greeted me.

"Do you know where Press is at this moment?" The man stepped outside and pointed toward the corral. "He should be down there with the horses."

I looked toward the corral. Another three hundred feet in my condition and on my swelled feet didn't interest me.

"Gracie, you will apologize to Press, now," I silently commanded myself. "No excuses." I walked the distance to the corral, laboring over each step and wondering how I'd get back up the long hill to the ranch house. On the way, I found the garden, passing neat rows of vegetables and several barrels of water.

Press and Jorge squatted on the ground looking at a horse's hoof. My slow approach didn't alert them to my coming. "Press."

At the sound of his name, he jumped to his feet and turned to face me.

"I— Oh!" Pain made me clutch at my stomach and double over with its severity.

The two men rushed toward me. "Gracie, what have you done? You shouldn't have walked this far from the house." An anxious Press took one arm and Jorge the other.

"I'm sorry. I needed to talk to you." I said, gasping to catch my breath. The pain went away, and I stood straighter.

"We need to get you back to the house, but how…?"

Jorge solved the problem. "The stretcher we used when Whitson broke his leg falling from his horse."

"Jorge you're a genius. Run to the bunkhouse. Hurry back and bring two more men to help us bear her. We have a long walk and a heavy burden to carry."

Jorge ran toward the bunkhouse.

"Gracie, sweetheart, how are you feeling? Any more pain?"

"No, but I feel weak."

"Do you want to sit down here or try walking back to the bunkhouse?"

"I don't believe there's a decision to be made. I can't sit down on the ground so a slow walk is necessary."

"What possessed you to come down here?" He seemed angry. "You might harm the baby."

What did he care? I thought crossly. The baby wasn't his. I didn't apologize as another pain hit me. I doubled over again.

Jorge arrived with the stretcher and two men. Loaded aboard, I was unceremoniously carried up the hill to the house. Hefting me over the front porch steps proved to be a struggle and terribly embarrassing. I held on for dear life, fearful of sliding from the stretcher to the ground.

"Maria," Press shouted as we entered the house and passed the kitchen. "Please hurry."

The four men attempted to carry me to the back wing. "No, no, I can walk by myself," I declared, trying to swing my legs over the edge of the stretcher. "Put me down. Put me down!"

"Put 'er down boys. Let the lady do as she pleases." Press acquiesced, exasperated.

Maria appeared wiping her hands on her apron. Her smile turned to shocked fear when she saw the empty stretcher. "*Señor* Press, what has happened?"

I closed my ears to the explanation as I waddled to the privacy of my bedroom, holding onto furniture or the wall to steady myself. Maria caught me, mumbling something under her breath about me being *loco* and threatening the birth of my baby. Even Maria was angry with me. All right, so I was angry at me too.

"Is too early to have labor pains, *Señora* Gracie. I put you in the bed."

Maria nodded to Press. "Go get *Señora* Julia, and hurry, *Señor* Press." The loud thump of hastening cowboy boots echoed down the hall as the men left the house, carrying the stretcher.

We entered my bedroom. As I held on to one of the posts of the bed, Maria turned down the beautiful quilt with the colors of the Texas sunset. I'd lost the fight to take the coverlet off the bed. Maria stripped my clothes, pulled my nightgown over my head, and gently helped me between the white sheets. Another pain caused me to pull my knees to my stomach.

Still mumbling, Maria left the room. I caught parts of her words, "too early to have pains...*loco*...hot water and towels."

I'd been foolish to walk so far in my condition. Would I lose my baby because it would be born too early?

When Julia Marshall arrived, I burst out crying as she bent to hug and kiss me.

"Don't worry, my child. Maria and I'll take good care of you. Chances are these contractions will stop." She reassured me with her presence.

Julia stayed the rest of the day. My pains turned out to be a false alarm, but Julia and Maria were determined to keep me in bed until the baby was born. "You don't want this baby born too early—too many complications may occur," cautioned Julia. "Today is a warning for you to rest."

My birthday passed without fanfare, because I told no one it was my special day.

Last year, I'd been at Stinnett Station on my birthday. I wondered what Ronald was doing. And my Wooly lamb, did she miss me." Pitying myself, I sobbed into my pillow.

The following day, Maria came into the room with a clean nightgown. "*Señor* Press says you are angry with him most of the time."

I looked at her. "Maria, if I'm not angry at him, I'm bawlin' at something he's said. We never had an argument before I came to the Glory B. Is irritation normal in the final stages of having a child?"

"*Si*, probably. Every *Señora* is different. Time for a bath." I watched as Maria busied herself with getting hot water for my basin, clean towels, and soap. No more tub baths for me. This little Mexican woman was taking good care of me. I pulled her to me in a quick hug as she prepared to help me bathe. She and I both had tears in our eyes.

REBA RHYNE

❦ 45 ❦

Mr. Stockton returned to the Glory B on July 22. Press came by my room to tell me he planned to leave the next day to fetch water from Comanche Springs. After my annoyed exchanges with him on our previous meetings, he stuck his head in my door for two or three sentences. I reckoned he didn't want me snapping at him again.

On the day he was supposed to leave, my labor pains started again. This time they didn't stop. The time had arrived for my child to be born. When Press found out, he hurried to my room.

"Gracie, I'm not goin' to get water. I'm stayin' here with you. I'll be outside in the drawin' room if you need me." He leaned over and kissed my forehead, caressing my face with his hand, concern showing in his eyes. I wondered if he was remembering from our long talks that my own mother had died in childbirth and my brother along with her.

In the safety of my bedroom at the Glory B, I thought back to where I'd been on this day last year. Pa, Mr. Ormand, and I had traveled within one day of Fort Smith, Arkansas. The rain started to pour the following day, and driving became a nightmare as we entered the frontier town. Sitting in the wagon waiting for Pa and Mr. Ormand to find shelter from the rain, I'd heard the exchange between Jedediah and Hurricane Bailey. Their unexpected presence and altercation had changed my life.

Now, many months later, my unborn child had become the result of seeing the two men again.

Julia and Maria bustled around the room, getting the cradle ready for a new life and piling bed clothes on top of my dresser. I wondered what they were for, but figured I'd find out soon enough.

The first contractions weren't bad. Julia or Maria sat by my bedside holding my hand and wiping sweat off my brow and body.

On the occasions the door was opened, I caught glimpses of Press with his father. The older man sat in an armchair. The younger paced around the room or in front of the couch I usually rested on.

My labor went on all afternoon as I tossed and turned in the huge bed. Finding a place of comfort didn't happen. My water broke after dark, and the pains started to be severe. In the early hours of the morning, I couldn't help but scream with each one.

"Gracie, you're close to delivering. We're going to put you in position for the baby to arrive." I heard Julia's quiet voice saying. I felt them tugging at my body, pulling me at right angles in the bed, and placing more linens around me on the mattress. I didn't care what they were doing. I was ready for this to be over.

"Here... Bear down on this." Maria placed a small piece of rolled leather in my mouth. My screams slowed with the rawhide in place.

"Push," came Julia's calm voice. "Push, Gracie."

I pushed and pushed and pushed.

"Relax until you feel the next pain starting."

What did she mean, I thought? When did they stop?

"Gracie, I see the baby's head. You're doing wonderfully well. Keep pushing with each pain."

More pains and more pushing. *Please, God. Help me.*

"Maria, hand me the receiving blanket. Gracie, it's almost over. As soon as I can grasp under the shoulders, I can pull the baby out."

Two pushes later, Julia exclaimed, "You have a baby girl."

She handed the baby to Maria. I heard a slap, and the baby screamed in shock. I don't know what happened after the baby cried. I lay back on the pillows, too exhausted to care.

When I regained enough courage to open my eyes, Maria stood in front of my clothes chest cleaning the baby with water from a small tub, and Julia was cleaning me. "Gracie, do you have enough strength to change your nightgown?"

"I'll find it." I loved the cool water as it touched my skin. When Julia finished, I smelled of soap and lavender.

Several minutes later, I stretched out in a clean bed with my new daughter tucked in my arm. "You will need to suckle your child, Gracie." Julia helped position my infant. The baby seemed interested but didn't eat.

"Don't worry, she'll come around. It may take a few hours for her to learn."

"What will you name your little girl?"

"I've been thinking about a name, and I've chosen Ruby Eliza Bailey. She'll be named for my husband's mother." What better way to honor Jedediah's mom?

"What day is this?"

"Sunday, July 24, Gracie."

"Julia, you missed church."

"I think the good Lord will forgive me." Julia smiled at me.

I ran a finger over the soft skin of the baby's ruddy cheek. Love for her flooded through me. "Ruby Eliza, you were born six days after your mother's eighteenth birthday." I gave her a gentle squeeze, afraid I'd break her bones if I held her tighter.

Julia and Maria looked at each other. "You didn't tell us about your birthday."

"I've been a cantankerous and unhappy lady these last few days. I'm so sorry if I've been a difficult patient. I didn't intend to hurt either of you."

"Gracie, we haven't noticed any difference in your attitude." I knew they were only being courteous.

A knock on the door stopped our conversation. "Is everything okay in there?" Press's voice sounded anxious. After Ruby's loud birth scream, the room had become quiet.

"Yes, come on in," responded Julia. "We're decent."

Maria and Julia headed out as Press came inside the room.

Julia paused before closing the door. "Gracie, I was right."

"About what?"

"You did have a baby girl."

I nodded, and she left, giving Press and me a private time together.

Instead of standing by my bedside, he sat on the bed. Leaning forward, he embraced me and baby, Ruby, gently but forcibly. I felt his warm cheek nuzzling my forehead. He raised his head, and his lips lingered on mine. He drew back, looking in my eyes and waiting for my response.

A thrill ran through my tired body as realization came. *I loved him.* Had loved him since he kissed me goodbye on the Butterfield Trail last year. With my free hand, I drew his face to mine and kissed him back.

We pulled apart. "I love you, Gracie. Since the minute I laid eyes on you, I—"

The baby cried in my arms, and the words he might have spoken died on his lips. He turned his attention toward my red-faced child, running his forefinger gently over the baby's face. "What did you name this little girl?" he asked, leaving his previous sentence unfinished. I felt cheated, because there were other words I wanted him to say.

"Ruby Eliza is her name. She's named after Jedediah's mother."

Ruby grabbed Press's finger and held on.

"I see," he said.

The silence between us grew awkward.

"Would your father like to meet her?"

Press smiled. "I'll get him."

Press left the room, and his father came in with Maria. "Julia's gone home. Said she'd be back this afternoon. She'll help out around here and let Maria rest. Press said to tell you he'd see you tonight. He's getting ready for another trip to get water."

The early signs of daylight appeared outside my bedroom windows. Exhausted, Ruby and I slept the rest of the day except when Maria came in to help me with the baby's nursing.

Maria told me that Press came in to tell me goodbye. But even he could not wake me from my sound sleep.

🎗 46 🎗

Ruby and I were great friends by the time Press came back from his trip to get water. She recognized me as the one who fed her, bathed and diapered her.

Down the hallway, I heard his voice greeting Maria. He was coming to see me. I arose from the sofa, my heart jumping in my chest. What would he say to me? I couldn't wait. I ran down the hall to meet him.

"Press…" My words stuck in my throat as I eagerly greeted him.

"Gracie." He held out his arms, then apparently thought better of it and dropped them by his side. "I'm home."

"I'm happy to see you. Come and see Ruby. She's starting to grow." Confused at his cool response, I led him to her cradle.

Was this the man who'd said he loved me only ten days ago? He seemed almost cold toward me, but baby Ruby he cradled in his arms, giving her the gentle kiss I expected. "Hello Ruby," he said, tweaking her cheek. She smiled. The first one she'd given any of us. He continued to hold her as he talked to me.

"When will you go for more water?"

"Tomorrow. We're in a crisis situation. Pray for rain, Gracie."

"I pray for your safety."

He looked at me. I saw a flicker of love before he dropped his eyes.

"I've got to go into town and get supplies." He handed Ruby to me and gave me a quick hug.

"When will you be back?"

"Ten more days."

"Will you be able to stay longer this time?"

"We'll see."

Four days later, Ruby and I took the Glory B buggy to town. We ate supper with the Marshalls. After dinner, Julia and I decided to take Ruby and hike the well-used trail to Moses Mountain. I wanted to see the view from its top. Pastor Marshall waved goodbye to us.

"Watch out for thunder and lightning," he teased.

Julia took a small pack with water and cookies inside. The sweets were our dessert from supper. I carried baby Ruby Indian-style on my back. We walked under the shade of the pines and hardwoods. After a mile of ups and downs, we arrived one hour before sundown. The view was spectacular but hazy. To the north, Julia spotted smoke from one large fire and two smaller ones. To the south, the peaks of the Glass Mountains poked into the sky. What caught my attention were clouds, hanging low in the western sky. One in particular interested me.

"When Pastor Marshall said to watch out for thunder and lightning, he wasn't joking." I pointed to a thunderhead on the horizon. The dark-gray and white monstrosity towered over the others.

Julia followed the line of my finger. The sun was behind the cloud, causing the edges of the billowing wonder to seem like they were on fire.

"Looks like a streak of jagged lightning got frozen in the sky," observed Julia of the cloud's ragged halo.

Other clouds floated around the big one, some white and some gray. "Do you think we'll have rain out of this line of clouds?"

"Maybe," Julia responded. "Let's pray for it."

Julia's prayer was brief but to the point. "Father we ask for rain from these clouds. Will you hear our prayer? Amen."

"Amen." I echoed her ending, remembering Press's request.

The clouds moved slowly into the Glass Mountains. During the next day, the rain partially filled the watering holes bringing a brief relief from the ranch's drought problem, and the cold front lagging behind the downpour was refreshing.

Ten days after Press left he returned. His demeanor toward me seemed the same. At times, I caught him looking at me. I wondered what was going on behind those handsome eyes.

Press loved Ruby, and from her reaction, the feeling appeared mutual. At the sound of his voice, her head turned in her cradle, and she tried to focus her eyes on him.

He always came to the drawing room after supper. We talked about the ranch operations, the weather, and his future plans for the town and land. He never mentioned the word love to me.

The day before he intended to leave for his regular water run, Press suggested a picnic. He drove the buggy to the front porch of the ranch house. Maria appeared with a basket covered with a red-checkered cloth. The bundle was placed under the seat smelling thickly of fried chicken. Maria knew this was my favorite.

Earlier, she had volunteered to sit with Ruby, so Press and I would be alone on our outing. "Just so you are back in two to three hours to nurse the baby."

Press drove the wagon through town, past the church, past the sawmill, and down into the valley on the other side of Moses Mountain. He stopped at a steep ravine and climbed out. "Gracie, we'll leave the buggy here and walk the rest of the way. Are you strong enough to do it?"

"Yes, of course." I took his hand, and he helped me out.

We stood face to face at the edge of the ravine, and I thought for a brief moment he would kiss me. I wanted him to kiss me. Instead he turned and led the way to a trail, barely seen, down the side of the ravine.

"This is deep. Only the noon sun hits the floor," he explained.

Fifteen minutes later, we came out into a green, grassy area. The air was cool, and I could swear I heard running water. "Is there a—"

"Spring nearby? Yes, but the water runs above ground only a few feet. Come and you'll see."

He was right. I stood by the trickle of water, flowing around and over mossy rocks before vanishing thirty feet downstream. "What a lovely place for a picnic."

"Do you see why bringing Ruby would be impossible?" he called.

"Yes, but one day she'll be able to walk down by herself." I turned around. A single sunbeam lit the area where Press spread our tablecloth on the ground. The area had seen use before. He set the wooden basket in the middle and stretched out beside it, leaning on his elbow.

"I'm at peace here, Gracie. The gurgle of the stream, birds singing, and flowers growing remind me of you and The Pinery." He closed his eyes. "When I wanted to remember you, I'd come here and imagine…" He seemed embarrassed by his admission.

"Hard to picture a place like this in the middle of the vast Chihuahuan Desert." I walked over and sat down gingerly. I'd regained most of my strength, but sitting and rising from a floor position tested my muscles.

"Are you hungry?"

"Famished."

"Gracie's back." He grinned, showing dimples, and my heart did flip-flops.

"I haven't thought about food since I arrived at the Glory B." I said this wondering when my habit of loving food had changed. I couldn't put a finger on it.

I helped Press spread our food on the cloth between us. He took two china cups to the spring for water, and I filled my plate with food.

We spent the afternoon much like those days on the wagon train, talking about whatever came to mind. Instead of riding horses, we sprawled on the tablecloth or rolled on our back.

"Have we been here two hours?" I asked, suddenly mindful of the need to nurse my baby. A chill came over me, and I realized the sun had escaped from our eating place.

Press pulled out his pocket watch. "Yes, we'd better go." He put his watch back in his vest pocket and started to replace the picnic items into the basket.

"I'll be returning to The Pinery soon."

His hand stopped mid-air, and his eyes searched mine. "Is that what you want?"

How could I answer? He hadn't given me another option. "Yes, of course." I lied.

After supper that night, Press came to the drawing room and gathered Ruby from her crib. Cradling her in his arms, he walked outside under the trees, keeping a running conversation with her as he strolled along.

"I'm going to help Maria in the kitchen and wash a few clothes," I called to him from the open drawing room window.

"Sure, go ahead. We'll be fine."

About an hour later, I decided to check on the two of them. Quiet reigned from my end of the house.

A new hall rug muffled the sound of my footsteps. Press had returned with the piece of carpet from Fort Stockton, saying reducing the noise would allow Ruby to sleep soundly.

No one occupied the drawing room.

Were those two still outside? It was dusky dark, and the mosquitoes would be swarming. I headed for the veranda but stopped again.

Someone was snoring softly. The sound came from behind the sofa. I tiptoed around the couch, and there on the floor in the semi-darkness lay Press sound asleep, a pillow from the sofa tucked under his head. Ruby's blanket covered her legs. And my little girl was stretched out on his chest, her open mouth drooled a puddle of milky slobbers on his clean shirt. Her little body rose with each breath he took.

I caught a lungful of air at the sight of Press loving another man's child. How could I not be in love with this man? I fought the loud sob, which threatened the peaceful moment—the sight touching me to the deepest part of my soul.

I started to wake him. *No, let them sleep and be together.* Our time at the Glory B shortened with each day.

❧ 47 ❧

Two days after Press left, I sat on the front porch nursing Ruby, rocking in my favorite chair, and humming nothing in particular into her ears. Autumn—always my favorite time of year.

I treasured the scenery below me. Each tree, distant mountain, and familiar rock I loved. Closing my eyes, I listened to the birds and grasshoppers on the slopes nearby. I'd miss this place after I left.

Ruby gave a contented sigh, and I gazed down at her. She looked like me. I ruffled her curly black hair, looked into her dark eyes, and pushed her chubby nose. "You're a sweet baby girl," I told her while wiping her milky mouth. I pulled her to my shoulder to burp her.

Looking northeast, a rolling line of dust appeared to be rising from the valley road. Had a catastrophe befallen Press and his crew? Were they returning for some reason? My eyes were riveted on the advancing plume. Minutes later, a column of mounted riflemen appeared with the infantry guidon fluttering from its long lance. I recognized the flag. It belonged to Captain Tom Stephens and his troop.

I rushed into the house with Ruby. "Maria take the baby. We have visitors on the road below the house."

"Who is it, *Señora*?" Maria took Ruby to her makeshift cradle in the kitchen.

"The mounted riflemen from Fort Davis," I called over my shoulder.

I returned to the porch. The horsemen were halfway to the house. Coming along behind them was a small Conestoga wagon like the one Pa and I had driven from Memphis, and a smaller farm cart behind the big one.

I watched as the procession came closer, weaving in and out of the woods below. The figure of the man driving the smaller wagon looked familiar. I glanced at the larger conveyance. Were my eyes deceiving me?

Pa! Mr. Ormand must be in the one behind him. I ran down the front steps and downhill to greet Captain Tom Stephens and the column from Fort Davis. He grinned. "Gracie, I see you've had your baby. Boy or girl?"

"Girl," I yelled, running past his troop of smiling soldiers and coming to the Conestoga. Dust flew from my long skirt.

Pa jumped down and ran toward me. Picking me off the ground, he twirled me around.

"Pa, what are you doin' here?" I caught my breath and held him at arm's length. He looked tired.

"I have some sad news."

"Did The Pinery burn down...or did the Indians attack it? Where's Wooly and Ticksy." The wagon appeared packed to the canvas top.

"Whoa. One question at a time. The route for the Butterfield Overland Stage has been changed."

"Changed?" My mouth flew open.

"Yes, it'll run through Fort Davis and points south."

"You mean The Pinery's closed?" I couldn't believe my ears.

"Yes, that's just it." Pa shook his head. "Broke my heart to leave there."

I noticed his moist eyes.

"I don't understand. Why? Why change the route?"

"It seems more people are taking the Southern Route, because forts afford more protection from maraudin' bands of Indians. And water is more plentiful on the overall route." Pa raised his hands, showing resignation.

"Where are you headed now?"

"To Fort Davis, we'll run the station next to the fort. Are you going with us?" I thought his question out of place. Of course, I'd go with him.

While Pa and I were talking, Mr. Ormand walked from his wagon with Wooly scampering beside him. "Couldn't keep her in the wagon once she heard your voice."

"What happened to your hair, little girl." I knelt to give my lamb a big hug. She'd been sheared from top to bottom.

"She was hot, so I told David to get rid of the wool. She's been steppin' higher in the air since then."

I grinned at Mr. Ormand. "Thank you for takin' care of her. How about Ticksy?"

"Oh, she didn't take kindly to the wagon. We had to crate her to bring her. She's in my wagon."

"Where are Caleb, Cephas, and Ben?"

"Laggin' behind, as usual. Exploring the countryside," said Pa. "They've got the rest of the stock."

"Are the twins and Ben goin' to Fort Davis?"

"I reckon so. Gracie there's another question I want to ask you. Boy or girl?"

"Pa! Didn't you get the letter I sent?" In the excitement of seeing Pa and Mr. Ormand, I'd forgotten my baby. "You have a granddaughter."

"Whoopee," yelled Pa. "I love girls. Where is she? I want to see her."

"Come on to the ranch house. I'll take care of the introductions."

"Ride beside me on the wagon." Pa gave me his hand. "It'll be like old times."

I mounted to the seat.

We passed the Fort Davis Infantry, making their camp next to the bunkhouse.

"I see they've been here before," Pa observed.

I filled Pa in on my life at the Glory B. "No one's here to greet you. Mr. Stockton's out with the cattle, and Press has gone to Comanche Springs for water. He won't be back for several days."

"Not havin' water's hard on everybody. Even the flow from Pine Springs diminished somewhat. How is Press?" Pa looked sideways at me. I knew this question didn't cover the entire information he wanted. He was digging for something.

"He's fine, workin' hard as usual." I tried to be nonchalant when I answered.

"I see." I had a feeling he didn't see. But he only said, "Now let's go meet my grandchild."

We pulled the wagon in front of the house. After securing the teams and wagons on the sloping drive, Pa, Mr. Ormand, and I ascended the steps into the front room.

"Maria, I'm bringing someone for you to meet."

Maria appeared from the kitchen, wiping her hands on her apron. "This is my pa, Jay Tipton, and our best friend, David Ormand."

"Oh, *Señors*, happy to meet you. Gracie's *padre*." Maria rushed forward to shake their hands, examining them at the same time. "I feel I know you."

"I'm lookin' for my granddaughter." Pa grinned widely, obviously eager to see her for the first time.

"Ruby's here," said Maria, throwing her hand toward the kitchen and leading the way.

"Ruby, huh?"

"I forgot to tell you. I named her Ruby Eliza after Jedediah's mother."

Into the kitchen we trooped. Maria pointed to the makeshift crib. Pa tiptoed over and peered in. "Why Gracie, she looks like you."

"Who'd you expect her to look like?"

"I-I don't know."

"She's takin' her nap. When she wakes, I'll feed her and then you two can get really acquainted." I winked at Mr. Ormand.

Supper became a time of catching up, loud laughter, and tall tales. My heart swelled to see my father with little Ruby cradled in his arms. Later, in the drawing room, Pa, Mr. Ormand, and I discussed the move to Fort Davis.

"You didn't answer my question, daughter. Are you goin' with us?"

I thought about Pa's question. I didn't want to go, especially if Press loved me. But Press hadn't asked me to stay.

"Yes, Pa. I'm going."

"How long will you need to pack, Gracie? We should go as quickly as possible." He sat watching Ruby sleep on his knees, tracing the shape of her ears and chin with his finger.

"Can you load my things tomorrow?"

"Shouldn't be a problem with Caleb, Cephas, and Ben's help."

"Then I should think day after tomorrow."

❧ 48 ❧

"**G**racie, we're almost one mile high. You'll find our temperatures here moderate and nights cool." Lt. Colonel Seawell and I were standing on the parade ground looking south toward the small town of Chihuahua. The smoke from several buildings blew east in the continuous breeze.

"Does the wind ever stop?" I asked the fort's commander whose well-clipped, snow-white mustache and beard always fascinated me.

"Only rarely does the wind not blow. Keeps our area pleasant even in the hot summer, but I'm not sure the camels like the cool weather."

We turned to look toward the north end of the parade ground where six camels grazed on field grasses. My first sight of the hump-backed animals had surprised me upon my arrival at Fort Davis. Now, I'd come to expect seeing them on patrol with the troops.

The continuous *tap-tap* of a hammer came from behind us. I looked in the sound's direction. A full-time carpenter worked hard to keep the older wood buildings in repair. Newer stone buildings with thatched roofs sheltered the officers and troops.

Seawell noticed my interest. "I built Fort Davis five years ago from slab lumber cut from a Page Circular Sawmill pulled by twelve mules. I did this thinking the government would construct a permanent fortification in a different location. I'm still hoping for this to happen. Trouble brewing in the East may put my hopes on hold."

I nodded.

"Your father is worried about the continuation of the Butterfield Overland Stage should there be war."

I looked at Seawell in surprise. Pa hadn't mentioned this concern. "Do you think the war will come to Texas?"

"It might. Sam Houston's resolve is to keep our state from seceding, but most of our inhabitants have slaves and they'll fight him."

"Pa says Houston will be elected governor again."

"We'll know when this month's election is over."

I pulled in a breath and let it out. "I wish it would rain."

The Colonel studied the cloudless sky. "Not likely today."

"Colonel Seawell, thanks for the fresh garden vegetables. I brought seeds from Tennessee, and I have a hoe, but they may never be planted."

"How's the little one?"

"Pa says she's growing like a weed. He's taking care of her while I'm here today."

"Bring her to the fort to see the wife. She misses her grandchildren."

"I will one day soon. Good afternoon, sir."

"Good afternoon, Gracie."

I could see Davis Station from the fort. My half-mile walk wouldn't take long.

Davis Station wasn't The Pinery. I stopped my walk home and looked west. I didn't see the face of El Capitan standing sentinel at the western end of our home. Instead, the tall rocks of a box canyon and several rock homes of the Eighth U.S. Infantry guarded our position in the Davis Mountains.

Music echoed down the canyon. Strict times of bugling, marking changes in work related fort activities punctuated the silence and reverberated between rock walls—sounds not familiar to me, which took getting used to. I walked on.

Our cramped quarters couldn't start to compare to the spacious stockade and fortress we formerly lived within—a place built of stone with an adobe roof. Pa and I had hung a sheet to separate my bedroom from the rest of the common areas where travelers congregated. We had plenty of visitors.

I was back in my feather bed, and Ruby occupied a quickly put together cradle next to me. The Stockton cradle had remained at the Glory B.

Pa and the others slept in tents behind the main building. He made no attempt to build permanent quarters. This puzzled me.

"Pa," I called as I entered the low dark doorway. "Where are you?"

Two small, uncovered windows accommodated a breeze coming west to east, but did little to let in the sunlight. I waited until my eyes adjusted to the dim light inside.

"Out here, Gracie."

I walked across the flagstoned floor and out the back door where Pa and Ben sat under a small oak tree. "Hey, you two, where's my daughter?"

"Here," said Ben, indicating a large, black cooking kettle. Ruby's blanket lined the bottom, and she slept peacefully inside as Ben fanned her with the paper fan Julia had given me when I was expecting Ruby.

I doubled over with laughter. "Are you planning to make stew of her?"

"No. Quiet," Pa shushed me, but he and Ben were smiling broadly at their joke.

"I brought your vegetables, Ben." I walked over and placed the food on our outside kitchen table. Across the field, Mr. Ormand and Cephas were giving the stock a special treat of dried corn.

Behind them, the Davis Mountains looked more like the Glass Mountains with pinion pines, juniper, and oak trees.

One big difference I thankfully accepted. Limpia Creek ran through the area, its crystal clear waters supplied drinking water and bath water. I climbed into my porcelain tub for a good scrubbing each week. Otherwise, I used a washrag and soap.

"Where's Caleb?"

"Said he intended to go into Chihuahua."

"Bet he doesn't get there," said Ben.

"Why?" Pa and I said together.

"Could only be a female," Ben replied. We didn't get any more information from him.

Another major difference in The Pinery and our station next to the fort was the amount of traffic traveling the San Antonio to El Paso route. James Birch ran a rival company, carrying mail west to California. His mail route converged with ours outside of town, and the Army's express to Fort Davis brought supplies monthly. Wagons and men on horseback rolled through at all times of the day and night.

New stations appeared along the Butterfield route from Fort Chadbourne to Fort Davis, traveling west of the Glass Mountains and bringing the mail closer to the Glory B.

Both routes brought marauding bands of Indians and highwaymen, preying on the vulnerable stages, necessitating the troops guarding both mail lines.

I managed to get through the waking hours at our new station, but the cool, pleasant nights in the Davis Mountains reminded me of the Glass Mountains and of Press. Sitting in my rocking chair with baby Ruby in my arms, I told her of missing him, of the deep love I had for him.

"Ruby, we could still be at the Glory B."

She looked at me with her dark eyes, watching my face and holding my finger tightly in her fist, becoming my comfort when I thought of him. I pulled her perfect face to mine and kissed her.

Not impressed with my affection and love, her eyelids drooped, and she yawned.

"Ruby. When the rains come, I hope we'll see Press. If he comes, I'll know he truly loves me. Do you want to go home to the Glory B—see Maria and Julia?"

Press couldn't come until the rains filled the ponds with water. He had responsibilities. He and his father fought to save their livelihood, the garden and cattle. What assurance did I have he would come after the crisis was over? I'd left without saying goodbye.

Ruby put my finger into her mouth to suck. "Are you hungry, little girl?" I smiled at her. "I'm jealous. Grandpa calls you his 'little girl' now."

I loved watching my father fawn over her, reminding me of...

Every thought, emotion, and action was about Press. "Why had I left him? I loved Press. I was sure of this."

A thought struggled in the back of my mind. Something to do with...rushing to love. I hurried to love the first time, and love didn't prove trustworthy. Yet, my heart yearned for Press, pled for him.

The continuous motion of the rocker caused Ruby's eyes to close, again. Soon she was a heavy lump in my arms. "You're growing, Ruby girl," I whispered.

⚝ 49 ⚝

We'd been at Davis Station a month when I woke one morning with clouds piled heavy in the southwest. The sight caused excitement throughout the residents in the area.

All day, the ominous gray thunderheads crept closer until the western sun set behind them. Flashes of lightning followed by loud cracks of thunder announced the storm's approach.

One jagged streak went from the sky to the ground. The earth jarring thunder woke Ruby. She began to cry at the terrifying sound. I nursed her and she went back to sleep, assured of her safety.

Dusk came early.

At exactly sundown, the skies opened and rain came down fast, pelting the hard earth, and running in rivulets down the dusty road. The smell of water-settled dust permeated the air until the earth became drenched in the flood.

Pa and I sat inside the open doorway of the station, watching the road turn to glorious, wonderful mud. "The coaches will be late tomorrow because of slick roads and over-flowing streams," Pa observed.

"The stagecoach will need to be washed when it pulls in here."

"Only a woman would make such a comment." He chuckled. We watched the rain ease off to a steady downpour.

I felt close to Pa as we sat watching the rain water the earth. Because of resettling our life, he and I hadn't had a serious conversation since moving into our home in the Davis Mountains.

"Gracie, I feel like I've been plucked out by the roots and transplanted where I don't want to put down new ones. Do you understand what I'm saying?"

The admission of his unhappiness here at Davis Station didn't come as a complete surprise. I'd been watching him. And remarks made by Seawell and Mr. Ormand prepared me for this comment about his feelings.

"The Pinery spoiled us. We both had every intention of remainin' there permanently."

"The Davis Mountains are remarkable, and I've no reason to be unhappy here, but my heart wasn't set on this place." Pa sighed.

"Could we go back to The Pinery? Stay there on our own."

"No, the area's too dangerous, too isolated. Do you remember my hesitation at bringin' you to Texas, Gracie? Do you see why I didn't want you to come? Don't get me wrong," he continued. "You've survived everythin' the frontier threw at you and done admirably. I'm proud you're my daughter." He reached out his hand and patted my knee, a gesture I knew well.

"If I hadn't come with you, you'd still be intendin' to send for me." He and I both knew this statement to be true.

Another flash of lightning and a loud crack of thunder shook the earth, stopping our talk. The wind blew past the doorway, and brush and leaves rolled down the wet road.

I stood and went to check on baby girl.

"How's Ruby?" Pa asked when I returned.

"Still asleep in her cradle." I sat down. "What are you going to do, Pa?" A chill ran through my body at the thought of leaving Press. At least, he could find me at Davis Station...if he wanted to.

"I haven't decided, but I don't intend to remain here. I wanted you to know."

"Thank you, Pa."

"What about you, Gracie? Press loves you. He told me so. Don't you love him back?"

This was the first time he'd mentioned Press since we left the Glory B. "Pa, I love him. I ache for him, but he didn't ask me to marry him." The wind moaned through the pines, matching my heart feelings.

"Do you have any idea why not?"

"No, I gave him opportunities to ask, but he didn't."

"Did he tell you he loved you?"

"Yes."

"Did you tell him of your love?"

"Not in so many words, but in actions he should have known."

"Gracie, Press is no ordinary man. He doesn't need a woman who likes him. He wants one who loves him—loves him deeply. He wants to be told those three words, 'I love you.'" Another crack of lightning and thunder shook the ground. "Are you over Jedediah?"

"Yes. I understand why I married him. He's a sweet memory, and Ruby's father, but my attachment to him is gone."

"Does Press know this?"

"I never said so to him. I didn't understand saying it was necessary."

"I think Press believes you still love Jedediah. Press may feel you like him but don't love him."

"If the ponds on the Glory B fill with water, he may come for Ruby and me. He loves Ruby."

"Gracie, I wouldn't guess about such an important happening. If you love him, go to him. Tell him of your love. Don't hold back. For God's sake, don't lose him. Press is reputable and persistent, following you from Fort Chadbourne to The Pinery to the Glory B. He'll make you a fine husband and Ruby an amazing father. He's waiting on you to make up your mind."

I remembered Mr. Stockton's words, *I believe the best marriages happen when you love someone who's secure and established as a person. Find someone like this and you'll be happy.* Pa was saying the same thing. Did Mr. Stockton know of Press's feelings? Was he pleading for his son like my father was pleading for him? Of course he was. Press talked to his father just like I talked to mine.

"You've always liked Press."

"Yes, he's the man I would have picked for you, little girl." He reached over and patted my arm as he always did when the conversation was over. "Press will always love you."

"Pa, I need to get back to him." My heart was pounding in my ears—harder than the rain upon on the ground.

"I'll see what I can arrange."

❦ 50 ❦

"**G**racie, in two weeks there's a regular scouting patrol riding the Butterfield Trail to Fort Stockton. Colonel Seawell says you're welcome to travel with them, and they will assure your safety clear to the Glory B."

"Pa, that's wonderful news. I'll start packing for the trip."

"Mr. Ormand will lend you his wagon. He and I will stop on our way to Fort Chadbourne as soon as we can arrange for someone to take our position here."

"You've decided to leave?"

"Yes, but we haven't decided where to put down our roots. I've sent word to Mr. Coburn to find other people to man the station. As soon as I hear back from him, David and I'll head out."

"Oh Pa," I cried, flinging my arms around his neck. "Don't go too far."

On Sunday, Pa and I walked to Fort Davis. Colonel Seawell supplied a rickety slab building as a place for Mr. Ormand to preach. Hastily made benches allowed the worshippers to sit.

After greeting the officers and soldiers alike, Pa and I sat down on the front pew. Mr. Ormand stood, welcomed his listeners, and opened the service. I watched Pa gently turn the pages in our Holy Bible to the chapter Mr. Ormand announced, and we stood for the reading of the Scripture taken from Isaiah 30:18.

Mr. Ormand read the verse. *And therefore will the LORD wait, that he may be gracious unto you, and therefore will he be exalted, that he may have mercy upon you: for the LORD is a God of judgment: blessed are all they that wait for him.* Let us pray. Dear Father, today we wait for your divine guidance to the meaning of this Scripture. We ask you to be present among us and to bless the message to be preached. Amen.

Mr. Ormand looked straight at his audience and asked, "What happens when we don't wait upon the Lord? When we run ahead trying to accomplish our will instead of his? What are the consequences of our actions? Are we blessed when we don't wait? The Bible says those that wait are blessed."

I sat thinking about the Scripture, feeling it particularly spoke to me, especially his chosen word.

God had provided two young men on the Butterfield Trail to the Guadalupe Mountains. I'd felt drawn to both.

One of them He specifically sent to be my husband, the love I'd hoped for. Press didn't need me in a clutching way, but he loved me because I fulfilled the image of the woman he wanted to marry—an interesting woman with a mind of her own. I was someone who could be his helpmate—a woman to admire, strong and resourceful, who would remain so throughout their marriage.

I opened my Bible and turned to the passage in Proverbs. *Who can find a virtuous woman? For her price is far above rubies. The heart of her husband doth safely trust in her... She will do him good and not evil all the days of her life.* Pa always told me my mother could stand on her own two feet like this honorable and worthy woman. His favorite part of the thirty-first chapter pertained to her. *Many daughters have done virtuously but thou excellest them all.*

In contrast, Jedediah was needy, holding on to me as a liberator. So needy, I'd mistaken helping for love, rushing in to pry him from his abusive father, thinking I could save him. I pushed Jedediah to go against his father's will. Demanded he come and marry me. I didn't wait on the Lord to work through the situation.

Still thinking, I closed my eyes and shook my head. I should have waited until Jedediah gained enough strength on his own to make a clean break from Mr. Bailey. I should have waited for him to stand for himself.

There were times of sweetness in our relationship. I couldn't deny this. And for Ruby's sake, I was grateful.

I knew now what God had intended for me as I left Nashville, Tennessee. My home wasn't in the Guadalupes, although I loved The Pinery, Pine Springs, and the fortress. My home was at the Glory B as Press's wife. I saw the answer plain as day. Any hesitation I'd been feeling before flew out the window of the slab building. Press wouldn't believe the Gracie who would show up at his door.

Mr. Ormand finished with another verse from Isaiah 64. *For since the beginning of the world men have not heard, nor perceived by the ear, neither hath the eye seen, O God, beside thee, what he hath prepared for him that waiteth for him.*

My whole body tingled at the realization of my thoughts. Surely the Spirit had revealed this truth to me, and God had blessed the message I'd received.

On the walk back to Davis Station, Mr. Ormand caught Pa and me. "Gracie, the message today, I preached for you."

"I figured you did, and you were right to do so."

"Sometimes we reckon we know how God wants us to act. We don't wait until He's finished with His work. Then we make decisions based on knowin' half of His mind. Most times we're wrong."

"I know what He intended for me, Mr. Ormand. I'm at peace with my decision."

I started packing.

One afternoon the following week, I stood before my chest, humming to Ruby, placing items she and I would not be needing before we left into a wooden crate sitting on my feather bed.

Momentarily, I heard the sound of a lone horseback rider hurrying by the station. The pounding hooves faded into the distance, a sound so familiar I didn't give the hastening rider another thought.

My heart was singing as I worked.

Busy at putting clothes in the crate, I didn't hear light footsteps or notice a slight flutter of the curtain separating my room from beyond.

"Gracie," a familiar voice uttered.

My heart leapt into my throat, and instant tears rolled from my eyes in a flood rivaling last week's storm. Every nerve in my body tingled.

"Press!" I ran to him, throwing my arms around his neck, clinging onto him, afraid he'd disappear. "I love you! I love you!"

"Gracie, my sweetheart. You don't know how I've longed to hear you say those three words." His voice broke. He gently pushed me away to look into my eyes. "You do love me. I see it in your eyes. I worried you still loved Jed—"

I put my finger to his lips and a tear slipped down my cheek. "I have mourned him, Press. But he is gone. Now there is only you. Never anyone else but you."

"Then before you vanish in a wisp of air, I must ask you a question. Will you marry me, Amazing Gracie Tipton Bailey?"

Smiling, I shook my head, shaking loose more tears. I couldn't believe he'd said the words I longed to hear.

"Is that a no?"

"No, silly. It's a yes. I'd love to marry you, Press. I want to marry you with all my heart."

"Strangest *yes* I've ever seen," he kidded me. But he bent and kissed me on the lips—a tender, gentle kiss. "Oh, Gracie," he pulled me to him, hugging me close and whispering into my ear. I trembled at the passion in his voice.

"Press, I knew you'd come."

"I couldn't stay away from you. I've loved you since I saw you beside your pa on the Conestoga. You sat there with your hat pulled down over your wild curls and your blue eyes smilin' at me. Melted my heart right then. I loved our rides with the wagon train and hated the thought of leavin' you. On our last horseback ride together, I wanted to speak to you about our future, but somethin' in your demeanor stopped me. My men ribbed me all the way home. Someone had finally caught Preston Stockton, Jr." He laughed. "And I happily embraced the thought. I went home, built a wing for us on the Glory B. I told Pastor Marshall to get ready for a wedding."

I regarded him. "That was the reason for a new wing on the ranch house complete with new furniture."

"I wanted everything to be fresh and new. I even built bookcases and stocked them with books, because I knew you loved to read. I ordered Maria to pull the quilt out of our cedar chest and put Mama's gift for my bride on my bed. When I came to The Pinery with Bossy and found out you were married, the bottom dropped out of my heart, but I decided to wait for you. I didn't know how long that'd be. I believed God brought you into my life, and He would make a way."

I started to cry again, sobbing into his shoulder at the wonder of his love. Press kissed my forehead and my cheek.

"I'm sorry about Jedediah. When I came north with the cattle, you told me what happened. I wanted to beat Hurricane Bailey to a pulp. There you were expecting a baby and no husband to take care of you. I talked to your father. Told him I loved you, which he already suspected. Asked permission to take you back to the Glory B when I returned from driving the cattle to Kansas Territory. Told him I wanted to marry you. Without urging, he offered his blessing."

"So that's what was going on. I wondered why you weren't gone as long as you told us, and Pa had a secret."

"As soon as I found someone to take the cattle on to the gold fields, I sold them and hurried back to The Pinery. I stopped for a moment and headed on home. I needed to ready the Glory B for your arrival and get our wagon to haul your personal possessions back to the ranch. I didn't intend for you to ever leave me."

"Did you know we'd made arrangements to go to El Paso for Ruby's birth? I remember Pa being anxious as the day drew closer. I didn't know he anticipated your arrival."

"Knowing your stubborn streak, I was afraid you wouldn't go, but you did. The rest you know, except you became cranky and short with me. I thought you regretted coming to the Glory B—thought you didn't love me."

"But I did love you. I didn't realize how much."

"Why didn't you speak the words?"

"I don't know. I guess I was stubborn. I..."

"I told you when Ruby was born."

"Yes, and I waited for you to ask me to marry you."

"How could I ask a woman who didn't love me? Do you remember our trip to the spring? After our enjoyable day together, you told me you wanted to go home."

"Oh Press... Let's put it all behind us and look to our future together."

"I intend to do exactly that, with a kiss from my intended, lovely Gracie." Press bent his head close to mine. "I'm waiting, sweetheart."

I lifted my lips to his and gave him a short peck. He drew back and chuckled—a happy laugh. Pulling me close, his lips brushed mine, gently at first and more passionately. "I've waited a long time to find you, dearest. I'll be the best husband you can imagine and a good father to Ruby."

With arms around each other, we sat on my feather bed and planned our future together. "Do you want Mr. Ormand to marry us?"

"No, I want Pastor Marshall *and* Mr. Ormand to hold the wedding service."

"Your father told me he's planning on leaving the Davis Station and heading for Fort Chadbourne."

"How did you know?"

"I didn't stop here but rode by when I saw him out in the field with the mules. He told me his plans."

"That was you I heard earlier. You went galloping by the station."

"I rode hard to get here after the rains filled our waterholes. I would have come the minute I got home from Comanche Springs except for the critical water shortage."

"I felt as much. I told Pa you would come."

"I'm not bashful, my love. I intended to tell you everything, but I needed to know you returned my love. That's the only reason I hesitated."

"Oh, Press... What should we do now?"

"I'll go back to the Glory B and wait for you to come with your father and Mr. Ormand. Everything will be ready when you arrive."

❧ 51 ❧

Two weeks later, Pa, Mr. Ormand, and Captain Stephens's troop from Fort Davis pulled up to the front of the Glory B. Maria came running down the steps to greet me.

"*Señora*, I've been missing you. Everyone, come inside."

We dismounted from the wagons. She bustled through the front door into the living room, waving her hands, indicating places to sit.

I heard Captain Stephens give orders for his soldiers to bivouac next to the bunkhouse. He joined us inside the ranch house.

"*Señor* Press and his father are in town. They should be here shortly. Come, *Señora* Gracie."

I followed her into the kitchen. She gave me a hug and took Ruby from my arms, "My, this *bambino*, she is growing." While Maria and Ruby got reacquainted, I went to the new wing.

Fresh wildflowers graced the tables and mantle. Through the glassed doors leading to the veranda, the colorful leaves of autumn fluttered in the breeze, and a squirrel scampered under the pinion pine and junipers. What peace I found in the room.

I paused at the spot where Press and Ruby had lain asleep together on the floor. I went into the bedroom where everything sat as I'd left it, except there was a large, ornate crib for Ruby.

How had it gotten there?

I walked over to the large four-poster bed, and on the coverlet with the colors of a Texas sunset sat an open box with a ring inside.

Two arms stole around my waist. "I love you, Gracie."

I turned in his arms. "If you don't quit sneaking up on me, you'll be sorry."

"Sorry about what."

"You'll find out." I raised my mouth for a kiss. "Where did the crib come from?"

"Fort Stockton, I brought it back on my last trip. You were gone, and Ruby wasn't here to use it."

"And the ring?"

"Your wedding ring. It was my mother's. Father gave me the circlet months earlier when I told him I intended to marry you. Will you wear it now? I'll buy another on our honeymoon."

"Honeymoon? We haven't discussed one."

"We'll go toward the end of October."

"Where?"

"That's a secret."

"If I took a branding iron to you, would you tell me?"

"No."

The town church bulged at the seams. People stood outside the door as my carriage pulled to the entrance. The fall sunlight streamed down from heaven, and I felt like a panicky angel on this blessed day. My heart jumped around in my chest.

Floating to the ground in the beautiful rose-colored dress Pa had given me for my seventeenth birthday, I pulled off my bonnet—the one Mr. Ormand bought to match—and nervously held it by the strings. Taking my father's arm, we headed for the church house door. Maria followed with Ruby.

"Are you ready, little girl," asked Pa, holding my arm, knowing my trepidation.

"Yes," I managed as we walked into the foyer and paused.

The church was decorated with pungent pine and lighted candles. The men and women wore their best clothes. In front, Pastor Marshall and Mr. Ormand stood in black suits with string ties and stiffly starched white shirts.

Smiling at me, Julia sat on the second pew from the front, craning her neck toward the back. Mr. Stockton sat beside her. Maria joined them.

And Press, he took my breath away and settled my nerves at the same time. If the occasion hadn't been solemn and serious, I would have laughed.

"Steady, girl," said Pa, noticing my quick breathing and trying to keep a straight face. "This'll be over soon." *Those two! Always pulling some stunt.*

I remembered Press's words from last night as I'd paced the floor before the sofa in our drawing room. "Gracie, sweetheart, they're people you know. Don't worry, tomorrow I'll think of something to help calm you down. Do you trust me, my love?"

I hadn't responded.

"Gracie?" He got up from the sofa, put his arms around me, and held me still. "I can't believe my sweetheart—the fearless girl who chased off warring Indians—is afraid of crowds."

"I didn't know I had a problem either. Why did I want a big wedding with all the trimmings?" I moaned.

Couldn't I face a church full of people and marry the man I loved with all my heart? Press was right. I'd licked everything from the Comanche to having Ruby. "Right now, I'd rather be married in the middle of the vegetable garden," I'd told him.

Press had laughed, shaking his head. "I'm going to kiss you. I won't see you until you walk down the aisle tomorrow morning. Remember, I intend to set you at ease."

Now, he stood in front of the congregation, smiling and handsome—in the same clothes he'd worn on the first day we met.

He wore the light-blue cotton shirt, sleeves rolled up to the elbows, with a striped vest of a darker blue and red, and a red bandana tied loosely around his neck. Brown britches covered a pair of expensive cowboy boots, well-scuffed with wear. His brown felt hat sat atop his head.

On cue, everyone in the church stood to greet me.

As I approached, he removed the hat and placed his old favorite on the front pew. My eyes were riveted on his hazel eyes. Mischievousness and love looked back at me.

I walked down the aisle, knowing God truly had provided my wedding dream with this man. I'd hoped and prayed for him for many years.

As we joined our hands, the two pastors performed the wedding ceremony. I looked at Press, tracing his face with my eyes. In a few minutes, we would start our lives yoked together. He whispered, "I love you."

"I love you," I whispered back.

Somewhere beyond us, Pastor Marshall said, "I now pronounce you man and wife.

We'd asked Mr. Ormand to pray before the traditional kiss. Everyone in the congregation bowed their heads.

"Father, what a glorious day you've given for two special young people to start their married lives together. I ask you to bless this union and give them a long life together based upon your Scriptures and your son, Jesus Christ. Amen.

Preston Stockton, Jr. looked at me and bending his head to my uplifted face, he kissed his bride.

ACKNOWLEDGMENTS

During one of the many writer's conferences I attended at Ridgecrest in Asheville, North Carolina, Deb Raney urged me to keep writing my novel, *Butterfield Trail*. If not for her comments, I would not have kept at it.

In May 2017, everything came together and she agreed to edit my book. I'm sure that editing a new writer's manuscript is a labor of love, and she'll never know how much I appreciate her patience. Ken Raney, her husband provided the wonderful book cover and inside copy for publishing. He was a joy to work with. It just seemed that God provided the perfect couple for this project.

Cherie Cowell, and her crew at EA Books Publishing, took the readied manuscript and worked their magic.

So many people, who manned the historical sites I visited, gave interesting tidbits about the area and the stages.

Ms. Marsha Nelson of James Price Library in Tipton, Missouri copied articles and was very helpful in suggesting places to see in the town.

Also, two people helped by reading the unedited text. My cousin, Nancy McLemore and Sue Marsden, two avid readers, agreed to give me feedback on their view of the story.

Learn More about The Butterfield Trail, The Pinery, and The Guadalupe Mountains

To make sure my readers would have an accurate account of the Butterfield Trail into Texas, I set out to travel as much of the true path as possible. I found some of the road is still called Butterfield Trail or Stagecoach Road. I took notes of the areas I traveled through. There are maps on line of the original route and if you stop and ask, many will take the time to point and comment or take you to the original tracks.

I visited Tipton, Missouri where a picture of a stagecoach is prominent at Townhall and a monument to the trail is on the main road. Another monument or plaque is at Springfield, Missouri, smack in the middle of town.

The Texas Forts Trail offered many stops for the stagecoaches. At Fort Chadbourne, I was given a lesson, by the owner, on the Hawken rifle. A wonderful museum and restored mail station exists on these grounds.

Other places, museums, libraries, and Welcome Stations provided written information and the employees were gracious and interested…Fort Belknap, Fort Phantom Hill, Fort Davis, and others mentioned in the book.

To learn more about John Butterfield's great adventure, established before the Pony Express, there is much information online, including maps. *Frontier Trails of the Old West* or Wikepedia, is a good place to start. Buzz words such as stagecoach, overland mail, home and swing stations, and stage drivers will introduce you to a wealth of information.

Books to buy are *The Butterfield Overland Mail* by Waterman L. Ormsby, *900 Miles on the Butterfield Trail* by A.C. Greene, *Fort Chadbourne-A Military Post-A Family Heritage* by Ann Pate, and *Roughing It* by Mark Twain has a chapter of a trip when he rode the stagecoach.

Child of the Fighting Tenth by Forrestine C. Hooker will give you an overview of life during this time period.

Contact me at rebarhyne@gmail.com

For three-quarters of a century, Reba Rhyne's home has been in East Tennessee. During this time, she was married for 25 years, had a daughter, and established a business of her own. Writing began as a hobby, while she spent months on clients' locations as a consultant, developing prototypes for boat upholstery. This is her first published novel, but not her last. Writing in a style reminiscent of Laura Ingalls Wilder and Janette Oke, Reba Rhyne, tells stories based on real history, much if it inspired by her own ancestors. For sixty years, she has been a Christ-follower who believes her responsibility is to follow the Great Commission found in the Gospel of Matthew. Retired, she shares her fifteen acres in the Smoky Mountain foothills with Phil the groundhog and numerous other animal friends.

79086355R00220

Made in the USA
Lexington, KY
17 January 2018